"Resonant ... vivid and compassionate ... A timely, disquieting reflection on mortality, war, and the startling dichotomy between the affluent West and the impoverished Third World."

—*Kirkus Reviews*

"Lyrical, moving, gripping ... A dark, compelling story about moral ambition and its pitfalls — a necessary book for this moment in America's imperial history."

—Andrew Solomon, author of the National Book Award-winning *The Noonday Demon*

"Dr Huyler's writing is quiet, precise, spell-binding from beginning to end ... Easily holds with the best contemporary fiction."

—*New York Times*

"Frank Huyler creates a thrilling drama out of a few well-chosen elements."

—*Harper's Magazine*

"He writes in a surgical fashion — with precision and care, making no sudden metaphorical movements. Huyler's protagonist resists easy answers or self-congratulatory axioms in examining the ethics of humanitarian intervention."

—*The New Yorker*

"A fascinating and heartbreaking meditation on healing and motivation."

—*Minneapolis Star Tribune*

ABOUT THE AUTHOR

An emergency physician in Albuquerque, New Mexico, **Frank Huyler** is the author of the essay collection *The Blood of Strangers* as well as the novel *The Laws of Invisible Things*. He grew up in Iran, Brazil, and Japan.

RIGHT of THIRST

FRANK HUYLER

RIGHT of THIRST

A Oneworld Book

First published in Great Britain and the Commonwealth
by Oneworld Publications 2010
Reprinted 2010

ISBN 978–1–85168–734–3

Cover design by vaguelymemorable.com
Printed and bound in Great Britain by CPI Cox & Wyman

Oneworld Publications
UK: 185 Banbury Road, Oxford, OX2 7AR, England
USA: 38 Greene Street, 4th Floor, New York, NY 10013, USA
www.oneworld-publications.com

From the war of nature, from famine and death, the most exalted object which we are capable of conceiving, namely, the production of the higher animals, directly follows. There is grandeur in this view of life.

—*Charles Darwin*, The Origin of Species

PART ONE
HOME

CHAPTER ONE

She let me lie down beside her. But she didn't want me to touch her, and she didn't want to talk. I suppose we'd talked enough by then.

She looked up at the ceiling, and blinked. The shades on the bedroom window were open, and it was early in the day. The morning nurse was gone, and it would be hours until the evening nurse arrived.

"How long will it take?" she asked.

I fumbled out of my clothes before getting into bed. For an instant I considered remaining dressed.

"Not long. A few minutes."

"Please, Charles," she said, glancing at me, then away. By then I think even her fear had been taken from her. She was calm, and asking for calm.

Her eyes were gray, her hair black where it had grown in again. Despite the hollows of her temples, and the spikes of her cheekbones, it was still her face.

She'd drawn up the bedclothes to her chin—a plain blue quilt, white flannel sheets—as if it were cold outside. Even then she wouldn't reveal her body, and I had not seen it uncovered for weeks. As I eased in beside her the plastic crackled beneath us, and I felt the cold point of her hip against mine.

I tried to put my arms around her. I tried to hold her close, and whisper. But she shook her head.

So I lay on my side and faced her, and took her hand, and held it against my chest. I tried to stroke her hair, also, short and brittle and dry, but she shook her head again. I brought her hand up to my cheek, and held it there, which she allowed. The room was full of fresh air, but underneath the sheets there was the faint smell of urine, as her kidneys continued on, in ignorance. That was the line she had drawn. When I can't get up to the bathroom, she'd said, that's when.

I don't know if I can, I'd replied.

Then her last flash of intensity, turning toward me, sitting up—please help me, Charles. Don't make me do this alone.

Her hand lay easily in mine. It revealed nothing at all, and I held it—neither warm nor cold. Her breathing was steady, and she blinked up at the ceiling. I could smell the apple juice on her breath. If she lay thinking, if she lay gathering herself, I couldn't see it. For the first few minutes, each time I forgot myself, and started to whisper something, she shook her head. And so I did my best, as I had promised her I would. But I was weak anyway, far weaker than she. I shook and trembled, and she lay as still as a sunbather.

On they went—the minutes, the long steady breaths, and we lay there together, and she let me hold her hand against my cheek. I began to wonder whether it had been enough. She continued, minute after minute, breath after breath. I held her hand and waited, my heart pounding, though I tried to empty myself as she did—I tried to follow her, if only for a little while. But I began to sweat beneath the heavy quilt. Soon there were rivulets on my chest and belly, and her hand grew damp in mine. I closed my eyes for a long time. I held her hand as though it could save me, and then I felt it loosen.

Her breathing changed and the gasping began. I had dreaded that gasping for so long, and there it was at last—a steady hiss of inhalation, and then a long, mirror-clouding sigh, and then another, the spaces between growing longer, and then a cluster of breaths, and the beginnings of gray, as my fingers slid to the slow pulse in her wrist.

Six breaths, then four, then none. Her heart continued on, and her face began to change. A light blue, at first, in the lips, but then spreading, like water spilled on a table, darkening to the color of slate. Her heart was strong, but then it too began to go, and I knew exactly what was happening beneath my fingers, the skips and shudders, the pauses and returns, and then, as more minutes passed, nothing at all.

The yellow soap shone on the dish, the grains of dust lit up on the blue tiles below it. I heard the sound of a tractor in the corn-field behind our house. From the corner of my eye I could see my body standing in the mirrors over the bathroom sink—not young, with gray hair on its chest and thickening at the waist—not young, but healthy nonetheless. I tried to clear my head, I leaned my face briefly against the glass door of the shower stall, and then I opened it, and stepped inside, and turned on the water.

All the details that awaited me, the telephone calls, the pa-perwork, the crunch of tires on the gravel, the prepared expla-nations—I was in the next room, I came and found her—and finally the bundle carried out, light as a girl—I let all of that dissolve in the steam, as it clouded the door, and encased me.

Only a few days earlier, when she was still able to sit in a chair by the window, she'd told me that she loved me. Her words had caught me by surprise, and as I stood in the shower I tried to cling to them. I hadn't replied, but I'd put my hands on her shoulders from behind, then bent and kissed her cheek. She was trembling, but soon she stopped and looked out through the window and made a casual comment about the dry state of our trees. It was a warm day, and the industrial sprinklers in the fields were on again. At times, I'd look out at them—the sunlight, the wide curtains of water and the millions of sheaves of green corn—and wonder how it had come for her there, through all of that.

The water fell.

We were on a trip to the Pacific Northwest. We were staying at an inn, high in the forest, a few months after our marriage. The hike was a loop through old-growth trees to an overlook. Round trip took about two hours, and the path was wide and easy, with mossy stones at the sides and split-log bridges over the streams.

It was spring, the off-season. I remember the enormous wooden lobby overlooking the snowcapped peaks in the distance, with its chandeliers of antlers and its crossed skis and snowshoes on the walls and the standing stuffed hides of grizzlies shot seventy or eighty years earlier. Leather furniture, cool in the height of summer. A large fireplace made of stones from a river. A hunting retreat, sold for a hotel when the heirs were gone.

The rest of the patrons seemed old to me then. Mostly retired couples, as I remember. The place was nearly empty.

We set off after breakfast. The hotel sat at the edge of a meadow on top of a hill, and the path descended across the grass into the trees below. The trees closest to the hotel had been logged, and so were close and thick above us, but a half mile into the forest we were in old-growth timber. The change was abrupt and clear, like stepping from a hallway into a large room—the spruce, in their immensity, rising hundreds of feet above us, the long spaces between them full of shades and stillness and cool heavy air. The path wound along across the needles and decaying logs as soft as paper, where mushrooms of all kinds grew— off white, deep yellow. There were patches of snow. We were alone on the path, and the forest absorbed our footsteps entirely.

It was just a snapshot, but I remembered it with such clarity—Rachel, ahead of me, walking lightly across the forest floor through columns of sunlight from the high canopy, as I hurried to catch her. Just that—her figure, twenty or thirty yards ahead, among the trees and the empty spaces between them, as I followed. There were so many other moments I might have remembered from that time, but that was the one that never washed away—Rachel, pushing on, without waiting, which was very like her. She was young, and she was not afraid, and we did not know each other quite so well, and we had the first of our many years to fill together.

"Please, Charles," she'd said. That was all.

CHAPTER TWO

Our home is an old two-story clapboard farmhouse twenty miles outside of town. We bought it many years ago, straining our budget at the time. Despite the bad plumbing and the wires, which took years to replace, and the constant work on the grounds, we both loved it, and it's odd to think that a material thing, a house, would resonate as it did through our lives. It was something we could not have afforded elsewhere, and though there were many times when Rachel wished the town was larger, and the fields were smaller, and that we had family nearby, the house at least was something we could agree upon.

It's white, with a dark shake roof, and green trim, and flower boxes at the windows, and it sits on eight private acres at the end of a narrow lane. There are trees around it—pines and willows and oaks—and sheets of green grass, and a small stream, and a few winding paths I put in. A wide porch at the back opens to several hundred open acres of cornfields, and though the land around us eventually filled up with equally expensive homes, even now, no other house is visible from the property. I don't think there's ever been a time, driving in, pressing the automatic button in my car to close the gate behind me, when I didn't feel blessed to have it. It was exactly what my mother always dreamed of, and never had, and never let my father forget. It made me feel like a man of substance, that all my efforts had been for something in the end. And yet it was only a house.

But in the days and weeks that followed Rachel's death, with nothing to do but live there, to wait for the bell of the microwave—*ping*, you must eat—the house became something else; peaceful and sustaining on the one hand, shadowy and unearthly on the other. It was late spring, with the first of the cicadas beginning to shriek in the trees, and the earliest fireflies opening and closing over the wide lawn stretching out to the white gravel driveway, which shone for long minutes as darkness fell.

When people die, there is work that must be done. There are phone calls to make and to receive, and documents to sign, and there are closets to be emptied and bags to be packed, as if one is moving away. That, at least, I understood. I gathered up her dresses, her shoes and slippers, her coats, her jackets, her underwear, her nightgowns and mittens and jeans, her ice skates and cross-country skis, her bicycle, her lipstick, her gauze and plastic sheeting, her syringes, and every prescription in her name. I did it over one long day, and divided it all in piles on the porch— Goodwill to one side, trash to the other. When I was done only her studio was left.

But then the funeral had been held, the guests had come and gone, the casseroles trickled off, the cards were fewer, and the attention of even our closest friends started to turn away. I was alone with my dog, an elderly Labrador retriever I've had since he was six weeks old, who used to run with me and Eric through the fields beside our house when he was young. And though many people were kind to me during that period, he was my single true source of comfort, steady and gentle in the background, heaving himself up onto the bed beside me in the guest room where I slept. In the afternoons, when it rained, he would rise at the first clap of thunder and ease himself under the bed. I'd get on my knees, and stroke him, because even then, or perhaps especially then, his fear never failed to touch me.

I went to work. I fed us both. I couldn't read. A few times I tried to exercise on the treadmill in the garage. I went for drives in the countryside. I'd roll the windows down, and let the manure-laden air of the farmland pour in against me for an hour or two, past miles of soybeans and corn and sleek cattle, with tractors in the fields, and during that time I felt like a stranger in a waking dream, as if each day had become an elegy to a world I would never see again. Sometimes there were trains to stop for—boxcars and grain carriers, battered and dignified and identical, their brown iron wheels spinning slowly enough to see. They were going from granary to granary, I suppose, and it was animal feed, mostly, for the stockyards, but they seemed like something more, something stately and wise and redeeming. Then the gates would lift, and I'd drive on.

Eric had left the morning after the funeral. I'd driven him to the airport. We said little to one another, but I'd embraced him before we got into the car, and for a moment, as we drove, I'd reached over and gripped his hand.

"I don't understand why you didn't tell me she'd gotten so much worse," he said, turning to me, his face thin and pale, his green eyes shining. "You said she was going to make it until summer."

I watched the line on the road before me.

"I'm sorry, Eric," I said. "It was very sudden. I didn't expect it to happen when it did."

"I wanted to be there," he said. "You knew that. You knew how important it was to me. I told you a hundred times."

"Please, Eric," I said.

"I never got to say good-bye to her," he continued. "I always thought I would be with her at the end. I was thinking about it all the time."

A moment passed.

"How can you just sit there and not say anything?"

"I don't know what to say."

"She called me. She left a message on my answering machine the night before she died. She must have known how bad she was. You should have told me to come home."

He was crying in earnest then, wrenching sobs, for the first time. During the service, and afterward, he had contained himself, but now, with the last of his childhood passing through the windows on either side of the road, he let himself go, which he had never done before in my presence. I reached out again, and put my free arm across his shoulders, and pulled him close to me. Finally, he gave in, and leaned against me like a child.

CHAPTER THREE

When I was just starting out as a cardiologist, I used to wear a bow tie, round gold-rimmed glasses, and a starched white coat, and I let my childhood accent flower in my voice again, and as I led my little cluster of residents and students on rounds I must have looked both ridiculous and affected. I felt a thrill, a flush of pride, standing there outside the door on rounds, claiming the power behind it, and there is no denying that I took pleasure in grilling the medical students and residents before we all entered the room. Tell me, Mr. Jones, what are the laboratory findings that one would expect in hyperthyroidism? Is that what this patient has? And what might you find on physical examination? Dr. Smith, what are the cardiac effects of hyperthyroidism? And the treatment? Is it the same as the treatment for other kinds of heart failure? And so on.

Mr. Jones, the medical student, and Dr. Smith, the intern, might fumble with their papers, or hesitate and stammer, or they might speak up boldly, with confidence, and either way I would stand there and watch them and make sure they understood that my judgment was upon them, as if to say—these are important questions, and we are important men and women, and no part of that rheumy-eyed supplicant behind the door, not his eyes, his ears, his throat, his skin, not his chest, not his belly, his arms, his legs, not even his gray withered haunches, will go unexamined or overlooked.

In my bow-tie years, the stammerers and fumblers both wearied and annoyed me. It was only much later, when I'd long since lost the bow tie and the fountain pen, and only the round gold-rimmed glasses remained, that I began to sympathize with them. Increasingly, when I cut them off and made them start again, blushing and flustered and shuffling their notes, or asked them questions I knew they could not answer, and impressed upon them again that the stakes were real, and this was not a game, I felt myself the lesser for it. Perhaps that sympathy, in the end, was what experience had brought me. And those who stood up straight, and reeled off all the answers, those to whom I would grant my highest recommendations—even as my pen checked the boxes, even as I took them aside, as I did on occasion, and urged them to consider a career in cardiology— even as I did all of the things that were expected of me, in my heart they began to annoy me more and more. They exhausted me, with their tedious narrow energy, so young and strong and full of the pretense of confidence. I knew that I was looking at my former self, that I'd been no better, but the game wearied me by then. All that posturing—the fumblers were more honest by half. But that world has never been a place for honesty, and fumbling got you nowhere. The confident ones would do well, and move on, like me, and they would go to conferences, and present their research, and stud their offices with plaques, and the engine would move forward just as it had done for a hundred years, and then it would wash over them, and it would be their turn to look back at those lining up without reflection in their path.

• • •

My appointment with the chairman of cardiology was at five o'clock on a Friday afternoon, the only opening in his schedule that week. I made the appointment on Monday morning. I wasn't entirely certain, then, what I would say to the man, or what I expected from him in return.

But during that week, as I stood on rounds, and tried to listen, and tried to guide them as I always had, as the world of the hospital flowed around me—the laughter of nurses in the break room, the lines at the coffee stands, the dozen or so nods I made each day to acquaintances in the hall, and all the many patients to see, filing in and out through the clinic doors with their worries, with their breathlessness and palpitations and their swollen ankles that felt like clay—as all of that passed, I realized that it was the knowledge of the meeting that kept me going. All week I felt its presence, and as it drew nearer I somehow grew lighter. The meeting felt like a secret, like a small dark stone in my pocket, cool to the touch, mysteriously reassuring.

The chairman of the department had been recruited from an elite institution only a few months before, and he was my junior by half a decade. New blood, the dean had said, will be good for us. A year or two earlier it would have been a bitter blow, but by then I cared only a little.

"Charles," he said, standing from his desk in welcome. He looked the part, with his smooth black hair, his pressed white coat and immaculate blue tie. His office had a fine view of the town. I didn't know him well, and had not invited him to the funeral.

I asked if he'd finished for the day. He said that he had. He sat down behind his desk again, and gestured to one of the overstuffed chairs in front of him. I sat as well. There was a penny of a coffee stain on the cuff of his coat, a single sign of imperfection, and I stared at it.

"Thanks for fitting me in," I began.

"Of course."

It struck me that I was looking at a slightly more successful, slightly younger version of myself. His walls were full of honors—framed diplomas and certifications and prizes, which sooner or later would be taken down and replaced with someone else's. In another time, I thought, they might have been flags, or the heads of animals.

There was a folder on his desk. It had my name on it, bold and black, and I realized he'd been reviewing my file.

"Were you reading my CV?"

He smiled, quickly.

"I always do that before I meet with faculty," he replied. "It helps me keep track of what everyone is doing."

I nodded.

"Yours is very impressive," he continued. "You've given a lot to this department."

He shifted in his chair. A moment passed.

"So, Charles," he said. "What can I do for you?"

I didn't know how to answer him.

He had started to watch me closely. Past him, through the window, I could see the spire of the nearby church over the rooftops. Leafy streets, handsome brick buildings, the haze of green fields in the distance.

"Are you all right, Charles?" he asked.

"No," I replied, finally. "I don't think I am."

"I see," he said, looking down at his hands for a moment, then up at me again.

"I'm sorry for your loss," he said. "I want you to know that."

I didn't reply.

"My father died recently," he continued. "I thought I was prepared for it. But it was much harder than I thought."

He took off his glasses, rubbed the bridge of his nose, then put them back on.

"Losing a parent is hard," he said. "But he lived a full life. He was eighty-four."

I remained silent, but he carried on nonetheless.

"I know that you kept your wife at home and took care of her yourself."

"Who told you that?"

"One of your clinic nurses."

"I had help. We had hospice care."

He shook his head, dismissively.

"I don't think I could have done that."

I shrugged, and looked away.

"Tell me why you wanted to meet with me, Charles," he said, gently. "Do you need some help? Do you need to take some time off?"

"I thought working would help me," I said. "The structure. It's always helped me before."

He nodded, slowly, as if considering.

"Well," he said, "sometimes that's true. But sometimes it's not. Have you reached that point?"

"Yes," I said, finally, admitting it at last. "Yes, I think I have."

I could see his mind working—call schedules, lectures to be given and clinics to be staffed, consultations to be done.

"Well," he said. "Then we'll need to get you some time off. How much do you need?"

"I don't know," I said. "A few months, I think."

"You don't have to decide right now. We can see how it goes."

"Thank you," I said, and suddenly realized that I was blinking back tears. "Without pay is fine. I'm sorry I've put you in this position."

My words must have pained him, because he grimaced and looked down.

"Please don't apologize," he said. "You've nothing to apologize for." After a while, he added, "You'll get through this, Charles. And there will always be a place for you here as long as I'm chairman. I want you to know that."

It was his decency that did it. Had he been otherwise, had he been faceless, bureaucratic and indifferent, I'm certain that I could have kept my composure. But his kindness undid me. I tried as hard as I could, and for a brief moment the effort alone sustained me. Don't give in, I told myself, because then your weakness will be there forever. But it was an irresistible wave nonetheless, followed by the cold recognition that this was what I had been waiting for all along, that this, of all things, was the stone I had been carrying in my pocket for the last five days. And something else came to me as well: I thought of Eric, in the car beside me.

I broke down, right then, in the chairman's office. For the first time in my adult life I wept publicly, and I've never been able to think back on those minutes without a sense of deep and bitter humiliation. Had I spoken, I might have said that my life was in ruins, that I had failed those closest to me, and that my hopes had come to nothing. But I didn't speak, and I was thankful for that. I felt as if my only strength—my restraint, my discipline and determination—had snapped with a single sharp report beneath me. And why it happened there, in that office, with that man, instead of with Eric, I could not understand. It was the place, after all, where I'd done the best in my life. It was the place where I'd never had doubts.

Later—how much later I could not exactly say—I was standing. His face was pale and troubled, and he was offering to drive me home. But the worst of it had passed by then, and I was shaky and cool and felt as if I had been swept clean. The recriminations I would later unleash on myself had not yet begun.

"Are you sure you can drive?" he repeated.

"Yes," I said. I did not apologize again. He watched me like the doctor he was, and I must have looked all right, because he let me leave. But to my astonishment, as I turned toward the door, he took a step forward, and gave me a quick, awkward embrace. It shocked me, to feel his arms around my shoulders, and to smell his aftershave, which lingered as he stepped away.

I cleaned myself up in the bathroom down the hall. I washed my face, and dried it with paper towels. I gripped the sink in my hands for a while, looking down at the silver button of the drain, and then I straightened, and combed my hair with my fingers in the mirror, and when I left I looked almost as if nothing had happened.

I walked down the carpeted hall, and out of the offices, into the main hospital. People passed me: residents in scrubs, nurses, a cluster of giggling high school girls, with handwritten name tags—Charlotte and Crystal and Wendy—on what I assumed was an after-school field trip. I walked past them to the elevator bank, and pressed the button, standing in my white coat with my name and title embroidered in blue beneath the pocket, and my plastic hospital ID dangling from its clip beside it, and the black coils of my stethoscope draped around my neck.

The elevator doors opened, and a handful of medical students, in short white coats, stepped out together. The elevator behind them was empty.

"Hi, Dr. Anderson," a young woman said, smiling cheerfully at me—a medical student I'd supervised the year before, whose name escaped me. She had that Scandinavian hair common in the Midwest, so light and fine it was nearly translucent. A chubby, friendly girl, with a wide, open face, who intended, if I remembered correctly, to do a residency in family medicine. An average student at best.

"Hello, Mary," I said, with the briefest flick of my eyes to her name tag.

She smiled again, and passed me, and as I stepped into the elevator I heard her talking to the other students around her.

"He was my cardiology attending," she said, in a proprietary way.

It was a casual comment, but alone in the elevator, descending toward the parking garage, her words nearly undid me again. I couldn't find my car, and for a while I wandered through the rows, until finally I held my keys up in the air, pressed the button, and let it blink and chirp and lead me to it.

As I sat in the car, I thought of my file lying naked on the chairman's desk, written down in black and white—all the papers I'd published, the conferences I'd attended, the committees on which I'd served. The truth was that nothing I'd done had changed the practice of cardiology in any way. Yet the man was correct; it was an impressive CV. It spoke to decades of blind, relentless work. It spoke to a thousand sleepless nights.

CHAPTER FOUR

I'd met Rachel three weeks after I'd left home for my residency in Chicago. It was the annual hospital fund-raiser, a black-tie affair. The estate was a few miles north, by the water.

The owner of the estate was a spry old woman with piercing blue eyes and a silver wave of hair. She invited the interns and residents because she liked young men in tuxedoes in her house, or out on the flagstones of her veranda overlooking the lights of Lake Michigan, where ships passed, and foghorns could sometimes be heard, and she liked young women in evening gowns beside them. I knew this because she told me so, as I stood with a glass of wine in the corner. She had been circling the room, and spotted me.

"I'm Mary Spruance," she said, advancing with her hand out-stretched. "And you are . . . ?"

"Chuck Anderson," I replied.

"Dr. Anderson?"

"I just started my internship."

"Congratulations," she said, with enthusiasm. "What are you going to specialize in?"

"Cardiology, I hope."

"A cardiologist! Well, good for you. Where are you from?"

I said that I was from Atlanta, Georgia.

"Atlanta!" she said, as if the city evoked wonderful things in her mind. "I've never been there. Of course now I'm too old to travel. It tires me out."

I said that she didn't look too old to me. I thanked her for the party, and I told her that her house was beautiful.

"So," she said, looking me over with approval, taking a sip of wine. "Dr. Anderson, did you bring a date?"

I said that I hadn't.

"Why not?"

I reddened. I said something about being new in town and not knowing anyone.

She thought for a moment, studying me carefully.

"Then why don't you come with me," she said, taking my arm. "This is why I really give these parties, you know," she added, in a conspiratorial whisper. "I like young people. I'm tired of all these rich old farts. Even though I'm an old fart myself, I can remember when I wasn't. That was much more fun, believe me."

When we reached the middle of the room, she stopped.

"You wait here," she said. "Don't move a muscle."

She laughed, and though it was early in the evening I realized that she was a little drunk.

Rachel had gray eyes and short black hair, tapered at the back, and brushed forward across her forehead toward her cheek. She seemed both dismayed and amused as she allowed herself to be led over to me, but she looked exactly as she must have intended nonetheless, a figure from the twenties, tall and languorous in her long blue dress, with a slender neck, and a glass of wine in her hand.

"Chuck, this is Rachel Adams, my art teacher," Mrs. Spruance said firmly. "Rachel is a classically trained artist. She paints the most wonderful portraits. Rachel, this is Dr. Charles Anderson, the cardiologist."

She gave me a wink.

"Rachel, that's a lovely dress," she continued. "Where did you get it?"

There were tiny black beads woven into the fabric. The beads caught the light, and the effect was shimmery—at first, the dress looked like ordinary blue cloth.

"At a thrift store."

"I had one exactly like it years ago. How much did you pay for it?"

"Twenty dollars, I think."

"Ha!" Mrs. Spruance said. "Good for you."

Then she patted me on the arm.

"Excuse me," she said. "I have to go cheer up that poor man over there." She pointed to a severe elderly figure standing alone with his drink, staring moodily out through the windows toward the water.

"He's so rich I have to invite him. He always comes, and he always does exactly what he's doing now. Doesn't he look absolutely miserable?"

She laughed, then turned to face us.

"You two get to know each other," she said. "It's a lovely night, don't you think?"

"I'm sorry," I began, when she was gone. "She just grabbed me. You can go back to your friends if you want."

"We have to talk a little," Rachel replied. "Otherwise she'll be offended."

She made a show of waving at a group of old ladies across the room who were studying us keenly. They laughed, and waved back, but then one of the group said something to the others, and they all elaborately looked away.

"They're my students," she said, shaking her head. "She invited the whole class. First they made me wear my flapper outfit and now they're giving me a hard time."

"So you are her art teacher."

"She doesn't take it seriously. She's just there to have fun with her friends."

"And are you really a classically trained artist?"

She rolled her eyes.

"I went to art school. That's all she meant. Are you really a cardiologist?"

"No," I said. "I'm just an intern."

It might have been awkward. But over the next few minutes of our conversation I felt as if my rented tuxedo was speaking for me—my tuxedo, and a few glasses of wine. I had nothing to guide me, and did not yet understand how radiant real money can be, how it can infuse everything around it with a sense of promise and significance.

Place settings were assigned for dinner. She sat with her students, and I was with a group of residents, most of whom had partners. I hardly knew them, and throughout the pleasantries, the introductions and the various courses, the flurry of speeches before dessert, I was aware of her sitting a few tables away. I watched her profile out of the corner of my eye, and once she looked over and gave me a quick ironic smile before turning her head.

But later, after dinner, I lost her in the crowd, and thought she might have gone home. I'd only spoken to her for a few minutes, but I felt an acute sense of loss nonetheless, as I wandered out onto the veranda with a glass of whiskey. I leaned on the heavy stone railing overlooking the water, feeling the cool air against my face, sipping my drink and watching the lights. I didn't want to go back to my studio apartment in the city, with its street full of sirens, and I felt very far from home. I thought of my father and mother, standing together on the driveway as I drove off in the car they had given me.

"There you are," she said, appearing out of the dark. "I was looking for you."

"I thought you'd gone," I replied, unable to hide my delight.

"No," she said. "I usually hate parties like this. But I'm having a good time tonight. My students are fun. They sent me out here to find you."

She lit a cigarette, and I sipped my drink. For the first time there was a strained silence, and then I asked her about her family, her parents and all the rest, and where she was from.

"I grew up here," she said. "My father teaches art history at the university. They're in Europe right now on sabbatical."

"Are you going to go visit them?"

"I've been before," she replied. "But I have a few commissions right now and they take a lot of time."

"Commissions for what?"

"For portraits," she said. "That's what I really do. I just teach the watercolor class on the side."

She paused.

"What about you?" she asked. "Is your father a cardiologist?"

For a moment I was tempted to lie to her, and invent grander circumstances for myself. But I didn't. Instead I told the truth.

"No," I said. "He's a pharmacist, but he's been out of work for a while. My mother's a schoolteacher. To be honest this sort

of thing"—I gestured to the house behind us—"makes me a
little uncomfortable."

"I wouldn't have guessed," she said. "You fit in fine."

"I do?"

"Yes," she said. "You do."

"Well," I replied, thrilled by her words. "So do you."

"I know," she said calmly. "That's why Mrs. Spruance introduced us. But I only came tonight because of my class and
because I'm hoping she'll ask me to paint her husband's portrait
someday. Plus it was an excuse to dress up and I was bored."

"Isn't her husband dead?"

"Lots of my subjects are dead. I use photographs."

"What do you do if they were unattractive?"

She laughed.

"That can be awkward," she said, "but the first rule of por-
traiture is kindness."

Later, we walked down the steps and out onto the lawn leading
to the water's edge. She took off her heels, and held them in her
hand. I'd had another glass of whiskey by then. The lights of the
house cast our shadows out onto the grass, and her necklace—
tiny triangles of linked stained glass, green and blue and dull
orange, framed in pewter—sparkled as she turned her head.

"The grass feels good," she said.

"It's beautiful, isn't it," I said. "This place. It doesn't seem
real."

She thought for a moment, looking at the house behind us,
shining like an ocean liner in the dark, with a quarter mile of
private beach stretching in either direction.

"For people like us, it isn't. It's out of reach. Mrs. Spruance is
a nice woman, but I only get to come because of the watercolor

class and because my father is a professor at the university. You get to come because she likes young doctors and she likes giving money to hospitals. We're the decoration."

"Nothing seems real tonight," I said, looking at her.

She smiled.

"I'm just an art teacher," she said. "Don't be fooled."

"Maybe you'll be a famous artist someday."

"I'm a woman," she said, with a hint of bitterness. "And portraits are always out of style."

"You could paint something else."

"I could," she said. "But I like portraits. They matter to people. They mean more than other kinds of paintings."

We reached the dock.

"Okay, then, it's your turn," she said, as we stepped out onto the wooden planks. "What do you want?"

"It's nothing complicated. I want a better life than my parents had, I guess. And I want to make a contribution."

"To what?"

"To cardiology if I can. A lot of specialties don't do very much. But cardiologists actually make a difference."

"So you're ambitious."

"Yes," I said. "I guess I am. Maybe it sounds silly."

At the end of the dock, where I might have kissed her, she stopped suddenly and looked at her watch.

"Oh, no," she said. "It's late. I have to leave." My heart sank, but then she turned to me.

"You're easy to talk to, you know," she continued. "I like you. You don't sound silly. You sound honest and you have a real job. It's refreshing. Plus you're not bad-looking and you're not too old. That's always a plus."

With that, she reached for her purse, withdrew a card, and handed it to me.

"Here's my number," she said. "Call me if you'd like to."

I held it up in the dim light. Rachel Adams, it read. Artist. Portraits and Private Classes.

"Are you sure you have to go?"

"I really do," she said. "I'm sorry. I have to take my class home. None of them can drive at night."

She hesitated, her eyes on my face, and she must have seen how disappointed I was, because she stepped up and kissed me lightly on the cheek.

"Good night," she said, simply. "It was nice to meet you. I hope I'll see you again."

I watched her walk away down the dock. As she stepped out on the grass, she turned, and gave me a friendly wave, her pale arm leaping out of the dark, and then she disappeared into the heavy shadows cast by the veranda on the lawn. But a few moments later I saw her again, slim and elegant on the well-lit stairs leading up to the veranda, and I realized that she'd put her heels back on.

For her, that night can't have meant very much at the time. It was only another party, after all, and I was only another young man. But I think I realized right then that I had a chance to become someone else.

CHAPTER FIVE

I'd seen the announcement in the local paper. The lecture attracted me, and I must have been doing better that night, and I hadn't drunk too much wine, because I shaved, and dressed, and got into my car, and drove the thirty minutes to the university campus just past the hospital. The first of the summer classes were in session, the students were out in the warm evening, and the air was full of honeysuckle from the flower beds along the old brick building where the lecture was held. I'd been to lectures there before, and I knew that many in the audience would be my age or older. The college kids had better things to do on a Saturday night.

The hall in the basement was half full. I took my place high up by the projectionist's booth, and looked down at the podium below me, hoping for a few minutes' respite. The talks were held weekly, on a wide variety of subjects.

The speaker stood waiting. He was in his early forties, trimly muscled, lean as a long-distance runner, with well-cut salt-and-pepper hair, a black T-shirt, loose tan cargo pants, and an erect, military air. He wore rubber sandals with burnt orange straps. He looked tanned, sternly athletic, and impatient, as if he had work to do.

He tapped the microphone a few times to make sure it was on.

"Let's turn down the lights," he said, after a minute or two, "and get started. First slide, please."

The projectionist, an elderly gray-haired woman who I knew volunteered her time, turned down the overhead lights from inside her booth, and lit up the podium where the man stood. An image appeared behind him on the screen—an emerald green valley, deep between snow-covered mountains. A village stood in the center of the valley; mud homes, an orchard, with trees rising above the brown walls. Around the village, a ring of delicately terraced fields.

"My name is Scott Coles," the man began. "I'm going to talk to you tonight about an earthquake.

"This village was over three hundred years old," he said, pointing to the screen. "It hardly changed at all during that time. The people there have much more in common with the ancient past than they do with the present."

He paused.

"Next slide, please."

There was a click from the projectionist's booth behind me.

It was a photograph of a damaged Japanese city. Sheets of broken glass, whole structures moved off their foundations, tangles of black wire coiling everywhere, though many of the office blocks seemed intact. The photograph must have been taken shortly after a rain, because there were puddles on the black asphalt streets, which were strangely empty, and the glass sparkled and shone.

"This is what a big earthquake will do to modern steel buildings," he said. "Next slide."

It was the mountain valley again. The fields remained, but the village itself was gone. The whole of it was a low pile of earth and stones, like a burial mound. Only the trees in the orchard were undamaged, though the walls around them lay in pieces at their feet. No human figures were visible.

"This is what a big earthquake will do to a mountain village made of mud-brick and stones," he said, pausing for effect.

"It happened early in the morning," he said, "when everyone was asleep. More than one hundred and fifty people were buried here. Only a handful escaped, and most of them were injured. They tried to dig out the survivors. But they had no tools. It was cold. They used their hands. By the time help arrived, pretty much everyone trapped in the rubble was dead. Imagine what that must have been like."

He paused again.

"There were hundreds of villages like this," he said. "And now they're all tombs. Tens of thousands of people are gone. We don't even know their names. Whole extended families were wiped out."

He began to pace, his voice grew louder, and even from the back of the lecture hall I could see the cords of his neck standing out, yet I was sure he'd given this lecture many times, working his way across the country, stopping at college towns and rotary clubs and libraries, while the audience sighed and wrote handfuls of modest checks when he was done. Watching him, I wondered what it was, exactly, that filled him with such outrage and intensity. It was a tragedy, certainly, even an unimaginable one, yet another cataclysm neglected by the papers of the West, but the world is full of such events: tidal waves, earthquakes, and the fires of illness, sweeping back and forth across continents like the light of the sun.

The content of the lecture was, I thought, predictable. The earthquake had come and gone many months ago, but thousands of survivors remained, high in the mountain country, with nowhere to go and little to eat, with winter approaching, and these were deaths that could be prevented. The paths were blocked; the roads were shaken away down the hillsides, and there were not enough helicopters. Camps were needed, resources, awareness, money most of all. The world's attention was elsewhere.

After a while, as I watched him from my perch high up in the back, the content of his words began to fade away for me. I knew what he was saying and what he'd say. I knew what slides he would eventually show—a blackened baby pulled like a plum from a hole, an outstretched grasping hand protruding from the earth. I knew all of that, and yet the man himself, clipped and incantatory, on and on—he compelled me nonetheless. I watched him, as he paced a few steps one way, then the other, delivering his sermon, and I envied him his certainty and his righteous anger that washed up over the rows of seats against my face like the heat of a campfire. How nice it would be to have such conviction, I thought, like a revivalist, a man with passionate knowledge, as opposed to knowledge alone.

It was a short talk, and he concluded, as I knew he would, with an appeal for donations. Perhaps forty minutes had passed before the flutter of applause, and his sip of water from the glass on the podium, and his request for questions.

A hand went up. Something about other relief organizations. He shook his head.

"Most of them are hopeless," he said. "They've put in some large camps near the cities, where it's easy for them, but the problem is that people can't get out of the mountains. They have to walk. We need smaller temporary camps in the high country to help them along, where they can rest, get food and medical attention, then continue. That's what we're trying to do right now."

Another hand, no doubt a student. Did they need volunteers to help out? In the summer?

He smiled, took another sip of water. His hair, black and gray, sparkled under the lights.

"No," he said. "We don't do disaster tourism. I'm sure you mean well, but unless you have a particular skill we can't use you. We can't assume the responsibility."

The young man persisted. What kind of skill?

"We need doctors and nurses," he said. "We also need contractors. Carpenters. People who know how to build things. People who really come to work, not just travel. This is serious business. Lives depend on it."

His tone was self-righteous, superior, and I knew that he was borrowing the significance of the event. I could see it because I'd done the same thing more times than I could count, as Dr. Anderson, the rigorous one, pausing on rounds in the doorways of the sick, turning to the medical students and residents beneath me.

At the end of the talk, just after the collection plate had gone through the rows and he was packing up to go, I found myself descending the stairs toward him. I wasn't alone; an old woman was praising him effusively for his efforts, her voice thin and quavering, and he glanced at her abstractly, as if he'd heard her words a thousand times before and had little use for them. A few others handed him last-minute checks. He smiled and pocketed them without looking at the amounts. The room was nearly empty by then. I hesitated, a few feet back, waiting, but then he saw me, and before I could retreat he spoke.

"Did you have a question?" he asked.

"I enjoyed your talk," I said. "But I didn't bring my checkbook."

"We have a Web site where you can contribute."

"I'm a physician, actually," I said, which caught his attention.

"Are you interested in volunteering?"

"I'm not sure," I said. "Maybe."

"We could probably use you," he said. "Let me give you my card. Please contact me anytime."

He pulled it from his shirt pocket, and handed it to me.

"How did you get into this work?" I asked, taking the card. It was thick cream, embossed with gold letters, like something a banker might offer, or a lawyer.

"That's a long story," he said.

"When are you going back?"

"Not any time soon," he said. "It's where I belong. But I'm much more useful here. Someone needs to raise the money. That's what keeps us going."

I was about to reply when the projectionist, who had descended from her booth, touched him lightly on the shoulder.

"I don't usually do this," she said, shyly. She was a small, thin woman in her late seventies, and I'd seen her before, from a distance, at other lectures. Standing beside her, I realized that she had a fine tremor in her left hand. It leapt out at me like a flag: she had early Parkinson's disease. I knew it at a glance, and I was sure that no one around us, least of all Scott Coles, had any inkling of this fact. I've had that experience many times over the years, the sense of secret knowledge that my profession has given me, and yet, as she opened her checkbook, I found her affliction unexpectedly moving. She hunched over the podium, and wrote a spidery sum carefully on the line, the final check of the evening.

He thanked her sincerely, and smiled, and then she turned away and filed out with the others. I waited as he picked up his bag.

"Where are you going now?" I asked.

"I was going to get something to eat," he said.

"Let me buy you dinner," I said, impulsively, though I'd already eaten. "I'd like to hear more about what you're doing."

He gave me a quick, assessing look.

"All right," he said, after a moment. "If you're serious I'd be happy to talk about it. But I can't stay long. I need to get an early start tomorrow."

"I understand," I replied.

"I didn't catch your name," he said, extending his hand. "I'm Scott."

CHAPTER SIX

It was the most expensive restaurant in town, along the main street, an easy walk from the lecture hall. It was the kind of place visiting parents took their newly grown children, and the negotiations of adult roles began. Sons and daughters, boyfriends and girlfriends and introductions. We'd taken Eric there a lifetime ago, for his high school graduation, and toasted him.

We stood outside in the warm evening.

"This is fine," Scott Coles said, glancing at his watch. It was a little after eight. Though the restaurant was only half full, it took nearly fifteen minutes to be seated, and five more before the waiter appeared.

As I ordered a salad, I expected him to choose something similarly modest. But without hesitation he ordered the fillet medium rare, a full bottle of merlot, and an appetizer.

"You're not eating dinner?" he asked.

"I ate earlier," I admitted.

He let his gaze drift out across the dining room, with its white tablecloths and blue china plates, and the glitter of silverware. Low conversations washed around us. A young blonde waitress walked past, her dark slacks clinging to her body, her white dress shirt tight against her breasts, and he watched her for a long moment before turning away. I wondered if he slept with the college girls he met along the way, easing them into bed with his stories of saving the world.

"Well," he said, as we waited for the meal. "What would you like to know?"

"How many camps you have, I suppose. The kind of help you need. How you got started."

"I thought I covered most of that in my talk," he said. "We have two camps at the moment, but they're in the lowlands, and they're already staffed. We're starting a third in a few months up in the mountains. That's where they're most needed, but logistically it's much more difficult. Everything has to be flown in. It's incredibly expensive. There are tensions along the border, also. Whenever they flare up everything stops for weeks, and no one moves. It's almost impossible to get things done sometimes. It took me months to get the army to agree to a new camp. I had to meet with a high-ranking general at least a dozen times, and even then he insisted on a liaison officer to oversee things. We have to pay for him, too, of course, even though he'll do nothing useful. We have to pay for everything. That's why I'm always on the road."

He closed his eyes for an instant, as if overcome by weariness. Just then the waiter appeared with the bottle of wine and the appetizer—tiny chicken kebobs, roasted in garlic. He set the dish on the table between us, poured each of us a glass of the expensive merlot, and asked us if there was anything else we needed.

Scott Coles shook his head, waved him off without speaking, and took a sip.

"Not bad," he said, twirling the wine around in the glass in a practiced way. He took another sip, and I looked at him. He put a skewer between his teeth, and pulled a piece of chicken into his mouth. The muscles of his jaw stood out in his cheeks as he chewed.

"Right now we have openings for a few volunteers to get things started. Later we'll bring more people in. We haven't done this before, so we're learning as we go."

"Is it really that different from the other camps?"

He nodded, impatiently.

"It's completely different. Like I said, this one is in the high country. It's in the middle of nowhere. It's a way station. The whole purpose is to give them a few days of food and rest so they'll be able to continue. No one will stay for long. We'll need to keep the numbers low so we can feed them. We can't afford a bottleneck up there."

"How many people are you talking about?"

"We have enough tents for two thousand people at full capacity. But no more."

"So you're going to tell them to leave?"

"Yes," he said. "They'll have to keep moving. They'll have to keep going down."

"What if they don't want to?"

"I doubt that will happen," he said. "But there will be a military presence, just in case. I hope it doesn't come to that. If they're sick, they'll need to stay longer, of course. In the lowlands, we can usually get them to a local hospital. But in this case we'll be the hospital. That's why we need a doctor."

I studied him, and took a sip of wine.

"Who else will be there?"

"At the moment there will be the liaison officer from the army, and a friend of mine. She's doing a research project on genetics, but she's also taken classes in nursing, so she'll be

useful. I'm recruiting some other people with practical experience, but they'll mostly be needed when the camp is up and
running. I'm planning to go also, but I can't be there in the
beginning."

"That's all?"

"For the moment, yes. But like I said, once the camp gets
going we'll increase the staff. At this stage it's really a pilot pro-
gram. That's why, if you're serious, someone like you would be so
valuable. You could tell us what we'll need for the other camps.
I'm hoping this will be the first of many."

"How old is your organization?" I asked. "Did you start it
after the earthquake?"

"Yes," he said. "It was something I wanted to do for a long
time. But the earthquake made it a necessity."

"A necessity?"

He smiled, thinly.

"Yes," he said. "A necessity. If you'd seen what I have you'd
understand what I mean."

I nodded.

"So," I said. "What did you do before this? You must have
had another career."

"For a long time I was a mountaineer," he said. "A climber.
I've given that up now."

"Why?"

"I had an experience in the mountains that made me realize I
was on the wrong path."

I took a bite of salad.

"Are you going to tell me what it was?" I asked, after a moment.

I knew it was the question he'd been waiting for. But he took
his time nonetheless, finishing his glass of wine, pouring himself
another.

"Do you know what it means for a climber to climb an eight-thousand-meter peak?" he asked.

"I think so," I said.

"It means you're among the best in the world. Only a few thousand people have done it."

I waited.

"We were a small expedition," he continued. "We were climbing alpine style. That means fast and light, with minimal equipment. But my partner couldn't go on summit day. He'd twisted his knee. It was so swollen he could hardly bend it."

He took a swallow of wine.

"So I went for the summit on my own. I was stupid back then. We weren't the only expedition on the mountain. There were other climbers going for the summit that morning, and I thought they could help if anything happened. I convinced myself it was safe to go, even though it wasn't. I'd sold almost everything I had to get there."

As he spoke, I realized that the pace of his speech had increased, and again I got a glimpse of how he'd been in the lecture hall—a glint in his eye, incantation in his voice.

"The weather was good," he said. "It wasn't that cold. But there was a lot of fresh snow. So I waited for the other group to leave, and then I followed their tracks. They were an hour or so ahead of me. They broke the trail. I followed their route. They put in protection, and I used it. I couldn't have done it otherwise."

He shook his head, as if marveling at his younger self.

"I made good time because they'd done the work. It was a perfectly clear day, and there was very little wind. I could see for hundreds of miles. There aren't any other peaks around that mountain. I could see fields, I could see valleys. I felt as if I could see the entire world. I was alone. It was beautiful. All I could hear was my own breathing and my own footsteps in the snow. I was scared, also. I felt as though death was all around me."

He smiled.

"I was at almost eight thousand meters by myself. Not many people can say that."

"What mountain was it?" I asked.

"That doesn't matter," he replied. "It's not important."

I looked at him, puzzled.

"Did you catch up to the other group?"

"That's the point of the story," he said. "I was on a ridge just below the final snowfield to the summit. I was about four hundred meters below them. There were three of them, roped up. I could see them. They were Polish, and really strong. They were at the top of the game."

He paused again.

"The snowfield scared me," he said. "It was loaded with fresh snow. It was obviously unstable. But the summit was right there, and they couldn't resist it. They went for it. I didn't know what to do. So I stopped and watched them. They knew the risk they were taking. They moved as slowly and as carefully as they could, and they almost made it."

He shook his head a final time.

"It was a huge slide. It took all three of them down the face. They fell at least three thousand meters. One moment they were there, and the next they were gone. I was safe on the rock band. It just went by me, and there was nothing I could do."

"Didn't you go get help?"

He laughed.

"They fell almost ten thousand feet. They didn't need any help." He paused. "Do you know what my first thought was?"

I shook my head.

"I thought, there's no avalanche danger now."

He closed his eyes again, then opened them.

"My first thought was that the summit was wide open. Three hours away at most. Perfect weather. Early in the day. No problem."

"Then why didn't you do it?" I asked.

"Because my second thought was that I'd just seen three men die, and I realized it was for nothing. If I hadn't stopped to watch them, and had started up the snowfield, I would have been dead as well. My death also would have been for nothing. I'd been lucky as a climber up to that point. I hadn't seen anyone get killed. But suddenly I learned what it really is, what kind of risk I was taking. And I realized that I'd become someone I didn't want to be. Someone who would think of the summit first, and human life second. Someone who defined everything in terms of his own personal ambition and accomplishment. The only person in the world who would care if I climbed that mountain was me. No one else. And climbing it wouldn't have mattered any more than dying in the avalanche. I saw all of that on the ridge that day. I sat there, and looked down at the view for a while, and then I turned around, and went back to the high camp, and helped my partner down like I should have from the beginning. I gave up high-altitude climbing after that."

"And you started to do relief work."

"Not right away. It took me a long time to understand what I wanted to do. But I realized I wanted my life to mean something. I wanted it to have significance. I didn't want to be just another dead mountaineer. Or even just another famous one. There are lots of those.

"It's terrible to say this, I know," he continued. "But in many ways the earthquake was the best thing that ever happened to me."

I didn't know how to reply. If he noticed my unease, however, he gave no sign. He ate the rest of the appetizers quickly, washed them down with the wine, and refilled his glass from the bottle on the table. He tapped his fingers on the table.

"They're slow here," he said. "I hate bad service."

If anything, my confusion about him deepened.

"So," he said, finally. "Tell me why you're buying me dinner."

"As I said, I'm curious about your organization and what you're trying to do."

"It's quite simple. We're trying to save a population at risk. You can do two things to help us. Give us money or volunteer your time. Or both. Or, of course, you can do neither."

"Yes," I replied. "I understand that."

For the first time since we'd sat down, he looked at me directly. He smiled, wearily and quickly.

"I'm sorry," he said. "I appreciate your interest, I really do. I'm just tired."

I nodded.

"Why don't you tell me about yourself," he said.

"What would you like to know?"

"What kind of doctor you are, for one. And why you're interested in this."

"I've been practicing cardiology for almost thirty years. I'm on the faculty here at the medical school. I'm taking a few months off. I'd like to do something useful."

"How much time do you have?"

"At least three months, possibly more."

"Good," he said. "A week or two is pointless. It's tourism."

He looked at me.

"There won't be much cardiology up there," he said. "You'd be dealing with problems like diarrhea and malnutrition and skin infections. Nothing fancy like cardiology."

"I realize that."

He nodded.

"So why don't you tell me," I said, "why I should volunteer with you and not a more established organization?"

"A good question," he said. "The best answer is that while we are small, we are much more efficient than some other groups, and you would have a lot of autonomy. We keep things simple and pure. We keep staffing to a minimum. We don't waste anything. We empower our employees and volunteers to make decisions as they see fit. Individual initiative matters and we value it. That's why we need to screen people so carefully."

He took another sip of wine.

"It's an astonishing place, it really is," he continued. "It's beautiful and wild. It's like going to another world. It's about as far away from this"—he swept his hand across the room—"as it's possible to get."

The meal arrived. He curtly thanked the waiter, lifted his knife and fork, and started in on the fillet. We were quiet for a while as he ate. I picked at my salad.

"It's nothing personal," he said, finally. "But we need people who are serious and come to work. We've already had one or two bad experiences."

"Such as?"

He swallowed.

"People who like the idea of relief work more than actually doing it. People who think it's a vacation. It's not a vacation. It's a reduction to the essentials. You see exactly what is important and what isn't. It's deeply satisfying to dig a well for a village that hasn't ever had one before. Or build a school. It really is like nothing else."

He wiped his mouth with his napkin, took another swallow of wine. He jerked his chin toward the other tables.

"These people here," he said. "They have no idea. They have no idea how big the world really is. They're thinking only about themselves—their own lives and careers. Maybe they're thinking about their children's lives and careers. They're telling their kids to become lawyers and bankers and stockbrokers. They're telling them to compete and win and get rich, that's it. They're oblivious, they really are. They don't know what's important. They think you get a prize at the end, and you don't. But saving people from hunger and disease, that's important. That actually matters."

He had a look in his eye again, and hadn't finished chewing, and I could see the red meat and wine in his mouth. The profusion of individual gray hairs on his head stood out in the dim lighting against the youthful black of the rest.

"How old are you?" he asked, bluntly.

"I'm fifty-eight."

"Do you have any health problems?"

"Nothing significant."

"Conditions are rough. You should understand that. You'd be living out of a tent. There won't be any modern conveniences."

I took another sip of wine.

"Do you have a family? Even three months is a long time up there."

"I've had some personal issues recently. I'm alone now. My son lives in New York."

"Ah," he said, as if something had become clear to him. I felt my cheeks flush.

"It's not a bad way to start again," he said, thoughtfully, and not unkindly, after a moment. "It worked for me."

I did not reply.

He finished off the last of the meat, eating with evident pleasure, drank the rest of the wine, and then, as he wiped his mouth for the last time, he thanked me for dinner.

"I hope you'll join us," he said, after I paid the bill, and we stood outside the restaurant in the warm night. "I've talked to a few others, but they're much younger, and have very little experience. We need someone like you. We need someone who knows what they're doing."

With that, he shook my hand, firmly.

"You have my card," he said, looking me in the eye, bringing the evening to an end. "I hope to hear from you."

"Do you need a ride to your hotel?" I asked.

"No, thanks," he said. "It's not far. I'm used to walking."

I said good night, and watched him for a moment as he strode off purposefully toward the center of campus, head up, as if he had an appointment to keep.

As I stood on the street, I felt as though I was on the cusp of an untraceable disappearance, that I was very close to being swept under entirely. I'd lived in that town for nearly thirty years, and right then it meant nothing to me, no more than the Atlanta of my youth. It was just another place, another stop along the way, full of strange young faces, ten thousand at a time, in four-year cycles, passing through.

I suppose another world was what I wanted most.

PART TWO
THE VALLEY

CHAPTER SEVEN

The days were blinding and bright and deep. Silent, also, except for the wind and the river in the background. When it was still, at night, the air was like a pane of ice. Sound carried a great distance—footsteps on the gravel, voices from the cook tent. There were birds—a kind of small brown gull, sweeping in for the garbage. Apart from them, and the villagers below us, the place was empty. When I first stepped out of the helicopter, I felt as though I'd landed on the surface of the moon.

Our five tents sat clustered around one another on a field of boulders at the base of a thousand-meter cliff. Two of them—the cook tent and the dining tent—were canvas, tall enough to stand in. The other three were modern two-man domes, one blue, one yellow, and one green, where we slept. They were the single source of color on the field.

It was the flattest place for miles, a few hundred yards of gently sloping ground, between the steep flank of the wall rising above it and the path descending sharply through the boulders to the river below.

On the far side of the river, immense gray granite walls swept up to the tips of the ridges. There were patches of snow, icefalls, streams of running water. Deep in the valley, the day was shortened by the ridges on either side, and the escarpment of snow-covered peaks I knew was there, stretching northward, could not be seen.

Above it all, the sky presided like the most radiant of blue pools, stained with the faintest hint of black.

A mile or so below us, beside the river, stood a village of some thirty homes, and if we walked to the edge of the field and part-way down the slope we could see it. Less than a hundred miles to the north, countless identical villages lay in ruins, and tens of thousands of people lay dead. But there, just south enough, nothing had been touched.

The villagers grew barley and wheat on terraces and apricots in orchards and the sudden emerald and yellow fields leapt up around the houses. From a distance, the village was entirely lovely, with the gray and white snowmelt of the river, and the polished granite boulders, and the brown-walled orchard full of apricot trees, and the high-altitude sun pouring down over everything. In the early evenings, the gentle yellow of the lanterns flowed out of the windows of the mud homes, and sometimes I'd catch a whiff of smoke in the air. But the lanterns didn't burn for long, and a few minutes after sunset the village went quiet and disappeared into the darkness.

For the first few days I had a headache. My pulse pounded in my temples, and when I bent forward to put on my boots I could see the afterimage of my retina, in black and white—blood vessels pulsing in my own eye. A distortion of the globe, perhaps, due to the lower pressure at altitude. That, and dehydration—the dry air sucked the moisture out of us, even without exertion, and it was an effort to drink glass after glass of cold, iodinated water from the river, although I got used to that as well.

At night, when I woke up, I'd listen to the wind rustle against my tent, warm in my sleeping bag, watching my breath enter the air. I soon gave up on the effort of going outside to urinate; when the urge came I made do with a bottle I kept for the purpose, screwed tight, in a pocket sewn to the wall. Despite the cold, I often kept the door partly unzipped, so I could look up from where I lay into the night sky, which seemed active and alive. The sky was entirely unlike the skies I knew—the skies of green trees and cornfields and thunderstorms. I saw shooting star after shooting star, and what appeared to be satellites—silver points crossing rapidly from east to west, or west to east. The Milky Way, also, white as a brushstroke when the moon was down, and then the moon itself, rising over the ridges like a perfect circle of ash. It looked entirely cold and inanimate to me, with none of the tenderness it had in the lowlands to the south. The people here lived at the edges of what was possible—only a few places had such high permanent towns, though the village below us was hardly a town. It was more a rough collection of hardship and unwritten history, and the villagers themselves seemed like visitors as well despite all their centuries of presence. When they left the confines of their village it was with a singular purpose in mind—the gathering of wood, the collection of wandering animals.

That tiny cluster of tents on the windswept field of stones, the altitude, the ridges, the sky overhead, the knowledge that I was as far away from anything I knew as I could possibly be, out beyond the edge of the modern world—it filled me with unease, but also, at first, with a profound sense of relief. For a little while I was gone, and had another role entirely to assume, in a place where no one knew me, where I might be anyone, or anything, like an anonymous traveler in a foreign city.

If ever there was a place for the imagining of ghosts, that was it. I've never been superstitious, but up there, on the wide high reaches, with so many thousands buried alive only a few miles to the north and only a few months ago, absorbed into the ground as if they'd never been there at all—I thought about them, or tried to. It was difficult to imagine them. What I felt instead was a nameless sense of presence, of clarity and empty space.

Sometimes I'd try to read by a tiny light on a wand clipped to the fire-warning tag on the wall of the tent. I hadn't brought many books, and had gone for density and small type as a result. *A History of the British Raj, 1800 to 1900. Islam, an Introduction. Birds of West Asia.* But the books bored me, and I'd wished I'd been more honest in my choices. All that talk of pig grease on cartridge cases, all that dry commentary on the Black Hole of Calcutta, all those steam locomotives and transformative institutions (bureaucracies, universities)—it seemed almost entirely irrelevant. But Genghis Khan was only thirty generations away, as Elise, the German geneticist, had told me at dinner. Only thirty men and women separated his time from ours.

I could only wonder what the villagers talked about as they lay down in their dark houses to sleep, and what they thought of us in our tents above them. On the day we arrived, the chartered Russian pilots, in their white dress shirts with blue epaulets, had roared over the village one by one before landing on the field. We'd sat in the windowless back, on jump seats with the cargo.

I've always loved things like that—industrial machines, helicopters and ships and heavy equipment. I remember a childhood trip to the Hoover Dam, and how pleased I had been to be deep beside the turbines, with steel shafts the size of backyard oaks spinning like mirrors beneath my fingers, and the vast cool presence of Lake Mead above me. At times I wonder whether I would have been happy as an engineer, the kind of man who could look at a mountain of rock and say—*the diverting channel will go here, and then we will start on the spillway. A thousand men and five years should do it.* The world allows hardly anyone such acts, though, in anything.

For the first time in months I was not alone.

CHAPTER EIGHT

Sanjit Rai, our liaison officer, was a few inches taller than I was, with broad military shoulders, a trim, narrow waist, and a black mustache that he had a habit of stroking. His features were sharp, his black eyes set narrowly beside the curve of his nose, with a receding chin, and a prominent Adam's apple that one noticed when he swallowed. When one looked at him directly he was handsome enough, but in profile his nose was too large and his chin too small. His skin was brown, his hair curly and black, his irregular teeth a little yellow from the cigarettes. He had a quick intelligence, and took obvious pleasure in his English, which, though accented, was nearly flawless. It was clear from the start that he enjoyed matching wits with me.

We had many conversations in the dining tent. When the wind was up, and in the evenings, in the cold, we'd keep the elegant Japanese kerosene heater going full blast, sit close to it, and sip a little of the cheap local rum he'd brought with him. Every so often I'd smoke one of his cigarettes, which I hadn't done in decades. At first, before we knew each other, every conversation was another performance. I was trying to pretend my life was something else, and he was giving voice to his ambition, though I don't think he realized it. I believe he thought he was demonstrating our equality, that he was a man of substance also. Once, early on, I made the mistake of answering his inappropriate question of how much money I made each year. I realized my error immediately, but only magnified it by saying that it wasn't really a great deal back home. He was a little drunk, which is undoubtedly why he asked the question at all, but he simply nodded and said nothing, and we both got a little drunker. Even then I couldn't help myself, I couldn't stop myself from entering the dance of men, with all its assessments and judgments and subtle assertions of power. Instead I took to it as eagerly as ever, relieved to find the instinct within me still. Elise left us to it, retreating with her tea to her tent, or writing in her journal in the corner, though occasionally she would roll her eyes at something one of us said.

Sometimes, no matter his care, his comments took on an edge that flashed all the more brightly when he took them back, or made a joke.

"What are you doing here?" he asked. "A rich man like you. Why did you come all this way?"

"I needed an adventure," I replied. Elise looked up from the corner for a moment, then turned back to her journal.

"An adventure?" He didn't laugh, but he smiled. "I thought it was for good works."

"That, too."

He pointed to the heater. "You see this?"

"The heater?"

"The heater. Yes. In this country, we never build that. We just burn all the wood, then we freeze. And then we do not understand why we are freezing. And then we turn to God."

"Ah," I said. "You're a patriot." It was the kind of comment I'd regret the next day. A certain deliberately arch tone, a struggle for cleverness with a man more than twenty years my junior.

He didn't answer at first. Instead, he poured himself some more rum.

"I am a patriot," he said. "But I also hate my country." He took a drag on his cigarette, smiled, and handed me the bottle. "Here, Doctor," he said, "have some more."

"Why do you hate your country?"

He stroked his mustache, and thought for a moment about his answer.

"I hate what we are not," he said, at last, and took a sip from his glass.

For him, the rum was significant. Technically he was on duty all the time, though no one was there to tell him so. But as time passed I came to recognize the small changes in his demeanor. In the day, he was more formal, his gestures to the cooks curt and imperious. He was less familiar with me as well. But after dinner, in the privacy of the dining tent, he relaxed and began his journey westward—the rum, the occasional talk about women, the photograph of his wife and daughters he showed to me more than once.

He asked me about my family also.

"My wife died recently," I said. "I have a grown son."

"Oh," he said, with a sympathetic look.

Impulsively I reached into my wallet, as he had done, and removed the photograph of them both together, taken when Eric was a small boy. He sat in her lap, and Rachel smiled for the camera. She looked happy. I handed him the photograph, and he studied it for a few seconds.

"She is very beautiful," he said. "And your son. I am sorry."

"Thank you," I said, and put the photograph away again.

"I also hope for a son," Rai said, after a moment. "I have only girls."

I smiled politely, and suddenly wondered why on earth I'd showed the photograph to him.

He wore his pistol all the time. It looked crude, but I knew firsthand that it worked well, because one morning, with nothing to do once the loads had been dropped from the helicopters, we went out and shot it.

We passed the piles of provisions—mostly tins of food strapped to wooden pallets—and made our way to the cliffs several hundred meters from our cluster of tents across the sheets of gray boulders and gravel.

Each of us had an armful of empty brown glass and clear plastic bottles. We set them down at the sharp edge of the shadow cast by the cliff. The cliff was silent and dark, not yet touched by the sun. He turned, and took twenty paces back on the sunlit ground.

There was no wind. It was almost warm standing in our jackets in the sun. He took off his sunglasses, breathed on the lenses, polished them with the corner of his shirt, and put them back on. Then he reached into his pocket and took out a clump of cotton wool, which he tore into four pieces.

"For the ears," he said, rolling the cotton into balls and handing two of them to me. I followed his lead, and put them in.

"Okay," he said. "Look at the front sight. The bottle is blurry. Put the front sight just below the bottle."

I hadn't fired a gun since childhood. He took the pistol out of the holster, and pulled back the slide to chamber a round.

"Arms straight," he said, extending the gun. "Both hands. Feet and shoulders parallel. The bottle is blurry. Look at the front sight. Understood?"

His expression hardened.

"I will show you," he said, and fired.

His first shot missed—a jet of gravel leapt up a few inches

from the bottle—but then he was on. The glass exploded, and he turned for the next. Two rapid shots; the plastic bottle whipped one way, then the other. On to the next, two shots, then three more, and suddenly the gun was empty, locked open and smoking, the sound of the shots slapping against the cliffs and echoing down the valley. My ears rang, despite the cotton.

"You're very good at this," I said, speaking loudly because of the cotton in my ears, and his face softened with pleasure.

"I am regiment pistol champion," he said. "But this gun is for military service, not for targets. I have a better one for matches."

"What kind of gun is it?"

"Russian Makarov. We make them also. Very simple and reliable."

Later, he would tell me that colonels and generals were given modern European weapons, jet black and expensive, as a sign of arrival. But he was only a captain.

He slapped in a new clip, chambered a round, and handed the warm gun to me.

"Okay," he said. "Arms straight. Look at the front sight. The bottle is blurry."

I stood awkwardly, trying to imitate the ease of his stance. He stood just behind me, eyeing me critically, and then he reached out and adjusted my shoulders.

"Use one eye only," he said, "and look." He waited a moment. "Okay," he said.

I pulled the trigger, and the pistol cracked and jumped in my hand—a good-natured punch, no more. I was aiming at the glass, because I wanted to see the bottle shatter. But I missed, and the bullet went off into the shadows, and I heard the distinct shriek of a ricochet.

"Too high," he said, and I fired again, closer this time, into the sand on the right.

"Deep breath," he said, and I did as I was told, focusing on the little black line of the sight, aligning it as best I could beneath the vague brown form of the bottle. I felt the trigger give, and as the jolt traveled up my arm, the bottle exploded, just as it had done for him.

"Good," he said, and clapped me on the shoulder.

Later, when the glass was all in pieces and the plastic water bottles were full of holes, and I could still feel the satisfaction of the pistol's recoil in my hands, Elise gave me a stern, disappointed look. She was sitting in the dining tent, and as we passed the open doorway, her eyes met mine. She said nothing, but I felt it, and felt faintly ashamed. The first of the refugees were expected any day, and the tents had not yet been set up. Rai had spent the time going through the provisions, leisurely checking his manifest, and drinking tea. If he felt any urgency, I did not see it.

The villagers stayed clear of us from the start. I didn't know why, in the beginning.

"Shouldn't we start setting up the tents?" I asked, that afternoon. Rai glanced at me, and inclined his head.

"There is no hurry," he said, finally. "But perhaps you are right."

With that, he stood, ground out his cigarette, and put on his jacket.

"I am going to the village," he said.

Elise immediately asked if she could come with him.

"It is better if you do not," he said.

"Why?" she demanded. "I would like to draw their blood. At least to ask them."

"They do not know Western people here," Rai said carefully. "Women especially. They will be suspicious if you want to collect your specimens from them. It is better if we wait until they are used to us. Later, perhaps."

"I do not understand why they will be suspicious of me," she said, looking back and forth between us.

"It's all right, Elise," I said.

She looked at me with annoyance. Rai glanced wearily at me, and left the tent.

"Why did you say I should not go?" she demanded, in her excellent state-funded school English.

"Because he didn't want you to. He must have a reason."

"I do not like people telling me what I should do and what I should not do."

"We don't know anything about them, Elise. We should listen to him."

"I am bored, you know?" she said, grudgingly, after a few moments. "I want to get started."

We were quiet for a while after that, and then she yawned.

"If I cannot go to the village, then I will go to my tent," she said. "I am sleepy."

With that, she stood up from the table and stretched. She was small, thin, and lithe, with a hint of sexuality all the same—curves, subtle but undeniable. I noticed this from the beginning, and it reassured me to feel it—to glance at her, sometimes, in that way, as if I were taking sips of water.

She wore her blond hair short, tapered at the neck. She had pale perfect skin, and blue eyes that leapt out against the fleece vest she wore most of the time. Her gestures were precise and delicate. She stood up straight. Her teeth were small and neat, and only a tracery of lines at the corners of her eyes suggested that she was older than she first appeared. She was working on her Ph.D., and by no means a girl, though she looked like one. In the beginning she was quiet, and when I met her I suspected her of both earnestness and dogmatism. It took me a while to see her playfulness, her humor and irreverence; at first, she was distinguished mostly by the attention that even modestly attractive young women receive when they are alone in a world of men.

Rai was gone for several hours. I sat in the dining tent alone, listening to the wind, restless, trying to read. Elise was in her tent when he returned. He stamped in out of the cold, blew on his hands, poured himself a cup of tea, and promptly lit a cigarette.

"Always they are difficult," he said, shaking his head. "Always. But they will come tomorrow."

I thanked him.

Early the next morning the men appeared. Eight or nine of them. They were bearded, dressed in a strange mixture of cheap Western clothes—worn and blackened tennis shoes, T-shirts—and traditional local cloaks. They wore tight woolen caps, which they touched in deference to Captain Rai. They hardly spoke. They were filthy. They did not resemble Rai, who was from the lowlands. Their skin was paler, with a distinct Asian cast to their features. Some of them had light eyes. They smelled strongly of smoke and a little bit like animals. As individuals they were young, but as a group they looked a thousand years old.

Rai looked at them and sighed. "I need some soldiers," he said, and led them out from the shadows of the camp into the sun on the field, where the tents lay waiting, mildewed and cracked and unfolded for years.

It was cold, especially in the shade, and the wind was picking up and flowing down off the peaks. Everyone's breath was visible. Elise and I retreated to the dining tent for another cup of tea. There was nowhere else to go, and nothing to do but sit there, reading and talking, standing up every so often to stretch. We left the door open, pulled our chairs close to the heater, and watched them.

"We should help," I said. "Don't you think?"

"I don't know," she said.

They seemed to be learning quickly; after only a few minutes of instruction the first tent was being staked into the ground, and Rai was simply standing and pointing. Every so often he'd stamp his feet and walk in a little circle to keep warm. The villagers, though, seemed utterly untouched by the cold, pounding in the metal pegs with stones in their bare hands.

After a few minutes, when the second tent was up and Rai had run his gloved hands across the ropes again to make sure they were tight, it was apparent that he'd had enough. He turned and walked toward us, in his green army jacket, the sun reflecting off his mirrored sunglasses, until he crossed into the shadows again. He stamped into the dining tent, and made straight for the kerosene heater, which was already up and hissing.

"It is very cold," he said. "And time for breakfast."

"It doesn't seem to bother them," I replied.

"They are like that," he said. "We have a brigade of them for mountain duty."

The men had begun to speak. We could hear snatches of words and laughter—a local dialect that Rai told us he did not fully understand. But they kept on, the tents rising one after the other in a neat line. An hour passed, the band of sunlight slowly flowed across the dining tent, and soon we took off our jackets and turned the heater down.

For a while, despite the draft, Rai watched them through the open door as we had done. He took out his watch and timed them—ten minutes, give or take, for each tent. They were identical to the dining tent, designed to sleep perhaps a dozen soldiers, and tall enough to stand in. He took a bite of bread, a sip of tea. He dabbed his lips with his napkin. Then, apparently satisfied, he lit a cigarette, and closed the door.

"How are you paying them?" I asked. "By the tent or by the hour?"

He shot me a look.

"No money," he said, after a pause, "but I will give them some kerosene."

Elise made a soft dismissive sound.

"How much kerosene?" I was curious, mostly because of his reluctance to discuss it. This isn't your affair, he seemed to say. This is a local matter.

"We will see," he said, finally. "Perhaps a few liters per man when the job is done."

It wasn't hard labor, but it was work nonetheless. The villagers, I suddenly knew, had not been given a choice. Captain Rai had gone down to the village, and that was that.

Later, after we'd eaten breakfast, and the valley was fully lit by the sun, Elise stood up and announced that she was going to take a shower. I wanted one as well; already nearly a week had passed, the walls of the dining tent felt close and warm, my hair was sticky, and my underwear needed to be washed. Not entirely unpleasant, not yet, but I wanted to be clean again. The villagers, the men in the field, looked as if they had not bathed ever in their lives and it was easy to understand why: the river was all snowmelt, only a degree or two above freezing.

Elise had come prepared; she had a black neoprene bag with a nozzle that held ten gallons of water, with a collapsible aluminum tripod to hang it from. The whole apparatus was light and modern-looking, with a digital thermometer woven neatly into the bag: it was, it seemed, her single personal luxury. I'd noticed her unpacking it outside her tent several days before and asked what it was. Filled with water, the bag was heavy, and I offered to help her carry it out into the sun to warm.

"It is only a little way," she said, gesturing toward a few

boulders that stood lit up in the sun. "I will sit on the rocks."

The boulders were only a few meters from the tents, and all who cared to look would have a full view of her, back turned or not. Rai glanced at her, but said nothing.

"Elise," I said, "come with me for a moment."

She followed me out the door into the cold. I kept walking into the sun, and the sounds of the workers—stones on metal pegs, the rattle of canvas, and murmuring voices—came to us clearly. When we were out of earshot from the tent, I turned to her.

"Elise," I said, "I know you don't want to be told what to do, but you can't undress and take a shower in front of these men. Don't you understand that?"

She looked at me with her startling blue eyes, in her red hat, and suddenly she seemed terribly young to me, unused to the world as it is. Not naïve, exactly. But uncompromising.

"Dr. Anderson, you are not my father," she said.

I sighed. "That's true, Elise," I said. "I'm not your father. But this isn't a beach in Spain, either. It's asking for trouble. If you want to take a shower, do it where no one can see you."

She pursed her lips, her forehead wrinkled a bit, and I could see her struggling between resenting my comments and acknowledging that perhaps there was some sense to them.

"You are right, maybe," she said, finally.

In the end I helped her carry the bag several hundred yards to an alcove in the side of the valley, close to the base of the cliff and concealed from the camp. The earth beneath our feet was nearly the consistency of sand, and there were many small gray stones that sparkled in the sun. Some kind of mineral—mica, perhaps—was mixed within them. The alcove was sheltered on three sides from the wind. It was quiet, and almost warm. I was out of breath—the bag was ungainly to carry, with only one handle, and we had held it awkwardly between us. After a few moments of rest, she set up the tripod, and we hung the bag high from its hook.

"How long does it take to heat up?" I asked

"Two hours," she said. "But it can get too hot. Once I burned myself."

She had softened toward me, apparently, because as we walked back toward the camp she said I could use it when she was done.

"Thank you," I said. "That would be nice."

A few hours later, after she had come back smiling and clean and flushed, more cheerful, it seemed, than she had been in days, I took her up on the offer.

Standing in the alcove, it felt very odd to undress and stand naked in the hot sun and the cold air, stuffing my dirty clothes in the plastic bag I'd brought for the purpose. I crouched beneath the bag, under the tripod, in the cold circle of mud from Elise's shower, adjusted the nozzle, and let the hot water fall on my hair and back, lathering myself thoroughly with liquid soap that smelled of peppermint and tingled and mixed with the swirling gusts of wind that blew a sheen of dust against my legs. I let all the water run out, until the bag above me lightened and began to flap against the poles, and my wet hair squeaked between my fingers. Then, quickly, before I got cold again, I stepped out onto the dry ground, toweled myself dry, and dressed in clean clothes. Walking back toward the camp, I felt as though I was beginning to wake up at last.

CHAPTER TEN

I asked Captain Rai to direct me to the pallet of medical supplies. Earlier he had deflected me—let us wait until the tents are up before we open the tarps—but the tents would not be ready for days. He sighed and reached for the manifest on the table before him.

"There is no hurry, Doctor," he said. "There is plenty of time."

"It's hard to sit around doing nothing," I replied. "I'd like to get started."

It was too cold to rain, and the pile of provisions and equipment had been left out in the open, dropped in slings by the Russian pilots conveniently close to the dining tent. The pallets themselves all looked alike, and were numbered—twelve heavy burlap bags, wrapped tight in blue plastic sheeting and strapped to a crude platform of soft yellow wood.

Rai paced around the pile, consulting his manifest, before he found it. The pallet weighed at least a thousand pounds, and I stared at it helplessly for a few moments.

"We'll need to set up a tent for the clinic," I said, finally. "Then we can see what we have."

"Okay," he said, and began walking purposefully out toward the line of tents in the field, where the village men had gathered once again.

Rai returned with four men. They walked behind him, the heavy canvas tent rolled in a line on their shoulders. Rai himself carried nothing at all—not so much, I suspected, because of personal unwillingness, but rather for the message it might send. There are those who carry loads, and there are those who do not. I'd chosen a spot perhaps twenty-five yards from the dining tent.

"Is this where you would like it, Doctor?" he said, formally.

"Yes," I replied. "Thank you."

He nodded imperiously at the men, pointed to the ground, and they let the tent fall heavily off their shoulders onto the gravel. They kept their eyes on their feet, and worked silently as we stood and watched—there was none of the laughter that came across the field when Captain Rai was elsewhere. In a few minutes the tent was up.

The mildewed green canvas released yellow shadows on the ground. There was no floor. It was decades old, and would have leaked badly in any kind of rain. A heavy snowfall, too—I could see it sagging under the burden, dripping and giving way. But for the moment the weather was light. Wind the tent could bear, staked tightly as it was to the ground. The door closed with buttons, the poles were dark brown wood.

It was the first day of clarifying work, carrying the frozen bags of IV fluid, the boxes of needles and tubing, the donated samples of antibiotics and anesthetics, the scalpels and suture kits and white coils of gauze. Elise and I did it together—I declined Rai's offer of villagers, feeling a distinct sense of superiority as I did so. I was surprised by how I threw myself into the task, bending and lifting, breathing hard. And my eagerness made me realize that I truly had come for a reason, that the simple freedom of experience was not what I sought. I needed something else, something clear and redeeming and larger than myself, whatever it might be, and in that moment I knew it.

By the afternoon, the tent was stocked; there were even cots for imaginary patients, and IV stands, an examination table, and chairs. A lantern, and another kerosene heater. The wind rattled the sides. I thanked Elise for her help, looking at my empty ward.

"It is nice to do something," she said. "I would like to start my research, but I can do nothing now."

I lit the second kerosene heater to make sure it worked, and sat beside it on an aluminum folding chair for a good while, listening to it hiss, warming my cold hands and knees. She sat beside me, and did the same. I was sore from all the bending and lifting, and breathless from the altitude.

"Are you married, Dr. Anderson?" she asked.

I turned to look at her.

"Please call me Charles," I said. "I was married. My wife died a few months ago."

It was still something I was not accustomed to saying.

"I'm sorry," she said. "That is terrible."

"Thank you."

She paused, but then her curiosity got the best of her.

"Why do you wear your wedding ring?"

"Because it's comforting," I said, after a moment. I had not been asked that question before.

She nodded, as if my answer was a practical one.

"Do you have children?"

"I have a son. He's only a few years younger than you."

"Is he a doctor also?"

"He's an actor. At least, he's trying to be an actor."

"Yes," she said. "It is difficult, I think."

"Not many can support themselves doing it."

"Do you give him money?"

"I do help him, yes," I said, surprised again by her bluntness. Her questions felt like muffled blows.

"Do you think he will succeed?"

"I don't know," I said. "I hope that he will."

I wondered what he was doing at that moment, and realized that for him it was very late at night, and that he must be sleeping.

At his college graduation, as I'd stood with Rachel in the crowd, and he crossed the stage to receive his diploma and his drama award, so young and far away, I could hardly bear to look at him. I did not expect it, but I'd been nearly overcome as we stood with the other parents in the audience, watching our children go, and it was a struggle not to give too much away when his drama teacher—an intense, bone-thin woman with severe gray hair—took me aside at the reception afterward and told me point-blank not to make it difficult for him because he genuinely had a chance. I'm sure she had no idea that her words were precious to me.

I'd seen him onstage a year earlier, howling and screaming in an experimental production written by one of his friends, to which, despite his resistance, I'd invited myself during a quick visit for a conference in the city. The play, at least in my eyes, was not good at all. Eric was the lead. I both pitied and admired him for struggling and storming as he did. It was something I could never have brought myself to do, yet he yelled and swore and flung himself all over the stage. Afterward, there was far too much applause in the small theater full of friends and acquaintances, and too many congratulatory remarks, and a bouquet of roses, and then the playwright himself crept with tentative arrogance out onto the stage for the question-and-answer session. The playwright blinked in the lights. He seemed both painfully young and painfully sincere, and it was hard to reconcile the torrent of brutal language in the script with the boyish author on the stage. My heart both sank and went out to all of them, as I stood and clapped for their bows with the rest. Oh, Eric, I thought. You've got a long road ahead of you.

He'd been drawn to acting in high school. We didn't talk much about it, but that night, over dinner in an expensive restaurant overlooking the lights of the city, I did ask him why he was so compelled by it, why he kept trying while one by one his peers drifted away into the professions.

He replied that there had been a few times, during one performance or another, when he lost himself, when he felt as if he were no longer fully conscious. It was as if he were somewhere else, in the lights, the presence of the audience in the shadows, like standing next to the sea at night—he couldn't even remember the passage of the lines through his mouth. It felt athletic, somehow, or meditative, as if he had stepped beyond himself entirely—he said he couldn't really describe it well, only that it was powerful and strange, and nothing else he'd ever done was like it. He understood why many felt that acting was a self-absorbed pursuit, with little practical use, but those moments made him think otherwise. Somewhere below all the pretense and falsity there was something selfless and profound. In this way, his teacher claimed, acting was a kind of metaphor for our lives. We all assume roles in the everyday world, and though the roles may vary, and though we may be unaware of them in our conscious minds, we endlessly fall into character nonetheless, and let them sustain us, and carry us along. He repeated his teacher's words to me with the sincerity of youth, and as I listened to him it struck me that perhaps his teacher was a more interesting woman than I had thought, one who examined her choices rather than just making them, but also one who undoubtedly sought to impose significance where none, or not so much, existed. It was only acting class, I thought, full of kids who dreamed of being movie stars. It was hardly a metaphor for life. But he meant what he said, and I could see it, and so I was careful to keep my comments as mild as I could.

"Well," I'd said, "if that's true, then how do we tell which role is real? Doesn't that mean that everything is just a kind of game?"

"But that's exactly what we do," he said, looking intensely at me. "We're just not aware of it. We construct our own identities all the time, and our identities always change depending on circumstances. There's no such thing as one identity, really, when you think about it. Acting makes you realize that. You can be anything. It's liberating."

He took a swallow of wine.

"You know," he said. "I can feel it. I really can. I'm feel like I'm just one phone call away, and the phone's going to ring, and that will be it."

"It's never one phone call, Eric. For anything. That only happens in the movies."

"You know what I mean. I'm as good as a lot of people. There is no reason why it shouldn't be me. I've had encouragement here, too. It's not just my teacher."

"You're better than a lot of people," I said.

He smiled then, his face lighting up. He resembled Rachel in some ways—the same coloring and gestures, the same physical ease within himself. But he had none of her restraint, none of her wry watchfulness. He was the opposite of that, another pole of the magnet entirely, and if he had news, I knew it at a glance. He smelled of cigarette smoke, and a single black coil of the tattoo he'd gotten a few months earlier was just visible below the cuff of his shirt at his wrist, and his earring, a dull pewter stud, gleamed a little in the soft lighting, but for an instant, with his dark curly hair and his green eyes, he looked like a boy again anyway. I knew that he was a little spoiled, that he assumed good things would come to him because they always had, and we had given him a bit too much over the years—a new car in high school, trips with his friends, generous sums for clothes and music and all the rest. And though his intelligence was plain, he had little tolerance for work that did not interest him, and his grades in high school had not been good enough for a first-rate college. My own had always been more than good enough, and yet I'd gone to a state university on a scholarship, and part of me resented him for squandering the opportunities I had not been given. But I was also proud to give them, even as I envied him the freedom that he felt was his. With his privilege came something else, something I'd lacked at the same age: he was kinder than I had been, even-handed and generous to his friends, with hardly an ill word toward anyone. I envied him that as well.

In what he'd chosen, though, he was as driven and as disciplined as I ever could have wanted, and that was where I saw myself in him. My handsome, good-hearted son—who was I to deny the possibilities, which perhaps were not impossible, not entirely out of reach?

"Have you been in touch with your teacher?" I asked.

"Yes," he said. "I talk to her every couple of weeks. She's really optimistic for me. She really believes it will happen."

"Tell me," I said, after a moment. "How do you feel when you audition for a part you really want, and you don't get it?"

"Disappointed," he replied. "Of course. Sometimes I'm crushed."

"Which role are you playing then?"

"The role of the waiter," he said, and we both laughed, and I wondered how much Rachel's illness had prompted him to seek solace with that woman, who believed in him and encouraged him, so nearly his mother's age, offering what passed for answers. He was so young, I thought, and so confident, and so full of passionate ideas that would not endure the test of experience. But on that night especially I didn't want to be the voice of caution.

When I finally told him that he was the best thing in the play, that I thought he'd been terrific, he smiled uneasily and confessed that he was embarrassed by the script, and that had in fact been the reason he'd agreed to the role. His teacher had said that in order to develop as an actor he must be willing to immerse himself even in work he was uncomfortable with, and that my presence in the audience had been a still greater test. He must learn to become a chameleon, and lose himself no matter who was watching, and only later indulge in the luxury of choice, and he was trying to follow her advice.

I'd been relieved a little by his words. But it also occurred to me that the world is not so pure, and does not respect or appreciate such trips to the monastery, and what would serve him most of all would be to choose works that would put him in the best possible light at every opportunity. But I said nothing about that, and only raised my glass of wine and touched it to his.

I knew that the trip had surprised and troubled him. When I had called him, and told him of my plans, I could hear it in his silences. He wanted to know how long I would be gone, and when I would return, and though I think by then he understood that I was suffering more than he had realized, to see such evidence of it did little to comfort him. Instead, it disturbed him further, as if the constancy of both my presence and my restraint had sustained him more than he knew.

A few days before I left, a package arrived at my door. It was from Eric, and when I opened it, I saw that it was a gift—a beautifully made, expensive utility tool, stainless steel, full of blades and pliers and tweezers. I imagined him wandering through a sporting goods store, wondering what to buy.

He sent a note, also, neither addressed nor signed. *Please be careful*, it read. Nothing more.

CHAPTER ELEVEN

"What's wrong?" she asked, and I was in the present again.

"I'm sorry," I said. "I'm a little tired, that's all."

"Here," she said, handing me her water bottle. "Maybe you are not drinking enough water."

"Thank you," I replied, taking it. I must have been thirsty, because I drank nearly half the bottle before handing it back.

"That's better," I said, wiping my mouth on the back of my hand.

"Maybe you should lie down."

"I'm fine, Elise. Let's talk about something else."

"All right," she said, puzzled.

"Why don't you tell me about your research," I said, less sharply. "I'd like to hear more about it."

"It is very exciting," she replied. "When the refugees come, I will draw their blood and later we will sequence their DNA. They are isolated populations. They have been in the mountains for a long time, but we do not know how long. We know very little. We will look at the mutations and see where they have come from. From East or West or South. Probably it is a combination. But we do not know. No one has done this here before. It is a new technique. And this camp is good because many people will come through. Better than the camps where they will stop. It is an excellent opportunity.

"I would like to get started soon," she added, wistfully. "I must collect many samples."

"How are you getting permission?"

"I will pay them," she said. "It is only the men, so I hope this will not be a big problem."

"Why only the men?"

"Here we are looking only at the Y chromosome," she said. "It is passed down from father to son. It is a straight line back. We can follow the mutations. It is a very elegant technique. The other chromosomes can come from both men and women. They are more complex to study, you know? Too many possibilities."

"So you're not studying women?"

"For women, we use mitochondrial DNA," she said. "It is also a straight line back. But it is more difficult. So we have decided not to do this for now."

"I'm curious," I said, a bit more bluntly than I intended. "How did you convince them to let you come here? You're doing research, but they told me that they only took people with practical skills and didn't have time for anything else."

"Yes," she said, uneasily. "I feel a little bit bad about this. But Scott let me come if I take some classes. So I am a nurse assistant also. I will do this first, and only then take the blood. I made this promise."

I studied her for a few seconds.

"I'm not really sure where my ancestors were from," I said. "I think they mostly came from Holland and England. My grandmother was Russian. She immigrated as a child. But I don't know much about the rest past a generation or two."

"The United States is interesting for genetics. People came

from so many places. Anderson is a Scandinavian name. Were your ancestors from there?"

"They were English Andersons. Though maybe they were from Scandinavia before that. I don't know."

"Where were you born?"

"Georgia. I spent my childhood there."

"Georgia," she said. "That is the South? Where there were slaves?"

"Yes," I replied. "One branch of my family had slaves a long time ago. But I think most of the others were sharecroppers, although my mother never talked about them."

The lithograph of the family plantation, circa 1840, was one of my mother's most treasured heirlooms. There were slaves in the lithograph—stylized figures, at work behind the oxen in the fields.

"Well," she said, smiling, "that is interesting. Maybe you are even a little bit from Africa. There is always mixing. More than everyone admits. Or maybe some of your ancestors are Indians. This was very common also. If you want I can draw your blood and you will see. We have a large database. It would be easy."

"I know they're mostly from Europe."

"Of course. But in the U.S., often there are surprises."

We were quiet for a moment.

"Okay," I said. "I'll do it. Draw my blood. I'm curious."

"Will you care if some of your ancestors are from Africa?" she replied.

"I've never considered it. Did you think I'd be upset?"

"No," she said. "But sometimes people are upset by these things. So it is good to ask subjects about this first."

She spoke very seriously, and I smiled.

"Well," I said. "My mother wouldn't have liked it, I admit. But I think it would be fascinating."

"Okay," she said, cheerfully, "then I will get my case. Also it will be good practice for me to draw blood. I have not done this since my course."

She stood, and left the tent, and I sat there for a while, thinking about the work she was doing—how all of human history could, in part, be measured in this way. It was astonishing to think that modern men and women had the signs of those ancient journeys within them. I envied her, in that moment, studying that, and suddenly I wished those opportunities might also have been mine.

She returned with an oversized black aluminum briefcase, like the kind photographers use for traveling. I had not seen it before. She knelt on the ground at my feet, undid the clasps, and opened the case.

Inside were hundreds of tiny glass vials, each lying in its own indentation on thin sheets of dark foam rubber. The vials were smaller than those of my experience, smaller even than the ones used on children.

"Do you always have to draw blood?" I asked. "Can't you take hair, or epithelial cells?"

"Yes, you are right," she said. "But blood is better. There is more to work with, and we can repeat the tests if there is a technical problem. Of course, if they are afraid I will swab their cheeks instead. For children also I do this."

She pulled a pair of latex gloves from the case, and an alcohol wipe, and then the syringe, with its capped needle. I watched her, and rolled up my sleeve, feeling a hint of childlike dread as I did so. Then she was readying the syringe, tying the yellow rubber tubing around my upper arm, handing me a square of gauze. My forearm looked very pale beneath me, nearly translucent as I clenched my fist, and braced myself, like diving into a pool.

She crouched before me, ran her naked fingertip gently over

my white skin, and then, finding a blue vein coiling up from the hollow of my elbow, she tore open the alcohol pad with her teeth and touched it there, tingling and shining in the cool air of the tent. She looked up at me, the needle poised in her free hand.

"Okay?" she asked, and I nodded, forcing myself to watch as the needle drew hesitantly near, as she steadied herself, and let out a little hiss between her teeth, and eased the tip of the needle into my vein a bit too slowly. The sting of a thorn, her hand tight on my wrist, the smell of medicinal alcohol in the air, and suddenly there it was, red and warm, springing into the glass vial. In an instant she released my wrist, undid the yellow rubber strap from my bicep, the jet lessened, and blood rose in the vial like an hourglass. I felt her breath against the alcohol on my arm, her nearness, intent on the task, and then the vial was full, the needle was out, and she was done. A few drops fell from the tip, a few others gathered in beads on the sides of the glass. She wiped the vial carefully with the alcohol pad, then held it up between her fingers, and I flexed my arm, pressing a tiny square of gauze to the oozing circle. In the vial, my blood looked black.

"You did that very well," I said, and she smiled.

"Thank you," she said. "I'm a little bit nervous."

"Why?"

"Drawing blood from people you know is different," she said, simply.

"Insert the needle a little faster," I said. "Flick your wrist."

She nodded, seriously, carefully placed a sticker on the vial, and wrote a number on the label with an indelible marker she also took from the case.

"There," she said. "You are the first in my study."

She placed the vial carefully into a slot in the foam rubber beside the empty vials. I looked at it, full as a tick with my blood, and all the men and women whose residue somehow remained within me.

She reached beneath the foam rubber in the case and withdrew an oversized loose-leaf notebook with a red plastic cover, with stenciled black German lettering on the front. She opened the book, then placed another sticker carefully on the page, and wrote down first the number, and then my name.

"What are you doing?"

"I must keep a record of each sample," she said, "so I do not confuse them. This is very important."

"But I'm not really part of the study."

"No," she said, "but the specimens look the same."

I looked over her shoulder at the page.

"It's a book of family trees," I said.

"Yes. For three generations only," she replied. "Grandfather, father, and son. These are the most I will see, I am sure. And so I can keep track of their relationships more easily."

There were several hundred empty pages in the book.

"Do you need that many samples?"

"As many as I can," she said. "Many will be cousins, if they are from the same village. So I have a new page for each village."

She closed the case, and locked it again.

"When do you think they will come?" she asked.

"Rai said in the next week or two," I replied. "They have to spread the word. He said they're dropping leaflets into the villages from the air."

"You know," she said, "we have evolved from things like this earthquake."

"What do you mean?"

"When life is not so hard," she said, "traits are not selected so strongly. But when there is a catastrophe, that is when new traits emerge. Without these events, we would not be the same. If life were simple and easy we would be something else."

"That's interesting," I replied. "I suppose I never thought of it quite that way."

We were in the same companionable moment, in a tent on the most remote hillside imaginable, on the other side of the world. For a while at least it didn't matter that there was nearly another whole adult lifetime—Eric's, for example—between us.

"I've been thinking," I said. "Why don't we give a clinic to the village? Until the refugees show up there's nothing to do. Maybe then they won't be so suspicious, and you can draw their blood."

"Yes," she said, with sudden enthusiasm. "That is a good idea. I will pay them also, of course."

"I'll talk to Rai about it," I said

"This is a very good place for research," she said. "Europe is not so interesting. Families usually come from nowhere else."

"Where are you from in Germany?"

"I am from Munich. I was born there, I went to school there. That is all."

"Your parents?"

"My father is a professor. My mother is a professor, too."

"And now you're going to be a professor as well."

"Yes," she said, and smiled. "Of course. Was your father a doctor also?"

"No," I said. "He wasn't. He injured his back in the war and most of the time he was out of work. It was difficult for him to stand."

"Was he a soldier?"

"He was in the navy. He fell down a flight of stairs on a ship."

"And your mother?"

"She taught school. She supported us, really."

"So you didn't have much money."

"No," I said. "We didn't."

"That is better, then," she said, cheerfully.

"Better for whom?"

"For you, of course," she said. "It is always better to earn things than to be given them."

CHAPTER TWELVE

Elise had gone to bed. We were sipping rum and talking about rifles.

"Western armies," Rai said, "most of them use 5.56. It is too light in my opinion. You need something with more punch. You need to drop him right away."

I have no guns myself, but I've read about them, their nuances and characteristics, their endlessly argued differences.

"It still kills you," I said.

"Of course. But with full metal jacket, 5.56 is like a needle. It just goes through. He can still fire back. Not like 7.62. That will stop you in your tracks."

"A soldier can't carry as much ammunition, though," I replied. "And the recoil is harder to control."

He looked at me with surprise.

"How do you know this?" he asked.

"I like military history," I said, thinking of my study, and how I used to sit with a glass of whiskey and let the blur of the hospital recede into my books—Shiloh and Ypres, Normandy and Tet.

"Yes," he said. "That is the traditional objection. But one round of 7.62 is as good as a burst of 5.56. That is all you need. Just one." He held up a finger.

"What rifle does the army use here?" I asked, pretending to myself that I was humoring him. But in fact I was interested.

"G3," he said. "German. Heavy, but very reliable, very good weapon. We make them under license."

"In 7.62?"

"Of course," he said, and smiled.

"How far away could you hit someone with it?" I asked.

He pondered as if it was a serious question.

"With a scope?" he asked.

"With the basic rifle issued to an average soldier. Nothing more."

I think he was struggling for honesty—he might have made any claim. But he wanted his answer to be true. He thought about it. I saw his youth in the effort.

"The target is standing?" he asked, and I nodded.

"With a G3, assuming good light and no wind, with iron sights, and from a prone position," he said, finally, "five hundred meters. Perhaps a bit more. But a sniper rifle, 7.62, with a scope, much farther, of course. One thousand meters in good conditions, no problem."

"Are you a good shot with a rifle as well?"

"I am better with handguns. But I am okay with a rifle also."

We sipped at our rum, and he lit a cigarette.

"In the old days there was tourism in the northern areas," he said, after a bit. "And mountain climbing. Now there is much less."

"Is it really that valuable?" I asked. "Does it matter which side has it?"

"It is complex," he said. "There are resources, but also it is about other things."

"Such as?"

"It is about national interests," he said. "About wrongs. These are important."

I made a dismissive sound.

"When you look at your country," he replied sharply, "and the wars it has fought, how many were not the same?"

"Some were just, and some were unjust," I said. "Which one is this?"

"A just one, of course. There have been many provocations. And it is not so much a war."

"What is it then?"

"It is an almost war."

"I was never in the military," I said, after a while, "but it seems to me that in order to be a good soldier you have to enjoy it."

"What do you mean?"

"You have to enjoy killing the enemy."

He thought for a moment.

"You must enjoy aiming the gun," he said at last. "But pulling the trigger—that is duty. It is not the same."

"Do you enjoy pulling the trigger?"

He looked uncomfortable, and, suddenly, a bit sheepish.

"I don't know," he said.

He chewed on the corner of his mustache.

"I need to do it," he continued, finally. "At least once. For the experience. It is important to understand what it is like in combat. That is where you find out who you are. Whether you are cool under fire."

"What if you're not?"

"Yes," he said, and smiled. "That is a big problem."

His desire for the experience of war, even to kill another soldier, would have disgusted Elise. I could picture her shaking her head, looking away. But I understood him perfectly.

"Just imagine," I said, "all the young officers on the other side thinking exactly the same thing."

He inclined his head, and didn't answer me. No doubt it was a strain on him—small talk with foreigners, the ambivalence he must have felt toward us and toward himself as well, so far from the action.

"My English," he'd said, "is helpful to me in many ways. But sometimes it is not so good to speak so well." I'd been complimenting him, shortly after we first met.

"Why is that?"

"I am a soldier," he'd replied. "But really this is civilian work."

I didn't press him, but I was reminded of a television interview given by the leader of the country I'd seen before I'd left. The general spoke perfect English—I'd seen him on TV before—but he gave the interview through an interpreter. He talked about national identity, of past wrongs, of provocations. But, he said, he was a man of peace. He said he was looking forward to a fruitful discussion with the foreign secretary, and hoped only that the other side would be as open to compromise. He wore his uniform, he looked drawn and severe, he was speaking to the endlessly restless crowd at his back—of that I had no doubt—and every word was in his native tongue.

The tea had gone through me. I stood, retrieved my jacket from where it lay on the top of the table.

"You are going to bed?"

"I'm going to the bathroom."

"Oh," he said. "Then I will go with you."

We stepped out of the tent together, into the darkness that had abruptly fallen over the valley. The moon was half full, and I didn't need the headlamp in my pocket.

To the south, all the stars were up. For an instant I thought of those long-ago summers on the Michigan lakes, where I'd sit with Eric in our canoe and try to pick out constellations that trembled through the haze that rose from the surface. We'd sit quietly, and drift among the fish rings, shining our flashlight on the book, feeling the cold of the water seep through the aluminum at our feet.

But at that height, the stars were close to their pure state, untouched by anything, let alone the forests of the upper peninsula, or the voice of my son as a child, or other people's fires in the campgrounds through the trees.

To the north, however, the sky was blank, and I realized there were clouds moving toward us through the darkness.

"There is a front coming," Rai said, pointing. "I listened to the radio this afternoon. There will be snow, I think."

"The tents look old," I replied.

"They will be okay," he said. "The snow is very dry."

Elise's tent was dark, and we walked past in silence so as not to wake her. Soon we were out in the field, the dining tent glowing in the distance behind us. The rest of the camp was invisible.

Rai stopped then, turned carefully away from me, and unzipped his fly. His urine splashed loudly on the ground, and it must have embarrassed him, because he stopped midstream and walked farther into the dark before continuing. It was not the kind of thing a Westerner would have done, I thought, as I emptied my bladder into the ground at my feet. His physical modesty, his unease—had women been present, his discomfort would have been natural. But there were only the two of us, on a dark night. He must have been listening to me, also, because he returned only when I'd finished.

I kept walking, and he followed. The blank part of the sky lent promise to the air. We walked for a while, in silence, and then he lit a cigarette, letting out a stream of smoke that mingled with his breath in the cold.

"When are they going to come?" I asked. "Why aren't they here?"

Rai sighed.

"It is difficult to communicate with them," he said. "They are scattered across a wide area. It will take time. We must be patient."

"At least a few of them should have shown up by now," I said, but he did not reply.

We reached the first of the shadowy tents on the field. No wind, for the moment, but I imagined that would change soon, and by morning they would all be flapping and shaking.

"Does it ever rain up here?" I asked.

"Not at this time," he said.

"So the trees in the village and the crops—is that all irrigation?"

"Yes," he said. "Irrigation from the river. They have many channels. It is an old village."

"How old?"

"I don't know. A long time, I think." He paused. "They are very backward people."

"They've stayed away from us. I expected them to be more curious."

"They do not like us," he said. "They are afraid."

"Why? What are they afraid of?"

He turned to look at me.

"They are afraid of the army," he said. "And also they are afraid that when these tents are full they will have no wood and their animals will be stolen."

"How do you know that?"

"Because I know them," he said.

I thought for a moment.

"Are you worried about them?" I asked.

He laughed.

"No," he said, "I am not worried. There are too few. Perhaps forty men. And they have nowhere else to go. And they know I have a satellite phone." He smiled. "I told them that I can have a company of soldiers here in two hours if there is any trouble. It is always the same in the tribal areas."

"Is that why the camp is by such a small village?"

"Yes, Doctor, that is why. There are some larger villages in this region. But there are always more problems then."

The moon began to pass back and forth behind clouds. It would get very dark for an instant, then brighten again.

Rai stretched, then pressed a button on his cheap watch to light up the time. It was early, but I felt the day's work catching up with me.

"I'd like to give a clinic to the village," I said. "I'm doing nothing. I'm sure some of them could use my help."

He hesitated in the darkness.

"If you wish," he said, finally. "But if you give them anything, they will ask you for more. Always they are this way. You should know this."

"Can we do it tomorrow?" I said.

He took a last drag on his cigarette, then threw it down and ground it out with his boot.

"If you wish," he said, finally.

"I know Elise wants to draw their blood for her study, also. She'll pay them to do it. Will that be a problem?"

"If you pay them," he said, with reluctance, "probably it will be okay."

"Good."

He stared moodily out into the dark.

"Well, then," I said awkwardly, "good night."

"Good night," he replied, and I left him there, standing among the rows of empty tents. I wondered what was in his thoughts, as I took out my headlamp for the first time, and let it play over the ground at my feet on the way back to my bed. Probably he was simply planning ahead, thinking of all those who soon would be sleeping in the empty tents all around him—the water they would need, and the fuel, the problems of the latrines, and how they would be fed, and when they would learn that we were there.

CHAPTER THIRTEEN

The next morning the sky was a low steely gray, with swirling mist at the tips of the ridges. It was cold without the sun, and clammy, as if the sea were nearby. There was no wind.

"It is going to snow," Rai said, at breakfast. "Maybe it is better not to go to the village today."

"If it starts snowing too much we can come back," I said, wondering why it had come over me so strongly—the need to work, to get started at last.

Elise nodded eagerly as she finished her bowl of oatmeal.

"I am ready," she said. "I have my case."

Rai sighed, and shook his head, but then he stood.

"Okay," he said. "If you want to go, then we will go."

I had a bag—antibiotics, ointments, a few rolls of gauze. Antihistamines and anti-inflammatories. I'd filled it before breakfast, enjoying the heft and sense of purpose it gave me.

"It will be cold today," Rai said. "Dress warmly."

He put on a green wool hat, and produced mittens from the pockets of his army parka, and then we all stood up and left the tent.

Already the villagers were out on the field, working on tents, and we paused to watch them for a moment.

"Do you need to stay here with them?" I asked Rai, realizing that our departure would require them to work on unsupervised. But Rai shook his head.

"They know what to do now," he said. "They will be okay."

There was no path leading from the camp to the village. As we picked our way down the rocky slope toward the river, the sky grew darker, and for the first time there were a few tiny flakes of snow in the air. The sound of the rushing water came up to meet us as we descended to the bank, where a thin path appeared before us. Looking up I saw that the mist now covered the tops of the ridges entirely.

Soon the village was in plain sight. The houses stood at a bend in the river, where the water widened and slowed. Beyond the village lay the terraced fields, with their new green crops, dull in the gray light and the low clouds. Smoke rose. Beyond, in the fields, figures were working.

As we neared the village, a dog barked, and the first of the children appeared. They seemed to come from nowhere—one moment we were walking alone, and the next they were upon us. Four or five of them, with their high-pitched voices. Unlike the adult men, there was no wariness, and in a moment they were tugging at our sleeves and peering at us and pulling at our day packs. Rai turned on them, shouting fiercely, and they fell back.

The children looked perhaps eight or nine. Their hair was reddish black, their eyes dark and wide. For the moment they looked fed, but this, I knew, was seasonal, and I had no doubt that they'd gotten by on the barest of food at times, and that their growth was stunted as a result. So they were small for their ages, and this gave them an odd, preternatural air. If they moved well, and quickly, and spoke in long passages, it was because they were far older than they appeared to be. There was nothing attractive about them. They hardly seemed like children at all, in fact, but some other human form altogether. When they stepped up close, pulling at my clothes, with their flowing noses and red-black hair and grubby fingers, the desire to shove them off with inappropriate force was difficult to resist.

Elise fumbled in her pack, then pulled a bag of candy from it with a look of expectation on her face. She opened the bag and began tossing the hard candy to the children, who followed us closely.

They fell on it. A kind of reflex, I think—they must not have had much experience with such gifts in the past. They snatched off the wrappers and put the candy in their mouths. But after a few seconds, with dismay on their faces, they began spitting out the candy on the ground and wiping their mouths on the backs of their hands.

"What did you give them?" I asked. I was tempted to laugh, but Elise looked crestfallen.

She handed me the bag. I put one in my mouth.

"It's sour," I said. "Maybe that's it."

Rai looked on, and said nothing.

"Do you have any caramels? Maybe they'd like those better."

"I have some at the camp," she said. "But I only bring these now."

From the heights of the ridge, the village had looked lovely and clean, but up close it was as filthy as the children it produced. We followed the main path to the center, with narrower alleys branching off between the houses beside it. An overflowing stream ran through the middle of the path, diverted from the river, turning the earth to freezing mud. Offal, somewhere, and the vague odor of excrement, and little bits of refuse carried by the clear water out toward the fields beyond. There was the smell of smoke and snow in the air, and the gray sky seemed close and thick overhead. The children were shouting, and a moment later the men began to emerge from the homes beside us. There were six or seven of them, bearded, restrained, murmuring to one another. They had weapons on their shoulders—mostly antique rifles, a century old or more, but several carried battered AK-47s. There were women also, watching through the windows, or standing in the doors, but they did not approach. Other dogs barked, but we did not seen them, and I imagined that they were tied up behind nearby walls.

Rai addressed one of the men. He spoke calmly and at length as we stood there, the villagers gathering steadily around us. We'd reached the village center, at a confluence of paths. The houses around us were brown mud, with narrow slits for windows.

The man Rai addressed wore a dark blanket over his thin shoulders, and a tight wool cap. His teeth were yellow and long, and his eyes, like his beard, were gray. Unlike the others around him, he was unarmed.

The man listened intently, and then he bowed and came forward, and took Rai's hand in both of his own, and shook it gently. The others stared at Elise and me, murmuring to one another, as the children milled around them. The man spoke, and gestured, then spoke again.

"What's he saying?" I asked Rai.

"He is the head of the village," Rai replied. "He is offering us some tea."

"Did you tell him why we're here?"

"Of course," Rai replied.

More discussions ensued. A few minutes passed, and then the young man who had entered the house returned with a plastic tray. On it were a few clear chipped glasses, and a single charred and battered metal teapot.

He poured it for us one by one. I blew on the small hot glass in my hands, smiling and nodding, hesitating, but then I sipped, as did Rai and Elise and the village headman. The tea was black, bitter, and hot.

The headman spoke again.

"He is sorry they have no sugar," Rai said. "He is apologizing."

"Tell him not to worry," I replied. "That the tea is very good."

Rai did as I asked. We stood and drank, as they watched us. I wondered why we had not been invited inside.

The minutes dragged on. Rai went back and forth with them, gesturing, and each time he spoke the men would murmur among themselves in low voices, as if discussing his words. Elise and I stamped our feet in the cold, waiting, and my impatience grew.

"What's taking so long?" I asked Rai.

"They are always like this," he said. "They are deciding what to do. Everything takes time with them."

"We should start," I said. "Or we can come back later if they like."

To my surprise, Rai translated my words.

The head of the village looked at me, and then he turned and said something over his shoulder to the others behind him.

A light snow began to fall. We waited, and finally a man emerged from another house with a rough unstained wooden table in his hands. Two boys followed, carrying a similar wood bench between them. The headman spoke again.

"He says it is best if we go to the orchard," Rai said.

The orchard had high mud walls, and stood pressed against the village. We wound our way through one of the narrow alleys to a pair of unplaned wooden doors in the wall. To my surprise, the doors were padlocked, with a rusty link of chain between them. The headman produced a key, opened the lock, heaved aside the doors, and gestured for us to enter.

"Why is it locked?" I asked Rai.

"So the apricots will not be stolen, of course," he said. I wondered who the thieves might be, and who owned the apricots, but I said nothing.

The wall around the orchard traced a rough circle perhaps thirty yards in diameter. The wall was high—nearly ten feet, smooth and brown. Part of the creek had been diverted beneath the wall, and then divided again into a dozen or so smaller channels, like a bed of capillaries, before converging again and flowing out beneath the wall toward the fields beyond. The ground underfoot was soft with old leaves. Tangles of calf-high grass and weeds grew in profusion.

The apricot trees stood at irregular intervals, ten or so feet apart from one another, and cast their branches out above our heads. The trees themselves were perhaps thirty feet high, and oddly delicate, with their gray-green leaves, and their trunks little larger than my waist. Overhead, in the density of the trees, hundreds of yellow-orange apricots hung from the branches, glowing against the heavy gray sky overhead.

The headman led us out to the center of the orchard, where the trees were larger and spaced more widely, and gestured to the man with the table. They stamped the grass a bit with their feet, and then they put both the table and the bench on the ground.

The crowd of villagers flowed in through the doors, and began fanning out along the walls on either side. I could hear them moving through the trees behind me, chattering excitedly, encircling us.

I put my pack down on the table, and then turned to the headman, who watched me impassively, glancing occasionally at Rai. Elise put her case down on the table as well, and put her hands into the pockets of her jacket.

"Okay," I said to Rai. "Please tell them to get in line, and I'll see them one by one. Then Elise can draw their blood and pay them."

Elise looked hesitantly at Rai. Rai thought for an instant, chewing on his mustache, as if deciding what to say. He turned to the headman, and spoke at length. There were no women in the crowd. One of the nearby men lit a cigarette with a match, took a long drag, and then passed it along to the others.

The headman watched Rai as he spoke, his face unreadable, and again he turned to the men behind him and spoke. They answered, and he listened carefully to the replies. Back and forth, for a minute or two, as we waited. Then finally he turned to Rai, a question in his voice.

"He wants to know why you want to take samples of their blood and what you will use it for."

"Please tell him that we are doing a scientific study to learn where their ancestors came from," Elise said, "and that if they do not want me to draw their blood I will not. And that I will pay them for each specimen."

"They will not understand," Rai said. "I will tell them only that you will pay, that it will not hurt them, and that they do not have to do it unless they wish."

Rai spoke carefully. A few seconds passed, and again the men discussed this with themselves. The head of the village asked a single question.

Rai turned to Elise.

"How much will you pay?"

"One pound for each vial," she said.

Rai grimaced.

"That is a lot for them," he said. "It is too much."

"It is okay," she said. "There are not so many of them. I want them to agree."

He stared at her for an instant, then shrugged and answered the question.

His words had dramatic effect. The men went quiet, and if anything became more watchful.

"Tell him," I said, impulsively, nodding toward the headman, "that since he is the head of the village we will give him two pounds for his blood."

Rai did as I asked. The man turned and spoke to the others behind him, and then they all began talking at once.

"Please tell them again that they don't have to get their blood drawn if they don't want to," I said. "And that I'll see them anyway and give them free medicines."

Again Rai did as he was told.

"Maybe Elise should draw your blood first," I said to Rai. "It might reassure them."

He looked at me with dismay.

"Why mine, Doctor?" he replied. "And not yours?"

"She's already drawn mine," I said. "I'll do it again if you want. But I think drawing yours might be more effective."

He glanced back and forth between us, then inclined his head in that characteristic sideways nod I'd seen so often among them, which Rai did only rarely, and only, as I'd come to realize, in moments of unease.

"If you wish," he said, finally. His voice was cold.

He spoke to the men again.

"What are you saying?" I asked.

"I am telling them I will show them what it is," he said, tightly, "so they know it is nothing."

"Elise," I said, "you're on."

Rai gave me a dark look before turning back to the men.

Then he took off his heavy parka, draped it over the table beside my bag, and rolled up his sleeve, exposing his brown forearm to the air. He did it quickly, forcefully.

"Thank you, Sanjit," Elise said, as she bent and quickly unsnapped her case, then sat down on the bench.

He extended his arm across the rough table toward her, beginning to shiver in the cold despite himself. Goose bumps had risen on his skin. Elise bent over his bare arm, readying the needle and the vial and the alcohol pad and the yellow rubber tourniquet, and all the while Rai kept his face impassive, determined to betray nothing. The men craned their necks, and moved closer.

To her credit, she did it well, better than she had for me. She snapped the tourniquet around his arm, and waited as he squeezed his fist as she asked, and the vein rose in his forearm. She cleaned his skin with alcohol, then flicked the needle in as I had told her to and released the tourniquet. The jet of Rai's blood instantly filled the vial, and then the needle was out, and he was folding up his arm, pressing a ball of cotton to the oozing spot, his face impassive. He put on his jacket, as Elise stood up from the table and held the tiny vial up in the air.

"That is all," she said. "Just a little. No more than a fly."

"Good job," I said to her, quietly, as Rai translated her words once more, and she labeled Rai's vial, just as she had done for mine, and noted its number down in her book, and placed it carefully in the open case.

"Thank you," I said to Rai, who did not reply. He held his hand pressed to his forearm through his jacket.

"Okay," I said. "Let's get started. Ask them to get in line. I will see them, and then Elise can draw their blood."

Rai did as I asked, but the men hesitated.

"Ask him," I said, gesturing to the headman, "if there is anything wrong. Ask him if anything is bothering him."

Rai spoke, and the man glanced nervously at me, murmuring a reply.

"His knees, I think," Rai said. "He is saying that his knees hurt him."

"Both, or only one?"

"Both, he says. But one is worse. And his back also."

"Is the pain greater in the morning?"

Rai asked the question. The man nodded in response, and began pointing to his knees and then to his back.

"Yes," Rai said. "He is stiff in the morning. His knees hurt him. But then they get better in the day."

The man looked down, his hands clasped together.

"Tell him I need to look at his knees."

I stood, and rounded the table. There was a ripple in the crowd around us.

The man fumbled with his cloak without hesitation, drew aside the blanket draped across his shoulders, rolled up his loose brown cotton pants, and extended his leg. It was thin and pale, his knee knobby and swollen. I crouched down, and took off my gloves, and reached out. The man's flesh felt cool, and I ran my hands over his knee.

"Ask him to bend it," I said, as the others gathered around him and began talking all at once.

The man's knee popped and clicked beneath my hand, a knot of gravel and bone.

"He has arthritis," I said, as I stood and reached into my pack, and found the bottle of pills.

"Tell him to take these when he eats," I said, and handed the bottle to the man. "Otherwise they might irritate his stomach."

The man said something to Rai.

"He wants to know if they will make him better."

I hesitated.

"Tell him yes," I said finally.

The man took the pills, and held them carefully against his chest.

"Okay, Elise," I said, and she smiled at the man, reached into her pocket, withdrew a roll of money, and carefully peeled off two worn bills and handed them to him. He stared intently at the notes, and then took them and tucked them away. A few seconds passed, and Rai's eyes narrowed, but then, to my relief, the man rolled up his sleeve and extended his arm as Rai had done. Elise opened an alcohol pad, withdrew a new clean needle, and without hesitation, as quickly and efficiently as she could ever have wanted, she found the vein, and filled the vial, and then he was stepping back with the ball of cotton pressed to his arm. The whole transaction was over in only a few seconds, and again I was proud of her—how steady she'd been, as if there was no audience at all. She asked his name then, and carefully wrote it in the book, and put the sticker on the vial, and looked up, smiling, at the others.

Without further discussion, the line formed, and just then the snow began to fall more heavily. The flakes were as large as moths in the air, and fell straight down, as dry as talcum, and when they struck our clothes they collapsed into powder. In a few moments the more distant trees of the orchard dissolved, and the figures in the crowd lost definition behind a curtain of falling snow. We sat on the bench, and one by one they stepped from the background up to us.

After the first awkward moments, it went smoothly. The figure would step forward. Rai would speak. I would listen, the man—they were all men—would answer. I would rise, and do a quick examination, and reach into my bag for some pills—I was careful to give each man something—and then Elise would do her work. None of them refused. I tried not to watch her, I tried to focus on the patient before me, but nonetheless there was a glint of needles beside me, the sound of the rubber strap and the rustling of sleeves. She did it well, easing each needle in and out as if she'd done it for years. One by one they stepped back, a bill in one hand and a ball of cotton in the other. As the minutes passed, I could feel them relax, and several times I heard laughter in the crowd.

"It is better to hurry," Rai said, as time passed. "It is snowing more. We must go back soon and check on the tents."

Periodically I would sweep the snow off the table with my glove, and stand, and shake it off my coat.

They had bad teeth. It was the single most common complaint among them—their teeth hurt. They woke them at night. And so on. A bottle of antibiotics, a bottle of painkillers. I know nothing of dentistry.

A young man with a superficial skin infection, a honey-colored crust on his chin, his thin dark beard, his eyes the color of mud.

"Tell him to wash twice each day with soap and warm water," I said, "and I'll give him some antibiotics."

As he took the pills, I wondered if he had any soap.

Another bottle from the pack. Already I was running low. Impetigo, nothing more. It would clear up on its own anyway.

A scarred hand, a finger that would not straighten.

"He was cutting wood," Rai said. "It was a long time ago, he says."

Another bottle from the pack. Ibuprofen again.

"There's nothing I can do for that," I said. "But these will help if he has pain."

They were thin, not starving. But I was surprised, once the floodgates had opened, at how eagerly they pointed to their mouths or elbows, or clutched their bellies, and how greedy they were for my bottles of ibuprofen and generic penicillin, which I knew would ease their aches only for a little while. I wondered what powers they had invested in me, and why, because even as I played along I knew better.

Then an old man, one of the last we saw. Wheezing, hunched over a stick, eyes wide and bulging, he appeared like an apparition. His beard was entirely white, his legs thick and doughy at the ankles, his lips dusky and pale. Two younger men helped him forward, and I realized that they must have gone to find him.

"He cannot breathe," Rai said, growing steadily more impatient. "He cannot walk far. He sits up at night to sleep."

I stood again, and rounded the table, and approached him. He looked up at me. I knew what he had before I touched him. I'd seen it a thousand times before.

I wiped the snow from my stethoscope, from where it lay draped around my neck, and when, after some coaxing, the man finally exposed his thin, dirty chest to the air, I pressed the cold metal to the skin beneath his left nipple, and listened. The odor of his unwashed body rose out of his clothes into the cold.

His heart, a jumble of clicks and murmurs, skipping and leaping, and then his lungs, full of crackles, wet and heavy and thick, as he wheezed on.

"What is wrong with him?" Elise asked, looking up from the table as the man covered himself again. "He looks very sick."

"He is very sick," I said. "His heart is failing."

"Why is his heart failing?" she asked.

"It's hard to say. He might have had a heart attack. Or he might have had rheumatic fever at some point. There are a number of possibilities."

The man spoke, with difficulty, to Rai.

"He is asking you to help him," Rai said.

"I will give him some pills," I said, finally, to Rai. "The pills will make him urinate. His legs will be less swollen and his breathing will improve. He'll feel better for a while."

I reached into the pack.

"Will he be all right?" Elise asked, staring at the man.

"No," I said. "He'll be dead soon."

"Maybe he should go to a hospital," she persisted.

I shook my head.

"It's too late," I said. "A hospital couldn't do much for him either. He's an old man with a bad heart and there's nothing anyone can do."

I handed him the pills. I didn't look at him very closely. I thought they were going to lead him away. But the man spoke again.

"He wants you to draw his blood," Rai said, evenly, to Elise.

She blanched. For the first time I think it struck her. She turned to me.

"It won't hurt him," I said.

She hesitated, and the man spoke again.

"He says his blood is still good," Rai said.

Elise bit her lip, but then she smiled at the man, and did as he asked, reaching for his wick-thin arm.

"I would like to give him more," she whispered.

"Then do it," I replied, and before Rai could speak she'd pressed a handful of bills into his hand. It surprised him, clearly, and he put the money under his cloak as quickly as he could. He touched his hat, and bowed several times, and then, finally, the young men at his elbows helped him away. If those watching in the crowd saw what he'd received, they gave no sign.

The last man was a repeat visitor. Rai smiled contemptuously.

"He wants her to draw his blood again," Rai said, "and pay him again."

Elise smiled also, but more kindly, brushed the snow from her hat, and shook her head.

"We only need one sample," she said. "Please tell him."

The young man looked down at his feet, murmuring his request again.

"You see," Rai said. "If you give them anything, they will ask for more." He turned to me. "We must go, Doctor," he continued. "I must check on the tents. The snow is heavy now."

"Tell them we will come back," I said, "when the weather is better."

Rai translated for the last time, as the snow fell around us and slid in clumps out of the trees, and the apricots shone in the branches overhead. We stood, quickly, and Elise closed her case, and then without saying anything else Rai led us out through the crowd to the alley.

They followed. Already the roofs of the houses were draped in white, and the mud beneath our feet had disappeared, as if the village had been cleaned and remade. The sense of windless, abiding quiet, the vague mass of figures behind us, in and out of the curtain—we walked, listening to their excited, muffled voices fade away as finally they thinned out by the edge of the village. A few of the children continued with us up the trail beside the river for a while, but then they too turned back, and we were left alone with the river and the falling snow. I could see only a short way, as if I were walking with a lantern on a dark night. The river led us back.

CHAPTER FOURTEEN

All night the snow fell, whispering against the sides of my tent, and in the morning there were nearly three feet on the ground. Only the cook, Ali, was waiting for me at breakfast as I stamped in and shook off my jacket. For the first time I looked at my watch and realized I'd slept late, and that the others had eaten without me.

Ali was a small man in his forties with bad teeth, a patchy black beard, and a wet, alert gaze. When his few words of English were exhausted—Tea? Omelet? Finish?—he would smile and bob his head. He seemed like a different species entirely from the villagers who had erected our tents, thin from weakness rather than from strength, a man whom everyone looked through. Rai claimed to know little about him, only that he was from a large city to the south and had many children. He slept in the cook's tent with his nephew, who did the washing up, the sorting and stacking, and all the rest. The boy rarely entered the dining tent. Ali and his nephew seemed to get along well—we never heard a sound from them, and the meals came like clockwork. Unlike Rai, they prayed five times a day, in front of the cook tent, on plastic mats, falling to their knees, bowing, bowing again. They did it every day, no matter the weather, and I found it touching to watch them—the faith of the poor, who understand that their fates are beyond them, and their rewards must wait.

"Omelet?" Ali said, smiling, as I brushed off by the doorway and stamped my feet clean and took off my jacket.

"Yes, please," I replied. "I'm sorry I'm late."

"Okay," he said, and was gone.

A few minutes later he returned with his battered aluminum tray. He stood behind me in the corner by the heater as I ate. Usually he left, returning later for the dishes. I suppose it was because of the cold, and Rai's absence, and the fact that he was dressed thinly, with a cheap-looking tracksuit under what appeared to be a green cotton army surplus jacket. No gloves, damp dark wool socks in worn, off-white plastic tennis shoes of the kind that are sold to the poor by the truckload in market stalls throughout the world. There was an odor in the tent, and after a while I realized that it was his feet. The smell was tolerable, but unpleasant all the same, and I ate the omelet quickly, and the heavy white bread with a hint of mold and a packet of jam, washing it down with another lukewarm cup of tea.

"Thank you, Ali," I said, as I wiped my mouth on the napkin.

"Finish?" he said, smiling, bobbing his head, coming forward to the table.

"Yes, finished."

"Okay," he said, and put my dishes on the tray. Then he was gone, out through the door into the snow with my dishes in his arms. The whole of it embarrassed me—his stinking feet, his obeisance, the way he stood and waited for me to finish my breakfast with such patience. He was poor, he was there for the money, and I'm sure it was going into the mouths of his wife and children somewhere in the slums, but I wished he hadn't stood there like that, and I wished I hadn't so utterly ignored him as

I ate my fill. Suddenly, I thought of Eric, standing in his white dress shirt and pressed black pants—yes, sir. There are several specials this evening. But of course it wasn't the same, not even close. Ali waited by a distance he could never in this world hope to cross. I was sure there was no dream behind his indignity, and I doubted whether he even felt indignity at all. He just stood there and watched.

Already the tracks I'd left from my tent were filling in. But it was only a few hundred yards to the main body of the tents, and if I missed them I could simply keep going until I reached the end of the field, then trace my way back along the side of the cliff. So I set off, in my hat and heavy down jacket. In a few minutes I was entirely in my own world, lost in my own breath. I felt as if I was wading through shallow water, with flakes as large as leaves falling to pieces as they struck my clothes, clinging to my eyelashes and eyebrows. I tried to walk straight ahead, paying close attention. Several times I turned around to examine my tracks, satisfying myself that I wasn't wandering in circles. But then I heard voices in the expanse before me, and followed them to the first of the tents.

It was three men from the village. They were knocking the snow off the roofs of the tents with spare wooden tent poles. At first, they didn't see me. One man, shorter than the others, was having difficulty reaching high enough with his pole, and the others were laughing at him. Their faces were flushed and damp from exertion, they looked young and happy and unreserved in their ragged clothes and their round wool hats and their off-colored eyes. For an instant I was tempted to retreat into the snowstorm—I felt abruptly self-conscious, as if I were about to enter a room of strangers at a black-tie affair—but then one of them saw me, and said something to the others. They turned around, and fell silent, and the door closed.

"Hello," I managed, with an awkward wave of my gloved hand.

"Hello," one of them replied, bowing his head before looking up at me again.

"Captain Rai?" I asked.

They didn't understand.

"Captain Rai?" I said again. The short man muttered something.

"Rai," one of the taller men said, as it came to him, pointing down the row. "Rai."

I thanked them. They bowed their heads; they smiled and did not meet my eye. It was many degrees below freezing, they were brushing the snow off the tents and banging it loose with wooden sticks, it was all over them, and yet they were hardly dressed. No gloves, the thinnest of shoes, and it didn't touch them. They were like birds, in the dead of winter, with pale bloodless feet clasped tight to the wire.

Rai and Elise were with the rest of the villagers at the northern end of the tent city. The snow made it difficult to set up more tents, so Rai had set them to work clearing the roofs. They walked back and forth down the rows with their sticks. How long he would keep them at it was unclear; the snow showed no sign of relenting. Elise held a pole, and was pitching in with the rest, but Rai stood empty-handed, hooded in his parka, some distance from the others.

"Good morning," I said.

"Good morning," he replied, shortly.

"How are the tents holding up?"

"It is snowing heavily. But if we keep the loads down probably they will be okay."

The tents were standing, but the roofs bowed beneath the weight, straining the lines that held them to the ground. The villagers were entering the tents with their poles, and lifting the roofs from within. From a distance, the tents swelled, and the powder slid off them.

"It's a good thing they're empty," I said.

"Why?"

"Can you imagine what it would be like if we had two thousand people here? In this?"

"Then they could clean their own tents," he said. "I would not have to do it for them."

He paused to light a cigarette, then continued.

"This will delay them," he said. "They will not be able to cross the passes until the snow melts."

"How long will we have to wait?"

"I don't know."

Elise had seen me.

"Here," she said, trudging toward us, handing me her pole. She was breathing hard, her face red and wet from melted snow. "Help us."

"Good morning, Elise," I said.

"Sanjit will not work," she said, looking at Rai. "He is lazy."

Rai smiled. I would have thought that such a comment would be an affront to his dignity, but he was playing along.

"If you were my wife," he said, "you would not be talking so much."

She laughed.

I smiled along, surprised by their playfulness. And I felt something else—a clear wave of jealousy. It came over me without warning. I had hardly seen them exchange two words since we'd arrived in this place, and yet now, suddenly they were joking like old friends.

"I'm going to rest," she said, handing me the pole. "I am going to the tent."

Rai shook his head and looked pleased as she walked away.

"Well," I said. "I'm going to get started."

I set off by myself. It wasn't heavy work, but it was enough to make me unzip the front of my jacket, and stop for a breather every now and then. I stepped alone into the cold dark interiors, one after another, pushing the broom slowly into the sagging canvas overhead, and let the snow roll off. It was far too cold for the snow to melt, and in that we were fortunate. Wet snow would have soaked the tents through. But Rai was right; the snow was dry, and poured off the roofs like salt.

The snow-covered canvas muffled all sound. I could hear nothing from the outside world. It was satisfying to stand inside them, and push the pole against the roof, and feel the weight of the snow slide off to nothing with a long sigh. As I entered them one after the other, with all the snow and quiet around me, they reminded me of ruins, or the cells of catacombs, deep underground, as if people had once lived there, and left long ago.

Back home, a few weeks before the trip, I'd rented a film about a biology professor who'd spent his life studying the burrows of ants. I'd liked the man, and his passion, and his awkwardness on camera, and the pleasure he so clearly took in his work. He was soothing, somehow, and I'd watched the film twice before I sent it back.

The professor's idea was both simple and elegant. He and his graduate student filled a wheelbarrow with their equipment and pushed it out to the ant mound. Then, carefully, the professor shoveled off the top of the mound until the central tunnel was exposed, ants flowing everywhere. Meanwhile, his assistant turned on the gas burner in the wheelbarrow and melted a bar of lead in a crucible.

It took a while for the lead to melt, and during this time the professor talked a bit about his research, in his slow Southern drawl, about the biomass of insects on this earth and ants in particular, how generally important they were, and how little was known about them. And yet they were among the most intricate of living systems in the world. They were born to their roles, and followed them without pain, without regret or choice or pleasure, and yet they were alive. They had fascinated him since he was a small boy. The assistant boiled and stirred the lead. It looked like molten silver, or mercury, and when it got hot it was runny and thin, not thick and slow like I might have expected. At night, I imagined that it would have glowed, but in daylight it was simply shiny.

Once the lead was ready, the assistant handed a galvanized steel funnel, with a handle attached, to the professor. The handle was long enough that the professor didn't have to bend. He held the funnel over the exposed tunnel, then nodded to his assistant.

"This is the delicate part," he said for the benefit of the camera. "The lead cools quickly, so it has to be done just right."

The assistant was careful with his tongs and his crucible, pouring the lead into the funnel as the professor held the funnel steady and let the single bright thread flow into the ground.

"It took us a while to figure out how much lead to use," the professor said. "And how hot to make it."

When the cup of lead was gone, the professor looked at his watch.

"Now we wait," he said, putting the funnel back into the wheelbarrow.

They walked between the narrow trunks of young pines. The earth was red. The biology professor digressed a bit—he talked about sawtooth pine and spruce pine, he talked about grasslands and periodic fires and the good they do for ecological systems. He talked about how one system is related to another, and how you can't change one without the other, which he said we were just beginning to learn even though I'd heard it many times before.

When the minutes were up, the professor and his assistant started digging. The hole was deep when they were done—nearly six feet, measured exactly with a string. By then they were using trowels, and finally heavy brushes, the kind with wooden backs that scrubbed the floors of the nineteenth century.

At last they had it, pried loose from the ground. A perfect cast of the ant burrow, with many branches, and a little ball at the bottom where the queen lay encased. It was a strangely beautiful object, a shining metal root, hot enough to be handled only with gloves. It looked like silver.

Back in his laboratory, many dozens of similar casts hung from the ceiling, with name tags affixed. It was, the professor said, the largest collection of ant burrow casts in the world. One could tell the species of ant from the shape of the burrow—the number of branches, the location of the queen's chamber. All the millions, working in the dark, and yet they were following a secret plan, a blueprint, which they carried in their genes and reproduced over and over again. Sometimes the burrows were abandoned, for mysterious reasons, and reoccupied, but only by colonies of the same species. The shape of the burrow, the professor said, was identical no matter where they were on earth, and had not changed for tens of thousands of years.

There was a movement in the doorway.

"Doctor?" Captain Rai said inquisitively, hood up, peering in the tent.

"Let them do this," he said.

"I don't mind," I replied.

"Already you have done too much," he said.

"It's good to get some exercise. I'm tired of sitting still."

"Yes," he said, and smiled. "It is also good to rest and have lunch."

Already it was a little past noon by Rai's watch. On the way back to the dining tent we passed a few of the villagers—they had broken into small groups for the job—and Rai stopped to speak to them. They emerged from the flurries, dark forms becoming whole, like a pack of wolves. Then they bowed their heads and were gone.

"What did you say to them?" I asked.

"I told them to go back to the village today. The snow is not so heavy now."

It was true—the snow was lessening.

"What did the radio say?"

"The front is passing," he said. "But they will not be coming now for some time. It will be very deep up high."

"How long will it take to melt?" I asked.

"I don't know," he said. I stared at him.

"Sanjit," I said. "Have I come all this way for nothing?"

He shrugged, and didn't answer.

CHAPTER FIFTEEN

So we were back in the dining tent again. Rai stamped in behind me, brushing the snow from his clothes in the entrance, and then he turned and shouted over his shoulder for what I assumed was Ali and lunch. The air was close and thick.

Elise sat comfortably by the heater, hat off, flushed, her hair, damp from the snow, sticking up at odd angles. She looked entirely cheerful, and smiled as we came in.

We took off our coats, and sat down, but Ali did not appear. Rai glanced at his watch again, then he stood abruptly, apologized, and went out into the snow.

"Have you seen Ali?" I asked

"At breakfast," she said. "While you were sleeping."

After a while we heard voices—Rai's, in anger, and then Ali's, lower and cajoling. A few minutes passed, then Rai returned to the dining tent in disgust.

"He was sleeping in his blanket," he said. "He said he was cold. Our lunch is late."

"Do they have a heater in their tent?" I asked.

"They have the stove. It warms the tent when they cook."

"But no heater?"

He inclined his head.

"It is okay," he said.

Ali entered the tent a few minutes later. He looked entirely wretched in his green cotton jacket and his tracksuit, bowing his head and murmuring his apologies. He was visibly shivering, and I realized that his clothes were wet. He looked chilled to the bone, miserable, and even as he apologized I could see him inching closer to the heater and the great mass of warmth it gave off.

"He's soaked," I said to Rai, who sighed in response and shook his head.

"It is always a problem with them," he said. "They are no good in the cold."

"Well," I said, "he needs to warm up. Let him sit by the heater."

Captain Rai said something curt to Ali, who bowed some more. Then he spoke, looking down at his feet.

"What is he saying?" Elise asked.

"Part of their tent collapsed because they did not clean it off," Rai said. "They got wet setting it up again. That is why our lunch is late."

"Where is the boy?" Elise asked.

"He is in the cook tent," Rai said. "He is wet also."

"Then he must come and get warm as well," Elise said, sitting up in her chair. "Tell him."

Rai shot a glance at me, then spoke. Ali bowed and bowed again, his voice rising in thanks, until Rai cut him off with a wave of the hand. Ali left immediately, returning a few minutes later with his nephew, who if anything looked even wetter and more miserable than Ali himself. He wore a thin cotton blanket over his tracksuit jacket, stiff imitation blue jeans, and plastic sneakers. I'd hardly noticed him in the weeks we'd spent together—he was perhaps sixteen, with the barest beginnings of a mustache, and a tangle of black hair that obscured his face. He was shivering violently.

Elise stood up then and gestured to her chair by the heater. Ali refused, however, and instead he and his nephew crouched beside it, rubbing their hands together. They got as close to the heater as they could, their faces turned away from us, and after a while the tent began to smell. Soon the odor was overpowering, and both Elise and I moved away and sat at the edge of the dining table. Steam began to rise off Ali and his nephew as they dried.

Elise wrinkled her nose.

"They smell bad," she said. "Really bad, yes?"

"Yes," I said.

Rai said nothing, but he looked intensely mortified, as if the presence of the stinking cook and his nephew reflected on him personally. And I suppose it did—they were his countrymen, after all, and he could speak to them, and he alone among us understood them.

Rai spoke, sharply again, and both Ali and his nephew flinched and stood.

"They are warm now," Rai said.

"Ask them if they have any dry clothes," Elise said.

Rai did so, and Ali and his nephew shook their heads.

"That is all they have," Rai said.

"Do we have anything?" I asked. "Blankets or clothes in the supplies?"

"I will issue them some blankets," he said, and shook his head. "They are useless like this."

He stood and left the tent. Ali and his nephew took the opportunity to instantly crouch down by the heater again.

"I have a jacket also," Elise said, "maybe it will fit the boy."

I did not have an extra jacket, but I had a sweater, and a soft fleece shirt that I was reluctant to part with. But I parted with it nonetheless, and the depth of their gratitude was painful to see, so raw that it generated guilt rather than pleasure. But not for Captain Rai; when he made a show over handing the blanket to Ali it was with a look that said *understand why you are receiving this*. I watched it carefully; I saw it for what it was. And in that moment I had no doubt that had we been absent, Ali and his nephew would have remained soaked and miserable all night, until the sun finally burned through the mist and warmed them up again.

That evening, before bed, I wandered over to where the pallets of supplies lay cloaked in snow beneath the tarps. I looked at them carefully, and finally did some calculations in my head, and for the first time realized that we had nothing close to what we needed.

CHAPTER SIXTEEN

The next morning the storm was over, and it was all blinding light again, and soon the avalanches were thundering gloriously down the walls across the river.

"It was kind of Sanjit to give Ali the blanket," Elise said. Already the villagers were at work, kicking places in the snow for the remaining tents.

I didn't answer at first. My stomach rumbled. I'd made several trips out into the rocks already.

"You do not think so?"

I turned to her.

"Yes," I said, after a moment. "It was kind of him."

She looked at me in puzzlement. We were walking out to check the tents. The sky was blue and hard and clear. The drifts we walked through were so soft and light that they barely resisted our passage, and our tracks fell in on themselves almost immediately. A minute or two of wind and there would have been no sign of us at all. It was quiet, full of the stillness that covers every wilderness after a snowfall.

The tents had held up well—none had collapsed, though snow had drifted between them and many of the doors were blocked. But there they were, intact, in their lines, waiting. Dozens of them now.

"We don't even have a single latrine," I said. "We're lucky the storm will delay them."

"Sanjit says they will dig the latrines when the tents are ready."

"The ground is rocky," I said. "Digging is going to be difficult. Plus there's no privacy."

"They can go at night," she said. "Then no one will see them."

"They won't have lights. And they probably won't use the latrine. If we're not careful it's going to be a mess. Water is going to be a problem also."

"There is the river."

"It's a half-hour walk. There are enough tents for two thousand people when they're all set up. But there's practically nothing to burn. There's nothing to cook with unless they have kerosene stoves. And there's hardly any kerosene, have you noticed?"

She shook her head.

"There's enough for our uses. But not nearly enough for two thousand people."

"They will have to bring in more."

"There is also not enough food," I said. "There are not enough blankets. There is not enough of anything except tents and medical supplies. That's because I arranged the medical supplies."

She looked at me, uneasy.

"Are you sure?" she said finally.

"I finally did some calculations last night," I said. "We don't have close to what we need. We're completely unprepared."

"We need to talk to Sanjit," she said.

"Yes, we do."

"It is not his fault, I am sure," she said.

"No," I said. "But they don't care very much, do they?"

She gave me a look, much like the one she'd given me the day Rai and I had shot his pistol.

"I am not a child," she said.

"I don't mean to patronize you," I said, "but if the villages were important to the army we'd have supplies. As it is we barely have enough to get started. I can't believe I didn't see it earlier."

"Scott also says this. He gets very angry. But he said there was enough to begin, and when the refugees come the army will have to do something."

"I hope that's true," I said.

"Do you think this is all for show?" she asked suddenly.

"I don't know. But there aren't any refugees, are there?"

I thought of the president, with his stern military eyes and his monotone, speaking in his native tongue. In the distance, the villagers were digging the last of the folded tents from the snow, as Captain Rai stood and watched.

"Maybe you are right," she said, pensively. "But there is nothing we can do now. And it is beautiful, you know? It is an adventure, like you said."

"I didn't come here for an adventure."

She nodded, and bit her lower lip, and looked young, and I felt a sudden wave of fondness for her.

It was inevitable, I suppose, that I'd begun looking forward to seeing her in the mornings, and thought about her when I was alone in my tent. If something caught my eye, I would wonder what she would think of it, and wish I were her age, or another man entirely, and sometimes I would pretend that I was. How predictable, I thought, and yet how little I resisted. She could easily have been my daughter, and had circumstances not placed us together I hardly would have noticed her. She would have been simply another of the young, a medical student, perhaps, whom I might glance at in passing. But then, up there, with my own body rising up against me, I felt far more than tenderness. My body, it seemed, cared nothing for the differences between us. It lusted on, and was afraid, or exhilarated, or hungry; it consumed, it excreted, it slept, it dreamed and wanted, and had no use for dignity at all.

CHAPTER SEVENTEEN

Rai was right. A few days later they asked for more. It was one of the men, one of the pack of wolves, as I'd come to think of them. Young, with a handwoven brown lamb's-wool cap and yellow-brown eyes. A wispy dark beard, a quick smile. A brown shawl over his thin shoulders. Perhaps he weighed 130 pounds. As we left the dining tent after breakfast, zipping up our jackets, the man was there. He wanted to speak to Captain Rai.

Rai listened, impassively. At first I wasn't sure whether he understood the man, whose voice was hesitant and soft. The man bowed his head, several times, then gestured toward the village below us and out of sight.

"What does he want?" Elise asked, as she came out of the tent behind us.

"Someone is sick in the village," Captain Rai said. "He is asking us to help him."

"Who is sick?" I asked.

"I am not sure. A girl."

"What's wrong with her?" A girl, I thought—I hope it's not a delivery gone bad. I hope it's not that.

Rai said something, short and curt in tone, and the man replied, touching his hat as he spoke.

"Her foot," Rai said. "There is something wrong with her foot."

The news relieved me. It's only a foot, I thought—something I probably can deal with. My stomach groaned.

"Tell him I will come and see her," I said. Captain Rai glanced at me, quickly, then looked away, his face unreadable.

"We should try to have good relations with the village," I said. "Don't you think?"

"Of course," he replied. "But this is a delicate matter. It is a girl. I am surprised that they have come to us."

"Why?"

He did not answer, but instead turned to the man and said a few words. The man replied quickly.

"She is his sister," Rai said.

"I will go also," Elise said immediately.

Captain Rai studied her.

"For this, it is okay," he said finally.

All these nuances that I didn't understand, all these questions of hierarchy and propriety and honor—the subject, at least, was clear—all of it annoyed me, though I hid it as best I could.

"What should we bring?" Elise asked.

"Let's just see what the problem is first," I said.

My stomach was rumbling again, and I felt a wave of nausea. I'd certainly caught it from Ali's cooking and for a moment I was tempted to go to the cook tent and see what they were doing. I imagined them rubbing mold from cheese with their unwashed hands and leaving the cracked eggs out for hours. But they'd been through enough, I thought, and as I imagined Rai, standing in the cook tent, putting on a show for my benefit, the temptation left me.

So we went, the three of us, Captain Rai tight and correct, with the villager leading the way. At first, the others tried to come along as well, but Rai stopped them in their tracks, and set them back to working on the tents.

By then the snow was melting rapidly in the sun, leaving pools of water in hollows as we picked our way down across the stones and gravel of the slope. The roar of the river filled the valley; it had doubled in size since the snowfall, and in places nearly swallowed the path that normally ran a safe distance up the bank. Near the water's edge, the sound was deafening, the river tumbled and poured, and we stepped into an icy mist that covered the stones like a thin layer of oil.

Rai was shouting at us over the rushing water, and I tapped Elise on the shoulder to get her attention. She stopped, and looked up at me, and then we bent our heads to hear him.

"Do not slip," he yelled. "Or you will be done for."

He was obviously correct—the violence of the river, as we stood beside it, shook the ground at our feet. Had any of us fallen in, we would have been carried away and drowned without a chance of saving ourselves—a flick of the eye, a red or yellow streak of a jacket through the white sheet of foam, and then gone. So we were careful, moving hand to hand and foot to foot, and then the path eased up the bank away from the river, and soon enough we were walking on flat ground and could speak to each other once more.

The sky was very blue above us, and then the snow on the banks began to give way to green undergrowth, and the first of the small pines.

"It is very nice," Elise said, and I agreed with her—the air, warm in the sun, and the cold breath of the snow against our legs, and the clear panes of ice here and there in the rocks along the river's edge. We walked in a line through the snow, with the villager leading us, and every so often I caught a whiff of him. But it was nothing like Ali, just damp wool and smoke.

The house was at the far end of the village, and they must
have been expecting us, because they were waiting in the doorways, and as soon as they heard the cries of the children, who
once again met us at the outskirts, they stepped out into the alleys and stared at us unreservedly, parting only to let us pass. We
followed the young man through the center of the village, past
the orchard, nearly to the edge of the fields. It was one of the last
houses, identical to the others, a low mud wall around it, narrow
slit windows like the rest. He stepped up to the door, knocked,
and called out.

A moment later a woman emerged through the door, wearing
a red head scarf and a ragged dark shawl. She looked at us with
a kind of ferocity, it seemed, and when she spoke it was with a
high, rough-sounding voice. Perhaps she was forty-five, perhaps
ten years younger.

The door was crude, made of many boards nailed together.
Local wood, unstained, planed by hand. All those boards wrung
out of the bent and stunted trees, then filed and nailed—who
knew how long it must have taken. It was probably a week's
worth of labor. The result was a bad, rickety door, full of chinks
and drafts. The ridges over the roof of the house were lovely in
the snow. I could hear the sound of birds at work in the orchard,
and the brook at our feet babbled and chuckled despite all the
cold flecks of excrement and trash it carried. The smell of mud,
the stronger smell of smoke, a goat knocking its pinpoint hooves
on the rocks at the edge of the path, moving from patch to
patch. The ragged crowd, watching. The woman wiped her nose
on her sleeve and coughed.

The woman and her son went back and forth for a bit. The
open door behind her gave way to a room so dark I could not see
inside. The men standing around us in a circle all began speaking at once, and then the woman turned to her son and spoke

hoarsely and rapidly. He nodded, then walked quickly through the door into the house.

"What's going on?" I said, to Rai.

"I am not sure," he said. "I think they are bringing her out."

I looked at the black square of the doorway. We waited. A few minutes passed, and finally the young man stepped out into the sun with a small blinking girl on his back. She was very young—perhaps seven—with a dirty face, and wide brown eyes. She had a small dried red flower in her hair. I wondered if she had just put it in, or whether it was something she always wore.

Her left foot was wrapped in a gray rag.

Rai spoke to the young man who had led us here. Halting, even to my ear, but he made himself clear enough, because there was an answering torrent from the woman, who had stepped aside to make way for her children.

"She was collecting wood," Rai said, gesturing to the steep slope above us. "A stone fell."

"When did it happen?"

He spoke again to the man

"A week ago," he said. "She did not come back for many hours."

"She was by herself?" Elise asked.

"Children here must work," he said. "It is part of life in these villages. All girls must collect wood."

She nodded, and then said nothing further.

"Is it only her foot?" I asked.

"Yes," he said.

The girl's mother interjected, speaking rapidly to Captain Rai, who gazed at her impassively.

"She says that if her foot is no good no one will want her."

"What is her name?" Elise asked. Rai glanced at her before translating.

"Her name is Homa," he replied.

"I need to look at it," I said, as a discussion ensued.

In the end the woman brought a blanket from the house and spread it out on the ground in front of the door. Then the boy let his sister down, gently, and she stood on one leg. She didn't make a sound, holding on to her brother for balance.

"Ask her to sit down," I said, "and please tell her I need to look at her foot."

Rai spoke to the woman, who in turn spoke to her daughter. Coldly, I thought, though I could not be certain.

The girl did as she was told. When I crouched down beside her, I saw that she was trembling. The crowd immediately pressed closer, craning their necks for the view.

"Please ask them to step back," I said, wishing I'd insisted on entering the house. But there was no light inside, only an oil lamp or two, and I needed to get a good look. Rai did as I asked, but they retreated only a few inches.

The rag looked as if it had never been changed. As I bent down, I could smell it.

The rag was stuck to the wound. The girl shook, but she made no sound. Elise, however, took a quick breath, a little hiss behind me, with each tug. I was as gentle as I could be, but it needed to be done. After a few seconds I pulled it free.

The girl's foot had been crushed. Her foot was nearly the size of my own—a hot black club. There was exposed bone, gray white, through the split foot, and a clear trickle of pus. Bleeding now, and smelling, the scabs torn away by the dry rag.

Of course I'd seen worse, so many times I've lost count, but never like that, so far from anywhere. The infection was into the bones; the bones themselves were splintered. Her foot needed to come off. At the very least it needed to be opened and drained and scrubbed to a raw and bleeding bed, which then, in turn, had to be kept clean. Weeks of antibiotics, also, and daily dressing changes, and something for pain. My heart sank.

I looked up at Rai.

"She needs an operation," I said.

Elise wrinkled her nose and turned her head away.

He said a few words, and then the crowd at my back began talking excitedly to one another. The woman went back and forth with them for a few seconds.

"They want to know if you can give medicine like you did for the others. They say the medicine has helped them."

I tried to explain as best I could—the foot was crushed, the antibiotics alone were not enough, the infection had spread to the bones, an operation was the only thing. How much they understood I could not say. The girl sat on the cloth, and said nothing.

"They need to take her to a hospital," I said.

Rai spoke. The woman listened intently, then replied, with her rough voice.

"She says there is no hospital," he said.

"Is that true?" Elise asked.

"They would have to go down," he said. "It would take perhaps one week to walk there."

"Then we must call a helicopter," Elise said, looking back and forth.

Rai looked at me, quickly, before turning to her. She understands nothing, he seemed to say. She knows nothing about this country or these people.

"It is not possible," he said.

"Why not?" Elise asked. Her tone was measured, but I knew her well enough by then to see her blossoming anger.

Captain Rai looked at her directly. His face was impassive.

"We are a poor country," he said. "One helicopter flight, do you know how much it costs from here?"

Elise shook her head.

"Three thousand pounds," he said. "More than everything they have. Who will pay?"

Elise flushed.

"I will pay," she said.

She caught him off guard. She didn't surprise me, though. By then it was the sort of thing I expected from her.

Rai sighed, and looked away.

"You do not understand," he said. "It is impossible."

"Why?"

"It is more than the helicopter," he said. "It is the hospital. The operation. The medicines. And someone must go with her. All the time it is like this in these villages."

"I will pay," Elise said again.

"Do you have three thousand pounds?" he demanded.

"I do not have so much here," Elise said, coloring.

He was getting angry as well, and turned to the woman, speaking rapidly. She answered him.

"She has nine children," he said. "Two of them died already."

"Yes," Elise said, with sudden ferocity, "and now you want to make three."

Rai was looking at me.

"Why can't you do it?" he asked. "You are an American doctor."

"I'm not a surgeon," I said. "I don't do surgery."

Rai shook his head, and looked away.

So there we were, and there I stood, looking at the girl as she sat on the blanket and trembled in silence.

"All right," I said, finally, because I knew I had to. "Let's take her up to the camp."

I was feeling worse. My stomach rumbled and groaned.

Captain Rai said his piece, and then everyone began talking all at once. A wave of cramps came again, and I knew that I would need to relieve myself before I could make it back up the hill. I felt intensely mortified, and suddenly the whole scene—the jabbering villagers, the girl on the blanket, even the sun and the snow melting out of the apricot trees, all of it seemed nightmarish and terrible and for a moment I thought longingly of my home on a winter's day, with its study overlooking the fields and the smell of a fire in the woodstove behind me. My dog, now staying with friends, a cup of coffee and maybe a long-distance talk with my son.

But there was nothing to be done, and so I touched Rai's arm and whispered my intentions, grateful that he simply nodded and said nothing. I stepped back from the blanket, and made my way down the alley, looking for a place, but to my dismay my departure did not go unnoticed. The children followed me, despite my best attempts to frighten them off. The alley opened into a field of barley, the green strands rising to my shoulders out of the melting snow. I pushed my way in, desperate now, and squatted down in the snow and the mud. I felt the children's eyes on my head as I struggled with my clothes. It was only then that I realized that the slush beneath my feet was mixed with human excrement, that the field served as the latrine for the village. Only the cold of the snow kept the odor at bay. The green field, so lovely from a distance, was this—a latrine, and the children were watching me, and a wave of cramps passed through me and expelled themselves in grotesque coughs as the ground sucked at my boots. In that moment I felt as if I would never be clean again, and I wondered what ever had possessed me to come to this godforsaken place, with all those eyes upon me as I crouched there, caught up with the indignity of the act—I felt entirely like an animal, revealed before everyone and everything.

I panted, and felt the barley brush against my face, and the cold against my exposed haunches, and I heard the children calling out to each other, craning their necks, drawing as close as they dared. It was as disgusting a moment as any I had ever experienced in my life.

When I was finished, and when I had cleaned myself as best I could, and washed my shoes in the stream, I found all of them waiting: Elise, and Rai, the girl on the blanket, the whispering villagers. As I approached, the child's mother said something, and then the young man took his sister's arm and helped her stand. He bent, she leaned forward and put her arms around his neck, and then he stood. It was the only moment of tenderness I'd seen that day.

Just then, as I rejoined the others, a man pushed his way through the crowd and made his way up to us. He was old, walking with a stick, and I didn't recognize him until he was reaching for my hands, and bowing his head repeatedly, and calling out. I took a step back, even as I let him take my hand in both of his.

"His is thanking you," Rai said. "He is thanking God for sending you."

It was the man with the bad heart.

"It is amazing," Elise said, smiling with delight. And it was—he could walk unassisted, the fluid in his legs had melted away, the blue of his lips had receded, and he could speak without pausing between each word to breathe. I watched him, and my stomach felt like a stone.

"He won't be better for long," I managed, looking at Elise. "The diuretics bought him a little bit of time, but that's it."

"Still," she said, her smile faltering only a little, "he is better now."

I did my best to smile at the man, and for a moment I debated trying to explain what the future held for him, that as soon as the diuretics were gone the fluid would return, that even with them he would probably be dead before the year was out. But then I looked at Rai, and the crowd around us, and the girl clinging to her brother's back, and chose to say nothing.

CHAPTER EIGHTEEN

Perhaps I should have done it that afternoon. But I wanted a few hours to gather myself, to read and plan. My stomach, also. And so I let her spend a night in the medical tent, on the cot with her foot propped up on pillows and a bag of donated antibiotics flowing into her little dark stick of an arm. Her brother slept beside her. Her mother remained in the village below.

I had most of what I needed—the sterile drapes and fluids, the sutures and needles and all the rest. I didn't have a bone saw, though. I would have to make do with the saw on the tool Eric had given me. The saw itself was perhaps three inches long, sufficient for the girl, though I would need to boil it in the morning.

The question, of course, was whether I had the nerve. I had the nerve to scrub the foot raw, and pluck out the dead tissue and fragments of bone, and get it all bleeding again—I was certain of that. I'd done such things before. But taking off her foot was something else entirely. She was not the old man. For her, it truly was a lifetime in the balance, and that night I felt the full weight of her future on my shoulders. It was what I had asked for, after all, and finally there it was.

For her I cannot imagine what it must have been like. Even though she was a child, she was old enough, surely, to comprehend something so stark. I checked on her before dinner to make sure the heater was working properly and her brother was comfortable beside her and that the antibiotics had gone in. I considered sleeping in the medical tent as well, but her brother was there, and I could see no reason to disturb her further. So I left her with her brother, and the hiss of the kerosene heater, on the green canvas cot made up tight with probably the first clean sheets she had ever slept on in her life. I debated bathing her, also, but thought better of it. I did not feed her, because I wanted her stomach to be empty in the morning.

We were mostly quiet at dinner, though the three of us ate together as usual. Through it all I could feel her presence in the medical tent just a few feet away. We ate our canned stew, and dipped in the crackers, and drank our instant lemonade as Ali came and went with the dishes. Outside the sun fell, as it always did, abruptly, casting the tent in shadow, and Captain Rai lit the lantern hanging from the center pole.

"I'll need some help tomorrow," I said to Elise. "I'll need an extra pair of hands."

She made a wry face, which Rai noticed because I saw him begin to smile.

"How will you put her under?" Rai asked, with interest.

"I'm going to use a drug that puts you out, but you breathe on your own. You are awake and not awake at the same time."

Rai looked intrigued.

"Will she feel any pain?"

I shook my head. "She shouldn't," I replied. "I'll just have to give her enough. It's one of the things I'll need help with. And I'll need someone to hand me instruments."

"Of course," Rai said, in a professional tone.

I could have shared my fears, I suppose. I could have told him that I had never done such a thing in my life before. I could have told him that I was only marginally more prepared to do this than he was. But I knew that I couldn't confess those things.

Usually I lingered after dinner, but that night I said my good nights and left them together, and if they noticed my change of mood they said nothing.

It was light enough to see the cliffs as I walked back to my tent. I hardly glanced at them. Instead, I did what I expected of myself—I looked through the surgical textbook by the light of my headlamp again and again, tossing and turning on the hard ground. For hours, later, I lay there, looking up through the fly at the veil of the Milky Way.

She lay there also, just a few meters from my tent, a dark slip, a shivering little figure, and though I listened carefully as the hours passed, and the air was still, I never heard a sound.

CHAPTER NINETEEN

Early the next morning, after a few hours of fitful sleep, I dressed quickly, and made my way to the dining tent just as the sun began to flood the valley. Elise and Rai slept on, but Ali and his nephew were awake preparing breakfast. As I waited beside the heater, and sipped the first cup of tea, I wished with a sudden passion that I'd never come. In some ways the stakes were low—whatever the outcome, nothing would happen to me. But in other ways the stakes were enormous, because even then I knew that I would carry her with me forever.

"Omelet?" Ali asked, in his usual way. I shook my head, which puzzled him, and then I waved him off. It took him a moment or two to realize that I wanted him to go. Finally he retreated, leaving me with my mug of tea.

Alone in the tent, I might have given in to my fears. But instead, as I waited for Elise and Rai, I felt a sudden wave of exhilaration, the source of which mystified me completely. But it was there, and I could feel it, as the wind gusted, and the band of sunlight flowed across the cold earth and dark shadowy stones. It came over me like recklessness, and gave no warning at all. Tremulousness, weakness—these things I understood and expected of myself. But the cold bath of confidence, of sudden ruthless conviction, caught me entirely by surprise.

Elise and Rai arrived. He was smiling, rubbing his hands together, and her cheeks were red and flushed in the cold, her eyes a piercing blue.

"Well, Doctor," he said, pointedly. "Are you ready?"

"Yes," I said, and met his eye.

"Good," he said. "When is the operation?"

"I'd like to do it soon. Now, even, if that's okay with you."

"Before breakfast?"

"The earlier, the better," I said, or rather found myself saying. Elise was looking at me.

"Very well," he said, formally, then glanced at her.

"Good," I said. "Let's go."

The girl and her brother were both awake. How much they knew I could not say. The girl lay there on the cot in the center of the tent just as she had the night before, her foot propped up on pillows and wrapped in plain white gauze. Her brother, the young man who had started all of this, sat beside her on the floor where he'd slept. The tent itself was warm, because the heater was working well—it was warm enough for shirtsleeves. The girl had cast off her blankets during the night, but now she drew them up again as we entered the tent, announcing our presence through Captain Rai's voice at the door.

Aside from the cot, the heater, a table, and several folding chairs, there was nothing in the medical tent but the piles of supplies, much of them wrapped in plastic.

The first order of business was to boil water on the table, and in a few minutes I had the little propane stove hissing away at a pan of it. Then, carefully, I took out Eric's gift, the all-purpose tool, and opened all the blades, the corkscrew and bottle opener and file, before dropping it carefully into the pot.

It would have to be the table. Perhaps I should have set it up the night before—in any case I hadn't, and during the next few minutes I lay out the packages of drapes, and placed the table in the brilliant square of sunlight flooding in through the open door. The water came to a boil and began to knock. The girl lay in the corner, watching us. It took quite a while; I needed to be sure I had everything in reach—the blue paper gown to be used only once, the drug, the needles and syringes, the liter bottles of sterile saline flown in from the other side of the world.

As I worked, Elise went over to the girl and knelt beside the cot, then reached out and took her hand. The girl did not resist, but neither did she respond. She looked to her brother. The expression on her face was that of terror.

Elise spoke to Captain Rai.

"Tell her it will be all right," she said to him. "Tell her we need to make her foot better."

The brother was standing now, a few feet back from the cot, taking it all in.

Rai surprised me then. He knelt down beside Elise and spoke with unmistakable tenderness to the girl. His voice was low and soft. For a moment it was the three of them—Elise and Rai on their knees beside the cot, and the girl, lit up in the sun through the doorway. Then I turned away, and finished with the drapes and the instruments and drew up the drug in my clear plastic syringe.

"Tell her," I said, "that I may have to amputate her foot. She needs to know that."

Rai looked at Elise, then back to me.

"She is afraid," he said, "and she is only a child."

"Does her brother understand?"

"I don't know," he said.

"Then we at least need to tell him," I said. "The family needs to understand this."

Captain Rai moved his head in that particular native way, as if it slipped out of him. But then he spoke to the brother, and asked us to step outside.

We stopped a few paces away, out of earshot. Elise remained with the girl.

"Tell him," I said, "that I may need to cut off her foot. Her foot is very bad."

Rai translated. The man stood looking down at his feet, murmuring his answers.

"He understands," Rai said.

"Tell him I won't unless I have to."

They murmured.

"He says that he is grateful that God has sent you to help his sister."

I've heard the sentiment before, of course, many times. As well as I know anything, I know it to be nonsense, to be empty. God had also sent the stone, and the teeming microbes after it, and the poverty to do nothing. Did he thank Him for that as well?

"Tell him there are risks," I said instead, and turned away.

There was no need to delay any further. I was as ready as I could hope to be, and the book was open, and through it all, I knew, the girl's foot pounded away with her pulse as if it had just been boiled.

I gave her the drug before I moved her. I gave her a good dose, quickly, before I could do any more thinking. No one understands such things—the overwhelming absence, the roving eyes and emptiness and steady breath no matter what is done. Just her eyes, drifting back and forth, with nothing to remember or forget.

We watched her intently, and just then she was gone; her limbs relaxed, her half-open eyes began their unearthly wandering. There was no transition that I could see—just here, then there. I waited a few more seconds to be sure.

"Is she out?" Rai asked, fascinated.

"I think so," I said. "Let's move her."

She weighed hardly anything, and I carried her easily to the table. Then I undressed her, quickly, and covered her in a blanket, until only her head and her entire left leg protruded from them. An odor, as her ragged dress came off—unwashed, vague. She was still a child. Her brother turned his head away, without speaking, and left the tent.

She breathed steadily, and her pulse beneath my finger was regular and slow and reassuring. For the first time I had the chance to see exactly what was there.

Her thigh, the little dark knot of her knee—all normal, but then, just above the ankle the skin went doughy and soft beneath my hands. Her foot was black, twice the size of the other. When I lifted it a trickle of pus began oozing from the deep, jagged, scabbed-over wound. I could see dirt ground into it, shiny flecks of gravel. The bones of her ankle were loose, also, and I felt them shift and grind together. The foot bent unnaturally, dangling to one side as I lifted her leg.

Elise took a breath behind me.

"It's very bad," she said.

The girl's eyes went back and forth in silence.

I knew then that there was nothing else for it, whatever I had hoped for.

I looked at her then—the little girl, suspended somewhere else, and a sudden wave of anger filled me. This worthless girl, so complete in her misery, and they in their complicity—the villagers, her brother, Captain Rai, the lot of them. Myself, also, standing above her full of inadequacy, in my gown and gloves, with my boiling water and steel tools, my age like a weight on my back. I was full of the anger of weakness, of the inadequate when they are forced to see themselves for what they are, and action is required.

"What are you going to do?" Rai asked, eagerly.

"I have to amputate her foot," I said, my voice harsh and foreign even to me. "What do you think?"

An amputation is a simple thing. But I'd never done one, and had only the dimmest memory, across a gulf of over thirty years, as a medical student, of standing beside a draped figure while the leg was lifted free and carried away. I could remember nothing more than that.

In a child, the incision is made some six or seven centimeters below the knee. Dissect down to the tibia, then laterally, to the fibula. Identify the neurovascular bundle that runs between the bones along the membrane between them. Tie off the vessels, above and below. Cut them between the knots. Cauterize the smaller vessels. Run the blade around the back of the calf, down toward the Achilles tendon, so that a flap of muscle will hang. Then the bone saw, up at the top of the wound, close to the knee. First through the tibia, then the fibula. Peel the bone free of the hanging muscle. File the sharp edges of the bone smooth. Then fold the hanging muscle of the calf forward, trimming as necessary. Stitch it up like a pillow beneath the bone ends. Elevate the leg. On the tenth day, remove the stitches. Nothing for a surgeon, but for me it was a foreign land.

I'd read it over and over until I was certain that I knew the steps. The difficulty lay in finding the vessels—the arteries and veins supplying the lower leg. If they got loose she might bleed a great deal. But again and again I told myself it was something I could manage. It should take only a few minutes—her leg was hardly bigger than my wrist. I thought of the past, of how surgeons were measured by the speed of their amputations, and how they timed themselves, with hourglasses, and drank bloody-handed toasts to the winner.

We step outside ourselves sometimes. Eric's birth, for example, when I drove home with him for the first time, or the day at the office when I first heard Rachel's news, which she told me in the most matter-of-fact of tones on the telephone. At the first bite of the scalpel, the drag on the blade as the brown skin spread like clay, her blood rose in points from the capillaries, and the sun shone, and she gave no sign at all.

I had a battery-operated cautery device, a thick white pen, and I watched myself touch it, one by one, to the points between the tiny yellow globes of fat. Each time, a crackle, a wisp of smoke rising in the sunlight from the red-hot tip, and on I went—the blade into the muscles of her calf, the muscle parting like strands of warm red rope, irregular slices, bleeding now, as I dabbed at it with squares of gauze. I carved a long ellipse from the back of her leg, down to the bone, and I clipped the white rubber of her Achilles tendon free from her heel with a pair of scissors. The end of the muscle was ragged, uneven, but it couldn't be helped, and as I watched the blood began to clot and go blue. Her leg was warm, and her blood cooled on my slick, gloved hands.

I was down to the bones of her lower leg—the tibia and fibula. It was a shocking sight—the gash, circling around and down her calf, the muscle hanging loose and dripping, then several inches of perfectly exposed white bone, and finally, below it, her dead black foot, which I'd wrapped in plastic to prevent it from contaminating the rest.

Then, finally, the saw, gummy on the bone for the first few strokes before biting. The sound of it, like someone brushing their teeth very slowly, and the rasp of it in my hands, the silver bar of the blade up and down, bloody and glistening from the bone ends, until, right before the saw went through, I stopped, and took the bone in my hands, and cracked it, gently, like green wood. I did the same for each, and finally only the blood vessels and the membrane between them connected the girl to her foot.

But I could see them, even without the guidance of the book, I could see the vessels, her pulse regular and slow within them, and then—I think this was the only time my hands shook—I tied them off with fine sutures, throwing in far more stitches than were necessary. The long half-moon of the needle, around them and through them again, above, and below. Then I cut them quickly, between the knots, with the smallest pair of scissors I had, and her lower leg was free, and I could hardly believe what came loose in my hands. It felt malevolent, like a dead snake, or a gun, and I covered it quickly with a towel.

I turned to the stump. I filed the bone ends as smooth as I could, running my thumbs across them over and over again. I thrust the needle in and out of the dangling calf, then pulled it by the hanging sutures beneath the exposed bones to pad the stump. I sewed it all to the front of her shin, trimmed the fat and dead tissue, smeared antibiotic ointment on the wound, and then I wrapped the stump until it was a cap of white gauze.

Later, I could not remember those minutes well. Just as I'd started, I'd given her another dose of the drug, to be absolutely certain, and it was as if the drug had found its way across her bleeding flesh into my hands and into my body as well. But somewhere in that brilliant square of sunlight and soapy foam from all the washing, I'd managed it, and though I'm sure a surgeon would have cast a critical eye upon it, even then I knew it was good enough.

We cleaned her up, and I took her leg and the bloody drapes

and stuffed them in a plastic bag. I threw the bag in the corner. We moved the table back to its position, and then we moved the girl, finally, back to her cot and out of the sunlight pouring in through the door.

Suddenly I was back again, soaked with sweat beneath my gown, light-headed in the heat. I murmured something to Elise and Captain Rai, and then I left the tent. The cold air struck me like a physical force, as if I'd stepped out of a shower.

Her brother was there, crouching down on his haunches on the gravel just outside the door. He looked up at me with his yellow-brown eyes, and then leapt to his feet.

"It is okay," I said. As I spoke, I must have looked terrible to him, dressed like that, in the surgical gown, with his sister's blood splashed across my belly. He gave me a long frightened look, and then he turned and stepped quickly into the tent.

I took a few steps away from the tent, feeling better with each breath. The peaks around me, the clear thin air, the grit of stones under my feet, the clarity of the sky—it steadied me, somehow, and by degrees I was myself again.

There are times when the weak inhabit the acts of the strong, and are therefore indistinguishable from them.

CHAPTER TWENTY

Rachel came up the walk from the mailbox with the magazine in her hand. It was a fall day, and leaves were coming off the trees. I'd been raking them most of the morning, and was taking a break on the porch, drinking a glass of iced tea. Eric was six years old.

"Look," Rachel said, her face troubled, stepping up onto the porch and sitting down beside me on the bench. "Mary Spruance died."

She handed me the magazine. It was the medical alumni review, and there she was—the woman I'd spoken to for five minutes nearly ten years before. The photograph had been taken decades earlier, but I recognized her nonetheless, and felt an unexpected pang of sorrow. "Philanthropist and Friend," the headline read, and below it, the bracketed years of her life.

"She lived a long time, but it's sad, isn't it? I still have that dress. It's in the closet in the guest room."

"Really? I thought it was long gone."

She started to cry.

I looked at her, puzzled, then reached out and took her hand.

"I'm not happy, Charles," she said, after a long while. "You're hardly ever home. I thought it would be better when you finished your fellowship and instead nothing's changed."

"I'll have more time when the grants are done. That's only a couple of weeks away."

"It's always the same, Charles. This grant, that study. They're always so important."

"Those grants pay part of my salary," I said. "They are important. We have bills. We have to save for the future. Do you think I'd rather be at work than here with you and Eric?"

"Yes," she said, quietly, drying her tears. "I do."

She stood up.

"Where is he?" she asked.

"I think he's playing with his toys in the living room."

"You *think*? This is your day off. Why aren't you spending it with him?"

"Rachel, all I'm doing is raking the lawn. It needs to be done."

She watched me some more, eyes narrowed, shaking her head, as if from a distance.

"I didn't know it would be like this," she said. "I thought you were someone else."

I threw up my hands.

"What can I say to that?" I replied, angry by then. "I'm doing the best I can."

"Who are you, Charles?" she asked, as she turned away. "Who are you really?"

"What are you thinking about, Doctor?" Rai asked, startling me.

"I was thinking about my wife," I replied.

"I am sorry," he said, in a sympathetic tone. "I often think about my parents also."

"Did they know your daughters?"

He shook his head.

"Well, then I'm sorry, too."

"There is nothing to be done," he said. "This is in God's hands."

He reached for his cigarettes on the table, and we were quiet for a while.

"Sanjit," I said, finally, as he lit the cigarette. "Where are the refugees? I can't wait for them forever."

"I do not know. Eventually they will be coming. Probably they do not know, that is all. And the snow also."

"We've been here for almost a month. I'm wasting my time."

"Of course," he replied. "But then I am also wasting my time."

"Why aren't there enough supplies?"

"There are enough to begin. And we will not solve this now."

Just then the satellite phone rang, and he stared in surprise at it for a moment. It had never rung before. He glanced uneasily at me, then picked up the phone, his voice coming to attention as he answered. He spoke a few words, listened, spoke again, his tone clipped and exact. The exchange was in his native language, so I understood nothing, and it was over in only a few seconds. When it was over, he took a deep breath, then let it out.

"What's wrong?" I asked.

"There is going to be an inspection," he said. "They are coming today."

"Who is 'they'?"

"General Said. He is in command of this sector." He shook his head.

"Is that a problem?"

"Of course it is a problem. He is a taskmaster, very strict. He is famous for these surprises."

"You haven't done anything wrong."

"No," he said. "But everything must be ready. Everything must be correct." He swore, and then he stood up and put on his jacket.

"Where are you going?"

"I am going to check on the tents," he said. "And the supplies."

"Do you want any help?" I asked.

He looked down at me, a flat, aggressive look in his eye that I'd seen before when he felt threatened.

"No," he said, dismissively. It struck me that three weeks earlier he never would have been so casual with me, or so revealing, or so inadvertently rude.

He left the tent, brooding and taciturn. I wondered about his wife in the city, and his little daughters, and what exactly it was that he seemed to want so much. I wondered why the only true refugee we had seen thus far was Homa. I wondered where on earth they were.

Rai spent the next few hours furiously adjusting the tents—tightening ropes, yelling at Ali and his nephew, who rushed to straighten up the dining tent. He shaved, also, badly, with a disposable razor, and then he changed his uniform. He looked unwashed nonetheless, as all of us did. And he looked concerned. Elise watched him with some amusement, which made him even angrier.

It was the kind of valley suited for echoes, and so we heard the unmistakable beat of a helicopter long before it appeared like a little dark bead in the low sky to the south. We were watching for it. I'd cleaned up a bit myself, trimmed the beard that I'd allowed to grow, brushing the gray clippings carefully off my jacket. I don't know why I bothered. Elise was not immune to such impulses, either—she'd put on a clean fleece pullover, and washed her face with a bowl of hot water Ali had given her. Her face looked red and healthy, and she stared at the helicopter with great curiosity.

We'd become comfortable with each other, I realized—comfortable enough that we didn't care about whether we wore a stained jacket to the dinner tent, or whether our necks were gray with dirt. And now this, a visitor, reminding us of our casual intimacy, and how it had crept up on us.

We stood outside the dining tent, hands shading our eyes, watching it grow nearer, and suddenly it was overhead, circling past us, out over the river, then turning back, sunlight reflecting off the canopy, the disk of the rotors above it shining like a coin for an instant.

It was a large helicopter, bulbous, foreign-looking, not at all sleek and light like Western machines. It looked strong and brutal and industrial.

"Russian," Rai said, when I asked him. "Mi-17. Very powerful."

I could see the pilots clearly through the canopy, wearing white helmets and sunglasses. They were looking at the ground, picking out a suitable place to land. They eased closer, into a hover, and the rotors began sending up billowing clouds of dust, drifting over the tents, and then, casually and gently, they set down on the gravel thirty yards away. A moment later the dust and small stones from the rotor wash struck us and we turned our backs all at once as the wind fell, and the helicopter relaxed heavily onto its oversize black tires, the green paint on its flanks dented and scratched, stained with oil and military markings, the shining canopy, as the turbines wound down in a slow descending moan. After a while the individual blades of the rotor flashed into view out of the blur, and I could smell the hot sweet exhaust, as the rotors swept to a stop and all was quiet again.

The machine seemed at home there, parked among the tents, and then the doors opened.

General Said was a short man with wide flat hips, sloping hunched shoulders, a little potbelly, a black mustache streaked with gray, and warm brown eyes—a handsome man's face on a small ungainly body. He wore a red beret with two gold stars on the center, a green sweater much like Captain Rai's, heavy green wool pants, a small black pistol on his belt, and leather combat boots. His feet were small, delicate. Perhaps he was sixty, perhaps a few years younger. He seemed pleasantly amused as he stepped easily down from the helicopter and began walking purposefully across the gravel to meet us.

Two soldiers accompanied him. They were also mustached, though broad shouldered and tall and stern. One of them carried an elegant bolt-action rifle with a telescopic sight slung over his shoulder. It was a civilian weapon with a finely engraved wood stock, and it looked out of place. I studied it for an instant, reading the words engraved on the black action—*Weatherby 7mm magnum*. The light caught the fine grains of wood beneath the varnish, and the brown leather strap was tooled and oiled and soft.

The other man held a notebook, its purpose unclear. The pilots remained in the helicopter, anonymous in their flight helmets.

As the general approached, Rai muttered something unintelligible under his breath, and then he came to full attention and saluted. He did it as sharply as he possibly could, and his boots came together with a muffled slap. On another occasion I might have laughed, but Rai's face was as stern and expressionless as he could make it, and he held the position until General Said stopped before us and waved his own hand casually near his forehead.

"At ease, Captain," he said, in English, in a pleasant tone.

"Yes, sir," he said. "Permit me to welcome you to our camp."

"All right, all right," the general said. "We are among friends now. There is no need for all that parade-ground nonsense."

"Yes, sir," Rai said again, attempting to relax. I'd no doubt that he would have much preferred to spend the entire afternoon formally at attention. Now he had to laugh, and move easily, and play the host, and the effort that this required was abundantly clear.

"And what do we have here?" General Said said, looking inquisitively at Elise. "Rai, you have drawn difficult duty. Up here with this beautiful girl so far away from home."

Elise opened her mouth, then closed it again. She clearly had no idea what to say, and began instantly to blush. Rai reddened also, but he managed to introduce them well enough.

I half expected the general to kiss her hand. Instead, he merely shook it, and said he was pleased to meet her.

"I have a message for you, young lady," he said, with mock severity. "A message that I am afraid you will not like."

"A message?" she repeated, confused. "What message?"

"You see, I must break your heart," he said, and winked. "Our mutual friend Scott Coles cannot come as planned. I am sorry, but he has been delayed. He has called me and asked me to tell both of you this."

Elise did not reply, but I saw the disappointment in her face nonetheless, and with it I felt a dark stab of personal reduction. I said nothing to her, because the general was turning to me.

"Where is he?" I asked.

"This I do not know, I am sorry," he said. "But he said he will try to come in a few weeks' time."

"We need to talk to him."

The general smiled and inclined his head.

"You must be the American doctor," he said, and extended his hand.

"Yes," I said, and smiled as best I could as I introduced myself. His handshake was firm.

"Thank you for your good works," he said. "And how has Captain Rai been treating you? Are you comfortable here in this wilderness? Is there anything you need?"

I said that Captain Rai had done an excellent job and could not be improved upon as a host. As I spoke, I saw Rai shoot a sideways glance in my direction.

"Yes, well, I am not surprised," General Said said, reaching out and clapping Rai on the shoulder. "He is one of our best young officers and so I expect this."

"Thank you, sir," Rai said.

"Okay," the general said, looking around, his hands clasped together. "I've come to inspect, so then I must inspect. But first perhaps I shall have a cup of tea." He made no effort to introduce his companions.

"Of course, sir," Rai said immediately.

Rai had anticipated this, and Ali and his nephew had been hard at work in the cooking tent since we'd first learned the news. They'd in fact produced an entire meal, and Ali was waiting just outside the tent when we reached it. The table we normally used held several covered dishes, and was laid out with a single setting of real silverware, and a cloth napkin, a fact that astonished me. Then the general entered the tent, glanced at the table.

"No, no," he said, with a dismissive wave. "Tea is all I want."

Rai spoke harshly to Ali, who in a flurry removed the dishes from the table and carried them back to the cooking tent.

The two guards remained outside. It was the four of us— Elise, and Rai, the general and myself. We drank tea by the heater. He talked about his time, as a young man, at a British university, and how he had come to enjoy beer a bit too much in those days. He spoke of how foreign beer had been to his youthful palate, how it was an acquired taste that he, he was ashamed to say, had proved very good indeed at acquiring. He said his father had threatened to cut him off until he realized that it was time to put away such frivolities—that was the word he used—and to dedicate himself to larger things.

"Not like Captain Rai," he said, winking. "He has always been very serious. Too serious in some ways."

Rai bowed his head and attempted to smile.

A few moments passed as we finished our tea.

"Tell me, General," I said then. "When do you expect the refugees to arrive? Where are they? We were told that they would be here by now."

He nodded seriously. "Of course this must be difficult for you," he said. "So much twiddling of thumbs. But I assure you they are coming."

"There are also not enough supplies," I said. "Not nearly enough."

Again the general nodded.

"You must talk to Scott Coles about why this is so. He has responsibility for this, you understand. I am only here today to show my support. But when the refugees come, we will bring in more supplies, of course. And personnel as well. Do not worry."

"Good," I said. "That's reassuring. But what is the army doing to let them know we're here? I was told that was part of the arrangement."

"We are doing everything we can," he replied. "We are doing our best. I understand, Doctor, your frustration. And I sympathize. There are many factors. Many do not know where to go, even though we have dropped maps from the air. They are always suspicious of paper, even if it is a map, because they cannot read. Sometimes they burn the maps to start their fires. I have heard reports of this."

"Have you sent anyone up there to tell them where the camp is? Wouldn't that be a good idea?"

"Of course, of course. But you must be patient. Eventually they will come, I assure you, but this is a new camp, and news travels slowly no matter what we do. The terrain is very rough. There are hundreds of villages, but they are very small and the distance between them is great. They are suspicious of outsiders, and also it is along the border. There are security concerns. There is the problem of transport in the mountains. And problems with weather. The recent snow. And of course many of them do not want to leave. Always there are these problems."

"Why don't they want to leave?" I asked.

"These are very backward people, Doctor," he said. "They have many superstitions and suspicions. They are extremely ignorant. They only know their villages, and it is difficult to get them to leave even when the villages are destroyed and soon it will be winter. They always think God will provide for them. They are always a struggle for us, and they never know what is best, even when they are told."

"Do you know what is best?" Elise said, suddenly. It was a provocative remark, and it got the general's attention, because his habitual half smile faded for an instant. But then it was back, stronger than ever.

"No," he said lightly, turning his head to wink at Rai. "It is only my wife who knows what is best."

I laughed, politely, and shot Elise a look. She met my eye, unrepentant, and began to scowl.

The general turned back to us with a smile.

"If you will forgive me," he said. "I must talk to your

young host about very dull things. I must talk to him about logistics."

"Of course," I said, taking the hint, noting Rai's pained expression as I did so. "We'll leave you alone."

"We will not be long," the general said. "Don't worry."

The guards remained outside, and as we left the tent they glanced at us, neither friendly nor unfriendly. I could hear the general's voice as we left, and realized that he wasn't speaking English anymore.

We walked toward the helicopter, out of earshot.

"I do not like him," Elise said.

"Why not?"

"He is trying very hard to . . ." She muttered something in German, which she rarely did. "I am not sure what the word is in English."

"To charm?" I asked.

"Yes. To charm. He is trying very hard to charm. And Sanjit is afraid of him."

"Sanjit is afraid of his rank," I said.

She looked at me.

"I am not sure why," she said, "but I am a little afraid of him also."

I thought about this, about why the general radiated such power. The easy answer would be that he had all the props—the helicopter, the guards, the subservience that every army affords superior officers. And it was easy—natural, in fact—to fear such men, however charming they might be, because one suspected them of being capable of terrible acts despite all their good manners and intelligence. I suppose that had he and I exchanged roles—we were not so far off in age, after all—and I had descended from the helicopter, and came out to greet Captain Rai, his reaction might have been much the same, and Elise's as well. Nonetheless, I didn't fully believe that the effect was one purely of circumstance. There was something else also, something harder to define. General Said was an intelligent man, of that there was no doubt, and yet there he was, presiding over a few ragged, worn-out tents, a few meager piles of provisions. Yet both of those men—Rai, and presumably the man he hoped one day to become—sat talking as if there were secrets to be kept, and forces afoot, and matters of great national importance drifting everywhere in the cold reaches around us.

General Said had something else as well: a sense of presence. There was something in his gaze, and his smile, and his firm-enough handshake, that didn't let you dismiss him so easily. No doubt he was exceptionally lazy, but if so his laziness was calculated and exquisitely refined, with discipline all its own. I wondered if he had ever ordered an execution.

"What do you think they're talking about?" I said.

"Sanjit will tell us," Elise said confidently.

The pilots had gotten out of the helicopter and were smoking and talking among themselves. I was tempted to join them, to ask them about the helicopter—how high it could fly, and was it as reliable as Western helicopters, and what was its range—all the usual questions asked by men and boys in such situations. Instead I looked out down the valley and wondered whether I should pack up and go. I glanced at Elise.

"How long are you planning to stay here?" I asked.

"I don't know," she said. "Until I am sure they are not coming, I think. But are you going to leave?"

"No," I said. "Not yet. But they were supposed to be here by now. At least some of them. And we haven't seen a single one."

She looked pensive, and I realized in that moment that I felt responsible for her, however resourceful she imagined herself to be. Of course I knew my concerns were old-fashioned, and that some would even have found them cause for offense. But I felt them anyway, looking up at the ridgelines and the snow.

To my surprise, she took my arm and impulsively leaned against me. I put my arm around her shoulders, and pulled her close for a moment.

"Don't worry," I said. "I don't have anywhere else to go."

Nearly an hour passed before they emerged. General Said looked well rested, entirely at ease, but Rai looked pinched, like a driven schoolboy who had just taken an important examination that he was not certain he had passed. Elise and I exchanged glances. In truth we had been inconvenienced, because there was nowhere else warm to sit. The guards, for their part, stood scanning the ridges behind us. We stayed clear of them, and I wondered what they were looking for.

The general was all smiles and apologies. He did not realize they had taken so long. He would like to make it up to us.

"There's no need at all," I said, doing my part.

"No, no," he said. "What kind of host have I been? A bad one, I will tell you."

"But you are visiting us," Elise said.

If he was surprised by her comment, he didn't let on. He merely smiled.

"Yes, of course," he said. "But you are the guests of my country. Please," he said. "Let me give you a tour."

"A tour?" I asked.

"Of course. I promise it will be very thrilling." He turned and spoke rapidly to one of his companions.

I realized that he meant to take us for a ride in the helicopter.

"Captain Rai has to write his report," he said. "We have been talking too much about serious matters, and so now let us enjoy ourselves."

"Would you like to see the tents and the supplies first?" I asked. He waved his hand dismissively.

"Believe me, Doctor, I have seen enough tents in my life. I am dreaming of tents. And supplies also. That is all I know. Come," he said, gesturing. "Let's go."

I could not resist. Perhaps I should have, on some principle or another. But it was too much to pass up.

Elise, to her credit, was reluctant. I could see her struggling with it. She wanted to, of course, and in that sense it was a foregone conclusion. But it gave her pause, where it gave me next to none.

The helicopter was rigged for cargo—a smooth metal floor, with rings for tying down supplies. Thin metal and canvas jump seats unfolded from the walls. It was a large machine—there were perhaps fifteen seats, excluding the pilot's. The seat belts, such as they were, were green canvas straps. As we approached, the pilots quickly extinguished their cigarettes and took their seats, but did not salute or come to attention—apparently the general did not stand on formality with them. They put on their helmets, and their glasses, so I could not see their faces.

Up front, the cockpit was wide and airy and full of glass. General Said ushered us in, insisting that we take the best seats, just behind and above the pilots, where he himself normally flew. His guards sat in the back, and the general did not sit down at all, but stood behind us. He made a show, also, of our headphones, carefully adjusting them for Elise and ensuring that she had placed them correctly on her head. He made certain her seat belt was buckled.

"I am sure," he said, "that you are the first woman who has ever been in this helicopter. So you see, this helicopter is a virgin."

He laughed, pleased with the joke, which made me wince,

and then turned to the pilots, speaking rapidly. They nodded, and one of them gave us a thumbs-up.

"I told them to give us a thrill," he said to me, with a smile, and just then the pilots began flipping switches on the large panel above their heads with practiced ease. The labels were in Russian, and the instruments looked somehow crude, old-fashioned, and well made at the same time. Dials with cut-glass faces, and white numbers, and heavy buttons everywhere that looked as if they would be very satisfying to push. The stick, sturdy and industrial, and the aluminum rudder pedals—all of it functional and purposeful, and I suddenly suspected that Captain Rai was right, that this really was a very good and rugged helicopter, and that I was not taking my life in my hands as I otherwise might have thought.

The engines came to life then, and the rotors began to turn, and as the sound rose to a shriek the reason for General Said's insistence on the earphones became clear. Just then his voice came through them, with a hint of static.

"Can you hear me?" he asked. Elise nodded, but did not speak.

"Yes," I said, my own voice loud in my ears.

The pilot said something I couldn't understand, but I felt the general grip the seat back behind me and brace himself, and then the pilot lifted his left hand sharply, and just like that the helicopter leapt straight into the air, the dust pouring out of the ground, and then the pilot nosed it over until the canopy filled with a heart-stopping view of boulders and stones, and then he sent us slinging across the field. It was difficult to believe so large a machine could move so quickly. I heard Élise gasp and felt her grab my arm, and then, in just a few seconds, we were at the edge, and then the slope leading down to the river dropped away beneath us, opening an enormous pit in my stomach, as suddenly there were hundreds of feet through the canopy beneath the pilot's legs. Then he banked, hard, and the canyon wall came up, and we were pressed deep in our seats as the rock wall began pouring by. General Said stayed on his feet without difficulty, grinning widely, and now we were circling back, climbing as we did so, above our camp, and the many empty tents. Then the pilot banked hard again, to the left, and we were looking down the full length of the valley. My hands, I realized, were clenched on the metal frame of the seat, my legs were braced, and Elise was holding on to my arm with all her strength. Back and forth we went, in long circles, higher and higher, until for the first time we could see above the ridges, north toward the epicenter. Somewhere out there the border lay claimed and reclaimed, but all I could see was the sky and wave after wave of jagged white peaks stretching off toward the horizon, shining in the sun, with no sign of damage anywhere, and no hint of human presence, like a kingdom of the dead.

CHAPTER
TWENTY-ONE

General Said's gift was a tiny mountain lake at the northern end of an adjacent valley. It was easy to see why the valley was empty of human beings—it would have been impossible to grow anything on the hillsides, jagged and steep as they were, and the valley itself was so narrow that only a few hours of sun could strike the center each day. But the lake at the end of it was like a perfect blue flower on a stem of thorns. Only a hundred yards or so across, it lay in the hollow of a snow-tipped peak. A small pine forest, also, at the water's edge, and then an acre or two of meadow where we landed. It was all in miniature, the lake and the forest, the lawn-sized grasslands, set down like an island in a sea of rock.

The meadow was covered with pinpoint white and red flowers, and as we landed no dust rose. I watched the grass flatten beneath the rotors, and felt the gentlest of nudges, as the engines wound down and the shadows of the blades spun across the grass for a few moments until they stopped. My ears were ringing, and felt full, and I swallowed to clear them and took off my headphones, and just then the guard with the rifle opened the sliding door at the back and jumped out onto the grass. The breeze came in, cool and warm at the same time.

"Well?" General Said said, as we'd walked down to the water's edge. "Is it to your liking?"

"It's beautiful," Elise said.

The water was an iridescent blue from a distance and like cut glass up close, spring fed, releasing a single stream into the wilds of canyon below. The breeze ruffled its surface, the air was full of the smell of greenery, which I don't think I've ever been quite so aware of. There were fish—I could see them, gray and silver, as long as my hand, nosing through the shallows and the slap of the water on the rocks.

"There are many fish in these lakes," the general said.

"And there are many lakes like this?" Elise asked, turning toward him.

"Yes, yes, of course," he said. "Only this is my favorite. But you must not tell anyone."

"How did you even know it was here?" I asked.

"That is a military secret," he said, and smiled. "But I will tell you. Aerial reconnaissance. That is how."

I imagined him, with the others, studying rolls of photographs taken at great altitude, bending over illuminated tables in dingy city rooms.

"Of all the secrets I know," he continued, gesturing to the lake, "I like this one the best."

"It is cold, but not so cold," Elise said, crouching down and touching the water with her hand. She cupped her hands, and brought up a palmful to her lips, and drank. It surprised me, that she would drink from the lake. I did not join her, but watched as she drank her fill, then washed her face and neck quickly, and ran her wet hands over her short hair until it began to stand up on its own. Then she stood, and stretched, and looked longingly out.

"I would like to swim," she said, impulsively, but then she glanced at General Said and just as quickly changed her mind.

"Do you know how deep it is?" I asked him.

"I am not sure, of course," he said. "But I think it is very deep. You cannot see the bottom from the air."

All that clear bottomless water, and the luxuriant green grass of the meadow underfoot, and the profusion of pinpoint red and white flowers—it was hard to believe, and suddenly I didn't want to go back to all the rocks and dust and snow of our camp, the oversweet tea and the limp moldy toast.

Elise walked off on her own then, and the general and I continued toward the stand of pines between the edge of the lake and the granite wall of the mountain. No doubt it was illusory, but the air felt warmer than on our side of the escarpment. Another fish jumped, a larger flash of silver.

He sighed contentedly.

"You know," he said, "our religion came from the desert. From Arabia. Water was very precious to them. And so one of our oldest laws is that we must give water to travelers. That is why we always give tea to our guests."

"Offering tea is an obligation?"

"Yes," he said. "In our scripture this is called the right of thirst. But as you can see, I am giving you this instead."

He made a show of breathing in the air, deeply, through his nose.

"Thank you," I replied.

"When I think of paradise," he continued, "I think of this place. Sometimes I imagine this lake when I am listening to long speeches. And so I look very peaceful and attentive, and do not fall asleep. It is very useful."

I smiled, on cue. A moment passed.

"Our artists always paint such scenes," he said. "If you go to any market, you will see many of them."

He knelt and picked one of the tiny red wildflowers, then held it up and studied it closely.

"Think of this," he said. "It is a perfect thing. How can one look at this flower and say that God has not made it?"

"I don't know," I replied.

He spun it off his fingers, and it fell.

The grass underfoot was soft, and for the first time in weeks I couldn't hear my own footsteps.

"We should have put the camp here," I said.

"Yes," he replied. "Of course. But this valley is too steep, as you can see."

Elise turned away from the water's edge, and crossed the meadow toward us.

"Ah, yes," he said, with appreciation, watching her walk. "And she is like the cherry on the cake, you know?"

Just then there was an excited shout behind us, and we turned. The two guards were pointing across the lake at the walls of the mountain.

At first I could not make out what they were seeing. Then, squinting against the sun, I saw tiny moving figures on the high granite wall.

The general's face lit up.

"Ibex," he said, excitedly. "A whole herd of them." Then he turned, and shouted something at the guards, one of whom immediately trotted back to the helicopter. He emerged a few moments later with a pair of oversized binoculars, which he quickly brought to the general. Said raised them eagerly, and trained them on the wall.

"Yes," he said. "A very good buck also. To the left of the rest."

He handed the binoculars to me, and the mountainside leapt up. The ibex were gray-brown, and heavily built, some with beards, all with dark curved horns several feet in length. They moved effortlessly across the steep face, leaping over stones, from ledge to ledge, like tree dwellers through a forest canopy. They were purposeful, heads down, and mysterious, as if they knew where they were going.

"Perhaps something frightened them," the general said. "Look behind."

I did, carefully, but there was nothing, only the gray clean stone, and the boulders, and the patches of snow.

"Can I see?" Elise, who had joined us by then, asked, and I realized that I'd kept the binoculars too long. I apologized, and passed them to her.

The guard with the rifle asked the general something. He sounded excited, and the general sighed, as if he did not like what he was about to say. Then he spoke, curtly, and the man bowed his head in acknowledgment. I thought of the rifle. But I said nothing—instead I asked him if there were snow leopards up there in the heights as well.

"Yes," the general said wistfully, watching the tiny figures round the high shoulder of the ridge and disappear. "Although I have never seen one. They are very rare. I have seen tracks only. Someday, perhaps."

The general turned, and said something to the guard with the notebook, who pulled a pen from his pocket and made a careful notation.

Elise handed him the binoculars.

"They are very fast, yes?" she said.

"They are very powerful," the general said. "They are believed to have many properties."

It was the first time I'd seen wild animals of any size since I'd been there. I'd seen what I assumed were marmots in burrows in the rocks, but that was all, and this sudden herd pouring across the cliffs, however far away, made the land softer in my eyes.

"The villagers hunt them," the general said. "And so you only see herds like this where there are no villages. Only in empty places."

We spent a few more minutes wandering along the meadow, around to the pines, and then back again. It was early enough, and the sun remained high above the ridges, but it was no place to fly at night, or in bad weather, and soon the general glanced at his watch and said that he was sorry to inform us that we had to leave. And so we got back in the helicopter. Unlike before, the pilot was gentle, and as we rose slowly off the meadow into the air I had a clear view of the blue center of the lake. The general was correct—there was no bottom to it that I could see, just the brilliant water, and our shadow passing through it, and then, for just a moment, the surface became a mirror, and I saw the helicopter with perfect clarity, suspended in the blue. I'd never seen anything like it before—a shadow, which then became the clearest of images before vanishing in the glare. By the time I'd turned to Elise to show her, it was gone.

CHAPTER
TWENTY-TWO

She could feel her leg sometimes. It came and went, and kept its own schedule. Much is made of such things—the ghostly presence. But I've had patients who've felt their absent legs for years, sometimes for decades, and it's something that no longer has imaginative power over me, though I understand its allure for others. Mostly it is simply a tingling, a pressure, the belief that one can move one's toes. Pain is uncommon, though that is what gets the attention of the larger world. Pain, the idea that something that is gone forever can nonetheless remain so cruelly alive.

It was Rai who told us. He was the only one who could speak to all of us. Her brother, who no doubt had responsibilities in the village, came to visit her each day, but he no longer slept beside her. Her mother, to my astonishment, never came at all. So the nights must have been long ones for the girl, lying in the tent full of shadows, getting better, even if she had been born in that valley, among the darkness and the oil lamps and the goats brought into the front room on the coldest nights. Elise moved into the medical tent as soon as she realized what had happened. The girl's brother never told us he was leaving her alone.

The stump was healing beautifully. I could hardly believe how good it looked. She was terrified of me. She would close her eyes, and shake down her whole length, in silence, as each day I removed the sterile gauze and put on the antibiotic cream and then wrapped her leg again. It took me only a few moments, and it can't have hurt her very much, but I know that she dreaded my morning visits. I could see it in her face whenever I entered the tent. She believed that she was at my mercy.

Her fear should have troubled me, I know that. It should have moved me to overcome it. But it did not—in fact, it had the opposite effect. It proved to me that I had done something profound, just as her phantom limb allowed me to claim her that much further. It is common in amputations, I might say. Yes, that is what we expect in such cases. It's all right, I'd say, softly, and she'd hold her stump up in the air as instructed. In truth I was no longer the man who had removed her leg at all. I examined the stump as if it was the work of someone else. The girl knew differently, however. She knew who I was. I debated showing Elise how to change the dressings, but in the end thought better of it. Elise could comfort her, and I could cause her the necessary pain, and there was no reason to confuse the two.

As a result, I spent little time in the medical tent during the day. I left that to Rai and Elise. But each morning I'd clean the girl's stump with peroxide, and white gauze, and bandage it again. She shivered, Elise would stroke her hair, and I took such pleasure there, in that quarter of blood soaking through at the tip, becoming a nickel as the days passed, and then a penny, and finally nothing at all.

When she was sleeping, though, I often visited her. I'd enter the tent, and sit on the folding chair next to her bed, and watch her for a while. She was a deep sleeper, and lay on the cot with the blankets pulled up to her chin, her breath steady and slow. Sometimes she would dream, and murmur, before settling again.

After a while Elise came to expect my nighttime visits. We would whisper a little, but mostly we were quiet so as not to wake her. Elise would read, or write in her journal by candlelight, and I would sit there for a few minutes beside the sleeping child, taking what sustenance I could, before getting up to go.

Soon she was hopping out to relieve herself, holding on to Elise's arm. Elise would deposit her behind some boulders, and retreat, and the girl would hold up her hand in the air when she was done.

Children are not entirely human. There is a lot of the animal left in them. Sometimes I think we're fully human only during the middle of our lives, when we are conscious, when we both feel what is coming and remain strong enough to fend it off. Sooner or later the old revert to helplessness, and the young are so effortlessly alive they are unaware of the debate altogether. It is only the middle-aged who can see both ends for what they are. Possibilities, of course, remain, but they are less glorious, and more true to the world as it is, and the past, for its part, shines for them also.

I've never had children under my care. I'm used to how the old heal—a slow crawl, even as the decline continues. The better and the worse together. And so she astonished me. She came back like fire.

"Is it common to feel a leg when it is gone?" Rai asked, curious and apparently concerned. I assured him that it was, and also that it was likely to improve as the years passed, though perhaps never vanish entirely.

"It wakes her at night," he said.

"Do you miss your daughters?" I asked him. He acknowledged the remark immediately.

"I miss them very much," he said. "I have not seen them in some time."

"How long has it been?"

"Two months," he replied.

"Well," I said, "it's kind of you to spend time with her."

He looked away.

"What did General Said say to you yesterday?" I asked, finally. "What took you so long?"

"They will bring us more supplies," he replied. "When we need them. Do not worry."

"Is that what you were talking about for an hour? Supplies?"

He smiled and looked away and for a moment I could see him wondering what to say. By then he trusted me, I think, as much as he could trust anyone from another world, which for all I knew was more than those from his own.

"He was talking about hunting," he said, finally.

"Hunting?" I asked, incredulously.

"Yes," he said. "He is telling me about mountain sheep. He is telling me also about ibex."

I wasn't sure what to say.

"He is telling me many details. The wind. The position of the buck. The range. That he is a very good shot also, that he made a very difficult shot."

Rai hesitated. No doubt he was weighing the propriety of the conversation. But then he came to a decision.

"He knows I am regiment pistol champion," he continued. "So when I see him he tells me about shooting and hunting. He is a very big hunter, he has traveled many places. That is why he comes so often on inspections."

"Do you mean he's hunting?"

"Yes. Sometimes he shoots them from the air. He shoots them right off the cliffs from the helicopter."

Rai shook his head, and made a shooting motion with thumb and forefinger.

"Yes," he said. "Right off the side of the cliff, and then they fall a thousand meters."

"You mean he doesn't even pick them up?"

Rai shook his head.

"No, no. He flies down and gets them. Unless of course it is impossible."

I remembered the general's face, lit up as he shouted to his adjutant for the binoculars, as the ibex flowed so effortlessly across the granite wall, and his comment about the buck, and how his adjutant had written it all down.

"So he's not really inspecting anything?" I said.

"He is inspecting. But he is also hunting."

"Aren't there rules against that sort of thing?"

Rai laughed.

"He does not do it too much," he said. "Just sometimes. And also only when he has another reason to go."

"Do you like to hunt?" I asked. He shook his head.

"No," he said. "It is too easy. It is nothing. He took several of us last year. But we were unlucky." He paused, looking out at the doorway of the tent.

"It is a big sign," he said, finally. "When you are an officer of my rank, if he invites you it is a very big thing. It means they have their eye on you. It means they know who you are."

Elise stomped in with her red jacket, taking off her hat and running her fingers through her short hair and smiling at me.

"It is cold, yes?" she said. "And time for the omelet." This was, more or less, what she said every morning—it had become a ritual with us.

"Yes," I replied, taking another sip of tea.

"What are we to do today?" she asked then.

"What we do every day," I replied. "Nothing."

She nodded seriously, and rubbed her stomach.

"How is Homa?"

"She is very good. She is eating her omelet now."

"Her stump is almost healed," I said. "We can send her back any day."

"What about her leg?"

"What do you mean?"

"A new leg for her? She must have one."

"The stump needs to mature," I said. "It must be ready to bear her weight. And she will need many legs, because she is growing."

"What do you mean, mature?"

"It must heal completely. Usually patients aren't fitted with artificial legs for several months after an amputation."

"Then where will she get her leg?"

"I don't know. She'll probably have to go down to the city."

"We will not be here in several months," she said.

I looked at her.

"We can't do everything for her," I said, more coldly than I intended. "She'll need a new leg every year. At least. Her family has to help her. If they won't there is nothing we can do."

"We can pay them, perhaps. To get her a new leg every year."

"We could. But they'd probably use the money for something else."

"Of course you are right," she said, after a moment. She paused. "We must do something about this. We must make them get her a new leg."

"You see," Rai said. "This is what I was telling you about them."

I didn't reply.

CHAPTER TWENTY-THREE

I thought it was thunder. A distant rumble, very far away, from the high country to the north. The ridges hid the distance, and it was impossible to tell whether another front was coming.

Rai, however, instantly came to attention, like a pointer—his head snapped up, he cocked his head, and then he rose rapidly and stepped outside and listened again.

"What is it?" I asked, as the rumble came again, barely audible, like wind through corrugated sheets of steel.

He motioned for silence, and listened again, and then he turned to me. He looked happy, excited and alive.

"Artillery," he said.

"Artillery?" I repeated, dumbly. "It sounds like thunder."

"Yes," he said. "But it is not."

"How do you know?"

He smiled a short smile.

"Because I have heard it before," he said. "And I know what it is."

It came again, in the direction of the wind. Not loud, but there, unmistakably.

"How far away do you think it is?"

"Thirty kilometers," he said. "A bit more."

"How do you know that?"

He looked at me as if I were a child.

"We have a base," he said. "A forward post thirty kilometers north. But everything has been quiet there for some time."

He turned, and went back into the dining tent, and picked up the satellite phone. He glanced at me, then spoke quickly into it. A few seconds passed.

"Yes, sir," he said, switching to English as he turned off the phone. Then he ran his hand through his hair and looked thoughtful.

"What was that about?"

He shot me a glance, but answered politely enough.

"There is a barrage under way," he said. "But I am to stay off the channel unless I am contacted."

"Who is doing it?"

"I don't know," he said. "We may be firing. But usually they are firing first. And then both."

I expected it to stop after a few minutes. I knew such flurries broke out from time to time along the frontier. No doubt they had a function—to remind everyone why they were there, why they stood in the deep snow of the ridges, and looked through their telescopes, why they huddled in their bunkers and spoke into their radios as they did. No doubt it was deliberate, to convince them that matters of vast importance were at hand, as they kept their heads down and their eyes up, thrilled and terrified and larger than themselves.

But it was something I could understand. The roar, the grandeur of it, ebbing and flowing across the northern ridges, carried through all the wind and snow and blinding sunlight of the high country—it was a human sound, but it seemed otherwise, like geology, or surf, and I understood the look on Rai's face as he listened and wondered, nearly overcome by his desire to call down again on his satellite phone and find out for certain what was going on. He spent the day hunched by the short-wave radio, listening to scraps—radios only carried a short distance, and we were in a deep valley surrounded by thousands of feet of rock walls. The pick-me-up was a satellite broadcast, and so it came through clearly, but the rest was line of sight and full of static.

"Wasn't the base damaged by the earthquake also?" I asked.

"A little," he said. "We lost some soldiers in the snow. But the bunkers are very strong. We dug them out and fixed them quickly."

It didn't stop. It continued all day, though there were lulls at times, and into the dark. My curiosity changed, over the hours, to unease, to a shifting of the ground beneath us. But it was exciting to feel that way; it infused everything with significance, like a rare spice, or the smell of smoke in a forest.

"It may be an offensive," Rai said, finally, by the light of the kerosene lamp. Forces were at work, and there he was, trapped and dumb as the rest of us, when all his adult life had been spent preparing for such an event. Now it was passing him by. Part of me pitied him.

"Has it ever gone on so long?" Elise asked anxiously.

Rai shook his head.

"It is rare," he said. "Usually it is only a few shells. But this is many hundreds of shells. Many hundreds."

"What kind?" I asked.

"What do you mean, what kind?" Elise asked, angrily. "All this talk of guns. And you are an old man. It is a terrible thing."

She stung me, of course, but in part I think I'd said it on purpose, to provoke her, and so I only smiled calmly and did not reply. She flushed, and bowed her head.

"I'm sorry," she said. "I did not mean what I said."

"Well?" I persisted, ignoring her, looking back at Captain Rai.

"Usually 105-millimeter howitzers," he said. "They are light enough to lift by helicopter. Some 155 millimeter, but those are more difficult to transport. They are carried up in pieces."

"What is their range?"

"Twelve thousand meters for 105. For 155, maybe twenty thousand meters. A bit farther at this altitude."

"So tell me," I said, deliberately, "how close does the shell have to fall to kill you?"

Rai looked uneasily at Elise.

"Fifty meters if you are unprotected," he said, finally. "That is for 155. For 105, high-explosive antipersonnel round, perhaps twenty-five meters."

"You mean if you're standing out in the open?"

He nodded. He couldn't help himself.

"Of course, it is different with entrenched positions. With a deep bunker, you can take a direct hit."

"So I assume they are in entrenched positions."

"Yes," he said. "But not all. It is difficult to dig in deeply in these mountains. Some of the time it is snow caves only. You must hope they do not see you."

I laughed.

"Yes," I said. "That wouldn't be good, would it? It must be cold up there with no lights and no fires, hoping they don't see you. It must make for a long night."

Rai looked at me then. I think he realized something wasn't right with my questions, but he wasn't quite sure what it was. We'd had similar conversations in the past, after all.

"How much does each shell cost?" I continued, pointedly.

"I am not sure," he said. "We manufacture them, of course. Perhaps one hundred pounds. Not so expensive."

"But that is very expensive," Elise said. "One hundred pounds. And now there are thousands falling. For what?"

He sighed, and looked at me.

"And Homa has no leg," she added.

"You are coming here on holiday only," Rai burst out angrily. "You are here for a few months, and then you are flying back home where there is everything. But we are here because this is our country and we must fight for it and there is no holiday for us."

There was a long silence, and then Elise flushed, excused herself, and left the tent.

Rai shook his head and lit another cigarette and took a deep drag and said something about women. I didn't respond, and we sat there in silence for a while. I thought about going after her for a moment because I knew I was in part to blame, but she'd stung me with her remark, and so instead I reached for Rai's packet of cigarettes. He tossed me his lighter, and we both smoked and didn't speak. The rumble continued in the distance. I thought about those men, high on the dark ridges, crouching beneath that sound, and I could not imagine them clearly. It was a new world for me, and I had nothing to draw on, no memories of my own. It was all thirdhand, it was all Gettysburg and the Somme and Tobruk for me, all names and abstractions. Nonetheless the roar continued, like trains in the distance, and it was real, and it felt like history.

"What is it like up there?" I asked, breaking the silence.

He took in his breath, sharply, and shook his head.

"It is very bad for them," he said. "They cannot hear one another. They cannot speak on the radios for too long. They cannot light fires or turn on any lights. They are pinned down in the snow. There are avalanches, also."

He took another drag, then continued.

"This is indirect fire," he said. "The batteries are many kilo-meters behind. The gunners cannot see the target."

"What is the target then? And who is aiming the guns?"

"There are forward observers on the ridges. They are calling in the fire. Probably they are shelling the ridgelines. But it is dif-ficult to be accurate in these conditions and especially at night. So most of the fire is ineffective. The shells are bursting in the snow and on the rock. But you must keep your head down, you cannot cook, you are getting cold and you are getting thirsty soon because all the water freezes. You cannot fly in provisions, you must hope it stops."

"So what do you do?"

"The enemy batteries are dug in well. In this terrain they are very hard to find and destroy, and they are firing from behind their own lines. So you try to find their forward observers. With night vision and infrared and telescopes. If they are exposed, sometimes you can see them. And then you call counter battery fire on their position. Or you use rifles if they are close enough. And if you cannot see them you guess where they might be and hope you are lucky. It is a game of cat and mouse."

"And they're doing the same."

"Yes, of course. They are trying to see who is looking for them also."

As he spoke, it struck me that what sounded like the work of thousands was really just a few men, perched high on moun-tainsides with all those stars in the dark, aiming volcanoes at one another. For an instant I did nearly picture them, in their dirty white suits, huddled among the sun-warmed rocks, mov-ing with reptilian slowness lest they be seen, offering rare terse sentences into their radios. And the barrage itself—from a dis-tance it was very likely to be beautiful, with all the hundreds of bright points opening and closing like a veil on the ridges, and snow falling in great cascades down the flanks into the echoing valleys below.

"Dangerous work," I said, and he nodded, slow-lidded and calm.

I was not calm. On the contrary, the sound was deeply unsettling, like the swell of a ship beneath us, or the moment before rain begins to fall. On and on it went, sometimes with a short lull, before starting up again. The radio hissed with static, and only rarely did scraps of voices come through, excited and high-pitched and quick.

"Are we in any danger?" I asked, later.

"No," he said. "We are many kilometers out of range."

"Maybe so," I persisted. "But there are dozens of army tents out there. It looks like a base, doesn't it?"

He thought about this for a while.

"An air strike, perhaps," he said, finally. "But that is a big change. That is a big escalation. From artillery we are safe."

I thought about it also. I was not afraid; instead, I was excited. It made me feel reckless, and it made me feel alive.

CHAPTER TWENTY-FOUR

Later that night, when there was nothing else to do but try and sleep, I heard footsteps approaching my tent. I'd been dozing, I think, and woke with a start at the sound of boots on gravel, and the glow of a flashlight through the nylon wall. I shook my head to clear it, and then there was a scratch on my door.

I unzipped the tent, and looked out, and it was Elise, looking very young with her headlamp and her rolled-up sleeping bag in her arms.

"I am sorry," she said, simply. "I do not like this noise."

"Is Homa awake?" I asked, for some reason.

She shook her head.

"Homa is sleeping. She doesn't know what is happening."

I paused for a moment, looking at her, and then I opened the flap wide and she crawled in beside me.

I made room for her, suddenly aware of my unwashed body in the close confines of the tent. For a moment I thought she would undress, but she only wriggled out of her jacket and nylon pants, revealing yellow long underwear, and had soon zipped herself into her sleeping bag beside me. She shivered a bit in the cold, and only her face and a few wisps of hair emerged from the mouth of the bag, and then she reached up and switched off the headlamp.

"I'm sorry," she said again after a few moments. "I could not sleep."

"What should we do?" she asked, after a while. "Should we stay here? I do not like this. I think maybe we should go down."

"I don't know," I said truthfully, after a while. "I'm not sure what we should do. If we left it would all be for nothing."

"This will delay them more," she said. "If they ever were going to come. And I'm thinking about what you said about the supplies."

"You mean that there's not enough?"

"Yes. Not enough. And the general coming. And now this."

She shook her head in the dark.

"It is always men who do this," she said. "Always."

"We'll ask Rai in the morning," I said.

"I am sure Sanjit does not know," she said. "I am sure they have told him nothing."

I didn't reply, and a few moments later she spoke again.

"How did your wife die?" she asked.

"She had a vague pain in her abdomen for more than a year. I thought she was imagining things. But she wasn't."

"Are you blaming yourself for this?"

"Of course," I said. "If she'd gone in earlier maybe she would have had a chance."

"I'm sorry," she said. There was a long pause. "I am sure it was not your fault."

"Not completely. But I was always working. Both of us were lonely after our son left home. In some ways we led separate lives at the end."

"What did she do?"

"She was a portrait painter," I said. "Bank presidents. Lawyers when they retired. That kind of thing."

I thought of them, also—the deans and partners who wanted

to leave a bit of themselves behind on the paneling, and were willing to pay for it. Still lifes as well—pears and apples and china. Watercolors of Eric as a child. The fields behind our house. The paintings were good, even excellent. But they were no more than that, and hanging on the wall of even a modest museum, as a few of them did, they hardly attracted a second glance. For her, in some ways, that was the most bitter truth of all.

"Were you ever happy together?" Elise asked, and again she caught me off guard. I paused for a while before answering.

"Yes," I said, finally. "More in the early days, before we realized how ordinary our lives would turn out to be. But we didn't appreciate what we had. Both of us made that mistake."

"She was unhappy with you?"

"Not exactly unhappy. But she was never completely content. Neither of us was. We didn't discuss things like that. We were like a lot of couples in that way. We tried to make the best of it."

And it was true. Many times I'd seen her looking out across the cornfields from the back porch, her thoughts so clear to me; bittersweet, taking her comforts where she could. They were not all that she hoped, I knew, but I'd like to think that it was tolerable enough for her, and if I had my failings and my distances, so, too, did she, and we had many moments of togetherness nonetheless, at times in spite of ourselves, as people always do.

One night, not so long ago, when I was well into my fifties, they had called me in from home. Usually the residents did not require my presence until morning, but the ICUs were full, and the ambulances kept coming, and they could not keep up, and they needed my help. I was just sitting down to dinner when the phone rang. Rachel gave me a long stony look, as she had so many times before, then stood and cleared my plate.

It turned out to be one of the longest nights of my career.

The first patient I saw was an old woman whose heart kept stopping. Refractory ventricular tachycardia, the sawtooth pattern on the screen, and her eyes would roll up in her head, the alarms would shriek, and we'd shock her, and she'd wake up again. Between shocks and the wisps of smoke, she asked us questions—Where am I? What happened?—until finally the electricity did nothing, and I could hear the sound of her ribs popping, one after the other, at the chest compressions. I watched, knowing it was no use, and after a few minutes I told them to stop and tell the family.

Then, without pause, it was on to the others. I'd been up since early that morning, and I was no longer young, and much later that night, as I stumbled through the ICU under the fluorescent lights, I couldn't ever remember being more exhausted. I had to force myself on, drinking cup after cup of coffee, and the EKGs before me, whose patterns had always been clear, seemed like a hundred black lines of calligraphy flowing from one patient to the next.

It was raining when I finally came home the next morning—a driving, cold rain, with low overhanging clouds. I nodded off in my car, then jerked awake and rolled the windows down. The air and rain poured in, staining the leather seats, fogging my glasses, and I could barely make out the road before me.

Our garage was separate from the main house. I was too tired to run across the lawn. Instead I walked, with my head down, soaked through and shivering.

Rachel was in the kitchen listening to the radio, and didn't hear me as I opened the front door. I left a trail of drops all the way down the hardwood floor of the hall. The lights were on, and the kitchen was warm.

I knew how sick she was of my absences, and that she was lonely, that she missed her son in college, that the town was small, and the commissions few, that somehow she was fifty years old and the art show she'd given a few months before at a local gallery had been attended mostly by acquaintances and friends, or students from her classes, that only a handful of the cheaper works had sold, and the others remained stacked in her studio along with the rest of her hopes—I knew all of that, and so I expected her to greet me with the familiar echo of those things, and I expected to reply in kind—helplessly, with weariness, as if to say, I don't know what else to do, and these are the choices we both have made.

But she didn't greet me like that. Instead, she sighed, and came forward, and put her arms around me, and pulled me close, and I was reminded of the early days again, when her face had lit up as I stood exhausted in the doorway of our apartment in Chicago, home for the morning, together for a few minutes before she went to work.

"You look awful," she said, as I put my head down on her shoulder. "You look a hundred years old."

She stepped back, and took a dish towel off the counter, and began to dry my hair.

Elise turned on her headlamp.

"Do you mind if I write in my journal?" she said. "I can't sleep."

"I don't mind."

I closed my eyes. I heard her fiddling with her bag, the rustle of pages, and then a ticking sound, like sleet against a window. I snuck a glance at her: it was a ballpoint pen, and she was writing intently in her small bound book, a faint frown on her face, in profile, the pages lit up by her headlamp.

She worked away, diligently, in a tiny, paper-saving hand. She wrote in German, and though I glanced over from time to time, and could see the sentences clearly enough, I understood nothing, not even a single word. I nearly asked her. But she was serious; I could see it in her face. I wondered who she was writing her story for, or whether she even thought of that at all.

As I listened to the pen, I realized that it was an important thing for her. I suspect it was not so much the act itself. I think for her it was more the formal collection of experience, and the dream of understanding it. I'm not sure how I knew this. Perhaps it was her discipline; she continued, without pause, for a long time. I wondered how honest she was being, and what she was saying. I wondered what she'd written about me, because surely I must appear there from time to time. Finally, she closed the book. Then, to my surprise, she leaned over, and kissed me tenderly on the cheek. Before I could respond she switched off the light, plunging the tent into darkness.

"I am sorry," she said, her voice catching, and after a moment, in the dark, I realized she was crying. But she composed herself quickly, and after a few more minutes she fell asleep, leaving me alone with my thoughts again.

I was so acutely and tenderly aware of her; the way she shifted, her breath, the smell of shampoo that came to me, her patch of warmth against the side of my sleeping bag. It felt strangely familiar, and I realized it was Eric, my son, as a very young child, that I was thinking of. Rachel and I had taken turns putting him to bed. He would shift and murmur beside me for a while—it was before he could speak—and then it would fall over him, his body would relax, his breathing would slow, and I would watch him sleep for a while before easing myself out of the room. It was the same feeling of tenderness, of intimacy and poignancy, and as I lay there beside her it came back to me. I could still feel him as the smallest of children beside me.

The sound grew when the wind blew toward us, and faded when it blew away. At times it was just at the threshold of hearing, and at other times as fully present as the river below us, the sounds merging together—the river and the falling shells—all night. As I lay there half asleep, I felt as if the sound was being poured into my unconscious mind. It reminded me somehow of the northern lights, which I'd seen decades ago, on a solitary camping trip, high on the Michigan lakes.

At first, it had simply been an odd glow on the horizon. It might have been mistaken for a distant city. But there was no city, just open water, and the vast sheets of forest stretching into Canada. The conditions, I learned later, must have been perfect—the right time of year, and clear weather, and sun flares trembling the ionosphere. I was lucky to have seen it, in such profusion—a true display of the aurora, and how it changed, as the hours passed, from a pale glow to a blue, swirling mass, like a deep and fragile creature in the sea. I watched it for hours, sitting beside my small fire. It was the kind of thing one expected to hum, but instead it was accompanied by a delicate and profound silence. It had no distance; it was both very near and very far away. The next night it was gone, and though I saw hints of it several times later in my life, once with Eric in nearly the same place, never again did it reveal itself to me so fully, and with such abandon.

In its own way, the sound of the barrage was as mysterious and as beautiful as the lights in the northern sky had been all those years ago. I knew it was a human thing, of course, that up close it was merely brutality and savagery, but from a distance it sounded like the work of God. In a sense I suppose it was.

CHAPTER TWENTY-FIVE

The next morning it was gone, but in the afternoon it returned, in fits and starts, and by evening it filled the air around us again. When I finally went to bed, I lay awake for a long time, waiting for her footsteps outside the tent. But she didn't come. No doubt she considered it. But something prevented her, and after a while, as the sleepless hours passed, I suspected it was pride.

I think that place, so unlike anywhere else I had ever been, so full of depths and absences and altitude—I think it was most true to itself at night. That is when the barrage was at its strongest, when it had the greatest reach, where it could carry me back into the past, and ahead into the future, with equal urgency. It showed me who I was most clearly, as if I had been deposited without context; and it made my mind tumble and spin, as if on a frictionless surface.

And as I listened, that second night, the ruined villages kept coming back to me. I imagined the dead, half frozen and rotting in the ground—so many thousands, stopped cold in a minute at four in the morning, the snow and stones on the mountainsides descending like surf, the earth a rippling sea.

The barrage, of course, was from a different instrument entirely. Yet lying there, it was hard not to think of it as a small dark cousin, an echo of a drum, another kind of phantom limb.

The following morning, in the cold clear air, there was only silence as I walked to breakfast, and a wisp of vapor from the cook tent, where Ali and his nephew were at work on our breakfast. My boots were loud on the gravel.

Something caught my eye just then. A flash, high on the ridge, on the far side of the river. I paused for a moment, looking up, but I could see nothing. I thought little of it, and continued, and just as I turned to enter the dining tent I saw it again. I felt a little prickle then, along the back of my neck, but I resisted the impulse to turn around and study the ridge—instead, I simply stepped into the tent, where Rai had already assumed his customary position at the table and Elise, who had arrived before me, stood rubbing her hands by the kerosene heater.

Rai looked up.

"Good morning," he said.

"Do you have your binoculars here?" I asked him.

"Of course," he said. "Why?"

"I think I saw something on the ridge," I said. "A reflection. I'm not sure."

He came instantly to attention.

"Are you sure?" he said.

"Yes. Something reflecting. Probably a piece of ice or a rock."

He gestured for me to step away from the door.

"What is it?" Elise asked.

"I don't know," I said. "Did you see it?"

She shook her head. Rai, meanwhile, had retrieved his heavy binoculars from under the table and stood up. He appeared to be thinking.

"Okay," he said. "I need you to open the door, just a little."

"Do you think someone is up there?" I asked.

"I don't know. It is possible, I think."

So I followed his instructions, and pulled the heavy canvas flap to one side. I understood his intention: from outside, the interior of the tent would have looked dark to any watching eyes.

"I do not like this," Elise said. No one answered her.

Rai crouched down, training the binoculars up on the ridge. He swept them back and forth for nearly a minute.

"What do you see?" Elise asked him, urgently.

"Nothing," he said, before standing and letting the binoculars hang from his neck. "But I am not sure where to look. You must try also."

We exchanged places. I crouched for a while, looking up with my naked eye at the sharp outline of the northeast ridge against the blue sky, trying to remember where I'd seen the flash. It was difficult to say how far away it had been—a half mile, a mile, distances were impossible there. I sat down on the earth floor, and rested my elbows on my knees, and brought the binoculars up.

The binoculars were large and heavy, like those that General Said had used to find the ibex. I swept them back and forth across the gray and tan rock, across the boulders and shadows, the patches of snow and hanging ice. I could see nothing also, but I kept on nonetheless.

"What do you see?" Elise asked again.

"Nothing yet," I said.

A minute passed, then two. I could sense Rai getting impatient, as he stood with the canvas bundled in his hands.

"You are sure?" he asked, finally.

"No," I said. "I'm not."

He kept standing there behind the door, and I went back and forth, like brushstrokes, across the wall.

And then I saw it. Barely discernable, a tiny point making its way slowly back up the gully to the top of the ridge. From that distance, the point was the exact color of the face. It was painstaking, and slow, immensely small, and every so often it would pause for long seconds and disappear against the rock. I looked as hard as I could, until my eyes began to water. I was reminded of sheets of cells on a microscope slide—the tiny boulders and shadows, so far away they could barely be seen at all, and the moving thing across them.

"There," I said, my voice louder than I intended.

"What is it?" Rai said.

"Something moving. I think it's a man climbing back up to the ridge."

"I need to see," Rai said, calmly. "We must change places. Elise, please hold the door."

She said nothing, but quickly did as he asked.

Rai crouched beside me, breathing, smelling like cigarettes.

"Start at the highest point," I said. "Then go left, about one-third of the way. There is a gully, a crack, with boulders below it. I think he's climbing up through the boulders toward the crack."

Rai took the binoculars from me, adjusting them quickly. He took a deep breath, then let it out slowly, to steady himself. He looked for a long time, saying nothing, convincing himself. The distances were so great, after all, and the forms so small, and it was so hard to be certain.

"I think you are right," he said finally. "I think it is a man."

He put the binoculars down, then stood up and began to pace.

"That was very good, Doctor," he said. "It was very good that you saw him. I did not believe you at first."

"But who was it?" Elise asked. "What is he doing there?"

"It is the enemy," Rai said, in the same flat tone.

"How do you know? He could be anyone. He could be from the village."

Rai shook his head.

"There are no villages across that ridge," he said. "And it is from the north, across the river. And he is going back. And the reflection means he is carrying field glasses or a telescope. Villagers do not have these."

He looked at me.

"They have come a long way," he said. "They are very far south."

"How many could there be?" I asked.

"Sometimes only one, more often three or four. They are observers."

Observers, I thought. But who knew what would follow, who knew what they would say into their radios when they were back and out of reach and entirely invisible once again.

Rai opened a case on the table, and withdrew a laminated map, which he spread out on the table and studied carefully. He looked out through the door again, and then, finally, he turned on the satellite phone, and spoke, quickly and urgently, in his native language. He paused, listening, then he looked at me for a long moment, and spoke again. Another pause, and then he recited some numbers, in English, which I realized must be coordinates from the map. Then he repeated them, slowly, as if on command, beginning to pace about the tent as he did so. He looked at me again, and turned off the phone.

"Well," he said, finally. "I hope that our eyes were not playing tricks on us."

"Why?" Elise asked. "Are they going to shoot the guns at them?"

Rai shook his head.

"No," he said. "But I cannot be wrong about this."

"Did you tell them you were completely certain?" I asked.

He met my eye. "Yes."

"Are you sure also?" Elise asked me.

I took a deep breath, feeling the weight of responsibility heavily.

"I saw something moving," I said. "I'm sure of that. But I'm not completely sure it was a man."

"It was a man," Rai said, looking directly at me.

I wondered then what it was that I had unleashed. Perhaps nothing, I thought, perhaps it was just another scrap of information pouring in, and no doubt the airwaves were full of them now—sightings, positions. But part of me wished I'd said nothing at all.

Rai paced, and I could see it in him; I knew that he wanted that moving point, so far away and elusive, to be a man. He wanted to believe they had finally come to him, that he was not there for nothing, wasting his time among women and civilians in the abstract name of duty.

"I should have a rifle," he muttered, stroking his mustache.

"There are things we must do today," he added, after a moment. "We need to take the girl back to the village. I am thinking about what you said. They might believe that this is a camp for reinforcements. For soldiers. It is possible."

CHAPTER TWENTY-SIX

Homa sat alone on her cot in the medical tent. She looked up at us. A plastic bag containing what little clothing she had lay beside her on the cot.

"Homa," Elise said, kneeling beside the girl, turning to Rai as she did so.

"Does she know she is going home?" Elise asked.

"Yes," he replied. "I have told her. But nothing else, of course."

Just then, the girl spoke, looking at Rai. Rai grimaced.

"What did she say?" I asked.

"She wants to know if she has done something wrong," he said, looking at me.

"No," Elise said, turning back to her and stroking her hair. "Tell her."

Rai spoke a few words.

"Tell her it is a happy day," Elise said. "That she is almost better and is going back to her family and soon she will have a new leg."

The girl listened solemnly as Rai translated, and then Elise began to cry a little. Elise composed herself after only a few seconds, but her tears clearly upset the girl, and she spoke again with urgency. Rai answered her gently.

"What did she say?" I asked again.

Rai sighed.

"She does not want to leave," he said. "She is afraid."

"What is she afraid of?" Elise asked. It was hard for Elise, I could see it—I knew that she wanted to offer the girl endless assistance, to offer her a new life entirely, had such a promise been hers to offer or to keep—I will save you from your fears. I will take you away from here. But of course it was impossible, and all of us knew it.

"She is afraid that she will not be able to gather wood and collect water from the river."

"Tell her," I said, "that soon she will have a new leg and that she will be able to do everything she did before, only a bit slower."

Rai gave me a questioning look, but then he did as I requested. The girl listened intently, then spoke softly to her brother. Her brother bent down to hear her, then spoke to Captain Rai, his off-colored eyes cool and foreign.

"She wants to know if she will need another operation to put it on again," Rai said.

I shook my head, and did my best to explain—her new leg would be like a stick, and it would not hurt to put it on again.

"She is afraid her mother won't take her back if she cannot work," Rai said. It was the sort of thought that came to adults when there was no one in the world to help them. It revealed a great deal about her life in that place, where a field of new barley was a latrine, and apricots drying on rooftops were full of tiny white worms that died off slowly in the sun.

Rai spoke again, firmly. Not without kindness, but leaving no doubt—the tone of authority, the tone of the world as it is. The girl looked down, but she did not, like Elise, shed any tears. She simply went somewhere else, as if dissolving before us, from presence to absence.

"What did you tell her?" I asked, grimly.

"I said that I will make her mother take her back."

Elise embraced the girl then—she hugged her tight, and stroked her hair again, and kissed her forehead. But the girl did not respond.

"Tell her good-bye," Elise said, finally, wiping a few tears from her eyes. "Tell her I will visit her."

Rai did as he was told.

"I do not think I can go with you," Elise said. "I think maybe it is too much."

Rai looked relieved.

Later, after Elise had retreated to her own tent, we gathered for the journey back to the village. I'd imagined this for some time, in spite of myself—the triumphant return, the thanks I might receive, the beaming girl released again into the arms of her family. But of course it was nothing like that—it was only Rai, carrying nothing, and Homa, on her brother's back.

I had a bag of dressing supplies in my pack, which I planned to show her mother how to use. I doubted whether she would ever do as I instructed, and in all likelihood the dressing would not be changed unless I returned to do it myself. But the wound was almost completely healed, with only a bit of scab along the suture lines, and was as good as done.

So we started, in silence, and without ceremony, down the path. It was hard to escape the feeling of being watched, of being terribly exposed beneath the heights, little figures that we were, standing so far out in the open. I knew it was unlikely, even if that moving point I'd seen, so small and far away, had been real. As time passed, I was less and less certain of this. But Rai did not allow himself to doubt. He'd changed possibility to certainty, just as I did the opposite. I suspected then that I would never know, that we would never discover where the truth lay, out there in all that blue sky and clouds and the immensity of the sheer ridges, so full of the inanimate, so full of boulders and patches of snow and silvery threads of water down couloirs never touched by any human thing. But the possibility alone of those dark eyes upon us made me feel uneasy and restless and afraid. It tapped into something, and filled me with a child's urge to hide, to creep out of sight, though there was nowhere to go.

Rai set a rapid pace, giving no thought to Homa's brother or, for that matter, to me. I struggled to keep up with him, and nearly asked him to slow down. Rai wanted it over and done with, that was clear.

Down we went, winding along the river. The river had receded since the snow had melted, but it was loud enough to make conversation difficult. But no one spoke, and Rai plunged ahead. I followed, breathing hard even as the trail descended and the village came into view once again. Homa's brother, however, made no effort to keep up with us, and began to fall behind. Rai realized this after a few minutes, although I said nothing to him, and slowed his pace, no doubt because he did not want to enter the village alone. He would have been required to wait, standing by the houses, the single object of attention. He was uneasy there—in most ways the village was as foreign to him as it was to me. But I could see the effort that slowing down required.

The mile passed quickly, the river went quiet at the wide bend by the village, and the path widened beneath our feet. This time, we arrived unnoticed, and were nearly to the edge of the village before the children saw us.

Rai had none of it. Two or three of them converged around me as before, pulling at my pack, but Rai's shout was like a shot into the air—they instantly went quiet, and fell back to a safe staring distance. By then, they had also seen Homa, and her brother. And so they followed, watching us, calling out, their thin voices like birdcalls in the air. Figures began appearing in the doorways, and then the men themselves emerged, joining the growing crowd. When we reached Homa's house, perhaps we had an audience of a dozen men and boys, but then, as the news spread, the entire village began to gather around us once again.

One of the children banged excitedly on the door, and I heard a woman's voice answering, but it was several minutes before the door opened and Homa's mother stepped warily into the alley. The cold stream down the center of the street had fallen to little more than a trickle, but still the sound of running water lent the scene an illusion of good cheer.

Homa said something then to her brother, who had stood silently with her on his back. He straightened, allowing her to slide lightly to the ground. Then he took her arm.

Homa, I realized, must have given thought to her return. She hopped toward her mother, doing it as well as she could. The crowd at our backs began to murmur, and her mother watched, making no move toward the girl. For the first time, I saw a resemblance between them—the same lightness of build, the dark eyes, the black hair that appeared in wisps from the edges of her red scarf. For an instant I could imagine the woman as a small girl, looking very much like her daughter. And now Homa hopped across the distance between them, the rough-handed hardship of years, toward her mother's scoured impassive face.

In some ways, I think it was as terrible a scene as I have ever witnessed. The crowd, the sound of her foot on the dirt, the girl's determination, and her mother, standing there, eyes narrowed, watching it all. It only lasted a few seconds, but it was enough, and for the first time I wondered whether I had done the right thing.

The woman took a step forward then, and bent down, and lifted the hem of her daughter's long dress, exposing the stump with its white cap of gauze. There was another murmur in the crowd, and jostling, as they strained to look, and then she turned to Rai and spoke, hoarsely. Homa stood there, enduring her mother's fingers on her dress just as she had endured everything else.

Rai answered her, matching her harshness with his own.

"What did she say?" I asked.

"She says so it is true that we have taken her daughter's leg."

"Does she understand that she would be dead otherwise?"

I heard the anger in my voice.

"That is what I have told her," he said. "But I do not think she understands."

"Tell her the foot was no good. That it was not possible to save it. So I saved her daughter instead."

Rai did as I asked. The woman listened, but then made an unmistakably dismissive gesture and began, suddenly, to shout at Rai. He tolerated it for a few seconds, but then he lifted his hand, and stepped forward, and shouted back a single word. The woman went quiet, and then, to my astonishment, there was a ripple of laughter from the crowd behind me. Rai shook his head in disgust, and turned to me.

"She says that she has lost her husband and now this. She is saying that now her daughter will never marry and is useless to everyone. She is saying that God has punished her."

"Tell her," I said, grimly, "that I'll give her some money."

Rai looked at me with surprise, but then he turned and spoke again.

His words had a dramatic effect. The woman opened her mouth, then paused, as if she did not know what to say, and in an instant her demeanor changed entirely.

"How much will you give?" Rai asked, looking at me, suddenly distant, with a hint of something else—suspicion, or wariness.

"I don't know," I said. "How much should I give?"

He looked away, thinking.

"Fifty pounds," he said, after a while. "That is enough."

"Tell that woman I will give her five hundred pounds," I said. "But tell her that we'll return in a year and if Homa is not here or if she has not been taken care of I will give her nothing else. But if Homa is in good shape and is well cared for I will give her another five hundred pounds. Tell her that I will do this each year until Homa is twenty-one years old. Tell her also that Homa is to receive a new leg and I will arrange that also. But if at any time Homa is not here or if I feel she is being mistreated she will receive nothing from me ever again."

As I spoke I realized it was an impossible promise.

Rai shook his head.

"It is too much," he said.

"It's nothing," I replied.

He shook his head again, with irritation.

"Maybe it is nothing for a rich man like you. But for her it is too much. She will have more than anyone in this village and much more than she needs. That will cause many problems. You do not understand this place, Doctor."

I thought.

"All right," I said, finally. "But it must be enough that the girl is valuable to her. It must be enough that she can't afford to mistreat her or cast her out."

Rai smiled.

"She cannot cast her out."

"Maybe. But I don't care. Just tell her. Make it two hundred pounds if you have to."

"Two hundred pounds is better," he said, and spoke to the woman again.

The crowd began talking all at once. And then, from the back, a man called out, gesturing, and they fell silent.

"What did he say?"

Rai turned back to me.

"He is saying that his animals are sick and that he needs money for his son and will you give him some also." Rai shook his head again, then continued. "You see," he said. "This is why there are problems. This is why you cannot give her too much."

"Tell him no," I said. "Tell them that no one will get anything else."

"Yes," Rai said, with approval, then turned to the crowd and spoke again. They shifted as he spoke, restless, and I felt a wave of hostility from them.

"You must be strong with these people," he said, turning his back again. "That is only what they know."

"Then tell her," I said, gesturing to the woman, "that God has blessed her and that she should be thankful."

Rai translated, but the woman did not reply. And then the man who had spoken earlier did so again, loudly, waving his hand in the air for emphasis. He spoke for a good while, and he had the crowd's attention. Rai listened, straining, I think, to understand.

"What is he saying?" I asked.

"I am not sure," Rai said. "I think he is saying if God is blessing them then why will all these strangers come and take their wood. And why is there fighting now."

There was a murmur of assent, and then Rai spoke up, loudly, clearly asking a question. The man answered, speaking more slowly, but no less intently.

"He says they will take their animals. He says they should go somewhere else."

The crowd shifted, and for the first time I was uneasy among them.

Rai spoke again, his voice loud in the air. He went on for a good while, as we stood and listened and tried to make sense of what he was saying.

"We must leave," Rai said. "They are angry now. They are blaming us for the artillery, I think."

He turned his attention once more to the girl. He spoke to her mother, curtly. It was my turn then, and I opened my wallet, carefully counting out two hundred pounds of local money. All their eyes were on me, and it was nearly all the cash I had with me. She watched me with the others, and when I handed her the bills, she snatched them from me without meeting my eye. In an instant the money disappeared into her dress.

She spoke, quickly, to her son, and he turned, holding out his arm for his sister. Then, without a glance in our direction, he led her slowly toward the doorway of the dark house. In was only a few feet, but it was the last of her journey, and she followed him, holding his arm with one hand. But just as they entered the threshold, she turned her head. She looked directly at me, expressionless, and I had one last image of her, with her flushed cheeks, her dark eyes and hair, against the weathered gray wood of the open door.

Her face stayed with me all the way through the village, and the resentment of the crowd, and the shouts of the children, emboldened, who followed us. Rai did his best, and walked slowly, but it was an undignified retreat nonetheless.

I thought of Homa's brother, so lean and tireless, gliding up the hillside from the village, giving nothing away, and I thought of the others—those men knocking snow off the tents, untouched by the bitter cold, and how they had gone silent at my approach that day. How little I understood them, and even now they watched us, through the tiny windows of their houses, or from a distance in the background. Only the youngest followed.

Just as we left the confines of the village, and began the slow ascent back along the river, something stung me on the back of the neck. My first thought was a fly, or a wasp from the orchard. I winced, and slapped the spot, and turned around, and suddenly there was a shout of triumph from the children in our wake.

It was a stone.

CHAPTER TWENTY-SEVEN

They came that night. I must have been very deeply asleep. Rai shook my tent, and called out. He had a flashlight, which he rarely used, and shone it at the door, printing a circle of light on the nylon and filling the tent with shadows. Elise was with him.

"What is it?" I asked, trying to wake up, my thoughts coming with difficulty. I unzipped the door.

"You must get up," Rai said. "Please get dressed."

"Why? What's going on?"

"I will explain," he said. "But you must get dressed."

"The army is here," Elise said.

I struggled into my clothes, and crawled out of my tent, and stood up. I could see the dining tent, lit from within, glowing in the darkness.

"The army?" I asked, dumbly.

"Yes," Rai said. "I am being relieved." He said it without expression.

"What army?"

"Our army, of course," Rai replied.

I blinked in the light, and then he turned it away, and began walking toward the dining tent. We followed him, in single file, and only then, I think, did I become fully awake.

"I'm sorry," he said, over his shoulder. "But I did not want you to hear them and come outside. I did not want any mistakes."

"What do you mean you're being relieved?"

"I will explain everything in a moment," Rai said, in a tone that suggested further questions would be unwelcome. So I said nothing else, and simply did as I was told, and followed the bobbing light in his hand. It was a clear night, dark in the absence of the moon.

There were armed men standing in the darkness. Two or three, I think, beyond the light from the dining tent door. Rai called out to them as we approached, and they murmured in reply. They appeared to be facing away from the tent, but it was difficult to see them well. They were not standing at attention, as best I could tell, but neither were they fully at ease.

"Why are they standing out there?" I said. "Why aren't they in the tent?"

"It is unnecessary, I think," Rai replied. "But they are keeping their eyes for the dark."

His phrase struck me.

There were two men in the tent, both seated at our table, both drinking cups of tea. Ali was there as well, serving them. As we entered, they looked at us, and only then, slowly, did they stand in welcome.

The older of the two wore a green wool sweater, identical to Captain Rai's, and a dark red beret over his weathered face. The obligatory mustache, also, beginning to go gray. He looked fifty, but I suspected that he was younger. He was a large, imposing man. He looked far harder than Rai, far more ruthless, stern and wintry, and I instantly realized that he had little of General Said's charm. Perhaps he was more intelligent than he appeared, but he had none of Rai's spark, none of Rai's alertness. He looked like a guard.

Rai saluted casually, and made the introductions.

"This is Colonel Raju," he said. "He is the commander of the regiment."

I shook his outstretched hand.

"Yes," the man said. He nodded at Elise, but did not offer to shake hands with her.

Colonel Raju said something to Rai.

"The colonel does not speak English as well as he would like," Rai said, translating carefully. "He hopes that you will understand."

"Of course," I said. "But there is no need for him to apologize. I don't speak his language either."

Rai translated, and the man replied.

"He is not apologizing," Rai said.

There was a pause. I looked at him, and managed to smile. The man spoke again.

"He says he is apologizing for the fact that you will have to go down in the morning, however."

"Ask him what is going on," Elise interjected.

Rai looked at her, clearly regretting that she had spoken, but then did as she asked. The colonel listened, and glanced at Elise. But he replied calmly enough.

"He says the situation has become complex. Beyond that he cannot go into details. But he says it is not necessary for you to be here any longer, and that tomorrow you must go down."

The other man stood, watching. He was about the same age as Rai, and similar in build and coloring, although his features were more classically handsome.

"Who is he?" I asked, gesturing to the man.

"I'm Captain Singh," the man said, in entirely fluent, British-accented English. "I'm the XO. Pleased to meet you."

He took a step forward, and shook our hands.

It must have been Rai's radio call that did it, I realized—the flash I'd seen, the point on the hillside. They'd sent in the army. It seemed laughable, absurd, and yet there they were.

Rai was as unreadable as I'd ever seen him. He was attentive, that much was clear, but he did not seem afraid, as he had with General Said. At first glance, Colonel Raju was a more formidable figure, much more obviously frightening, yet apparently Rai knew something that I did not.

Just then I saw Ali, standing in the corner with his tray. He moved, and caught my eye. He was being as unobtrusive as possible, but the expression on his face was one of despair, as if he had heard the most terrible news. For the first time he looked alert to his misfortune, not dulled to it, and I wondered what it was that had upset him so much. But then I looked away, because the colonel was speaking again.

"He says it is best if we stay together in the medical tent tonight," Rai said. "And to please not go outside in the dark. He does not want one of his soldiers to mistake you for someone else."

"Who else?" Elise began. She was angry, and I could see it.

"Elise," I said quickly. "Don't. Not now."

She shook her head, and I saw tears in her eyes. She shook her head again, and looked away. In that moment I realized that I didn't want it all to come to an end. I wanted to continue as we had been, waiting for them to come, drinking our tea and talking together. Now these men had made it impossible.

They did not invite us to sit down.

"Well," Rai said, finally, "we should go to the tent. There is much walking tomorrow."

So we shook their hands again, because we had to, and then

they were done with us, turning away to their strategies and their weariness, snapping their fingers at Ali when their cups were empty.

Outside, in the open air, Rai called out to the guards once more. Beyond them, in the darkness, there was movement, and rustling, and footsteps. I realized that soldiers were passing, just out of sight. Every so often one of the guards would call out softly, and each time there was an answering reply.

Rai led us away.

"How many men are out there?" I asked, finally, when we reached Elise's tent.

"More than two hundred," Rai said.

The number astonished me.

"Why so many?"

"It is a precaution only," Rai said.

I laughed, despite myself.

"They sent hundreds of soldiers up here because we saw something on the ridge that we weren't even sure was a man. Is that right?"

"It is a temporary matter," Rai said, more mildly than he might have. "They will only be here for a short time once it is clear."

"Once what is clear?"

"That we are not weak," Rai said. "That we will not tolerate their provocations. That there will be consequences for them if they violate our territory."

"I am supposed to pack now?" Elise said, sharply, interrupting us.

"No," Rai said. "Just your sleeping bag. We will pack in the morning. Tomorrow, it is important that we act the same. We will go to the dining tent early, we will eat breakfast, and then we will pack up our things and leave quickly. They do not know our soldiers are here. The soldiers will be in the tents, and so they will not see them."

"Why does it matter?" I asked. "I don't understand this. What are you trying to do?"

"These are my orders," Rai said, calmly. "There may be some risk now. It is possible. So you must listen carefully and do what I say."

"We should just call a helicopter," I said. "And fly out like we came in."

"This is too dangerous," Rai said, ominously. "They might have a missile. An SA-7. They are light enough to carry and effective against helicopters. They might fire on the helicopter if they think they have been discovered. They have done this before."

"In your territory? Wouldn't that be an act of war?" I asked, incredulous.

Rai laughed softly.

"What do you think this is, Doctor? A game we are playing?"

A deep anger came over me as he spoke. All of it, or nearly all of it, for nothing. I lay there in the dark beside them, wondering why I had ever listened to Scott Coles, when all along I knew that he was not fully what he seemed, that the promise he had offered was half a fiction all along, one that he had sold even to himself. He was out of his depth, and his organization was hardly anything at all. I knew better, and yet I'd fallen for it anyway. I'd come all this way for an empty tent city and a one-legged girl. A wind-scoured field of stones on the other side of the earth. The whole endeavor, as I saw it, had come to this; the whole attempt to start again. My plunge into the unknown, my step into this other world, where I hoped to lose myself in an abundance of need—and so few of my hopes had come true.

There was need, surely, there was need everywhere around me. But Homa alone had provided what I'd sought: redemption, the kind of clear personal triumph before which all the abstract questions recede. The rest of it, the cold roar from the heights, the absent refugees, the scraps of voices through static on the radio, all the questions of hierarchy and honor, the eagerness to spend precisely what they could least afford on conflict and war, to remake the struggle as one between men when it should have been one between hunger and food, between legs and stones— suddenly it infuriated me. I'd come for clarity, for Scott Coles's promise of a reduction to the essentials, because I'd assumed the two to be companions. Instead they were the most uneasy of bedfellows.

"Tell me," I said, coldly, to Rai. "What is wrong with you people? Why do you do this? I'd like to know why I came all this way for nothing."

"What is it that you would like me to say, Doctor? That we should let them take everything as they wish?"

"How many refugees could you have flown out of the mountains if you weren't airlifting hundreds of soldiers every time something sparkled on top of a ridge?"

"We are not like you," he replied, tightly. "We have not stolen everything to be rich."

"We didn't steal what we have. We earned it. And you're not even competent as soldiers. Any Western army would wipe the floor with you."

"You have not earned it," he said. "You are lucky, that is all. You have done nothing for what you have. We did not ask you to come here. And now that you cannot be a hero you are angry. You are trying to help yourself, not us."

The barrage rumbled on.

Early the next morning, in the dining tent, I finally saw why they had come.

It was windless and clear, cold, without a cloud in the sky, and the whole of the valley remained in shadow. The barrage, for the moment, had stopped. We left the medical tent together, and walked across the few meters of open ground.

Rai called out softly as we approached, then opened the door halfway, stood to one side, and gestured for us to enter. There was a flicker of movement within the tent, the scuffing of boots, as a figure stood up and moved away.

It was a soldier. As Rai let the canvas flap close behind us, I saw that a hip-high wall of sandbags had been stacked on the ground a few feet back from the door. Rising above the sandbags, a spotting scope, heavy and black, stood on a tripod. I realized that the soldier had been watching the ridges through a crack in the door, as Rai and I had done.

At our table, beyond the line of sandbags, Colonel Raju sat with Captain Singh, drinking tea. There was a radio on the table, and several pairs of binoculars. Both men looked up at us and nodded.

But it was the final soldier who frightened me. He lay on his back on a green rubber mat, next to the tripod behind the sandbags, staring at the ceiling, and he hardly glanced at us. Beside him on the mat sat a weapon—a heavy bolt-action rifle, with an oversized scope, its black synthetic stock scraped and battered. Two folding legs supported its thick barrel. It looked malevolent, functional; it had none of the elegance of General Said's ibex gun, with its tooled leather strap and varnished grains of wood. Directly in front of the weapon a firing slit had been prepared in the row of sandbags. They must have worked for hours in the dark, filling the burlap with gravel.

"What is this?" I said, sharply, my voice loud in the tent. Colonel Raju said something to Rai.

"Please," Rai said to me. "We will eat, and then we will leave."

"Why is there a sniper team in our tent?"

Rai's face tightened, and he reached out and grabbed my arm.

"You must keep your voice down," he said. "It is important that you control yourself now. Both of you."

Elise stood staring at the soldiers as I had done.

"I do not want to eat," she said. "I want to leave this place."

"Then we will pretend we are eating," Rai said. "Ali will bring us our breakfast. We will wait here for a few minutes. Then you will go directly to your tents, pack up your things, and we will go. Do you understand?"

"Send them somewhere else, at least."

"We cannot do this, Doctor," Captain Singh said, from the table. "If they see movement in the other tents they will know others are here. But if they see movement in this tent they will not."

"But where are the soldiers?"

"They are in the tents that are behind the others and more difficult to see from the ridge. They are lying down. They are not moving. But you are asking too many questions. Sit down, please."

With that, Captain Singh extended his hand toward one of the empty chairs at the table.

Rai turned away, opened the flap just enough to step through it, and began shouting for Ali. His voice was loud, designed to draw attention.

Elise and I looked at each other in bewilderment, then did as we were told, and sat down at the table. Raju ignored us.

Minutes passed, and with them came a rising sense of dread. The soldier reassumed his position at the door, eyes on the scope, sweeping it back and forth, patiently and slowly, again and again.

"If you shoot at them they're going to shoot back," I said to Rai. "You're putting all of us in danger. It is unacceptable."

"Even if they are there, which we do not know, it is very difficult to see where you are being fired at from long range," Singh replied, calmly. "It will be only one or two men, three at most. This is a prepared position and you are safe here, I assure you."

"You assure me? Based on what? You have no idea how many men might be up there."

Captain Singh smiled.

"We do not know if anyone is there at all," he said. "Though I am sure Captain Rai was not mistaken. If he was, then we are making fools of ourselves."

Rai looked at him, without expression, then turned to me.

"Please," he said. "You must calm down."

"We did not come here for this," I said. "If you want to start a war, why don't you do it somewhere else?"

Colonel Raju spoke for the first time.

"You will be quiet, please," he said, in English, his black eyes meeting mine again as he took another sip of tea. I felt the chill that he intended, and did not reply.

Just then Ali appeared in the doorway with our breakfast, eyes darting at the soldiers. His hands were shaking as he set the tray down on the table. Rai spoke to him. He bowed and nodded, nodded again, then turned and left the tent as quickly as he had come.

"What did you say?" Elise asked, her voice steady.

"I told him to pack our food," Rai replied. "I told him to be ready to leave."

"Nothing will happen now," Rai said, watching me. "This is a precaution only. You should not become carried away."

But he was carried away as well—he was as tense and coiled as I'd ever seen him. I knew what he wanted, and how afraid he was that he had been wrong. Every so often he glanced anxiously over at the soldier, expectant, like a fisherman watching a lure on the surface.

Rai looked at his watch. The soldier studied the ridges, back and forth and back again.

"In a few more minutes," Rai said, "we will go. But you should eat. There will be much walking today."

I shook my head, and Elise said nothing at all. The minutes ticked on—five, then ten. Only a little while longer, I thought, and we'll be gone. But then the soldier shouted, and surprised us all, because none of us, I think, truly expected them to be there.

It was a single word, one I didn't understand, but in that moment, despite all my doubts, despite how I had questioned my own eyes, I knew what was going to happen, and then with a single liquid movement the soldier rolled over on his mat and took up the rifle in his arms, inching forward beside the spotter, eyes to the scope, chin on the stock, finger extended past the trigger, the muzzle easing out through the slit in the sandbags.

In a instant Colonel Raju and Captain Singh were out of their chairs and beside the spotter. Raju whispered to him, bent to look through the scope, then leaned back again as Singh raised his binoculars. Raju spoke quickly to Rai, who had also risen from his chair. Rai crept around the wall to the canvas door, and eased it open, just slightly, then slightly more, on Raju's command.

Raju paused, as if thinking, and spoke again. Rai answered, failing to keep his excitement from his voice, all of them unaware of us now.

"What is it?" Elise asked, her voice startling. "What do you see?"

Rai looked back at her from the door.

"Quiet!" Rai hissed at her. "Get down on the floor. In the back of the tent. Behind the position."

I took Elise by the arm, and pulled her from the table to the ground a few feet directly behind the row of sandbags.

"Lie down," I said to her, on my knees, looking toward the door. Raju knelt beside the soldiers, his elbows resting on the top of the sandbags. The sniper spoke for the first time, but Raju shook his head, and answered, clearly telling him to wait. Long minutes passed—two, then three, until I could tolerate it no longer. I stood, and moved quickly to the table for Rai's binoculars, and then I was crouching behind them, lifting the binoculars to the ridge. I swept the binoculars back and forth, until I saw them also.

They were far closer than they had been before, much farther down than I would have guessed. They had reached the base of a sheer cliff, on a rock slope high above the river; two men, carrying packs and rifles, traversing slowly across the shadows of the slope toward a steep gully that led back to the top of the ridge. They were dressed like villagers. A few meters above them,

where the slope met the bottom of the cliff, was an opening—a
deep crevice in the base of the cliff, perhaps a cave; I could not
tell in the darkness of the face. And as I watched, a third man
emerged from the crevice, picking his way down, before following the others out across the slope. They moved steadily and
deliberately through the shadows, and had I not known where to
look I never would have seen them. But there was no doubt this
time; there were men up there, and they must have thought they
were safe enough, so early in the morning, in the deep shade of
the cliff before the sun fell on the slope. They must have thought
there was nothing to fear.

"Get down in the back of the tent," Rai said to me, from the
doorway, a look of triumph on his face.

"Don't kill them," I said. "Please. You don't have to."

"Get down," Rai said again, his voice rising.

The spotter pressed a button on the top of scope, and a green
light blinked, and then he spoke, and then the other man was
turning the knobs on the scope of the rifle. I realized that the
spotting scope had a laser range finder. I stepped back, as Rai
demanded, dropping the binoculars.

"Don't kill them," I said again, and for an instant I considered running out of the tent, shouting, waving my arms, but I
knew they never would have heard me. It would not have helped
them; they were out on the face, on forty degrees of rock, utterly
exposed, with hundreds of empty meters in every direction, and
nowhere to hide, and if they were going to be shot, there was
nothing I could do to prevent it.

"You don't know who they are," I said. "They could be villagers. They aren't wearing uniforms. They could be anyone."

Colonel Raju spoke again to Singh.

"They have packs and rifles," Singh said. "They are not villagers. They are the enemy, and they are in our territory. You

should not be here for this. But we are defending our country. Do you understand?"

"Yes," I said, as calmly as I could manage, struggling to think clearly. "But if you're right they'll have radios. What if you miss? Then they'll call for help."

"They are within range," Singh said. "Eight hundred meters. They have no cover. Their radios will not carry far enough unless they are on the top of the ridge. And now you must hold your tongue."

Rai crouched by the door.

Raju waited a little bit more. I ignored Singh, and raised the binoculars again, nauseated, unable to turn away. The third man was hurrying to catch the others, and each second he drew farther from the safety of the crevice.

"They were careless," Rai said, softly. "They slept too low and too close. They were in the hole in the rock."

"Maybe they're leaving," I said.

"Then they are leaving too late," Rai replied, for the benefit of the others, his hand tight on his fistful of canvas.

The soldier shifted the rifle against his shoulder, his left hand draped over the stock, close to his cheek, pulling it tight to his shoulder, and then he reached up with his right hand and worked the bolt.

Captain Singh tapped his fingers on the sandbags. Only Raju was at ease. They waited, letting them pass across the face, each step taking them farther from safety.

"You shouldn't do this," I said. "You should let them go. They must know we're not a threat or else they wouldn't have come so close."

Raju put his thick fingers in his ears, and gave the order to fire.

The shot was deafening, like the crack of an enormous whip,

the muzzle flash lighting up Rai's face. Instantly my ears began
to ring, and then the soldier worked the bolt again, and I was
looking through the binoculars once more.

They didn't realize at first. It took them many long seconds;
the first shot missed, and the sound of it must have been muffled
by the tent, because the men continued on across the wall as if
nothing had happened.

The spotter pressed the button on the scope again, fiddling
with the knobs, calling out the range, and then the soldier fired
a second time.

Once more the blast lit up the tent, and the weapon leapt
back against the man's shoulder, but this time I saw it, nearly a
second later—a little puff of dust as the heavy round struck the
rock wall a few meters below and behind the last figure.

"Ah!" Raju said, in fury, turning toward the man with the
rifle on the ground.

For a moment I thought it would be all right, that they
would get away after all, because they stopped, turning in uni-
son to look down toward the camp, and then, a moment later,
they began trying to run across the slope. They were fleeing for
their lives, and a few seconds later they cast off their packs. The
packs began to bound, little dark dots tumbling down the face
toward the river below. The figures began to scramble and leap.
But there were hundreds of meters to go, they were on a rock
wall steep enough for ropes, with all that empty space beneath
them, and running was impossible.

The soldier fired, and missed, for a third time—another puff
of smoke on the rock, no closer than before.

Just then one of the figures stopped, and reached up for the
rifle on his back, turning, lifting it to his shoulder, and I saw a
string of flashes, and an instant later I heard the distant rattle of
an automatic weapon.

"AK," Singh said, with elaborate, forced calm. "From there it is whistling."

But Raju swore, roughly, bringing his clenched fist down on the sandbags. He turned, shouting first at the soldier, then at Singh. Singh reached for the radio, and began to lift it to his lips.

In that instant Rai saw his chance. He left his place by the door, vaulted over the sandbags, and pushed the soldier aside. I watched in dismay as he lay down with the rifle, and brought up the scope to his eye, looked carefully up at the ridge, and twisted one of the knobs very deliberately, as if he had all the time in the world. The soldier stood helplessly for a moment, and then he took Rai's place at the door, and pulled it aside. Both Raju and Singh stared at Rai.

I could not stop myself from watching. They were nearly halfway across the slope, moving as erratically as they could.

Rai went absolutely still, as if he knew exactly what he had to do, and how much depended on it. He took his time, and when he fired the puff of smoke was far closer, nearly there, a hairbreadth below the first man's feet, but dead center, and the spotter was calling out, and then Rai worked the bolt, took a long breath, let it out, and fired again.

There was no puff of smoke. Instead, the man simply stumbled and fell forward. He slid a few feet down the face, rubbery and loose, and then he stopped. One moment he was moving, and the next he was not. That was all; I expected him to tumble, and spin, as the packs had done, but he didn't. It was like a long sigh, and from a distance it looked almost gentle.

The spotter cried out in triumph, and Rai chambered another round. The second man paused for an instant, studying the dead man before him—a reflex, I think, a kind of disbelief, but then he was off, and moving again.

Rai's second shot missed, and he ejected the shining cartridge, then turned to the spotter, his voice steady and cold. I
realized the rifle was empty. Raju nodded, and allowed himself
a tiny smile.

The spotter fumbled in a pack on the ground, then handed
Rai a fresh magazine. A few more seconds passed. Singh stared
at Rai. And Rai was calm, I thought, as calm as he could ever
have wanted, reloading, as my own pulse hammered in my ears.

The second man. He was running, stopping and starting,
but he was slower now, visibly tiring, and I knew that it was far
too late to say anything at all.

It took three shots. Two more puffs of smoke, one on either
side, missing by inches. Then the perfect third, timed for the
moment his pace slowed, the crack of the rifle less startling now,
though the tent was choked with dust, and the motes hung up in
the column of light from the door.

The bullet must have struck him low, in the spine, because
when he fell he did not stop moving. Instead, he began to crawl,
with his arms alone, his legs sliding down below him. As I
watched him, I expected Rai to shoot him again. But he turned
to the last man instead, his face expressionless.

Rai took another breath, and let it out very slowly. He had
all the time he needed. He had the range, the ammunition, the
audience, and the confidence that he could act, and the wall was
wide, and there was nothing to stop him. The figure on the wall
ran on, and Rai let him go, easing the rifle with him, waiting for
him to weaken, and then, finally, the man was bending down,
his hands on his knees, heaving his last few breaths into the thin
air in little clouds, the valley before him, and the river below,
winding toward the village. He sat down, and put his hands
high up in the air and waved them, back and forth.

For the first time Rai hesitated. Instantly Raju barked an

order. A moment passed, and then Rai spoke, questioning, looking up at the colonel from the gun. But Raju shouted again, rising from his crouch, turning toward him, leaving no doubt. Rai let out a sharp single breath, and then, as if denying himself the chance to think anymore, he fired. I had the glasses up, and I could see the man clearly. The bullet must have hit him somewhere in the face, below and between his hands, because his head flipped back as if struck by an invisible fist. It dropped him like a sack of meal, and suddenly, visible even at that distance through the binoculars, there was a tiny cloud in the clear air above him, a delicate settling haze.

Then, quickly, Rai swung the rifle back to the final writhing figure, worked the bolt, and pulled the trigger one last time.

CHAPTER TWENTY-NINE

The soldiers were out on the field. A swarm of them, as the tent city came to life for the first time, pouring into the open, their green uniforms dark enough that from a distance they looked black, with rifles in their arms, and hands shielding their faces from the glare, all of them staring up at the ridges above us, as if they had appeared by magic. Their boyish, excited cries carried across the gravel and stones, as the line of shadows eased eastward toward the river.

I was so used to the emptiness of the valley, to wind and quiet and the sound of the river, that even then, stunned as I was, I could hardly believe they were real. They were just far enough away to be dreamlike, as if they were made of something other than flesh and blood.

"You must hurry," Rai said, behind me. "I will help Elise. Get your things. Come to the dining tent when you are ready."

I must have put everything into my pack, and taken down my tent. I remember panting in the cold, and I remember the terrible sense of exposure, on the sunlit ground, certain that I was being watched from the heights.

Rai was waiting by the dining tent with Elise when I returned. A soldier stood with them, and Ali, and his nephew. The boy blinked, and looked confused. A pile of packs and duffel bags lay on the ground at their feet.

"Your packs," Rai said, pale and shaken, gesturing to Elise and me.

"Why is he here?" I asked, pointing to the soldier.

"He will help with the loads," Rai replied.

Rai opened our packs and spread the contents out onto the ground. Then he opened a duffel bag, and began stuffing our things into it, and then another, and finally a third, until our packs were empty.

"We can carry some of it," I said, but he shook his head, sharply.

"We must go quickly," he said.

Then he turned, and nodded to the soldier, and the man knelt, put his rifle down on the ground, then heaved the largest of the duffels up onto his shoulders before picking the weapon up again. He stood, young and blank, with sun on his clothes, and for an instant I imagined that his mind was as empty as his face. He seemed all body, somehow, without volition of his own, and whatever his thoughts might have been, watching us, he revealed nothing.

Ali stepped close to the boy, then bent down, and with effort lifted the next duffel in his arms. His nephew turned his back, and slid his arms through the narrow straps, and when Ali let go the boy let out a gasp at the weight. Then Ali turned, and began to struggle with his own load. For an instant no one moved to help him, and I found myself stepping forward as he had done for his nephew. The duffel bag was heavy. I struggled to hold it, and as he slid his thin arms under the straps I knew it was too much for him, that the morning would be a cruel one for them both.

The soldier was a different animal entirely. He stood effortlessly, and he was used to it, but Ali and his nephew had spent their days on small things—tea, washing up, or the breaking of expensive morning eggs into bowls. I glanced at Rai.

"It's too heavy for him," I said.

Rai scowled and said something to Ali—a question. Ali shook his head and mumbled in reply.

"He says it is okay," Rai replied. "We must hurry. Later we can worry about this."

Rai picked up his pack from the ground, and Elise and I followed suit. Then he set off, without a backward glance, and that was how we left the valley, ours no longer—without ceremony, one after the other, down the path. It was fully light by then, and in the distance I heard the first drumbeats of the barrage starting up again.

If Raju, or Singh, or the soldiers noticed our departure, they gave no sign. They ignored us completely, and watched the ridges. Apart from the intermittent rumble of the guns, the valley was as quiet as ever, the calm of the early morning just beginning to give way to the first gusts of wind as the sun warmed the dark swathes of air against the cliffs.

We walked as fast as we could down the track toward the river, and yet it seemed as if hours passed before the mud homes of the village came into view, with the apricot trees swaying behind their walls, and the sunlight falling upon all of it. The fields of barley looked vibrant and green and rippling on the terraces, and the river began to roar at our side, sending its cold breath into the air. For the first time there was no one at work in the fields, and the village was shut up tight.

We walked in order—Rai, then Elise and me, then Ali and his nephew, and finally the soldier. For the first few minutes, Ali and his nephew managed well enough, though the trail was easy along the river. No doubt as the hours passed their struggle would begin and something would have to be done. But just then, in the cold morning, with the miles stretched out before us, I simply walked behind Elise, watching her little white gusts of breath growing fainter as the air warmed, my legs shaking beneath me on the rocky hillside, which soon gave way to the first of the low trees. By degrees the walls receded, as we descended, each step taking us farther out of range.

Finally we were alongside the village, on the path beside the river, and Elise stopped.

"We must do something for her," she said, her voice rising. "We cannot just leave."

"We don't have time for this now," I said.

"We promised her," Elise said

"I gave her mother some money," I replied. "And I promised her more. And I said I would get her a prosthetic leg."

She looked at me, brushing a few angry tears from her eyes.

"But how will you do this?" she asked. "How will you get her a leg, and give her more money?"

Rai continued on down the trail, but the others stopped with us.

"I will arrange it with him," I said, nodding my head at Rai.

"But how will you arrange it with him?" she demanded. "How do you know he will come back?"

"Because I'll pay him. And I'll make him send a picture of her to prove he's done it."

"He will not want to. It will be difficult for him."

"You're right," I said. "So I'll just have to pay him enough. He can hire someone else to help him if he needs to."

"You must promise me," she said, turning toward me, reaching out and gripping my arm. "You must promise me that you will do this. I will help also. I will send her money when I get home."

"I promise," I replied. "But we have to go now. We have to get out of here."

She stood there for a while longer, staring at the village, but she had no choice, and she must have known it. The seconds passed, my unease increased, and Rai walked on. Finally, the soldier cleared his throat behind us, and, as I knew she would, she simply turned her head away and continued.

Soon we were beside the fields, stepping over the rough irrigation channels on the riverbank. We didn't speak for a long time, we just walked as quickly as we could, and after only a few minutes we'd passed the last of them. The slopes on either side went dry once more, and only the narrow strip of bushes and the rare gnarled tree reminded us that it was possible for things to grow there at all. The vegetation came to a sharp end a few feet up the hillside. It was a distinct line, from sufficient to insufficient, from presence to absence. But the strip of vegetation was a whole world unto itself, with tiny white, red, and orange flowers tucked here and there, and little round cacti, and a knee-high silvery kind of bush. High above us, the sun-filled granite walls, shining here and there with patches of water, and above it all, again, the blue and glacial depths of the sky. We warmed up as we walked, and I absently unzipped my jacket to my chest, and adjusted my pack on my shoulders.

The valley began to curve away behind us. At first I didn't notice it, but when my boot lace came undone, and I stopped to tie it, I glanced back along the river and realized that I could no longer see the village. Already it was hidden by the side of the valley, and now the only human sign was the path at our feet. Only then, finally, did I allow myself to feel the beginnings of relief. But I could not free myself from the image of those men lying dead on the wall—I saw them again and again, those scrambling figures, the puffs of smoke on the rock. It overwhelmed everything else—Homa, the barrage, the endless waiting, the righteous anger I had felt—all of it was washed away. My ears still rang from the shots. Only the effort of walking calmed me, and allowed me to think at all.

On we went, hour after hour, with only the sound of our own breath and footsteps, moving as quickly as we could. The river grew larger beside us. At times it boiled and roared, and at other times, when the angle lessened, it spread out and flattened and slid by nearly in silence.

Finally, at a bend in the river, when the sun was directly overhead and it was as warm as it was going to get, Rai stopped us to rest and drink. A handful of boulders had rolled down from the wall nearly to the water's edge, and we stopped there. It might have happened a thousand years ago, or it might have happened last month. It was impossible to tell.

We were miles below the camp by then. Surely we were far enough away, I told myself, surely we were safe now. The sense of threat was everywhere nonetheless, but for the first time that day I began to feel as though it was something I could master. The wind gusted against us from time to time, the river flowed on beside us. The water was an achingly cold gray, full of silt, but if left to stand in a pot it would clear, and could be decanted from the surface with hardly any grit. Rai pulled a cooking pot from the soldier's pack, then crouched at the water's edge and filled it. He carried it back and placed it carefully on the ground, then sat down a few feet from me, lit a cigarette, and smoked in silence.

Ali and his nephew had fallen a few dozen meters behind. For the first few hours of the morning they'd stayed with us, but as I sat on the boulder with my pack beside me, sipping cold, iodine-tinted water from the bottle, feeling the circle of sweat cool between my shoulders where my pack had rested, I could see that both were laboring. They shuffled together, heads down,

eyes fixed on the path. Ali, in particular, without the resilience
of youth, looked pale beneath the load, his forehead beaded with
sweat, his eyes wide and strained. A vessel in his neck flashed
along with his heart, and when he took off his pack he let it fall
heavily to the ground, which drew a sharp word from Rai, who
sat watching. His nephew collapsed beside him.

Ali nodded, vaguely, then crouched on his haunches and
leaned against the pack a few feet away. He let out a breath, then
wiped his nose crudely on the back of his hand. He closed his
eyes, then opened them again.

Rai said something to him, pointing to the pot of cold water.
Rai was steadier, more like himself. He repelled me then, and I
did not know what to say to him. All I could think about was
what he had forced himself to become.

"It's too heavy for him," I said, finally.

Rai scuffed at the ground with his boot. He didn't want to
look at me; for the first time he wouldn't meet my eye. Ali and
his nephew took turns gulping from the pot. Rai let them finish.
A few minutes passed, in silence. Lunch for Elise and me was
dry crackers, a few packets of cheese, and a tin of unappetizing
processed meat. I could hardly eat. We drank more water, but
Ali and his nephew drank most of all. They got up to lower the
pot again and again into the river. Their throats worked, and
water ran down Ali's beard onto his chest.

Finally Rai stood, wiping his hands on his thighs, and ad-
vanced toward Ali. He spoke.

Ali got to his feet, and did as he was told—he opened the
duffel and began spreading the contents out on the ground. Rai
spoke again, and the boy followed suit. The soldier, for his part,
simply watched, crouched on his heels.

It was mostly food. Our clothing also, and our tents and
sleeping bags, but the bulk of the weight was cans of condensed

milk and meat, the bags of rice—all that had sustained us for the past weeks.

"This is why I should not have brought them," Rai muttered, and though he spoke in English it seemed as if he was talking as much to himself as to me. "They are too weak."

He spoke to Ali again. To my surprise, Ali replied, protesting. Rai answered, his tone harder, but again Ali answered back loudly, gesturing. I had never seen him so animated. An expression of surprise passed across Rai's face. Ali, meanwhile, pointed to his nephew and talked some more, and then began, unasked, to put the tins of food back in his duffel.

"What's he saying?" I asked.

"He says that he can carry it, and his nephew also," Rai managed. "He says that they will be stronger."

"We can carry some of it," I said to Rai. "And there's too much there anyway. We can just leave it here."

"We need it," Rai said.

I hesitated.

"Did you tell him that he would have to pay for what was left behind? That you would deduct it from his wages?"

Rai did not answer.

"I can pay for the food if it comes to that. But Elise and I can carry some of it."

As he stood there, his mirrored glasses reflecting the blue sky and the ridges above us, I felt his anger, even though he said nothing.

"Why are you punishing them?" I said. "What have they done?"

"This is not your place," he said finally, restraining himself with visible effort. "But if you want to carry it, then carry it."

Perhaps, in the end, we took thirty pounds each, but it was enough for Ali and his nephew to stand far more easily, with palpable relief. Only the soldier's load remained unchanged. When finally we were ready, and standing, Rai threw his own pack effortlessly across his shoulders, and stalked off down the trail.

When Rai's back was turned, Ali approached me, quickly, bobbing his head, half bowing, and then, to my dismay, he grabbed my hand and tried to kiss it. I waved him off. The soldier watched impassively.

"Thank you," Elise said, looking down the trail at Rai.

I did not answer, and we continued in silence. My pack had weight now, but it was not unpleasant. There is something satisfying about a modest load, in its illusion of strength and possibility. And after a while, when we'd settled once more into the rhythm of walking again, the scene between Rai and me receded, as if it had never happened at all.

CHAPTER THIRTY

Late that afternoon, shortly before the sun fell behind the western ridges and cast the valley in shadow, Rai finally stopped us for the night. He'd chosen well—a bend in the river, along a sandy bank flat enough for the tents, where the current was slow and easy. I was tired, aching, and it was an effort to set up my tent. Rai looked at the low bank carefully—it was only a few inches above the water—and then glanced up at the sky.

"Probably is okay," he said, "for one night. But the river can rise up sometimes."

"There's been no rain," I said.

"Yes," he replied. "But sometimes the snow melts quickly in the mountains. I have seen it before."

"I don't care," I said. In fact there was little choice, since the walls rose steeply again a few feet away.

"I think it is okay," he said, then set Ali and the boy to work collecting water and lighting the stove.

The band of sun rose up the high walls to the east and disappeared. Once again, the transition was abrupt, from sunlight to the pool of shadows, and the temperature plummeted nearly as quickly. I sat there on the bank for a while, in front of my tent, with my rolled-up sleeping bag as a pillow, trying to get warm, watching the river and sipping the cup of tea that Ali's nephew had brought me. Elise had retreated to her tent as well, Ali and the soldier and the boy sat crouched beside the stove, heating more water, and Rai, for his part, paced uneasily at the water's edge, his cigarette blooming and fading like a firefly. The barrage was gone. Perhaps it had stopped, or perhaps it simply could not be heard that deep in the valley.

After a while, the ridges to the east lost definition—only their sharp, angular tips could be seen, printed against the sky, which glowed, and began to reveal, one by one, the brightest of the stars. And then too, the river began to shine, diaphanous, and the narrow strand of rapids below us leapt out of the background like white cloth. I sipped my tea, cool in my jacket, listening to the rocks knocking along the riverbed, wondering how on earth a man like me had found himself there. How unlikely it seemed, how enormous and strange the world was, and how unprepared I felt. By then my fear had receded to a dull and distant ache, and mingled with my physical exhaustion, so I could not quite tell where one began and the other ended.

I heard a sound, and looked up. It was Rai.

"Can I talk to you, Doctor?" he asked, quietly, reeking of cigarettes, his jacket buttoned up tight to his throat.

"Of course," I said, and moved over to make room for him.

He crouched beside me, then flicked his cigarette out into the river.

"I am having difficulties," he said finally. "I am sorry."

I didn't know how to reply.

"When you are an officer like me," he said, "you must distinguish yourself for promotion. Whenever there is a chance you must take it, or else you will have nothing. I am thinking about my daughters and my wife. Their education. Their food. Do you understand?"

"I don't know," I said finally.

He ran his fingers through his hair.

"I am paid very little," he said. "Every month we do not have enough, or only enough."

He picked up a handful of stones, and began tossing them, one by one, into the river.

"You didn't only do it for your family. You did it for yourself as well."

He kept throwing the pebbles.

"Yes," he said, tightly. "You are right. What you say is true." He shook his head.

"But there was no hope for them, Doctor," he continued. "I hope you understand this. They would not have escaped."

"If you had missed, how could anyone have stopped them?"

"Colonel Raju was ordering Singh to bring out the machine guns from the tents. That is what he was shouting when the corporal missed. Singh was reaching for the radio. It would only have taken a short time."

"Why didn't they then?"

"Because you cannot hide a machine gun. Without optics you must use tracer rounds at that distance. And so there is a risk for return fire, if there are others. But a single rifle, that is very difficult to see. They could not tell where the shots were coming from."

He threw more stones in the river.

"You could have captured them," I said.

"Perhaps," he said. "But this would be difficult. They were across the river. We could not have reached them quickly. And they were running."

We were quiet for a while.

"You could have captured the last man," I said, coldly. "The one with his hands in the air."

"Yes," Rai said, softly. "I am also thinking this. It is troubling me a great deal. And I don't know what to do."

He swore, and threw the remaining pebbles in his palm hard into the water.

"You know," he said, "when I was looking through the scope, I felt nothing. I thought only of the range, and the lead. I thought only of adjusting for the difference in elevation. That is all."

"You still pulled the trigger."

"Yes," Rai said. "And so now I know." He shook his head. "I must be stronger. They were spies in our country. They would have done the same to us if they could."

I said nothing, and we each stared at the river for a while. My body ached, my hips and back.

"Are they just going to leave them up there?" I said, turning toward him.

"No, we will recover the bodies. They will have no identification, but sometimes we find things. This has never happened here before. Probably they saw the camp with aerial reconnaissance, and that is why they came. But in other areas, active ones, this is common. This has happened many times."

"And you do the same. Send men into their territory."

"Yes," Rai acknowledged. "Sometimes we do this also. But not here."

"And both sides deny it, of course."

"Yes," he said. "These are covert operations always. That is why they were not wearing uniforms. It is so things do not get out of control."

"What am I supposed to say, Sanjit? What do you want from me?"

"I do not know," he said, falling silent again. We both watched the water for a while.

"Colonel Raju was talking to me afterward," he continued. "He was telling me that it is a difficult thing, but that I have done my duty. He was telling me that he has felt the same, but that I must calm myself. But I could not calm myself."

He shook his head.

"He is a good commander. He has also come from nothing. He understands my position. But I should have controlled myself better. I gave Singh another chance at me."

"Captain Singh?" I said, puzzled.

"Yes. Singh is nobody without his father. But that is enough. He can do anything he wants and he will be promoted anyway. He does not need his pay. He does not need anything. But he tries to damage my position anyway because I speak good English also and we are the same rank and in the same regiment. Always he is telling me to wash his car, or to clean his garden, as if he is joking. But he is not joking."

Rai spoke with great bitterness.

"If you had his advantages," I asked, looking at him carefully, "would you have shot those men?"

The question hung between us, and Rai thought for a long time.

"I do not understand what it is like to be given anything," he said, finally. "My father was nothing. A shopkeeper. He died when I was a child. But I think I would have let them use the machine guns. I did not want to kill them. I only wanted to do my duty."

He picked up another handful of gravel, and threw it into the river, and suddenly I could see how much he wanted my forgiveness.

A moment passed.

"How did your father die?"

"He was struck by a lorry in the street," Rai said. I'd expected something else, an illness, perhaps, a poor man's tragedy, untouched by the modern world.

"I'm sorry," I said. "Your mother raised you?"

"Yes," he said. "Our relatives helped us. My uncles and cousins. They made it possible for me to go to school. But they are nothing also. They had little to give us."

"I'm sure your father wasn't nothing. I'm sure he was a good man who did the best he could."

"He was a good man. It did not help him at all. Or us."

"You made a terrible choice," I said finally, because it cost me nothing. "I think it was wrong. But I understand why you did it. When I was your age I might have done the same in your place. That's the truth."

As I spoke, I thought how easy it was to absolve him, and how easy it was to absolve all the others, caught up in their fates, following orders, doing whatever was asked of them, no matter how dark, or hard, or merciless.

"Thank you, Doctor," Rai said, after a while, staring at the current. "Thank you for listening to this. It is difficult."

"So," I said. "Were you what you hoped?"

He laughed, briefly and mirthlessly.

"No, Doctor," he said. "I was not. Not at all."

He stood there for a while longer, as if he did not want to bring the conversation to an end.

"Maybe that's not a bad thing," I said.

"I must see to the others," he replied, finally. "Please, it is important to eat even if you are not hungry. We have much walking tomorrow also. And I am sorry I was angry with you today."

With that, he reached out, and touched my shoulder, and then he turned and walked back toward the stove, and the lantern, where Elise sat alone.

I watched the current a while longer, until it became difficult to make out, and the stars began emerging in the darkness of the sky overhead. It was strange, I thought, listening to the river, how this place had exposed him, just as it had exposed me. It felt like a blank screen upon which my entire life had somehow been projected. All that depth and absence, all that high empty country, and the waiting of the past weeks, giving way to something else entirely, something I never expected to be part of—I could hardly comprehend it. I had expected to lose myself in work, in a foreign land, freed from the burden of the familiar. Instead I felt as if I was gazing into a clear pool, bottomless, searching for signs in the depths, and all I found was the ghost of my own face, and the faces of all the others, in imperfect reflections.

I stood, stiffly, and made my way down to where Elise and Rai sat in strained silence, waiting for dinner. The small candle in the lantern lit up their faces. Ali and his nephew crouched a few feet off, and occasionally a bit of kerosene smoke made its way into the circle. Rai called out to Ali, softly, and then made room for me to sit beside him.

"It is chapati and dahl only tonight," Rai said. "I am sorry."

Ali had always prepared what he imagined was Western food for Elise and me. Cans of corned beef and cans of peeled white potatoes, or rice. Omelets for breakfast, stale moldy bread warmed on the stove. I knew there was a courteous intention there, and so I'd never requested anything else—I just ate what I was given, as did Elise, and Rai. For Rai, I think our monotonous diet was an opportunity to be, however subtly, one of us, as opposed to one of them. Ali and his nephew, however, ate chapati and dahl every day. They'd cooked the chapati—unleavened bread—on flat stones, which they heated on the kerosene stove and had chosen with care. I knew this only because I'd seen them scouring the rocky ground together when we first arrived, and I'd asked Rai what they were doing.

But now, because they were exhausted, they were serving us their own food.

As I sat beside Rai, I heard a slapping noise coming from the direction of the kerosene stove. I turned, peering through the darkness, and I realized that it was Ali, flattening dough against hot stones. After a while I began to smell it—the smell of baking bread. It smelled unexpectedly wonderful, and I watched him, plucking the bread off the hot rock, slapping another ball of dough flat between his dirty hands, then dropping it on the stone again, where it sizzled, hot enough to kill whatever lived on his fingers.

A few moments later, they brought it to us—dahl, and bread. The bread was cooked perfectly, crusty on the outside, soft and latticed in the middle, like a thick tortilla, made from rough white flour, and we dipped it in the stew, full of strange spices, peppers, thick and filling, leaving a pleasant tingle on the lips, which I washed away with cold gulps of iodinated river water. It was easily the best meal I'd had since arriving. It was the kind of food made for cold weather—dense and heavy. The food of the poor, but all the more sustaining for it.

The three of us ate our fill without talking, and the others did the same a few feet away.

"Why don't they come and join us," I said to Rai. "They shouldn't be over there in the dark."

Rai called out to them.

They were surprised—I could sense it in the long pause that followed Rai's invitation. But then they accepted—they could hardly refuse—and came out of the dark. Ali bobbed and smiled, uneasy, and his nephew looked only at his feet, although a few minutes later I caught him sneaking glances at both Elise and me. They settled on their haunches a safe distance from us, but within the circle of light cast by the lantern. We ate in silence—Elise and Rai and me with our spoons, our paper napkins, and Ali and his nephew with their fingers.

Rai reached down to the bottle at his feet, poured the rum into his tea, and took a long swallow.

"Don't leave me out," I said, extending my cup.

Rai passed me the bottle. It was only three-quarters full.

"Do you want some?" I asked Elise.

"Oh," she said, as if she had been somewhere else. But then she extended her mug. "Yes. Please."

The rest of them looked at us, uncertain.

"Do they drink?" I asked. "Can they have some?"

Rai said something in his own tongue.

I turned, and offered the bottle to them. At first, I thought they might refuse, or be offended, but instead Ali leapt to his feet, darted off into the dark, and returned within seconds with two battered cups—one for the soldier, and one for himself. Only the boy went without. I poured several inches into each cup, and we each began to sip at the rum, and finally we were all together, with thousands of empty square miles around us, gathered beside a single lantern. It was a moonless night, and the millions of stars overhead astonished me again, as they always did.

CHAPTER THIRTY-ONE

"Can I stay with you again?" Elise asked, later, as we walked to our tents after dinner.

"Of course."

She hesitated, and began to cry a little.

"I'm sorry," she said again, composing herself. "All I want now is to go home."

She retrieved her sleeping bag, and when we reached my tent I unzipped the door, and held it for her as she ducked inside. I waited for a few moments, giving her time to undress and get in her sleeping bag, and then I followed. I undressed as well, inside my bag, and we lay beside each other in the dark, listening to the river.

"I feel like I am somewhere else," she said. "I do not understand how he could do this."

I found myself thinking of the corpses on the wall, and whether they had been carried down, and how it had been done. I imagined wrists and ankles lashed to poles, pendulous necks and open mouths, blood dripping on the rocks. I imagined them laid side by side on the ground, and photographed, as the soldiers posed smiling above them.

"He knew what he was doing," I said. "He just didn't know what it felt like to do it."

"It does not matter," she said. "They are dead anyway for nothing."

"Yes," I said. "But his reasons were complex."

"Why are you defending him?" she said, accusingly. "He is a murderer, even if they ordered him to do it. I thought he was different, but he is not. All of them are the same. And now there is no camp because of them. No research, nothing."

I realized she was wiping her eyes in the dark beside me.

"And Homa," she continued. "Everything is terrible for her and that is for nothing also."

She was so young, I thought, so certain in her convictions, and so open to them. I envied her full heart, and the depth of her outrage, and wondered why I could not also rise, or rise fully. If I felt raw, raked and open, as I knew I did, it came upon me in secret ways, bubbling out of the deep, and caught me by surprise, and did not fully reveal itself to my conscious mind, like a flicker in the corner of my eye that vanished when I turned to look.

"I'm not defending him," I said. "I'm trying to understand him."

"Do you?"

"Yes," I said. "I think so."

"What did he say to you when he came up here earlier?"

"He was asking for my forgiveness."

"Why would he ask this from you?"

"His father died when he was young. He lives in a brutal and corrupt country. He can barely support his family. He looks up to me because he thinks I'm rich and successful, and he killed those men because he's desperate to distinguish himself. It's not that complicated."

"So you are saying that it is okay what he has done."

"No, I'm not."

"Did you forgive him?"

I thought for a while.

"Forgiveness isn't the right word," I said.

"Then what is the right word?"

"Sadness," I said. "I'm sad for him."

"Maybe you are right, that he is not so bad on his own," she said, a few moments later. "But together they are like monsters. They could do anything."

We stopped talking for a while after that, but neither of us could sleep. She shifted fitfully beside me. Long minutes passed. I listened to her breathing, and my own.

And then, without thinking, I was rolling over on my side to face her, and I was reaching out, and my hand was against her cheek, and then I was stroking her hair.

She took a breath, and then sat up in her sleeping bag. I froze, my face burning in the darkness. I withdrew my hand, and began to murmur my apologies, because there was no mistaking my intentions. For a terrible moment I thought she was going to turn on her headlamp.

But she didn't. Instead, she reached out, and pulled me down with her as she lay back again, and her own breath was quickening, and she was reaching for the zipper on her sleeping bag, drawing it down, and then I kissed her. It stunned me, to kiss her like that, as if I were plunging into a hot bath, and then I felt her arms around me, her hands finding their way beneath my shirt to the flushed bare skin of my back. I began to fumble with her thin fleece sleeping clothes, but she stopped me.

"Wait," she said, pushing me off gently, and I sat back as she asked, my heart pounding.

She undressed, deliberately and carefully, putting her clothes to the side. I listened to her breathing, and my own, and in the darkness of the tent I could just make out the white form of her body on the sleeping bag. I pulled off my shirt, and then she reached out and pulled me down against her, her mouth rising up to mine, the warmth of her body against me, and then it was the bath again, the pool, the breathing, the curves of her hips and her openness, my hands on her body, and then the lift of her pelvis and the deep, breathtaking shock, her upturned face beneath me, the heat of her breath in my ear, my hands tight on her hips, the rocking and the sound of it, and the gasps we both made.

It was over in only a few moments, but with her sleeping bag below us and mine above, I felt as though the world had changed entirely around me once again. It was dizzying, as we lay in that strange familiarity that men and women have at such times, both foreign and together.

We lay there, and I was careful not to overwhelm her with tenderness, or with speech. My hand rested on her belly, and during those minutes I felt as though I'd been emptied entirely, that nothing else was there—not the soldiers, not the corpses on the mountainside, none of it. It was just her body beside me, and my hand, and her warmth beneath it. She was wide awake, and I could see her blinking in the near darkness.

"I am thinking about my life," she said, after a long while. "About what I want to do. About having children. Many things. I can't stop. I'm just lying here and doing this."

"Do you want to have children?"

"Of course. When I have finished my degree."

She paused, hesitating, and I could feel it all begin to recede.

"I have a partner," she said, finally.

"You're talking about Scott Coles, aren't you?"

There was a long pause.

"Yes," she said. "But how did you know?"

"It was an educated guess."

"He's trying very hard to be good," she said. "He wants to be good. But then he sleeps with other girls. I do not know, but I think so. And he says he will come here to help us, but he does not come. Sometimes I think he likes giving his speeches more than he likes working here."

"He told me just the opposite," I said.

"Yes," she said. "He always says this. He does raise the money. He is very honest with the money. But he likes the audience also."

"How long have you known him?"

"I met him a few years ago," she said. "Before the earthquake. We were at a conference together. It was in Berlin."

"And you've been in a relationship since then?"

"Yes," she said. "But I do not see him so often. Always he is traveling, raising money. Always this is so important."

"It's hard to raise money for anything," I said.

"Yes," she said. "He started the camps. He provides money for them. He wants to do good. It's true."

"What did he do before all of this? He said he was a climber."

"He was a climber. He owned a climbing shop in California."

She raised herself on her elbow, and turned toward me in the dark.

"He is not young anymore," she said. "And his family, they are more successful than him. His brothers and his father. So he is angry with them. Very angry, I think."

"Was he married? Does he have children?"

"He was married. He has a daughter and a son also. I have never met them. They are young. He does not see them often either. They live with their mother."

"He told me he almost climbed an eight-thousand-meter peak," I said. "He told me he decided to do relief work when he

saw some climbers killed in front of him. He said that he turned
around when the summit was in his reach."

She sighed.

"Yes," she said, lying down again. "He tells this story. But I
am not sure about it."

"What do you mean?"

She thought for a moment before answering.

"He did try to climb an eight-thousand-meter peak. It was
a big mountain, very dangerous. And there were climbers killed
up high in an avalanche. But I think it was someone else who
saw them and turned back, not him. And he wants very much to
have this memory. So he says it is his."

"Why do you think that?"

"He is a good climber lower down," she said. "He is strong.
But he has problems with altitude. He gets sick. Some people are
this way. Some people who are strong lower down are weak up
high."

"Have you climbed with him?"

"Yes," she said. "We climbed Mont Blanc together. Not so
high. Only five thousand meters. But he had some trouble anyway."

"Altitude sickness is unpredictable," I said. "That doesn't
necessarily mean anything."

"I know," she said, anxiously. "But last year I met someone
who knows Scott also. A climber. It is a small community. I
asked him about Scott and the expedition. He said he heard
how in the beginning Scott is always saying how strong he was,
how fast. How he will be a famous climber. But when they got
to the mountain he could do nothing. He only reached camp
two and then he had to go down again. He tried this several
times, but each time it was the same. The others were laughing
at him, so he went home before they finished. That is what he

told me. He was not with them, but still I think this is what happened."

"Did you ask him about it?"

She shook her head.

"No," she said. "You must not tell him if you see him again. I feel bad for Scott about this."

I took a deep breath, and said what I knew I shouldn't.

"Elise," I said, "what are you doing with him? Can't you see that he's not what he seems?"

"I think you are a little bit unfair," she said, sadly. "And I am not so serious about him anymore. But he wants to be better. He wants to believe what he says. It is not all for show."

I was silent.

"I think I have said too much," she said, uneasily, after a while. "I like him, you know? I cannot help this."

She turned then, and leaned forward, and kissed my cheek, and then she sat up, and put her sleeping clothes back on.

"I am sorry," she said. "I'm a little bit cold."

CHAPTER THIRTY-TWO

The next morning we woke early, just after sunrise, and dressed, and left the tent. We said little. But from the first she didn't meet my eye, or kiss me again. Instead, she smiled and looked away. I saw it immediately, without a word being spoken.

We drank our tea, and ate some cold chapati, and then we packed up and started walking down the path by the river in the cold of the morning, as the valley narrowed around us, and the walls around us became closer and steeper.

As the light began to flood into the canyon I felt my attention turn to the days ahead for the first time. We were safe, and were going home, and the events of the past few days had receded just enough to let me begin to think of other things. I thought about Elise, and her silence, and what it meant. I felt entirely bewildered. The landscape around us felt both endlessly the same and infused with tiny details—a scarlet pinpoint flower among cactus spines, or the hump of glistening river as it rose unbroken over a deep rock. I imagined there were fish, as in the lake—silver streaks, cold and effortless.

An hour passed, and she began to whistle tunelessly, as if unaware of what she was doing. For most of the morning we were all like that; aware of one another, but also lost in our own thoughts.

The mind wanders at such times—it goes back and forth, as if released, here and there, present and past. Sometimes there was the outside world, the white stroke of a distant waterfall, or the sudden angular presence of a tiny tree on the rock wall two hundred feet above us, where somehow a blown seed had stuck, and other times there was nothing but the interior, whatever it may be—the unconscious mind, spilling out memories like so many colored marbles on the floor. In and out I went, thinking about the path ahead, or trees on hillsides, and then my dog at home, and what we'd manage for lunch, and the invading tribes of prehistory, with their Asian off-colored eyes, whose genes had somehow also been blown up these gorges and found purchase. It was dizzying, in a way, and impossible to keep track of, and I imagined a graph of my own thoughts, each thought a single point, scattered like seed corn on a table, some revisited again and again, glowing, and others only once. Elise whistled on, just ahead, and Rai, for his part, simply continued, deliberate and steady. The others felt like shadows behind me.

It went like that—flights of memory, then back in the moment. Over and over again I found myself looking at her, then at the ground passing beneath my feet. The ridges changed as slowly as an hour hand above us.

Later that morning, at a bend, we came to a footbridge across the river. The bridge was made from logs—four of them, irregular, rough, lashed together with rope, the whole of it resting on loose stone pilings. From a distance, it looked dark and unnatural. There was no railing of any kind, and the logs themselves were slick from the spray of the river, which boiled under them. The path itself was so little used that often there was no trace of it along the riverbank—it eased in and out of existence. But now this, a crude and miraculous bridge, like an artifact.

The logs were large ones, weathered and cracked, yet there

were no such trees anywhere nearby. Someone must have carried them there. The bridge was entirely unexpected, and reminded me somehow of Elise's solar shower, which she had lashed to the outside of her pack.

"Who put it here?" I asked Rai.

"The local people do this," he said, "where the river is too deep and you have to cross."

"How old is it, do you think? It looks like it's been here for a long time."

"I don't know," he replied. The bridge was not a compelling object for him, but it fascinated me. The logs might have been there for fifty years, or more—in the dry air, despite the spray from the river, the wood probably would last forever. No doubt the ropes lashing it all together needed to be replaced every so often, and the pilings repaired from time to time, but whoever did this work was nowhere to be seen.

"Is there another village around here?"

Rai shrugged in his familiar way.

"I don't know," he repeated.

It was a bad bridge, I thought—treacherous, the logs unimproved in any way, without a railing, over a section of river that looked both dangerous and deep.

We crossed it one by one, carefully. First Rai, then Elise and me, then Ali and his nephew, and finally the soldier. The logs were slick, and shook beneath our weight, and the rapids flashed in the gaps between them. I eased myself out, placing my boots carefully, knowing all the while that I wasn't going to fall off, that I'd make it fine, as the others had done.

The soldier, however, did slip midway out, and the weight of his load became evident, pulling him to one side for an instant, spinning his arms for an anxious moment. But he recovered well, and he joined the rest of us on the far bank, laughing as he stepped off the end of the logs onto the sheets of gravel again.

From the other side of the river, I could see why the bridge had been necessary—the bank disappeared just past the bend, and the river ran close along the valley wall, which was steep enough to make walking impossible. But where we stood, the valley widened, and there were more cactus and scrub pines, some of which came to our shoulders. The ground, in places, was sandy, and the ridges, on that side of the river, were several hundred meters away. For a while we were walking on a kind of plain. In a few minutes, the bridge was out of sight, and the path once more became difficult to follow.

"There are flies," Elise said, and as she spoke I was bitten also.

The flies themselves were unfamiliar to me—gray rather than black, longer and thinner than horseflies, they stung fiercely. Suddenly they were everywhere. We were getting lower, I realized—the vegetation was increasing around us, inching farther away from the river's edge, and now this. They came for us by the dozen. Several times, when I slapped them before they'd bitten, there was a scarlet smear of blood. Undoubtedly it was the blood of animals—mountain sheep, foxes, and birds— but I thought of the army also, passing that way only a few days before, and wondered if some of it was human.

We walked fast, slapping at them, waving our hands around our faces, but then, as the valley wall closed with the river again, as the pines thinned and disappeared, the wind picked up, and the flies vanished as quickly as they had come. It was a blessed relief. One had bitten me on the tip of my little finger, and it itched and throbbed until I dipped it into the icy river.

We slowed down again. The sun was directly overhead, and already, though perhaps we'd descended only a few thousand feet, it was noticeably warmer than it had been. Lower, I knew, it would become hot, but then it was simply pleasant, in the cool air, with the river clenching and unclenching beside us— strips of white water, followed by long sheets of calm. The valley had narrowed again, and was as it had been. Rai and the others moved ahead of us down the trail.

"You have these experiences," Elise said suddenly, turning to me. "And sometimes they are very strong ones. And then they are over, but you cannot say what they mean. And then you have other ones. And you cannot say what they mean. You just go on. Maybe you are happy, maybe you are scared, maybe you are sad. But you want to say, I learn this, or I learn that, or I understand better. But maybe you don't understand better, and it is not so easy to say what you learn and what you don't learn. Do you know?"

"Yes," I said. "I do."

We continued in silence for a while.

"I'm so glad I met you, you know," I said, quietly. "You're a wonderful young woman. You've given me hope. Whatever happens I want you to know that."

"Thank you," she said, awkwardly, beginning to blush in the sun. A moment passed, and then finally she turned to me.

"It is okay," she said. "What happened. It was nice. But no more. I need to tell you this."

"Why?"

"For me it is not the same," she said, simply. "I like you. But not so much in that way. And there is Scott, also. I am feeling a little bit guilty. It is too confusing. So I'm sorry."

I looked at her, and though my face flushed, I had been expecting her words all morning.

"It's all right, Elise," I said, after a moment, with difficulty. "But I want you to know it meant a lot to me. I hope I didn't take advantage of you, and please forgive me if I did."

She stepped up close, and put her hand on my arm.

"I did not do it because I felt sorry for you," she said, looking at me intently. "I did it because I wanted to also. And I liked it also. It felt very nice."

"Thank you," I replied, before turning away. I knew I was on the edge of tears, and I wanted very much to hide this fact from her. Her kindness, her concern for my dignity—I felt entirely naked before her, and a wave of longing passed through me. Not only for her, but for my own past as well, for Rachel, and the choices I'd made, and those early years, when I was handsome and strong and full of my own promise, when we loved one another, and our son was coming, when the future was bright, and the path was straight.

CHAPTER THIRTY-THREE

The river was growing larger as we descended, joined by thin streams tumbling off the walls, and we passed the mouths of several branching gorges that released little rivers of their own into the channel. Several times Rai consulted his map to be sure we were on the correct path.

I asked him how many days were left.

"We are not going fast," he said. "So perhaps four. But there is no hurry."

Both Ali and his nephew had adjusted to their loads, or so it seemed, and walked without much difficulty, talking to one another from time to time. Elise and I mostly stayed together, as we'd done since we started, and Rai kept a few paces ahead. For the most part we didn't speak, but I was always aware of her anyway, and from time to time, when I'd regained myself enough to struggle for normalcy again, I'd point something out—another bush high on the cliffs above us, a strip of ice, a collection of cactus flowers. She'd look with interest, intent, and smile at me, her eyes very blue against her burned cheeks, her hair growing blonder in the sun.

"This is very nice now," she said, at lunch, when the sun was out again for a while and the wind had died down. "I like these clouds."

It was, and I tried my best to focus also on the moment, to let time pass as slowly as I could. I felt as if I was paying very careful attention to something I knew I would think back on for years. By mid-afternoon, the valley had narrowed enough for the sound of the river to thunder back and forth in places between the walls, and the path began to rise up the rocky hillside above it. It became harder going, the trail undulating up and down, and the load carriers began to fall behind. Several times Rai stopped, tapping his foot, waiting for them to catch up, at which point he would set off again without giving them time to rest.

Sometimes the path rose quite a good way above the river—perhaps thirty or forty feet, and in places the hillside was steep enough that I could look almost directly down at the water. For the first time, however, the path had obviously been improved; it was wider, and better marked.

At one point, as we waited for Ali and his nephew again, Rai turned to me.

"I am sorry," he said. "I have made a small mistake."

"About what?" I asked, looking down the narrow gorge in the distance. It was a spectacular thing, the river churning in the canyon, spray in the air.

"We should have stopped earlier," he said. "I was not sure where we were. But now it will be several more hours before we can camp. It will be a long day."

I was feeling fine, and took a sip of water more from reflex than from thirst.

"It's all right," I said. "It's early enough."

"Are you feeling okay?" Rai asked Elise, who had joined us, breathing lightly.

"Of course," she said, giving him a look, peeling a strip of sunburned skin off her wrist and inspecting it. She let the skin fall, and it spun down to the ground like a tiny gray leaf.

Ali and the others appeared. They looked tired, and so Rai let them sit and rest for a while before continuing.

Rai had underestimated his mistake, however, because several hours later we were still walking and there was no end in sight. The trail, if anything, rose up and down even more steeply. My shoulders ached, and the sun was only just visible over the high walls of what had become a steep canyon. But there was no turning back at that point. Rai periodically apologized.

"I'm sorry," he said again.

"Don't worry," I replied. "If we have to, we'll just sleep along the trail."

But I could see that his error upset him. At times, we were high above the river, and at other times we were nearly beside it, walking in and out of icy mist. Nonetheless, the trail remained clear, and there was little sense of risk. Ali and his nephew were both wearing out, though. I could see it clearly in their faces, and the way they released themselves from their duffel bags when we rested. Even the soldier looked weary, heaving his enormous pack up and down and up again.

Then the sun retreated below the walls, and it quickly got colder, and the whole canyon retreated into twilight. By then Rai was clearly looking for any area that might serve as a resting place for the night. But it was all loose rock, a hillside steep enough to use one's hands, and a narrow corkscrew of a path along it. Soon it would be fully dark, and we would have to resign ourselves to sleeplessness, sitting on the cold trail with our legs off the edge, with nowhere comfortable to lie. My body ached, and Elise looked drawn as well, though full of the endurance of youth, and no doubt she could have continued all night if necessary.

It was becoming rapidly unpleasant. I could only imagine what Ali and his nephew must have felt—several times Rai called out to them, pausing for their reply before continuing on.

"Maybe we should just stop," I said. "It doesn't look like it's getting any better."

"When it is dark," Rai replied, "we will stop. It is only a few minutes more."

So we continued, in growing darkness. The path was too narrow to walk together. Rai was ahead of me, Elise forty of fifty feet behind, followed by the soldier. Ali and his nephew were last in line.

At one point, the path rounded a large boulder protruding from the hillside. The boulder was chest high, and extended a few feet out over the trail. I stepped around it easily, looking down at the river as I did so—it was a few dozen feet below, but the incline was not any steeper than it had been for hours, and I passed by it without a thought.

A few moments later I heard a cry, followed by a rattling of stones. I heard it clearly, and turned around to look back, but saw nothing.

Then someone began to shriek in the darkness behind me, and Rai came sprinting back toward me, his flashlight playing across the rocks as he ran. Someone had fallen in the river. For a heart-stopping moment I thought it was Elise.

After a few dozen seconds—it could not have been more—Elise appeared behind me, and I realized, from his nephew's screams, that it was Ali who had fallen. I felt a terrible kind of relief. The boy sat wailing and striking his head with both hands. The soldier, to my surprise, crouched sympathetically beside him, rubbing his shoulder. Elise stood a few feet away, clutching her arms tight, and I was shaking as well.

"Stay here," Rai said, quickly, turning away.

"I'll come with you," I said, but he shook his head.

"No. Stay here. I will look for him." And with that, he was gone.

There was nothing to do but wait. A few minutes later it grew so dark in the canyon, shielded from the stars, that I could barely see my hand before me. The dark pinned us to the ground.

It was the boulder—suddenly I knew it. The boulder must have caught his pack, and knocked him off balance. He was tired, the pack was heavy, and he'd lost his footing, fallen perhaps to a knee, the heavy pack rising up his shoulders, and then it had simply twisted him over the edge, down the slope, and into the water. I'm not sure, of course—no one saw the exact moment when he slipped. He had passed right under me, but I'd missed him. I must have been looking back along the path. Had I looked down, I would have seen him in the foam and spray, tumbling, all his chances gone. But I had not looked down, and he had passed like a ghost below me. He was tired, the light was bad. It happened quickly. And so on.

My chest felt thick and heavy. My fingers and lips tingled. I was breathing hard. I noticed all these things, even as I realized that there was no hope for Ali, that he had gone into the freezing torrent with at least fifty pounds strapped to his back. He would have had only an instant to comprehend what was happening before the first few breaths of foam, and the blows of the rocks, and the weight on his back, dragged him under. I'm sure he couldn't swim, though that hardly mattered. Probably he did not even feel the cold—only the shock of it, like the jaws of an animal, or a knife through a fingertip.

CHAPTER
THIRTY-FOUR

Rai, to his credit, took a very long time. It was several more hours before I saw the bead of his flashlight down the canyon. It came and went, winking on the trail, growing nearer all the while, splashing along the rocks, and finally he was back among us, his face drawn and strained.

"I could not find him," he said. He looked pale and exhausted.

"But maybe he is alive," Elise said. "Maybe he is on the bank. It is possible. We should not give up."

"He's not alive," I said, more bluntly than I intended. "But if he is, we'll find him in the morning. There's nothing more we can do tonight."

Periodically, Ali's nephew would wail and beat his fists against his head. He'd stop for a while, then begin again. At first, my heart went out to him entirely—his open grief, unrestrained, seemed purifying and honest. But as the hours passed, and the boy continued, I grew profoundly tired of it. I wanted him to be quiet, to stop reminding us, to let all of us settle back against the rocks in our sleeping bags, and get what rest we could. But he wouldn't let us. He sobbed on and off all night, moaning, and I nearly said something. I didn't, of course. Instead I crouched, and bore it, as we all did.

At Rachel's funeral, I had kept myself together, standing beside Eric, holding his hand, both in our suits. He had cried, but almost silently, and I had taken my own tears back to the house. All this wailing and gnashing of teeth—as the night passed, my view of it began to change, and I began to suspect that it was perhaps, in its own way, as dishonest as the stoicism I'd shown. Surely there was an element of performance there. If so, Ali's nephew did it well, and moaned all night.

We dug our sleeping bags out of our packs, and crawled into them fully dressed, but we were hungry, worn out from the walk, and the cold seeped out of the rocks and dirt of the path directly into us. We drank the last of our water quickly. It was impossible to get comfortable. My mouth was dry enough to burn. Elise leaned against me, though, and we talked in low tones from time to time. I put my arm around her once, for a little while, until my arm grew cold in the open air and I pulled it back into my sleeping bag. Even that gave me no solace. The hours passed with extraordinary slowness. I knew that I was not directly responsible. It was the dark, and physical exhaustion, and the boulder, the slope just steep enough—it had lined up so perfectly against him. Had he not been carrying a load, I couldn't see how it would have happened. Had he not been so tired, it wouldn't have happened. Had Rai simply known where he was, and stopped us earlier, it wouldn't have happened. And so on. But there was something else as well, and as I sat there on the trail I could not shake it. It seemed as if those dead men on the wall, the soldiers Rai had killed, had somehow struck back at us. I knew it was nonsense, that it was only a trick of my own mind, searching for patterns again, but it was there all the same. I had thought we were safe, I thought we were nearly there, and, as in so many things, I was wrong.

Rai was mostly quiet beside us, but several times I heard him cursing under his breath. We just sat and shivered, waiting for first light, listening to the river.

At first the lightening in the eastern sky was so faint I thought I was deceiving myself. We were too deep in the canyon, the walls too narrow and high above us, for any kind of sunrise. Instead, it was a gradual return to twilight, without warmth. We began to see one another—dust on our faces, and our tangled, matted hair, as we stood up shivering in our damp clothes.

Despite the cold I was as thirsty as I've ever been, but as the light revealed the trail and the slope down to the thundering river, I realized that even in daylight there was no safe way of getting close enough to drink.

Rai stood, stretching, stamping his feet, his face dark and angry.

"He was carrying the stove," he said. That was all. He felt something for Ali, that was clear, but in equal measure he was angry at himself, and the generalized misfortune that had fallen on us, full of the knowledge that he had not done well. Ali, in a sense, had been under his command, one of his soldiers, and he had not been equal to the task. So he was curt, quick in his movements, roughly stuffing his sleeping bag into his pack after lacing up his boots with quick, hard jerks, like tearing paper to pieces.

"We must start walking," he said, then switched to his own language and addressed the boy, who alone among us had made no move to rise.

The boy did not reply, but the soldier, again with unexpected tenderness, helped him with the blanket, and his pack, urging him, as one might a child, and after a while he stood up. I looked at Elise—her hair pressed against her forehead, her dirty face—but she did not meet my eye, expressionless, as if she'd exhausted whatever sentiments had washed over us all during the long night. I only wanted to get on with it, to get out of the narrows into the sun again.

We set off, shivering. But Rai, just ahead, was keeping a careful eye on the river, and so our pace was slow—he was, I realized, looking for Ali's body. The river, boiling and hissing below us, seemed increasingly monstrous. But we saw nothing anyway, and from the speed of the current, I knew that he probably had been carried for miles, and that we might never find him at all.

After a while, the walking loosened us, but it only made our thirst worse. My mouth felt full of nettles, my tongue tingled and throbbed, and I could feel the cold, dry air passing through my lips with each breath. The trail coiled up and down, and the canyon, if anything, grew narrower. Finally, after an hour or so, Rai stopped again, fumbling with his map, unfolding it on a knee and studying it.

"We should be almost out," he said, touching a finger to a point on the map. "Only one or two kilometers more, I think."

Elise joined us also, and offered a weary smile.

"Are you doing all right?" I asked.

She shrugged, her lips cracked and covered with gray paste.

I was as dry as I've ever been, yet the river below us seemed somehow detached from thirst, no different than the gray granite walls, or the gravel beneath our feet. It was a torrent, a crash of white—it almost didn't look like water at all.

So we continued on, one endless foot in front of the other, but Rai, finally, was correct. Less than an hour later, as we rounded a bend, the canyon abruptly opened once again into a valley, and the river slowed down and spread out into a gray sheet. And then, as we descended down the last steep and rocky slope, we crossed into the sunlight again. It felt blessedly warm as it fell on us. The banks were wide, and the river was nearly quiet, though the sound of whitewater in the canyon behind us was loud in the air. The river ran straight off into the distance as far as I could see. Though we were much lower, the hillsides were as dry and as featureless as before.

There was no sign of Ali. By then, he would have passed slowly, bobbing, rolling, bloody from the rocks above, staining the water around him like a bag of tea. By then, it was clear he wasn't alive, that he had not found himself gasping and coughing on the bank, delivered by a providential hand. I'd held out that dim hope despite myself. But then I stopped thinking about Ali—all I wanted was a drink of water. When we were close enough, all of us dropped our packs and trotted to the river's edge.

In the past, I'd always carefully treated my water before drinking. I'd drop in a little black pellet of iodine, and wait as it slowly dissolved in red and orange strings. I'd shake the bottle carefully, and wait some more—the instructions said an hour, if possible. But then I just plunged my bottle into the water, and drank again and again. The water was cold, and settled in my stomach like a stone. My teeth sang. But I drank, as did all of us—the boy and the soldier sucked it greedily out of their cupped hands. It was delicious, it was an indescribable relief, and it was scalding and painful at the same time. I squatted at the water's edge, my knees aching, and after I could drink no more I cupped my hands as well and washed my face as best I could. I could feel the grease in my hair, and my rough unshaven cheeks across my dirty hands, which were nearly numb from the water. I did it several times, but the water was too cold, and I hardly felt cleaner when I retreated to where our packs lay on the dusty ground and sat down against them in the sun.

I'd drunk too much, too quickly, and a sudden wave of chills and nausea passed through me. For an instant I thought I was going to vomit on the ground, but it eased after a few moments. I ran my wet fingers through my hair to untangle it, but after a while gave up, and simply sat there, shaking violently, looking absently at the rocks at my feet.

"We will stop here," Rai said. "We will rest today."

As he spoke, and my nausea settled, and as I leaned back against my pack on the gravel, trying to warm up, I realized how tired I was. I think the others felt the same; in any case, we simply murmured our agreement, and I managed to rouse myself enough to drag my sleeping pad from my pack, and unroll it on the ground, and lie down, with my jacket zipped tight and my sleeping bag over me and my hat pulled down on my face. I didn't want to talk to anyone just then. I was shivering, and I wanted only to close my eyes and get warm as quickly as possible. Only Rai was up and working, strong enough to be restless, compulsively going through the packs, sorting out our provisions—the rest of us simply lay down as soon as we could. We didn't speak. All I thought about, as I slowly warmed up again, with my eyes closed beneath my hat, was the sun.

CHAPTER
THIRTY-FIVE

Early that afternoon, after we'd dozed fitfully for a few hours, the prospect of staying there for the night became intolerable. I wanted to get down, I wanted to get out of there, and I wasn't alone. Without even discussing it, we started packing up. Rai had emptied the packs onto the ground, and hesitated over the heavy jugs of kerosene. Ali, after all, had the stove.

"We might use it," I said to Rai. He nodded, and stuffed the jugs back into the duffel.

The boy, for his part, had finally gone silent. He did not meet our eyes, but he'd wolfed down the meat, and drank, and washed himself like the rest. We busied ourselves with details, checking the ground, tying our drawstrings tight, filling our water bottles again, and blowing on our cold hands afterward.

And a few hours later, at the mouth of another canyon, in the shallows spreading out from the main channel, we found him. He lay half submerged, facedown on a gravel bar a few yards out from the bank. He was still strapped to the duffel. His head was underwater, as were his arms and legs—only his back, and part of the green duffel, could be seen. The smooth gray rocks on the bar were the size of eggs and melons.

Beyond him, the channel deepened and showed its speed, a

widow's peak of water running down the center, just starting to break.

Elise saw him first, and called out, pointing. Rai, though first in line, had missed him, and so had I, though he was out in the open, and fully visible. We all stopped when we realized what she was pointing at, then took off our packs and lowered them to the ground.

Rai shook his head, once, and suddenly he seemed very young to me, unprepared for what lay before us. General Said, I was sure, would not have batted an eye, but Rai was visibly shaken.

Ali would have to be pulled off the bar and through the shallows to the bank. Rai said a few words to the soldier. Both sat down and unlaced their boots, then rolled up their pants, their feet curiously pale and alike. The boy sat on the ground, rocking back and forth as he watched.

They pranced out awkwardly, slow and unsteady in the current, wincing at the cold and waving their arms for balance. The water came to their knees, rippling around their legs, and it might have been amusing had Ali not been lying dead a few feet away. They reached the bar, and stepped up on it beside him. The water rose above their ankles. It was clearly painful—each lifted one foot, then the other, up into the air, rapidly, as if standing on hot sand.

But still they hesitated for a moment before touching him. Finally, they grabbed the body by the shoulders, and tried to heave him off. But he was heavy, soaked through, pinned against the gravel bar by the current, and they only succeeded in lifting his back and part of his head—I caught a glimpse of black hair—above the surface. For a few moments they struggled with him, but then Rai straightened and said something to the soldier, though his voice was drowned out by the flowing water.

They crouched down, fumbling with the duffel bag and the straps, until the soldier pulled it free and lifted it, with a dripping curtain of water, wholly out of the river. Rai helped him, holding it to his chest, soaking himself, and the man turned and forced his arms through the straps. Then they both turned, and rushed back across the channel as quickly as they could. The pain was clear on their faces, and when they reached the bank, and the duffel bag fell on the ground with a wet, heavy cough, both of their feet were bloody and nearly white. They sat down in silence, and began rubbing them, first with their bare hands, then with a towel that Elise had quickly retrieved from her pack and handed them, rocking back and forth as their feet warmed.

Without the pack to weigh him down, Ali rode a little higher in the water—I could see his arms, waving and loose, and every so often his head would nod up out of the current for an instant before disappearing again.

Rai and the soldier exchanged a few words, and then, after a few minutes, they put their boots back on. Rai's chest was dark and wet from the duffel bag, and his face was thunderous.

"I never should have brought him," he said. "I knew this. I should not have listened to her."

"Listened to whom?" I replied, puzzled.

He blew on his hands, then glanced at me.

"My wife," he said, reluctantly, as if regretting his words.

"Your wife? How did she know Ali?"

"He was her cousin," Rai said, finally.

I didn't expect that at all. I never would have guessed that Ali was related by marriage to Rai. It completely surprised me.

"I'm sorry," I managed, after a moment.

He didn't answer, only nodded to the soldier, and then they both waded off again into the water with their boots on.

They struggled and cursed. Ali was a wet mattress, loose and slippery, and finally they simply grabbed fistfuls of cloth and dragged him without ceremony by the back through the shallows between them, stumbling on the uneven bottom. His head hung down, and left a wake. His legs flowed behind him. He seemed far heavier than he had been in life.

They paused at the edge of the bank, and then, grunting with effort, heaved his torso up and out of the water and onto the rocks. Then they stepped up beside him, reached down, and hauled him entirely onto the bank. Specks of gravel clung to his clothes, to his legs and back, to the matted, black mass of his hair—the river hadn't washed him clean. Instead, it had filled him with silt.

They left him there for a moment, catching their breath, but finally Rai bent down, and rolled him over by the shoulders as delicately as he could. His head followed, loosely, and for the first time I saw his face.

There he was—Ali, eyes cloudy, half open, expressionless. His slack jaw, his naked teeth, yellow and brown, above his patchy black beard, shot through with gray—a few scrapes, a bruise here or there, but otherwise his face was undamaged. I could read nothing there. No regret, no fear. It's always like that.

I was standing above him. But then I knelt down, and looked more carefully. The whites of his eyes were red, his pupils dark and empty. The gravel had left a fine tracery, like a watermark, on his cheek. His soaked clothes clung to the exact outline of his body—his thighs, the point of his hips.

I reached out and touched his neck, feeling for a pulse. It was more a reflex than anything, a kind of automatic act, the sort of thing one does at such moments.

His neck was very cold and firm, like a bag of flour left in a freezer. My finger left a dimple in the dead muscle, and I wiped my hand on my leg after I touched him. Then I stood.

Elise watched, her hand clenched into a fist, which she held gently to her mouth. None of us said anything at first.

Then the boy started up. It was as if he'd been waiting, gathering himself for the effort. He ran to the body, and fell on his knees beside it, and began wailing. He bent to kiss his uncle's face, and stroked his beard. He tugged at the sodden clothes, and shouted up into the air while everyone else was quiet.

I couldn't watch it. I turned my back, and walked away alongside the river. There was no dignity there. He was only a boy, of course. But Ali was not his father, nor his brother; he was only an uncle, and I suspected that they didn't even live together in the city. I knew my thoughts were far too hard. The shock it gave us, the calamity that had now so visibly descended on him, on his wife and his nameless numbers of children—I didn't care about any of it right then. But if I'd come for a reduction to the essentials, I thought, surely I had found it.

Rai called out to me, and I turned and let him approach. He paused before me, then lit a cigarette, cupping it in his hands, inhaling deeply, before he said anything. For a long moment he looked entirely lost, bereft and shaken.

"I am not sure what to do," he said, and I realized that he was asking me for advice.

"What do you mean?"

"I would like to carry him down," he said. "So that his family can have him. This is important to us."

"Do you think it's possible?"

He looked out over the river.

"I don't know," he said.

I thought about it. We had days of walking left. Even in the cold, the body would start to decay. I imagined the soldier, and Rai, and perhaps even myself and the boy, our packs discarded, struggling with him across the rough trail, as he began to stink and blacken and drip. It was not something I could face.

"We would have to leave a lot behind," I said.

He nodded. I wondered what Rai would have done had he not been related, however distantly, to the figure on the bank, and how much this fact revealed about him—his past, his poverty and struggle, his desire to be something other than what he was, in a world where the lines of class were never crossed. And there he was, in his army sweater, with that pistol on his hip, trying to cross them anyway.

"I think we should bury him here."

"It will be difficult to bury him," Rai said. "We have nothing to dig a grave. It is all stones."

"Then we'll have to cover him with rocks. We can put him at the base of the cliff."

Rai was uneasy, shifting from foot to foot, not meeting my eye.

"It is not a proper burial," he said. "There will be animals."

"I don't know what else we can do. We could cremate him, I suppose. We could use the kerosene."

Rai shook his head.

"That is forbidden," he said. "We do not do this."

"Why is this so important to you?" I asked him, carefully. "Is it because he was your wife's cousin? Or because you're blaming yourself?"

Rai ran his hand through his hair.

"He was clumsy," he said. "He was not paying attention. He is a foolish man. He was not carrying so much. It is God who decides this. But I should have known this anyway. I should have been more careful with him. So I am blaming myself, Doctor. I am blaming myself for everything. I told my wife I would help him and I did not."

He looked out at the river, then shook his head, and threw his cigarette down on the ground.

"We can't carry him down," I said. "We don't even have a stretcher. His body will decompose. So we either bury him or cremate him. Wouldn't your family understand that?"

"This is a very bad thing for them," he replied. "He supports them. His wife, his children. Now there is nothing for them."

"What else can we do?"

He shook his head.

"There is something," he said, quickly, as if to get through it. "We can call a helicopter."

It hadn't occurred to me. He had his satellite phone.

"Yes," I said. "Of course."

"There is a problem, however," he continued, in the same tone. "He was not a soldier. He is only a cook."

"So," I said, understanding at last. "They will not come unless we pay. Is that right?"

"Yes," Rai said, lighting another cigarette. "We cannot call the army. But we can call a civilian one."

"Then call them," I said. "I'll pay for it."

"It will cost two thousand pounds," he said.

"I don't care," I said.

"Thank you," Rai said, and for an instant he looked as if he might weep.

CHAPTER THIRTY-SIX

I imagined a long wait—a day, or even more. I imagined Ali, wrapped up and guarded against the animals at night. I imagined we were farther away.

Rai looked carefully at the map, and made the call from high on the hillside. There was no signal in the narrow valley, and so he climbed. Elise and I watched him, sitting a safe distance from Ali on our packs.

The soldier, meanwhile, went through Ali's duffel. We watched as he spread the contents out on the ground a few feet away. Tins of food. Pots, silverware. A blanket, and finally a few belongings—a black plastic comb, a cheap digital watch. A few pairs of blackened, threadbare socks. A blue polyester hat, a hand mirror. All of it soaking and dripping.

At the bottom of the pack, folded carefully, wrapped in a plastic bag, was my fleece shirt. The soldier laid it on the gravel. He looked up at me, questioning. I shook my head, and pointed to him.

"You can have it," I said.

He understood me well enough, and smiled, bowing his head at me. He lifted the shirt by the shoulders, and shook it, as one would a wet towel, held it at arm's length, and looked at it with a critical, appraising eye. He rolled the fabric between his fingers, then stood, and carefully draped the shirt across a nearby boulder, where it could dry in the sun.

Ali's nephew, if he noticed any of this, gave no sign. He sat by himself, staring dumbly off at the river, no doubt worn out by his display. A few minutes earlier Elise had tried to approach him, but he had not responded. He had simply shaken his head, and stared at the ground, and after a while she'd given up. Only the soldier, it seemed, had been able to offer him some measure of comfort, and now he was fingering my shirt and smiling with pleasure.

I didn't really want to think about my shirt, wrapped like a precious thing, in the bottom of Ali's pack. I didn't want to think about how little he had, or how pathetic and small it all seemed. He lay covered in a blanket now, his legs protruding from beneath it. I watched him for a while, then looked up again at Rai, a tiny figure high on the side of the ridge. He was descending toward us. As the minutes passed, we sat there, not speaking, watching his approach.

"They will be here in two hours," he said, when he reached us. "So we must get ready."

"Two hours?" I asked, incredulous. "I thought we'd have to wait until tomorrow."

"What time is it?" Elise asked.

"It is three p.m.," he said. "We will be in the city by seven. Maybe eight. But it will be light enough to fly."

It was very hard to believe, sitting there in the empty canyon, with no sign of anyone anywhere, with only the river, the rocks and distances, the sky above us, after all this walking and struggling. I could hardly conceive of it.

We waited, not saying much. Rai and the soldier spent some of the time rolling Ali up in a blue plastic tarp dug out of the soldier's pack, then tying it tight with a length of cheap white nylon rope. He looked vaguely like a rug when they were done. The tarp was large enough to wrap him completely, and they wound the rope around him over and over again. It was unpleasant to watch—Rai, on his knees, straddling the body, cinching the rope as tight as he could, then handing the loose end to the soldier, who lifted Ali by the feet, and flicked the rope under him for Rai to grab once more. Soon Ali was a bundle, wrapped in blue plastic and clothesline. When they were finished they stood, and wiped their hands on their thighs.

Despite Rai's assurances, I didn't expect the helicopter to come that day. I expected mistakes, inefficiency, incompetence, more phone calls—all of that. I expected to be there for the night.

But the helicopter came. We heard it first, to the south, in the distance, and only then did we see it—a tiny speck in the high center, following the river. Rai stood, and began waving. As it approached, all I felt was relief—it was here after all, and soon all of this, these brutal last few days, would be behind me. The helicopter seemed as slow as a swimmer, and seemed to approach forever, as we stood and watched.

Just then the pilot must have seen us, because he abruptly changed course, curving in a wide downward arc toward where we stood. It was a small machine, light, with a round Plexiglas bubble canopy. It was not General Said's piece of industrial equipment. It looked frail, delicate, and it came to a hover thirty feet or so above the river like a dragonfly. I could see the pilot clearly through the glass. He wore civilian clothes—a white dress shirt, dark pants. He was unhelmeted. I could see his feet moving on the pedals, as the machine bobbed and swayed. Rai waved with both arms, pointing to the gravel bank, and the pilot waved back, spun the helicopter effortlessly in the air, lowered it straight down to the ground, and settled, uneasily at first, onto the gravel—one skid, then the other. He shut off the engine, and it wound down, the rotors shining and skipping in the sun.

The pilot opened the door, then hopped out and walked toward us. He was very young—in his late twenties at most. Rai went out to meet him, and I followed.

They exchanged a few words, then switched to English. I looked at him carefully—his white shirt, his dark pants, his gold watch, aviator glasses dangling from a cord around his neck—and I guessed that he was a rich man's son, playing at boldness.

Rai made the introductions, and the man looked me over quickly before obviously and rapidly losing interest. He cheered up dramatically, however, when he saw Elise—he took her hand, and smiled with lots of white teeth, and ran his hand easily through his well-cut hair.

"How do you like our beautiful country?" he said to her.

She looked at him, removed her hand, and did not reply.

Rai said something, and the man's smile skipped a beat, and he looked over at the bundle on the riverbank, then back.

Though we stood out in the sun it was far too cold for a well-tailored dress shirt. The man glanced at us, and our gear.

"Only three can come," he said, not smiling anymore.

It was a small helicopter. I turned to Rai.

"Did you know about this?"

"They only have these. The Lamas. They have no big ones."

"I am cold," the pilot said. "Get your things. I will wait in the chopper." He turned, and walked away, then got in and closed the door, as Rai looked on with undisguised contempt.

"So," I said. "We'll have to leave the soldier and the boy. Is that right?"

"He knows the way," Rai said, gesturing to the soldier. "And I will give them provisions."

So that was it. Rai and the soldier dragged Ali over the

rocks to the helicopter, and laid him down along one of the skids. Then the pilot jumped out again with a length of chain, and padlocks, which he handed to them before getting in the helicopter again. We watched as they lashed Ali tightly to the skids with the chain, then with green canvas straps that the pilot tossed out the door to them. He was directing them through the window, but made no effort to help. When they were done, the pilot emerged once more, and bent down with visible distaste to heave on the bundle, assuring himself that it was tight enough, and would not fall, that none of the lashings would come loose and whip about in flight. He was shivering by then.

"Okay," he said to us, opening the door on the canopy. "Your packs."

He put them in the back himself, lifting them, clearly estimating their weight. He turned to me.

"Do you have a credit card?" he said. I fumbled for my wallet, pulled out the card, and handed it to him.

"Your passport also, please," he said.

"Why do you need my passport?"

"So that I know you will pay," he replied.

I gave it to him without a word.

"I do not like body recoveries," he said. "All the time it is like this in the climbing season. And sometimes the climbers, they have no money. They do not want to pay."

"We're not climbers," I said.

He shrugged, then turned back to the business at hand.

"How much do you weigh?" he asked me. I told him.

"And you?" he turned to Elise again.

"Forty-five kilos," she said. "Less now, I think."

He looked at Rai, who said something, and he nodded, doing the figures in his head.

"No problem," he said. "Let's go."

The soldier and the boy stood a few feet away. The boy looked disconsolate. Their packs lay at their feet.

Rai turned to the soldier, and said a few words. The soldier replied, and then, somewhat to my surprise, Rai reached into his pack and quickly counted out a sheaf of bills, which he handed to him.

The helicopter was no larger than a small sedan, and it smelled like a new car. Rai sat up front, and Elise and I were pressed together with our gear in the back. The pilot slammed the doors, tugged on the handles, then trotted around to his seat, put on his seat belt, and began flipping switches. He pressed a button, and the engine came to life, driving the soldier and the boy a few yards back. The din was higher pitched than the Mi-17, a more female shriek, but deafening all the same, and we had no earphones. With a glance over his shoulder, and no ceremony at all, the pilot lifted off, scattering the gravel with the rotor wash, and then we were away, over the river, out into the center of the valley, the two figures shrinking rapidly in the distance. They looked up at us, and I looked down at them, until they were specks, until there was nothing left of them at all—just two dots, at a bend in the river, invisible, had I not known precisely where they stood. To the north, a sea of empty country, full of peaks and snow and valleys, glimpsed in the gaps of the ridges. Meanwhile, inches away, Ali lay fluttering and shivering like a flag. Soon it was hot in the bubble, with Elise pressed tight against me. I thought—life on one side, death on the other, and how strange it all is, how utterly dumbfounding and mysterious.

The light sparkled in the globe of the canopy, and caught the grains of dust, and soon we left the course of the river, crossing slot canyon after slot canyon, the ridges rising and falling beneath the skids, with only the occasional streams sparkling below us. A dry land, a labyrinth below us, without landmarks to guide us. How casually the pilot flew, the tips of his fingers delicate on the stick, his eyes up, on the horizon, glancing down every so often at the instruments. He was following a compass heading, and had no use for the maze of shadows beneath us, as the machine swelled and sighed in the cold gusts above the ridge tops. Lower and lower, as Ali shook on. But Rai had tied him well, and none of the lashings came loose.

Rai saw something then, because his head turned and he looked down, and then he reached out and touched the pilot's arm, shouting above the engine, and pointing.

We were over a dry valley, studded with tiny bushes. From the air, the bushes looked black against the gray and brown earth. At first I didn't see what Rai was pointing at, and I leaned forward, against his seat, following his outstretched finger to the ground.

It was a rough line of them, walking together. They were to one side of us, ahead of us, and as I watched we rapidly gained on them, until they were abreast, and I could see them clearly, a few hundred feet away and several hundred feet below. They had stopped, and turned, and they were also pointing.

Rai shouted once more at the pilot. The pilot glanced over, and though it hardly seemed as if he moved the controls at all, the helicopter rolled steeply, pressing me against my seat, and then we were descending, my stomach rising into my chest. They came up fast, their faces lifted, and the pilot eased the stick back. The nose nodded up, the airspeed fell to nothing, and then he brought us to a hover thirty feet above the ground, almost directly over them. They scattered, hands above their heads, but then he backed away, like a horseman, light and easy in the saddle.

Perhaps there were thirty of them—men and women and children, all staring up at us with astonishment through the dust from the rotor wash. They were dressed like villagers. Many wore blankets on their shoulders, and they were carrying loads—rough burlap sacks, with coils of twine. But they were thin, so thin they startled me—their gaunt, drawn faces, their eyes open, their mouths agape, looking up. There were animals, also—a skeletal handful of goats tied to leads, the points of their shoulders like pins, their hides drum-tight across their ribs. I imagined they were all that were left, that one by one the others had been consumed, as the weeks passed. But they were nearly out of the mountains. They had only a few more days of walking left.

"Who are they?" I shouted at Rai.

"I don't know," he shouted back, over his shoulder.

For a few long seconds we stared at them, and they at us. I felt a terrible urge to laugh. They'd walked right by us, I thought. They never even knew we were there. But then the pilot tapped Rai on the shoulder, pointing to his gauges, and suddenly we were turning in the air, gathering speed, climbing away, and Ali resumed his eager rattle once again.

Twenty minutes later we were in the city.

PART THREE
THE CITY

CHAPTER THIRTY-SEVEN

That night I lay on clean sheets, on the fifteenth floor, listening to the sounds of traffic far below. It was fifty degrees warmer. Crowds on the streets. Dark buildings. Headlights, shop lights, along the sidewalk. Only a few neon signs—electricity, even there, was in short supply. Many horns, the heat, wet and thick, the smell of rotting fruit and sewers and roasting lamb on spits, in glass boxes, weakly lit by yellow bulbs. The sound of a thousand small motorcycles, like standing next to a box of bees. We'd passed through it, on the way from the airport in the cab, with the windows down.

The glass was thick, the curtains heavy, and the air-conditioner flicked on and off. I couldn't sleep; I felt strong and completely exhausted at the same time. I was alone. Elise was a few doors down, and I'd put her room on my credit card, just as I'd done with everything else. It was the most expensive place in town, and they charged like the West they pretended they were. Neither of us had eaten, nor had we wanted to.

The hotel felt like a bottle of clean water from an artesian well. It was a window to another world. The glass lobby, the concierge in his blue suit, the icy air after the sudden heat of the city, a few men in coats and ties, talking on cellular phones, sitting on dark couches with their tea—and we had walked in, with our packs and our boots, soaked in dust. They'd stared at us as if they belonged there and we did not.

After a while, showered and clean-shaven for the first time in more than a month, I got up, and reached for the phone. I didn't give any thought to time zones, to the fact that he was on the other side of the world, that it was daylight, and he was working. I just dialed, and listened to the ring, without a hint of static. The machine came on.

This is Eric. Leave a message.

And then a beep. I hesitated, like someone who finds himself unexpectedly required to make a public toast, after a cascade of spoons on half-empty glasses. But then, in the most normal tone I could manage, I said I was back in the city, and would be coming home early, that everything was fine, and I'd call him with details when I had them. I hung up the phone softly, even gently, and then wandered over to the minibar, where there were tiny bottles of imported whiskey.

I'd heard this message many times, and it always disappointed me. It was his slow, mannered, laconic tone that did it—deliberately indifferent, as if he could barely be bothered. It seemed both forced and unworthy of him, so unlike the friendly, excitable young man he was, and I suspected that he'd recorded it many times, with care. It revealed nothing of his true self. It was like his new tattoo, and his earring: it was studied, and just then I wondered what friends he had made, how many there were, and whether they had similar messages on their answering machines. I'd met only a few.

I drank the whiskey neat, because even there I didn't trust the ice. I pulled the curtains partly aside, and sat at the window on the executive chair, looking down at the street some fifty meters below. The hotel was the tallest building for miles, and I had a clear view of the city—the lights, the streaming cars on the dark roads. It didn't shine—it wasn't quite luminous, like the skylines of the West. But it was a city nonetheless, a vast one, with millions stretching out in their apartment blocks, in their shantytowns. No stars were visible; I had a sense of high clouds up in the dark. Several times I heard the sound of aircraft through the thick glass—the airport was nearby. Even through the air-conditioner, it felt as though it might rain, and that the rain would be warm and soft. With my face close to the window, I could see people walking in the streets, going nowhere in particular. Just out, idly looking into shops, men walking hand in hand, boys, a few women, in what passed for the comfort of evening. I was thirteen hours ahead of him, in another day altogether, and we were at opposite ends of the earth.

I drank two of the little bottles, sitting there in the dark. I nearly drank a third, but when I stood to urinate in the bathroom, careful not to switch on the light, because I had no desire to see myself again in the mirrors over the sink, I realized that I was swaying. It was good whiskey, smooth and silky to the tongue.

I drew the curtains, and lay down on the bed. For a moment I considered turning on the television, with its satellite service. But right then I couldn't face them, those men and women, so full of whatever it was that had happened that day, or that week. I didn't care what had happened, and in any case I knew I'd find out soon enough, because I was in the antechamber of my own world, and I could feel the money everywhere again. I could feel it in the cotton sheets, in the blanket, in the firmness of the mattress. Had I closed the curtains tight, I might have been anywhere. Oddly, I missed the sound of the river—the background murmur, the white noise that had accompanied us for so long, and now was gone.

I was tired of being lost, and I was tired of throwing still more experiences onto the bonfire of my own confusion. It was bright enough already, and cast its light as far as I could see. I wanted to go home, and I didn't want to go home. I wanted the idea of home. I wanted an end to my loneliness, and I wanted to be left alone. I wanted my wife and my son again. I wanted to do something decent at last, and I wanted to be rewarded for my decency. I'd amputated a girl's leg to prove that I could, and though I'd done it well—better than I ever expected—it had hardly been a selfless act. It had been something I'd mistaken for selflessness, when all along it was something else, something darker and smaller, that only I could see. I should have simply opened my checkbook, as Elise had wanted, and called a helicopter. Then Ali, a man whom I hadn't in my heart felt anything for. Yes, I feel sorry for him; yes, his life is difficult. In the meantime, please make him stop stinking up the tent. It was that kind of pity. On some level, I'd gotten him killed. Had I not come, he'd be alive as ever, bobbing his head at someone else, and the image of my shirt, wrapped in that plastic bag, would not keep coming back to me.

No doubt I was being too hard on myself. I was no worse than most, and better than many. I knew that well enough. Why, after all, should any of it make sense? It was a wash of images, it was all just stumbling and wandering, perhaps with some decency and tenderness along the way. Maybe, somewhere, in the beatitudes, were those who found something as lovely as a bell at the end, but I was not one of those people, nor did I know anyone who was. It was all biology anyhow, all X and Y—my flashy early conversations with Rai, that rivalry and preening, or the tingle of a woman, and what came with her, near my arm. It was just the human story again, flowing through me as it did through everyone else, and I'd mistaken it as my own. There I was, digging away in the dark, intent on the task, and now that

the boiling lead had come raining down upon me I was astonished to find that my burrow looked exactly like the others. With
one glance the professor could tell what species of ant I was.

Those were my thoughts. But after a while even they failed
to keep me awake—the whiskey overtook them. There is only so
much one can think, after all.

CHAPTER THIRTY-EIGHT

The phone rang loudly the next morning. I was already awake, lying in bed, a bit chilled under the blanket. I'd left the air conditioner on the highest setting, and the room felt both humid and cold despite the chinks of sunlight in the heavy drapes. The phone startled me, and my heart leapt—for a moment I thought it might be Eric. But then I realized that I had not left him the number of the hotel, or even the name.

It was Elise.

"Are you eating breakfast?" she asked. I said that I was, that I would meet her downstairs in the restaurant in thirty minutes.

I took a quick shower, shaved, then walked out on the carpet, wrapped in a towel. I was clean, but my clothes were not. They were full of dust and grime, smelling of kerosene and smoke, and I heaped them in a pile by the door, next to my stained pack. I called the front desk, and was told that they would be washed immediately. Then I picked through them, and dressed as cleanly as I could—a dark fleece shirt, like the one I'd given Ali, which hid the stains to some extent, and my spare nylon hiking pants, from a catalogue, which had been too thin for the cold. I shook them out as best I could. I combed my hair with my fingers, found the key on the nightstand and opened the heavy door, stepping out onto the thick wine-red carpet of the empty hall. I was ten minutes early, alone in the elevator as it slid smoothly down to the lobby.

In broad daylight, the lobby was not as splendid as it had seemed the night before. The desk clerk's blue uniform, with its ridiculous epaulets, was several sizes too big for him, and his starched white collar was ragged at the edges and hung down below his brown neck. The varnished counter, which had shone like a mirror in the evening, needed another coat of varnish. He directed me to the restaurant with great servility.

The restaurant was a large room, with dozens of tables covered with white tablecloths, red napkins, and plastic floral centerpieces. The room was empty, but wide bay windows opened on a garden with a terrace, where more tables stood. Each of the tables had a large blue umbrella rising from the center, with the name of the hotel stenciled on it with elaborate gold letters— *Excelsior.*

Everyone, it seemed, was eating their breakfast outside. The garden alone was immaculate—perhaps a half acre of perfectly mown green grass, red and yellow flowers in planters along poured concrete walkways. I asked to be seated there, with the others.

The hotel seemed both empty and overstaffed, with waiters and bellboys hovering in corners, ready to leap. And the shabbiness of the city had crept in, just a little. It could not be escaped completely. The scratched teacup, or the spots on my water glass in the sun. The desk clerk's collar, starched over and over again—I suspected that the shirt was his own, and that the uniform was not.

There was a Westerner as well—a pale bald man in a business suit, who sat a few tables away with a folder of papers, absently taking long sips of tea as he turned the pages. A contract, I imagined. He looked distinctly European, but somehow peripherally so—a Dane, maybe, or a Belgian. The rest of the men on the terrace were clearly members of the ruling class. I didn't look at them closely. I knew who they were. Had I stood and asked who among them knew General Said, I'm certain there would have been a show of hands. I could picture him there perfectly, throwing his head back in laughter, moving from table to table, greeting his friends.

"Can I help you, sir?" The waiter stood at attention before me.

"A menu, please," I replied. "And tea. Someone will be joining me."

"Of course, sir," he said. I hardly even looked at him. I only had an impression—thin, white shirt, pressed dark pants, a black tie.

It was pleasant and warm in the garden, looking out over the grass, the potted flowers—hibiscus, I thought, and marigolds, and red poppies. There were perhaps a dozen tables on the terrace, two-thirds of them full. There were a few bees, moving from pot to pot. I watched them reeling, pausing, reeling again.

The waiter returned with my tea, in a heavy white china pot. He poured it with a flourish, as if it were wine, and I thanked him absently, then added the milk, and the sugar, and took a sip. It was good, and dark, and I began to feel better.

Elise wore sunglasses, and, to my surprise, a long yellow dress. She walked through the dining room toward me, her pale arms bare from the shoulders, her hair shining in the sun. I'd expected something else, the kind of thing I was wearing. But she'd transformed herself entirely. When she stepped out onto the terrace, I caught the ripple in the men around her, like a stone into a pool. She was, after all, a pretty young woman, with very white skin, radiating otherness. The Dane, as I thought of him, barely glanced up from his papers. But the others, those entitled, powerful men, with their suits and mustaches, their strong profiles and uncoiling cigarettes, assuredly did. And so did I. Despite myself, I thought of Scott Coles.

I stood up. A day earlier it wouldn't have crossed my mind. I could feel their eyes on us as I pulled out her chair. Perhaps they thought she was my daughter.

"Thank you," she said, giving me a smile.

Up close, her dress was not nearly so glamorous. It was light cotton, made for traveling, the kind of thing young women take on warm foreign vacations, with their backpacks, in the summer.

"Where did you get that dress?"

"Everything else is dirty," she replied. "I bring this for when it is hot."

"Well," I said. "You look lovely."

She blushed.

"Stop," she said.

"Why?"

She gestured toward the other tables.

"Those men," she said. "I do not like walking in front of them, you know?"

"Then have some tea," I said, pouring her a cup.

We ate what passed for an English breakfast—eggs, toast, melons, tea—and looked out at the green grass and the flowers. We were in our own world again, I suppose, or what passed for it. For an instant I imagined the soldier, and the boy, still walking.

A gardener had made his way out onto the lawn a few feet from us. He was barefoot, wearing a kind of loincloth, and a rough brown cotton shirt. He crouched on his haunches, his back to us, and began cutting the grass with a tiny hand scythe. I don't think the others even saw him. He was perfectly in the background for them, I'm sure, but he fascinated me, as he cut a

few blades at a time with delicate, practiced strokes. The scythe
sounded like a whisk, and every so often he'd roll from foot to
foot, moving a few inches, and continue. He was an expert at it.
I realized that he cut the entire half acre in this way. The men on
the terrace ate, and spoke to one another, and I wondered what
on earth they were talking about. I wondered what they dreamed
of, there at the top of their house of cards—was it only to continue, to keep on as they were? Rai's dreams were clear enough.
But those men—what they hoped for, and what sustained them,
was far more difficult to see.

"Look at them," Elise said, gesturing toward the men around
us on the terrace. "It is disgusting."

"We're here also," I said.

"It is not the same."

"I'm not sure," I said.

And I wasn't. I felt like an owner of plantations, troubled by
the foreman's lash, who looks away over the green fields. Each
day they woke up, and crouched down, and rolled from foot
to foot with their little scythes, back and forth, tirelessly. And
those at their feet, those millions of blades of grass, did nothing, and were no more worthy for it. Homa's brutal mother, for
example—it was hard to imagine her as the victim of anything,
though of course she was. Nonetheless, hers was the heartlessness of poverty, which, it seemed to me, is different from the
heartlessness of wealth. Not that I forgave her, because I did not.
I had nothing but contempt for her, and if it weren't for Homa I
would never have given her a dime.

The waiter came with another pot of tea.

"Those people were like skeletons," she said. "They were
starving."

"They're almost down," I replied. "It's only a few more days
for them."

"Do you think they were refugees from the earthquake? Or was it something else?"

"Does it matter?" I asked.

"Of course it matters," she replied, looking out again at the men on the terrace. "They must not have known where to go," she said, shaking her head.

As she spoke, I wondered how many other bands were up there, struggling out of the high country without any help at all, and who they had been required to leave behind. I thought of the old man with the bad heart, and Homa, and then, suddenly, it all seemed too much to consider, or discuss, and I didn't want to think about them anymore.

"Sanjit said he would come this morning," I said after a while. "Do you think he will?"

"Why would he not come?"

"I don't know," I said. "He might be ashamed."

She shook her head.

"If he doesn't come, we will need to find him," she said. "We must make him help us with Homa."

I nodded.

As our breakfast came to an end, I did finally ask her the question that I'd put off since our return.

"When are you leaving?" I asked. "What are your plans?"

She looked down into her cup.

"I am not sure," she said. "At first, I think I will just go home. I do not have enough time left for the research. But now I am thinking of traveling."

"Where would you go?"

"I don't know. I think maybe Thailand. Or Cambodia. I have not been there. I would like to see those places."

"You'd go by yourself?"

"Of course," she said, then looked at me and smiled. "Unless you would like to come with me as my friend."

My heart leapt. For a moment the temptation was nearly overwhelming. But I was worn out, more or less completely, and she was simply tired. Soon she'd wake up feeling strong and good again, full of curiosity—she'd want to hop on trains, or the tops of crowded buses, and eat exotic foods, and rent bicycles for forty-mile trips through the rainforest. I could see it very clearly. She was young, after all, she couldn't help herself, and the world was full of wonders. But there I'd be, struggling to catch up, tagging along, like a schoolboy, or something worse. I reached out and took her hand, without thinking.

"You should go," I said.

"You are not coming?" She was smiling.

"It would be hard for me, Elise. I need to go home."

"Why? We will have fun, maybe. After this . . ." She let her words trail off.

"Thank you," I said, releasing her hand. "But I need to see my son."

Perhaps, after a few days' rest, I might have recovered. But I could not escape myself in the end. Would I lie there, at night, wherever we found ourselves, thinking of her in the next room, hoping she would give in again? Would I try to get her a little drunk, would I ask her to walk with me down the beach in the evening? It wasn't something I could face. And those we were sure to meet along the way—other travelers, full of adventure, full of physical things—they would have been too much for me as well. Seeing her talk to others her own age, or leaping into the sea off the green coasts—I couldn't picture myself there at all. Or perhaps I could. I was the ridiculous figure on the beach chair, with a book, watching.

CHAPTER
THIRTY-NINE

At one end of the lobby, just past the bank of elevators, there was a narrow hall, with a half dozen shops on either side. Over the entrance to the hall, a sign, in red cursive script—*Excelsior Bazaar.*

"I need to get a few things," I said to Elise, thinking of Eric. "Are you going back to your room?"

"I am sure everything will be too expensive here," she said, but followed me anyway.

There were dusty bottles of French perfume. There were Japanese watches, a few handwoven carpets, fake flintlock pistols with inlaid ivory grips, and photographs of the old city—piles of saffron, piles of almonds and apricots, columns of light in the old bazaar, and a stack of goat heads four feet high, all bulging eyes and bloody protruding tongues. The head at the top of the pile had horns. It was a shocking thing, nightmarish, yet there it didn't attract a second glance.

The shops were empty of customers, and the shopkeepers, undoubtedly hotel employees, sat bored behind the counters. A television was on—a cricket match. For an instant I stopped to watch the bowler, running down in his whites across a perfect sheet of brilliant green grass, straight-arming the ball toward the batsman at the wicket.

We wandered around for a few minutes, then entered the jewelry store, with its glass cases of gold chains and semiprecious stones. There were earrings, also, and elaborate brass plates, in-laid with silver, reflecting. A young man sat behind the counter, talking on a telephone. As we stepped in, a necklace in the center of one of the cases caught my eye.

It was simple, unadorned—four thin gold strands, braided together. The gold had a lustrous, rich look to it, as if it was nearly pure, and that was what caught my attention; everything else had the shine of modern times. The man looked up, then hurriedly hung up the phone and stood.

"Yes, yes," he said. "Welcome."

"How much is that necklace?" I asked, pointing.

"Yes," he said, in a practiced way. "That is a very old one. Very pure gold. It is from a burial mound."

"A burial mound?"

He nodded enthusiastically.

"Yes," he said. "How old I do not know. But very old, I think. More than one thousand years, perhaps."

"What kind of burial mound?"

"This I do not know," he said. "It is from the north."

"How much is it?"

He made a show of opening a notebook on the glass case, then tapped a few numbers into a pocket calculator.

"I can give this one to you for"—he paused—"nine hundred U.S. Or Euros if you prefer."

"Can I see it?"

"Of course." He eased himself out from behind the counter, then opened the case and picked up the necklace with both hands, as if it were an object of reverence. He held it out to me, and I took it.

It was austere and delicate at the same time, and though his story of the burial mound was no doubt carefully calculated, it seemed that it just might possibly be true. I turned to Elise.

"Will you try it on?"

She opened her mouth, then closed it again, and began to blush.

"Oh . . ." she began, uncomfortably, but stopped as I handed her the necklace. She undid the clasp, put it on, and stood there in her dress.

"Yes, yes," the salesman said. "It is very nice for your daughter."

I laughed, and Elise flushed some more, and the man looked nervously back and forth between us for a moment.

"I have a mirror," he said, reaching under the counter, nodding and bobbing. For an instant I thought of Ali again. She took the mirror, and held it up.

"I'll give you three hundred U.S. for it," I said, looking at him.

He winced, and shook his head.

"No, no," he said. "I am sorry."

"All right then," I said. Elise removed the necklace and handed it to him. He paused, as if he did not want to take it, and so she placed it carefully on the countertop.

"Seven hundred U.S.," he said, quickly, but I just smiled at him, and shook my head as well.

"I think we should go," I said to Elise, and she began to turn away with relief.

"Okay, okay," the man said. "Six hundred U.S."

"No," I said. "Three fifty. That's it."

Elise stood there, mortified, uncertain, and for an instant I regretted ever starting down the path—I should have just paid what he asked, and been done with it. But something stopped me, something quite strong, as if to say, when I am generous, it will be on my own terms, and not on yours, because you are trying to take from me.

In the end we settled for four hundred and seventy dollars. I put it on my credit card. He coiled the necklace in a small white box, and handed it to me with a smile that told me I hadn't bested him after all. I didn't care; it was the attempt that mattered.

We left the shop, and I kept the necklace tucked in my pocket for a while. Elise tagged along at my side on the way back through the lobby to the elevators, shooting nervous glances at me.

In the privacy of the elevator, rising toward our respective rooms, I handed her the box.

She hesitated, and I was afraid she wasn't going to accept it.

"It is too much," she said. "You know?"

"I do know," I said. "But I think it's beautiful, and I hope that you'll take it."

She took the box, holding it between her palms as if coming to a decision. I wished I hadn't done all that bargaining in front of her—it was no way to give a gift. I should have left, I knew, and come back for it. But it had happened so quickly, I'd had no time to plan, and there are so many things one can never take back, after all, so many choices and moments in this life that require resurrection.

"I knew I wanted to get it for you the moment I saw it," I said to her. "And I didn't care how much it cost. But I couldn't let that man cheat us, either. I had to make him work a little."

An odd sentiment, I suppose. It was only a necklace.

Finally she opened the box, and looked down at the necklace within it.

"Thank you," she said, softly, before closing the box again. "I think it is beautiful also."

"You're welcome," I said.

The bell rang, the doors opened, and we stepped out into the carpeted hall. She gave me a small uneasy smile, and then turned away.

There was an English-language paper hanging limply over the edge of the executive desk in my room. I was surprised to find it there, with my pressed clean clothes, folded in the precise center of the bed.

I sat down in the chair, and looked out past the open curtains at the rooftops. I thought of her smile, and felt the sting of my awkwardness. I shook my head, and picked up the paper.

The prime minister had hosted a conference on regional autonomy. There was a picture of him, at a podium. A school had been opened for underprivileged boys. Ruffians had clashed with police over the closing of a local mosque to make way for a road construction project. The army had committed more resources to earthquake relief. New Block D fighter aircraft were being procured after prolonged debate in Parliament, with considerable improvements in avionics and engines over the Block C export versions that had been promised some years before but never delivered. But there was not the slightest reference to the shelling, or to the soldiers, or to the corpses on the mountainside. It was as if it had never happened at all. I'd expected something, if only a cryptic reference to increased tensions along the border. But I was also entirely unsurprised.

Back in my room, with some time to kill, reading the newspaper, leaning back in the chair—all this might have made the events of the past few weeks seem far away, unreal, dreamlike. But the opposite was true. It was the hotel that seemed dreamlike and unreal. The valley did not seem far away at all. I could see it, in my scuffed boots, in the stained pack lying collapsed upon itself in the corner, even in my maid-folded clothes, which soon I'd change into again. I had no desire to go out into the city, to shop in the market stalls or what passed for bazaars. I had no interest whatsoever in the leftover forts, or the botanical gardens, or the grandeur of the financial district, home of many international banks and corporations. None of the Places of Beauty and Interest—this was the title of the brochure on the desk—tempted me in any way.

The air-conditioner clicked on and off. I lost interest in the newspaper, and put it aside, and then, almost without thinking, turned to the pages of hotel stationery tucked in one corner of the green blotter on the desk. I picked up the complimentary pen, and sat there for a while, trying to gather my thoughts, before I began.

Dear Eric,

I've been thinking a great deal about you and your mother on this trip, about my own life and the mistakes I've made. I failed you in some important ways and would like to do what I can to make up for it. I hope you will forgive me for writing to myself as well as to you.

I know that you haven't forgiven me for not telling you that your mother was at the end. I know you can't understand why I didn't ask you to come home. The reason is that I helped end her life. I will never fully recover from this, and I will have to face it forever. I helped her because she was suffering a great deal and I could not refuse her. But I couldn't have you there, and neither could she. She was ready to leave me and our life together. But she was not ready to leave you, and she could not have done it in your presence.

But that isn't the point of this letter. I'm writing to give you some advice.

Acting is seductive, and compelling, I'm sure, and I understand what your teacher meant when she said it was a metaphor for life. It's true that we choose roles, and let them carry us along. I spent most of my life doing this. But some roles are better than others. My parents struggled, and I had few advantages when I was young. I was determined to better myself, and though I chose a more conventional profession, I was just as ambitious as you are when I was your age. You were always closer to your mother than you were to me, but in some ways you are more like me than you may realize. Your childhood was far more privileged than mine was, and for a long time I was proud that I was able to do that for you, and proud that you felt free to follow your own hopes rather than more practical concerns. But the world is mostly practical concerns, and sooner or later this is something you will have to learn. I believe that I may have done you a great disservice by not making this clear to you long ago. I spent too much time congratulating myself on what I had provided for you, and not enough time thinking of your best interests in the long run.

I don't know your teacher, but I'm certain that what sustains her now is not acting, but teaching, and having students like you, whose lives she can affect. But please remember that her dreams did not come true, even though I'm sure they were encouraged also. At one time she undoubtedly expected to be more than what she became, and I wonder if she's still chasing those hopes through you and others.

It's hard to become a successful actor. It takes an enormous amount of luck, and talent and determination aren't enough on their own. The odds are against you, and twenty or thirty years from now you easily may find yourself bitterly disappointed. Right now you are counting on being blessed by good fortune, and this is a dangerous assumption. Like your teacher, I believe in your talent. But in a few years you should know if your dreams are realistic, and if they're not I hope you'll have the courage to see this and pursue something else. You shouldn't think that acting is the only thing that can give you purpose. You can always do it on the side, and most people have to settle for less than they hope. It was true for your mother, and it was true for me.

It's fine to try for a while. But don't try for too long. I know advice like this is unlike me. I have always loved you, even though I did not express it well, and I'm finding it difficult to forgive myself for neglecting you as I did. I spent too many years chasing something I couldn't even name, for reasons that I didn't understand. But in the end none of us are as complicated as we'd like to think. When I was young, I was the poor kid from the wrong side of town, and I realize now that I spent most of my adult life trying to prove that I was more than that, that I was significant in some larger way. What I didn't realize is that no one cared but me. I inflicted this on both you and your mother, and I can't tell you how sorry I am.

I hope the path you have chosen is the right one. I will help you as much as I can. But please remember that the world is indifferent not only to our fates, but also to the work we do. That matters only to us.

I can't tell you how much I miss you.

When I was done, I looked over what I'd written and knew it was something I could not send. I wanted so much to give him what I could, to steel him for the disappointments I imagined would be his, as they had been mine. But how limited my words seemed, as I read them again, how cynical and dispiriting.

I was one of a million distant fathers, and if my strengths did not distinguish me, neither did my weaknesses. I saw it clearly. I was guilty of the commonest of American failings, a modestly successful man, and no more, and there was so much I could not grasp, and did not understand, and I was old enough to know that I never would. If that was the best I could manage, I thought, it wasn't good enough, because surely there was more. Surely mine was not the only story to be told.

CHAPTER FORTY

When the time came to meet Rai in the lobby, Elise knocked on my door. She had changed out of her dress, and wore newly washed khaki-colored cargo pants, a freshly ironed T-shirt, and the open-toed rubber sandals of the casual Western tourist. Her small, orange, and very European-looking day pack hung over her shoulder. Her sunglasses hung from her neck on a cord. She had remade herself again, deliberately. I noticed it, of course, but as we rode down together in the elevator I said nothing.

The doors slid open, and there was Rai, standing by the leather couches, watching the elevators. I suspected that he had been there for some time. He wore what passed for a Western suit—pressed dark pants, a white collared shirt, a jacket, but no tie. I realized that I'd never seen him in anything but his green military sweater, his khaki pants, and scuffed black boots. He seemed distinctly reduced, in his civilian clothes, standing there by the couches as the waiters passed. When he saw us step out of the elevator together he offered a nervous half wave, which more than anything else revealed his unease. In the valley, we'd been close enough to one another, but now, in just an instant, the gulf between us had revealed itself again, and I could see it with absolute clarity before a word was spoken.

Up close, he looked tired. And his clothes were not good—his shirt was new, pressed, and clean, but his jacket looked cheap and thin. I had a sudden image of him, fingering the racks in an open-air market on the street. From a distance, in passing, he might have been mistaken, despite his young age, for one of the men on the terrace. But up close he would not have been—in truth, he looked more like one of the hotel's many employees.

"Sanjit," I said, and offered him my hand, which he shook firmly. "Thank you for coming."

"Of course," he replied, looking out over the lobby, with its gold-plated luggage carts, the bellman in his plumage by the revolving doors. The place looked increasingly ridiculous to me, garish and off. It had taken more than a day for my eye to regain itself, and see it. But for others, for Ali and his kind, no doubt it was as splendid and luminous as a medieval cathedral.

Rai, I think, was uncomfortable, but not so uncomfortable as to be fully impressed. He cast a contemptuous eye at the staff, and let his gaze drift around the lobby even as he spoke. He seemed elsewhere, distant and preoccupied, as if his mind were on other things, which no doubt it was.

There was an awkward pause.

"Would you like some tea?" I found myself saying. "Have you eaten?"

"I have eaten, thank you," he said. "But we can have some tea if you wish."

It was hot outside by then, in late morning, and so we had our tea in the lobby, on the leather couches. They brought us a tray, and put it on a side table, and each of us sat in the deep, dark leather, awkwardly holding our teacups in our laps. For a few moments we each busied ourselves with milk, and sugar, and tiny silver-plated spoons. When Elise leaned back in the couch, her feet came off the ground like a child's, and so she sat perched on the edge. Rai sat stiffly, holding the saucer on his palm.

"Is it all taken care of?" I asked, finally. "With Ali?"

Rai grimaced. He'd put us in a cab at the airport, as soon as he could, and sent us away.

"They will bury him today," he said. "They have the body." He looked down at his tea, then took a deliberate sip.

"Thank you, Doctor," he said, finally. "For the helicopter."

I felt my face flush, and I looked away.

"Is there a funeral?" Elise asked. "I think maybe we should go."

Rai shook his head.

"It is best if you do not," he said. "They are very poor people. They would not understand why you were there."

Elise opened her mouth to reply, but then apparently thought better of it. She took a sip of tea, her expression cold.

"So," Rai said. "You are going home soon, I think?"

"Yes," I replied, glancing at Elise. "Probably in the next day or two."

I wanted to ask him a great deal—I wanted to ask about the situation in the valley, the shelling, all of it. I wanted to ask him about the refugees, wherever they were, and what plans were now being made for them, and why I'd seen nothing in the papers, and whether he'd talked to General Said on his return. I wanted to press him about Homa, and the money I had promised her, and Ali's nephew, who no doubt was stumbling down the trail even as we spoke. But sitting there, in that strange place, swallowed in the cool black leather of the couch, I just took another sip of tea.

"I must leave soon," Rai said then. "I cannot stay this morning. But there is something else also. I would like to invite you to my home for dinner if you have the time."

"Oh," I said, surprised.

"Of course, your flights . . ." Rai began, but I cut him off.

"We haven't booked them yet," I said, matching his tone. "And we'd be happy to have dinner with you."

"I will tell my wife," he said, seriously. "She is not so good at Western food, so you must please forgive her."

"She should make us what she likes, and what you like," I said. "That's much better."

Rai drained his cup, then placed it with its saucer carefully back on the service. I wondered what he wanted.

"Yes," he said. "I think that is better also. But she is very shy. She does not know Western people."

"Please tell her not to worry. Is there anything we can bring?"

He looked at me, puzzled.

"What do you mean?" he asked.

"It is customary to bring something. Usually it is wine, or sometimes dessert."

"No, no," he said. "It is not the same. Please, bring nothing. You are my guests."

Elise had said nothing, I realized. She had hardly spoken to him since that day in the valley, and she was looking down at her feet, as if considering what to do.

"Where do you live?" I asked.

He looked uneasy.

"I am not a rich man," he said. "I have only a small house. I will give you the address, and perhaps you can take a taxi."

"Of course," I said, realizing in that moment that Rai didn't have a car.

Rai reached into his jacket and withdrew a pen and a small address book. He opened the book, and wrote down his address on one of the pages, then carefully tore the page from the book and handed it to me.

"It is not so far from here," he said. "Perhaps twenty minutes."

"When would you like us to come?"

"Tomorrow, if you like. Perhaps at eight."

"Tomorrow is fine," I said, glancing at Elise. "Thank you. I'm looking forward to it."

"I am sorry for what has happened," he said, looking down. There was a long pained silence, and then he hesitantly cleared his throat.

"There is something else also," he said, carefully. "I have a message for you. General Said would like to meet with you. Both of you. He will send a car."

"When?" I asked.

"He asked me to call him after we finished this morning."

I looked at Elise.

"I do not want to see him," she said, after a moment. "I have nothing to say to him."

Rai looked worried, and glanced at me, and suddenly I knew that Said would judge him by this. I turned to Elise.

"We should go," I said. "I have a lot of questions for him."

But she shook her head, leaving no doubt.

"You can go if you want," she said to me. "Maybe that is better. Just tell him that I do what you tell me, that I am a foolish young woman."

"Why would I say that?"

"Because that is what he thinks. He will ask you to be quiet about what has happened. That is why he wants to see us. He is afraid we will go to the media when we get home and say the army is not helping the refugees."

"You're probably right," I said, ignoring Rai, in his discomfort. "But the earthquake is old news now. I'm sure he knows it."

"Then go, if you want," she said. "I am going to my room."

She turned to Rai.

"I will come to your house," she said, looking at him with sudden intensity. "I do not blame you as much, even though you have done a terrible thing. But I will not see that man again."

With that she stood, and walked resolutely off toward the elevators.

Rai stood, watching her go. He looked wounded, and anxious, and then, finally, he turned to me.

"Thank you," he said, simply. "I will tell them to send a car for you."

"Are you coming?"

"No. The general wants to meet with you in private." He hesitated. "Please be careful what you say, Doctor. It could have great consequences for me."

He stood there, as afraid as I'd ever seen him, and waited.

"Don't worry, Sanjit," I said, finally. "I know what kind of man he is."

CHAPTER FORTY-ONE

They sent a small gray Asian sedan with tinted windows. The uniformed driver spoke no English. Despite myself, I could not shake the sense of dread as I got into the car, and we pulled out on the wide road, the lanes divided by a dusty hairline of bushes and painted white cinder blocks. The air-conditioner blew, the cloth seats were frayed. The car smelled like cigarettes.

Low concrete and tan brick buildings, alleys, market stalls. Shop fronts selling candy and photocopies by the page. Signs, in Arabic and English alike. Scooters, three-wheeled rickshaws, heavy trucks covered with battered finery—tassels, bits of tin, elaborate paint. Laundry on the rooftops. Clouds, heat shimmering damply on the roofs of the other cars. We moved at little more than walking speed. I sat back, invisible behind the windows, wondering what to say. Every so often a motorcycle would weave past, the rider's elbow brushing the glass at my cheek.

General Said's office was in a low concrete building, with a high wall around it, and guards out front, and the crest of the army on the front door. It stood on a side street near the city center, not far from the hotel, and as we pulled in through the gate it looked like nothing at all.

The driver led me up the steps of the building, and through the door, and down a long hall. The hall was lit by fluorescent light, and the linoleum underfoot was worn and scuffed. Other doors opened on either side, to offices, and we passed them, turning left, then right, then left again. The building was larger than I realized, and soon I was disoriented. A few men passed us in the hall, some in civilian clothes, but most were uniformed soldiers. They ignored us, walking by without a glance. I heard telephones, and, at times, typewriters. The building smelled of cigarette smoke and mildew. There seemed to be many empty rooms.

When the man stopped, it was at a door that looked exactly like the others. The door was numbered, in English—24. He knocked, opened the door, and gestured for me to enter. He did not follow. Instead, he waited in the hall.

Behind the door, in the corner of a small room, a soldier sat at a metal desk beside a modern telephone. There were papers on the desk, a Rolodex. The red wall-to-wall carpet on the floor was worn and scuffed, like everything else. Above the desk hung a large photograph of the prime minister, chief of the army, in uniform. It was the only decoration on the walls, which had once been white. In places, the paint was peeling. In one corner, against the ceiling, a yellow stain.

On the other side of the room, to my right, sat two over-stuffed chairs, a small glass coffee table between them. The chairs were a different shade of red. An ashtray sat on the coffee table, half full.

The soldier stood immediately as I entered, then gestured for me to sit.

"You will wait, please," he said, in broken English.

I sat down in the chair. The soldier returned to his desk. I stared at the door leading to the general's office, with its worn imitation gold handle. I could hear voices behind the door. They rose and fell, and sometimes they were punctuated by laughter.

The soldier did paperwork, checking boxes on a form with a cheap ballpoint pen. He ignored me entirely.

There was nothing to read. The coffee table beside me was empty save for the ashtray. The chair was comfortable enough. There was no clock in the room. I waited. The conversation continued.

Ten minutes later I'd had enough.

I stood, and the soldier looked up at me.

"Tell General Said," I said, "that if he wants to see me, he will see me now, or else I will leave. Do you understand?"

The soldier looked at me impassively, but then he pressed a button on the phone, and I heard the crackle of an intercom. The man spoke into it, and then Said's voice replied—a few quiet words, that was all. The soldier looked up at me again, then gestured for me to sit once more.

I didn't sit. I stood by the chairs, and made an elaborate show of looking at my watch. Perhaps thirty seconds passed, and then, finally, the door opened, and a man in his fifties walked through it. He was dressed in an immaculate suit, with a white shirt, and a fine blue tie, his thick black hair brushed elaborately back from his forehead. He had small eyes, thick brown jowls, and he was laughing at something the general had said. When he saw me he nodded pleasantly.

General Said followed, also smiling. He was dressed as he had been before, in khakis, as if he might be required to go on maneuvers at any moment. I watched as Said shook the man's hand, then whispered something to him that made him laugh again, and eased him out the door.

"Doctor," Said said, as soon as the man was gone. "I did not know you were waiting. I am very sorry. Once again I have inconvenienced you."

He shook his head, as if with deep regret, and then he extended his hand, smiling warmly, and I took it. His handshake was neither firm nor limp.

"Please, come into my office. Would you like some tea?"

"All right," I said.

He turned and spoke quickly to the soldier. The soldier picked up the phone.

Said ushered me into his office, and closed the door behind us.

"I am sorry," he said. "These businessmen. They are always asking for concessions. What am I to do?"

I didn't answer. Instead I looked around the office.

The only sign of luxury was a heavy antique desk, carved from dark wood, and a modern leather executive chair. The rest was battered bookshelves, the same peeling paint and worn red carpet, two identical overstuffed chairs, and another coffee table. The room was windowless, and seemed more like a colonel's office than a major general's. Part of me had expected antlers, or the feet of elephants, or humidors, but there was none of that. It was a place where business was done.

Said read my thoughts.

"Ah, yes, perhaps you were expecting something grand," he said. "But no, no, I am sorry to say. We do not spend our budget on finery. Only on what is necessary."

"That's very commendable," I said.

On the wall behind the desk were perhaps a dozen framed photographs. Most of them were of General Said shaking hands with someone else. Some of the faces were famous, faces that I recognized. But the rest were strangers.

"Please, you must sit down," he said, gesturing to one of the overstuffed chairs.

I did my best to smile politely, and did as he asked, expecting him to return behind the desk. But instead he sat down on the other overstuffed chair, and moved it to face me.

"Thank you very much for coming," he said. "I am sorry to impose on you in this way, especially after what you have been through."

He shook his head wearily.

"I can assure you that this has been a very unpleasant surprise for us. That area has been quiet for a long time. I am extremely sorry, Doctor, for what has happened. And I especially regret that the young lady was there. You are a man of experience, of course, but she is only an innocent girl. It must have been a terrible shock to her."

He paused, looking at me.

"I understand that you were both in the tent during the action?"

"Yes," I said.

"Where is she, if I may ask?" he continued.

"She's feeling unwell," I said. "She's resting in the hotel. It's been very traumatic for her. She's afraid to leave her room now."

"Of course," he said, his expression serious. "I do not know what I can do for her. But if she needs anything at all, you must tell her that we are at her disposal."

There was a gentle knock on the door.

Said rubbed his hands together with pleasure.

"Tea," he said. "It is a very simple thing, you know, but it is one of the joys of life." He looked at me, and smiled.

"Please," he said, gesturing, as the soldier put down a battered tray on the table between us, then filled two cups from a thermos.

"This is army tea," Said said. "It is the best. There is already sugar, and there is already milk, and so you can take both and feel no guilt at all."

I picked up the scratched cup, and sipped. The tea was strong, sweet, blonde from the milk.

"It's very good," I said carefully. "Didn't you tell me that offering tea was an obligation, like giving water to travelers?"

"Ah, yes," he replied, smiling broadly, the skin crinkling at the corners of his brown eyes. "You remember."

"And what about the refugees? Aren't they travelers?"

He nodded seriously.

"I see your point," he said. "It is very troubling, I agree. We are doing what we can, but unfortunately it is never enough, and there are other considerations, as you know. I wish this were not true, but sadly it is."

"Why did you want to see me, General?"

"To offer my apologies, of course," he said.

I put the cup down.

"And now that you've apologized, are you going to tell me what happened up there?"

He composed his expression, carefully, to suit my tone.

"There are no secrets, Doctor. They fired on our forward base. And so we returned fire. And then they sent a team into our territory. Or perhaps several teams, we do not know. You understand the rest. That is what happened."

He smiled, wearily, and sadly.

"I have been doing this for many years," he said. "And that is always the story. It is never complex."

"Why were they interested in us? A refugee camp? And why did they fire on your forward base?"

"I am speculating, you understand. I am only guessing. But I believe they saw the new camp from the air. They are always overflying the border, and now they have satellites as well, I am sorry to say. They were not sure what it was, especially since the tents were empty, and the area is so quiet. Nothing goes on there, you understand. This may have confused them. So they fired on us to send a warning, in case we are up to something. A shot across our bows. That is how they think. Then they sent in a team to look more closely. The team saw nothing, but they grew careless, and were discovered."

"Not just discovered, General. Shot and killed."

Said stood up.

"I understand how it must seem to you. You are shocked, of course. Please, I would like to show you something."

He led me to his desk, where there were several framed photographs. From the back, I assumed they were family portraits. He picked one of them up, and handed it to me.

It was not a family portrait. It was a close-up of three bodies, lined up carefully in a row. They lay in thick, luxuriantly green grass. The bodies were burned beyond recognition. I could make out gaping mouths, and teeth, and the bones of their faces. Their arms were coiled up against their chests, contracted by the heat. Their hands were like black mittens.

"They're children," I said.

"Yes. They mortared a school. With white phosphorous rounds. This was only a few years ago. Within our territory, you understand."

He smiled, his eyes eager, and studied my face, and in that moment I was certain that he had showed the photograph many times before, in the same way, to others. A trophy, I realized—he had one after all.

"I keep this photograph on my desk," he said, "so I will not forget what we are facing."

I handed it back to him.

"I've seen many similar pictures. Do you know who showed them to me?"

He shook his head, and for the first time I knew that I was irritating him.

"Scott Coles," I said. "They were taken after the earthquake. He said seventy thousand people had been killed."

"Of course," he said. "I understand what you are saying. A valid point. But you must understand, this is a different issue. This is something else altogether."

"How is it different?"

"When you are a doctor," he said, "perhaps you deal with God. But when you are a soldier, you deal with men. I am a soldier, I am afraid to say."

"And the earthquake was an act of God. Is that what you mean?"

"Here we take the long view. Many in your country believe that life is easy. But we know that it is not."

"I don't believe that life is easy, General. Tell me what you mean by the long view."

Said smiled, as pleasantly as ever, but this time he sat down in the executive chair and let me stand in front of the desk. He reached up, and rubbed the bridge of his nose. He thought for a while, hesitated for an instant, but then he looked up at me, and his smile was gone.

"Let us stop this nonsense," he said, as if he had come to a decision. "I will talk to you man-to-man. Scott Coles does not understand anything. He thinks that because he buys some tents, and some food, and tricks an American doctor into coming here, he will have a refugee camp and he will be a hero. A savior. He is very naïve in that way. Also he is not good at planning. He does not understand logistics. He does not understand anything. And

the people in the northern areas, they are like animals. That is
the truth. You have seen them. If we send soldiers up there, we
must send enough. They would kill us in our tents if they could.
Perhaps you think I am exaggerating, but I assure you I am not.
We do not govern them. And they do not want us there. When
we give them food, they eat it, and still they would kill us if they
could. There have been earthquakes in that region for hundreds
of years. Each time it is the same. The villages are destroyed. But
then, a few years later, everything is like it was before, and nothing has changed. That is what I mean by the long view."

"Then why did you agree to the camp at all?"

"I thought it could do no harm," he said. "It is a quiet area.
The site is some distance from the border, not a strategic position. And Scott Coles is always coming to see me, asking, asking. He is going to the international media also, and sometimes
he is saying unfortunate things. It is the only thing he is good
at. So I gave my permission. I was mistaken, as you can see. The
camp was too close after all, and they thought it was something
else."

"What is going to happen to it now?"

"We must remove it, of course. It has become a great deal of
trouble for us. And none of them will come there anyway now
because of this. Artillery always frightens them off. They will
stay in their villages as usual, and rebuild them. If they come
down out of the mountains, we must provide for them. But up
there, it is difficult. We do not have endless resources. We are a
poor country, as you know, and we are doing the best that we
can."

"Where are the soldiers now? Is the shelling still going on?"

"We are withdrawing them. Already we have taken down
the tents. And so the shelling is over with. It is quiet again, like
before."

I looked down at the floor.

"So," he said, with a smile. "You did not expect me to be honest with you. I know this. But you see, I am an honest man."

"Then tell me why you wanted to meet with me," I said. "So we can be clear."

He leaned back, and the black leather creaked.

"I would like to ask you not to go to the media when you go home and make negative allegations about us," he said. "Of course, I do not think the media will be interested. But I cannot be sure. It is a small thing, but it is worth a little of my time. I would like you to understand that you have caused this problem, not us. All of it, I am afraid to say. I know you have meant well, but you have cost lives here. At least eight lives, I believe. Four of our soldiers were killed by the shelling. And the three of theirs we caught in the open. And there is your cook, also, I was told. I am sure that our howitzers got a few more of them as well. I hope you will consider this when you return to your country. I hope you will explain this to the girl."

He stood then, came around the desk, and shook my hand.

"It was a pleasure, Doctor," he said, bringing our meeting to an end. "And please apologize to the girl again for me. I hope you have a safe trip home, and that you enjoy the rest of your stay in our country."

As I looked at him, I was certain that any appeal I made would be lost, that anything would be swept beneath the smile of his contempt. Even then, as he dismissed me, his face was warm and alert and untroubled, as if he enjoyed nothing more than my presence before him, and had all the time in the world. Again I saw his pleasure with the photograph on his desk, so like his pleasure with the tea. But finally I'd had enough, no matter what I'd promised Rai.

"Please," he said, as he began to ease me out of his office. "We are friends, and if there is anything I can do to assist you, you must let me know."

"Do you have a card, General?"

"Certainly," he said, and opened a drawer in his desk. His card was thin, and printed cheaply, his name in black beneath the green crest of the army.

"Thank you," I said, putting the card in my wallet. "I want to make sure the newspaper identifies you correctly."

"The newspaper?" he paused.

"Yes. When I tell them how you used a refugee camp as a pretext for military aggression toward your neighbors. Or how you use army helicopters for personal hunting trips instead of flying desperate and starving people out of the mountains. Or how you take attractive young German women sightseeing to beautiful alpine lakes in a time of crisis. I'm sure your superiors would greatly appreciate an article about that. Especially when I send it to them."

His pleasant look vanished.

"What is this nonsense?" he said.

"It's not nonsense. I'm completely serious, I promise you."

"So you are coming here and making threats?"

I didn't answer him directly.

"When you visited the camp, one of your soldiers had a hunting rifle. When you were in the tent I asked him what it was for. He pointed to the ridge. Then he pointed to the helicopter. He was very enthusiastic about it."

Said shook his head, impatient.

"You are imagining things. He was pointing to the enemy."

"He was pointing to ibex and mountain sheep. The rifle was a 7 millimeter magnum, and no military uses that. It's probably in your gun cabinet right now. Your guard wrote down the exact time and place we saw the ibex in a notebook. You were on a hunting trip, and if we hadn't been there, you would have shot that buck. I'm sure your superiors know all about your hobby. They've probably even gone with you. But I doubt they want it reported in the Western media. It would reflect badly on them, especially in times like this."

I paused, but I saw nothing in his face.

"Scott Coles is going to come back here sooner or later," I continued. "When he does, I want you to actually help him establish other camps. If you do, I'll keep quiet about all of it."

Said stared at me for a moment.

"Scott Coles is a fool," he said.

"Starving people don't care who feeds them."

He laughed, openly contemptuous for the first time.

"Do you think you are a savior also, Doctor?"

"Help Scott Coles. It will make you look good and cost you nothing. How hard is that to understand?"

And so we watched each other—two men, in late middle age, each of us as significant as we were ever going to get, each of us a few short years from being forgotten.

"Tell me," he asked, after a moment, "have you discussed this with Captain Rai?"

I met his eye, and answered steadily, determined to give nothing away.

"Of course," I replied. "He said he didn't know what I was talking about. I'm sure he was lying."

He watched me, and let a few seconds pass.

"Doctor," he said, "perhaps you think you are worrying me. But I assure you that you are not. You do not know what you are doing, and you are foolish to threaten me in this clumsy way. If you persist there will be consequences. But I will be honest with you again. This unpleasantness is not worth my time."

"Then give Scott Coles a few camps to keep him busy and your problem is solved."

He stared at me a while longer, and then he nodded once, as if it were nothing to him, and suddenly I knew that my dart into the void had struck something after all.

He gave me a small cold smile.

"Go home, Doctor," he said. "I will give Mr. Coles some assistance. I have several reasons for doing this. But you do not belong here, and you should never have come. You have cost lives and resources, and you have given nothing in return. So do not lecture me about people who are starving, or anything else."

I was tempted to reply in kind. But I knew I'd gotten as much as I could hope for, and so I said nothing. He pressed the button of the intercom on his desk, and spoke into it. Then he looked up, as if I were an afterthought, and extended his hand toward the door.

CHAPTER FORTY-TWO

That evening, the bellman flagged a taxi down for us out in the street and ushered it into the driveway through the gate. It wasn't even a car—it was a motorized rickshaw, a tricycle with a wide blue cab, with a bench seat for two in the back, and a single seat for the driver up front. It looked like a scarab, puttering in front of the hotel, the bellmen smirking to themselves, the driver—a wizened old man—blinking owlishly through the windshield in the floodlights. He seemed stunned to find himself there, peering out from his perch, working the throttle on the handlebars every so often to keep the engine going.

Elise was back in her dress for the occasion, and I was wearing the best clothes I had—a checked blue cotton shirt, my pair of khaki nylon traveling pants. My shoes couldn't be helped; I had nothing but my battered hiking boots. A light rain was falling. It was just dark, and I held a bouquet of flowers in my hand. I'd asked the concierge for them, and I'm certain they were cut from the garden—marigolds, red poppies, wrapped in tinfoil, damp from the vase of tap water.

I showed the bellman Rai's address, on the notebook page he'd given me, and he leaned in and said a few words to the driver, who nodded vigorously, then replied in a high crackle of a voice. The bellman stepped back, gestured for us to enter, and we clambered in, settling ourselves on the stained bench. I handed a bill to the bellman.

Once inside, I realized that the rickshaw was really a small motorcycle with three wheels and a roof. The driver's horned, gnarled feet, damp in their plastic sandals, rested on pegs, and he straddled a gas tank. There was a lip of bare metal for our feet, but beyond that the cab was open to the street below. There were no doors, and a single long wiper swept slowly across the windshield. He shot a quick, nervous glance over his shoulder at us, and then he twisted his right wrist, the engine rattled and whined, and we were off.

The nighttime streets were nothing like those of the day. The traffic, the hiss of the tires on the wet pavement below, the damp warm air and spray through the open doors, the headlights coming toward us, and the smell of rain, the driver working the handlebars, looking left and right as we swayed and bounced along—it felt suddenly exotic, as if jasmine were in the air, and strange temples were nearby.

The traffic was much lighter at that hour, and the sound of the tiny engine reverberated in the drum of the cab. It was too loud for easy talk. There were hardly any streetlights—simply the stream from our single headlight, which swept across the corners, catching on things—a railing, a cinder-block wall, a bicycle, a walking figure—draining them of color. Soon we were off the main road, into a maze of smaller streets.

The driver seemed to know exactly where he was going. He leaned into the bends like a jockey, even though a running man could have caught us. Elise's long yellow dress fluttered beside me, and for an instant I thought of Ali, wrapped in the tarp and lashed to the skid. But then I was back, in the gently raining night, going to a dinner party.

After some fifteen minutes, on one of the many small streets, he slowed down and began to crane his neck out the window. Then, abruptly, he swung the rickshaw to the curb and stopped.

I had a vague impression of a narrow, single-story house, with an unpainted cinder-block wall, and an iron gate, in a row of similar houses on the irregular narrow street—tan brick and poured concrete, flat roofs. I couldn't see it clearly in the darkness. I never could have found it again, or even recognized it in the day. The rickshaw popped and spat, the rain fell, and the driver peered out for a few seconds, then turned to us, and spoke for the first time.

"Okay," he said. A few motorcycles passed by, a car, but for the most part the street was empty.

I hesitated. I didn't want him to leave us there, only to find that he was mistaken. We were precisely on time.

But Rai must have been watching for us, because the door of the house opened to a square of yellow light, a figure passed through it, and then it closed again. I heard his voice, calling out to us over the patter of the rain, and then the unmistakable sound of an umbrella being opened.

"Remember," Elise whispered quickly in my ear. "We must make the arrangements for Homa."

"I think it's better if I take care of it privately with him," I said, and before she could reply Rai was there, opening the gate, slipping the driver a few small bills before I could stop him.

"Let me do that," I said, quickly.

"No, no. You are my guest." It wasn't much, I knew, and so I let it go, stepped out of the machine with my bouquet of flowers, then turned and took Elise's hand to help her up.

Rai stood awkwardly, holding the umbrella over our heads.

"Thank you," I said.

For a moment it was a comical scene, with Elise and me shuffling beside each other in the dark, as Rai tried both to open the gate and hold the umbrella over our heads at the same time.

"Sanjit," Elise said. "We do not need this umbrella."

"Okay," he said, sheepishly, and closed it. The rain fell softly on us all for a few seconds, but then he ushered us through, telling us to mind the steps, and up to the door. Behind me, I heard the sputter of the departing rickshaw, its beam like candlelight in the street, two tiny sapphire points at the back moving off into the dark.

The door opened to a narrow unlit hall. There were two pairs of plastic sandals on the floor, exactly like those the driver had worn. One pair was large, and the other was small. Rai leaned the umbrella against the wall, and slipped out of his shoes.

We followed his lead—I bent down to unlace my boots, and Elise was barefoot in an instant.

"You do not have to remove your shoes," Rai said to me, stiffly.

"Of course I do," I said.

Rai smiled at that, and my comment had its intended effect—it relaxed him a little. From down the hall, I heard childish giggling and whispers.

"There are sandals for you," he said, pointing to the floor. We put them on, but Rai remained in his stocking feet.

"Please," he said. "Let me introduce you to my family."

With that, he ushered us down the hall and into the single full-sized room in the house.

A young, slightly plump woman stood in the center of the room. She wore a burgundy skirt, a white blouse, and a loose dark blue head scarf. She also wore makeup—a modest amount of lipstick and eye shadow. Her eyes were deep brown, a shade or two darker than her skin, and a few black curls escaped from her scarf. Her lips were red and full. She wore elaborate gold ear-

rings, also—thin filigreed disks on chains, which had the sug-
gestion of a dowry about them. Despite her finery, she was not
beautiful, as I expected her to be. Rai's picture had flattered her.
But she had a pleasant, open face, and her cheeks were flushed,
and she looked at us and smiled both warmly and shyly as we
entered the room.

Standing in front of her, as if at attention, was the source of
the giggling and whispering—two little girls. Each had a luxuriant head of black curls, lovely brown eyes, and their father's
receding chin. They were dressed alike—blue blouses, looking
as if they had been made from the same bolt of cloth as their
mother's scarf, identical skirts to their knees, white stockings,
and shiny little leather shoes. Each had a red ribbon in her hair.
They stood in front of their mother, who rested her hands gently
on their heads. The eldest was perhaps seven, the youngest five
or six. They started giggling again, as soon as they saw us, and
their mother knelt down gently behind them and whispered
something.

The three of them stood in the center of a carpet. The carpet was small—perhaps six feet by ten—but it was obviously
old, and beautiful, all swirling reds and blues, with hints of
yellow, and instantly I knew it was by far the best thing in the
room. Behind them, a low couch, modern and shabby, with two
wooden chairs beside it. A large photograph of a mountain lake
hung from the wall behind the couch. The picture had a gold
frame, an airbrushed look, and the colors of the blue water and
the red and yellow leaves seemed as if they had been artificially
deepened. Across the lake stood a small white house, with an
ornate gold roof; a pavilion of some kind, or a gazebo.

To the right, against the curtained windows, stood a narrow
table with elaborate place settings—silverware and glass, and a
large brass teapot in the center, with a tiny blue flame beneath it,

and wisps of white steam rising from the spout. Around the pot, a half dozen or so small thick glasses sat on a tray. Above the table, clearly in a position of honor, hung the familiar photograph of the prime minister, the chief of the army, in full dress uniform.

In front of the couch, on its own stand, stood a small, though new, television, and beneath it an older-looking VCR. A tangle of wires stretched from them to the wall. The walls themselves were off-white, and the paint was chipped. There was a small bookshelf, and a battered-looking cabinet with a glass case, a few pieces of china within it. From the kitchen, the smell of food—curry, and something else. In the background I could hear the rain, falling more heavily.

"Please," Rai said to us, stiffly and formally. "This is my wife, Fatima. And these are my daughters, Saniyah and Rana." As he spoke, I was certain that he had rehearsed the scene in his mind.

At the mention of their names, the girls began giggling again, and their mother shushed them.

I stepped forward, and extended my hand to Rai's wife. She took it, her palm limp and warm, her wrist slack.

"Welcome," she said, and looked as if she were going to giggle as well.

I handed her the bouquet of flowers.

"Thank you," she said, and smiled, blushing.

I addressed what I imagined was a grandfatherly smile at the girls, then took a step back, and Elise followed, shaking Fatima's hand as well.

"Welcome," Fatima said, again.

Elise knelt down on the carpet, and extended her hand to the eldest girl—Saniyah, I think it was. She turned solemn for an instant, and Rai spoke softly from where he stood behind us.

"Saniyah, it is very nice to meet you," Elise said, smiling as the child gravely shook her hand.

"And it is very nice to meet you also. Is it Rana?"

The younger girl nodded seriously at the sound of her name, glanced anxiously at her sister, and extended her hand as well, which Elise carefully shook.

My heart sank in that moment. I was afraid it was going to be a long evening, full of pauses and formality. They had spared no effort; already that was clear. Rai's wife, in her best clothes, and the girls, as if on their way to a wedding, and the distinct sense of a day spent in elaborate preparation, with Rai no doubt pacing, watching over it all; for an instant I felt like General Said himself, come for an inspection.

I glanced down at the carpet, planning to say something about it. But instead the plastic sandals on my feet caught my eye; the hall had been dark, but now I could see them clearly. They were new, as if they had never been worn. Elise's were the same, and in that moment I was sure that Rai had bought them specifically for us, no doubt estimating the sizes of our feet in his mind. I could picture him, standing above the trays of sandals in the market, a wad of small bills in his hand.

"You have a lovely family, Sanjit," I said. "Thank you for taking so much trouble for us."

"It is nothing," he said. But he loved them; I could see it clearly, in the way he looked at them standing in their best clothes, in the softness of his tone. I felt a pure stab of envy for him at that moment.

"I thought you might live on an army base," I said.

He shook his head.

"No, no. Officers' housing is not so good. It is better for us. This was my father's house."

"Did you grow up here?" Elise asked, joining the conversation. Fatima looked on uncomprehendingly, smiling and uncertain, the bouquet of flowers in her hand.

"Yes," Rai said.

"And your parents, they are both dead?" Elise said.

"Yes," Rai said, without embellishment.

"It is very nice," she said, politely, looking around.

Rai smiled again in the same way.

"I know it is very little," he said. "But it is okay for us."

He was correct; the house wasn't much. A few small rooms—a kitchen, a bedroom or two—opened off the hall, but Rai did not show them to us. I could see the conflict there very clearly; pride in his family, shame in what he did not have. Once again his ambition was so clear, and so tangible, that it felt like a physical force.

Fatima smiled on.

"She does not speak English," he said. "She is not an educated woman. But she is a very good mother and a very good wife."

"Of course she is," I said. "And I think you're a lucky man."

He flushed, just a little, under his brown cheeks, and looked down. He looked young again in that moment, and vulnerable.

"Let us have some tea," he said. "And then we will have dinner."

We sat down on the scuffed couch. Fatima moved instantly to the pot on the table, and brought us each a glass of black tea, with a single cube of sugar beside it. We thanked her, somewhat too effusively.

"It is best if you drink it like this," Rai said, popping the sugar cube into his mouth, then sucking the tea through it.

We imitated him, with some difficulty, and the girls watched us with great fascination, alternating between solemnity and fits of laughter.

"What time do they go to bed?" Elise asked. "Is it late for them?"

"Yes, it is a little late for them," Rai replied. "But if they go to bed they will not sleep. They will escape to spy on us. So it is better they are here where we can see them."

Fatima sat down in one of the wooden chairs beside the couch. The eldest girl, who had been staring without restraint at Elise, turned to her mother and asked a question.

Her mother shook her head, quickly, glancing somewhat anxiously at Elise. She said something—clearly a reprimand—to the girl.

"What did she say?" Elise asked.

"She asked if she can touch your hair," he said.

"Of course she can," Elise said immediately, smiling and rising from the couch.

Fatima said something to Rai, eyes narrowed, but Rai simply waved his hand and replied in a casual tone. Still, she looked mortified, as Elise sat down cross-legged on the carpet in front of the girls, and bowed her head like a supplicant.

The girl—Saniyah—looked questioningly at her father, who nodded, and then she reached out and lightly stroked Elise's hair. In an instant her sister did the same, and for a few moments Elise sat there enduring their curious fingers. I laughed, and then Fatima did as well, biting her knuckle as she did so.

CHAPTER FORTY-THREE

Later, when Elise had been prevailed upon to help put the girls to bed, and all the many dishes sat piled on the table, Rai rose to the china cabinet, opened the door, reached up high, and pulled out a bottle of scotch from the back of the top shelf.

"It is only for special occasions," he said, showing it to me both tentatively and proudly. "Johnny Walker Black."

He opened the bottle, which was more than half empty, and poured each of us a generous portion. From the back rooms I could hear the girls.

"I must smoke," Rai said. "But Fatima does not like it inside the house. She is worried about the health effects.

"Let's go outside," he continued. "To the garden. And drink our whiskey."

I stood, and followed him into the dark hall. We passed the girls' room, a weak yellow bar of light flowing under the door along with the sound of their voices, and then to a door at the back of the house. Rai eased it open, and we stepped out onto a small concrete porch. It was completely dark; only when Rai struck his cigarette lighter did I see the rusty wrought-iron table with an ashtray, a candle, and two molded plastic chairs of the kind sold by the millions throughout the world. He lit the candle. The rain fell steadily.

The porch was narrow enough that we each eased our chairs back against the wall to escape the fine spray from the ground. He lit his cigarette, then handed the pack and the lighter to me. I didn't want a cigarette, but I took one anyway. For a few moments we sat there in silence, sipping the whiskey, listening to the rain fall.

The garden, as he called it, was a square of patchy half-dead grass, perhaps fifteen feet across, surrounded by a wall. In the candlelight I couldn't see it well—a few shrubs had been planted along the wall, but I could barely make them out. The houses on either side were dark, as if no one was home.

The whiskey tasted good after the meal—the endlessly prepared small dishes, delicacy after delicacy, the labor of hours. They'd spent a month's budget on us, I was sure. I let the cigarette burn in the ashtray. Then Rai spoke, breaking the silence.

"You are going home soon?" he said.

"I'm leaving tomorrow," I replied. "It's an overnight flight."

"Well," he said. "Then your adventure is over."

"I suppose it is."

"Do you think you will come back someday?" he asked, taking a drag, looking out into the curtain of water off the roof.

"I don't think so," I said.

He nodded.

"Thank you for the helicopter, Doctor," he said, as he had done at the hotel.

"You're welcome."

I sat back in the chair, which was unexpectedly comfortable, and finally puffed a little on my cigarette, and drank the last of my whiskey, and watched the candle for a while. Rai stood then, and excused himself.

He returned a few moments later with the bottle, and filled our glasses again.

"Are the girls asleep?" I asked.

"No," he said. "They are too excited."

For a few seconds I thought about it, the choices that we always have to make.

"Sanjit," I said, finally. "I have a proposal for you."

"A proposal?"

"Yes. About Ali. And the girl, Homa. I've been thinking about what to do."

"Of course," Rai said.

"I feel responsible for them. In some ways—"

"You are not responsible," he interrupted, but I raised my hand, and he fell silent.

"Let me finish," I said. "I am going to give them some money. I will give Homa what I promised her, and I would like to give Ali's family some money as well."

"That is kind of you," he said.

"I'll need your help to do it."

"Of course," he said.

I reached into my pocket, and withdrew the envelope. I was theatrical about it; I gave that to myself, because he was not the only one rehearsing scenes in his mind. I opened the envelope, and withdrew the checks. There were three of them, certified by the national bank, which had a branch office at the hotel.

"This is for Homa," I said, handing him the check. "I have made this out to you. I am trusting you to make sure she gets both the money and a new leg, even if it is difficult and inconvenient."

Rai started to speak, but I cut him off again.

"Please," I said. "Let me finish."

He looked perplexed, then took the check from my hand, peering at it in the dim light. He glanced up at me.

"It is more than you said."

"It's two hundred pounds a year for fourteen years, plus some extra for the leg."

He put the check down on the table.

"This is for Ali's family," I said, handing him the second check.

He glanced at it, then looked again, then held it up to the candle to be sure, the shock abundantly clear on his face.

"I think you have made a mistake," he said, shaking his head. "This is a very great deal of money."

"It's not a mistake," I said. "And you see that the check is also made out to you because I don't know Ali's last name or anything else about him."

He stared at the check in his hand.

"Have you lost your mind?" he said, looking at me with dismay.

"No," I said. "I haven't. That check is for Ali's wife and children so they don't have to worry about starving in the streets. I want it to go only to them. No cousins, no uncles, no one else. Just his wife and children. I want them to get all of it. I'm sure his wife is illiterate and uneducated. Someone could take advantage of her very easily. So I want you to help her with the money. Do you understand?"

Rai started to speak, in protest, but I interrupted him.

"I realize you could keep the money, and I'd never know. But if you steal from them then I've been completely wrong about you. You're partly to blame for his death. You made him carry too much, and if you'd read the map correctly he'd still be alive. This is your chance to make up for it."

Rai looked up at me.

"You are partly to blame as well," he said, tightly.

"You're right," I said. "It's something we share."

I reached into my shirt pocket, and withdrew my hotel pen.

"How do you spell your daughters' names?" I asked, before he could stir himself to anger.

"What are you doing?" he said, but of course he knew.

"Just tell me."

He opened his mouth again, as if to say something else, but then he thought better of it, and did as I asked, enunciating each letter clearly and carefully.

I wrote down the names on the third check, pressing it against the plastic table, and then I handed it to him.

He stared at it for a few seconds.

"You have given me the same amount," he said, in disbelief.

"Yes," I said, calmly. "But I haven't given it to you. I've given it to your daughters, to provide for their future. Do you understand?"

Rai looked stunned. He looked at the check again, then rose, and began pacing back and forth across the narrow porch. He lit another cigarette, drew on it, then threw it down and crushed it underfoot.

"I do not understand you," he said. "I do not understand why it is so much. A little, perhaps. But not so much."

"I can afford it," I said. "And it's my business."

Again Rai opened his mouth, as if to speak, and again he thought better of it. I knew it was too much for him to turn down. A little, and I would have offended him, or worse— tempted him toward the rest. But now, if he was what I wanted him to be, I'd given him no choice.

"You didn't have to shoot those men," I said. "Both of us know it."

He looked very confused, sitting there in the dark.

"So you have given my family this money because I shot the enemy?"

"No," I said. "It's the opposite. I'm giving you a way out.

General Said is the worst kind of man in the world. It sickens me to watch you try to impress him. And if he asks you about any of this, tell him I guessed about his hunting trips and you told me I was imagining things. And tell him that I gave you nothing."

Rai sat down again. He shook his head.

"You said you didn't know what it was like to be given anything," I said. "Now you do. You don't have that excuse anymore."

Rai thought for a long time, in silence, smoking. Periodically he would look up at me, then away.

"I do not understand why you have done this," he said.

I sipped at the whiskey, and took my time before replying.

"It's simple. This trip needs to mean something. Otherwise I can't go home."

I'd earned the indulgence of my words, I thought. Or at least I'd bought it. And if I enjoyed the power of my money a little too much in that moment, it could not be helped, because without it I had no power at all.

"Are you a religious man, Doctor?" Rai asked, suddenly.

"No," I said. "I don't believe in God. But do you think Ali's family will be able to tell the difference?"

He didn't answer.

"Will you do it," I said, "or not?"

"Yes," he replied, finally. "I will. I promise this. You are a very generous man, Doctor. Too generous, I think. You do not know what this means for us. You think you do, perhaps, but still you do not."

"Good," I said. "I want you to send me a picture of Homa in six months. With a new leg. If I don't receive it I'll write to General Said and tell him that you did in fact tell me about his hunting trips and his use of military helicopters for his own pleasure. I'll also tell him that you accepted a large bribe from Scott Coles's organization for services that you didn't provide."

Rai stared at me, and I drained the second glass of whiskey.

"Here's my address," I said, putting down the glass, reaching into my pocket again for my office card. "Don't lose it."

I put the card down on the table.

"Is this an arrangement you can accept?"

Maybe I was a fool, I thought, grandstanding to the last, forcing significance on a story that meant nothing. But that hardly mattered in the end. What mattered to them was the money.

He looked down. Perhaps he had tears in his eyes, and was hiding them. I couldn't tell.

"I must accept it," he said. "And you know this.

"You do not understand what life is like for us," he continued, his voice tremulous. "This country . . ." But then he stopped, and let the sentence trail off unfinished. He lit yet another cigarette before continuing.

"They have assigned me to a forward unit," he said, his voice steady again.

"Along the border?"

"Yes," he said. "I have been commended for my actions at the camp. And so they have rewarded me."

"Are you going to go?"

"Of course. I have no choice."

"If you get yourself killed it would all be for nothing."

He smiled.

"No, Doctor," he said. "It would not."

CHAPTER FORTY-FOUR

"Will he give Homa the money?" Elise asked me, as soon as we got in the cab. It was a proper car, a battered Japanese sedan that Rai had walked out with his umbrella into the rainy dark to find.

"Yes," I said. "He will."

"Are you sure?"

"As sure as I can be," I said. "He's going to send me a picture of her in six months. So then we'll know."

"Thank you," she said, and leaned against my shoulder. I put my arm around her, then turned, and gave her a kiss on the top of the head. It seemed natural, the kind of thing that neither of us would misinterpret. The driver, however, kept sneaking glances at us in the mirror.

"Stop looking at us," I snapped. He glanced anxiously back at me, and though he spoke no English he must have understood, because he kept his eyes fixed through the windshield the rest of the way back to the hotel.

Elise was crying.

"I am sorry," she said, wiping her eyes. "I don't know why I do this."

"It's all right," I said.

I kept my arm around her. At first she leaned against me, but after a few minutes she began to ease away again, and her tears ceased. I felt it, and let her go, and then we were back, and the driver swung in through the gates. He stopped without a word, and I handed him a bill as the bellmen converged, as greedy as pigeons.

But as we entered the lobby together, she took my arm. Music played at the bar, light reflected off glass, the concierge glanced up at us, watching, then down again at the desk, and we continued to the elevators. And this, I thought, would have to do; this was as triumphant a return as any I would have again. I was the high-roller now, I'd cast down the dice as if they didn't matter in the least. I'd allowed myself only so much, and no more, and that was my night to spend it all. A pretty young woman on my arm, in her willing yellow dress, as blonde as a wheat field—and everyone was watching, everyone was wondering who we were. I was a little drunk; the whiskey had gone to my head, as Fatima slept on, in ignorance, with the children. It was midnight, it was late, it was both the end and the beginning of my life, I was with Rachel, it was thirty years before, and she was a head turner then, she was an absolute knockout, gray-eyed and lovely as they come, far lovelier than this girl here, her hair black as the center of a vein of coal, her scapulas like cheekbones, that shimmery dress of hers, so long and dark and blue, and then she was turning toward me, down there in the deep, and she was looking at me, as unreadable as ever, as if to say, here we are together still, after all this time.

There was a *ping*, the elevator doors opened.

"Good night, Elise," I said, a short while later at her room. "Sleep well."

"Good night," she replied, composed again, and then she stood on her tiptoes and kissed me lightly on the lips.

On to the minibar, restocked. One and two, then three. My

mouth tingled despite myself. The streets below me, the shine of headlights on their anointed surfaces, less frequent, less frequent again, as formally it grew late. I was awake, head swimming, alert nonetheless, feeling the air-conditioner gasp from beneath the window against my chest.

I called Eric one more time, and once again he wasn't there, or didn't pick up. It was an effort to speak clearly. I gave him the details—the airline, the flight numbers, and arrival times. I enunciated well enough, I was sure, though I was also sure that he would hear something in my voice that he did not expect. Johnny Walker Black, I thought, but of course it was more than that.

Toward the end, Rachel turned to miniatures, to oils half the size of playing cards, with tiny matching frames. They were simple—flower petals, drops of water on a railing, leaves on a walk. She used her smallest brushes, and painted through a magnifying glass.

They were like the beads of a rosary. Her precise attention, dipping the filament into the paint again, and the freedom from thought that it gave her, the peace of otherness, and elsewhere—that is how she endured the last few months of her life. There were many times when I would peer in through the door, wanting to sit beside her, and yet I knew that my presence would distract her, would carry her back from that world to this, and so I slipped away.

When she was done, she had several dozen. They were gifts—to her family, to her friends, and to her students.

"Which one do you think Danielle would like better?" she would ask me, with two or three arranged on the table.

"I think she'd like the gold coin," I said.

"How about George?"

"I'm not sure. Maybe the fish in the pool."

She would nod, and make a note on a legal pad.

She left them in a gift-wrapped pile on the table in her studio, with names on each one. Her address book lay on top of the pile, and beside it, a sealed envelope.

I'd put it off for many weeks, but when I was finally done with that room, and the paint and turpentine and drop cloths and brushes and rolls of empty canvas were in the trash at last, I opened her letter.

Charles, it read,

> *I didn't quite finish. I'm hoping you can address these for me, and mail them. Please be careful with the packing—they should be sent in cardboard boxes filled with those Styrofoam beads I always use.*
>
> *There is a larger one for you, and one for Eric as well. They're not quite dry, so be careful when you unwrap them. They're in the closet. I like them, and I hope that you do too.*

Then her name.

I was going home to my dog, with his bad hips and the three-beat thump of his tail, gummy-eyed and stumbling toward my key in the door. I imagined my hand on his head, the warmth of his shoulder against my knee, the smell of the house, shut up for months, the cool white piles of mail at the post office, the fall scent in the air; and there I would be, standing in the doorway as if for the first time. Though of course he was staying with friends, he wasn't in the house, but I pictured him there anyway, sleeping off my absence, rising heavily from time to time to drink from the water bowl, coming to perfect clear-eyed attention at the sight of a squirrel in the backyard trees, the years falling off him for a few seconds, then finally the two-circled collapse back onto his elaborate sheepskin bed, which Eric had chosen for him out of a catalogue, and sent to him for Christmas.

And I imagined her there, too, looking out through our yard toward the cornfields, saying, the trees are dry, aren't they? And I reply—yes, I suppose they are—and put my hands on her shoulders again.

We come back, it seems, endlessly to the same place; we drink from the same well. How strange, I thought, that I would be faced with this, at my age. But it was required; it was what my life had somehow given me, despite all the plans, all the years and struggles and hopes.

I could feel the approach of the future, I could sense it like a mist on a winter morning, so delicate on the farms around my house, as the coffee warmed, and the sun burned through to the fences, and finally to the fields, laced with snow, the radio filling the warmth of the kitchen with the pleasure of the cold, the pride in the weatherman's voice, as if to say, yes, these are unusual times, and this is the coldest morning of the year.

When I was a young man, living with Rachel in that small apartment not far from the hospital, I remember the mornings especially, driving home after a night on call, the heavy black pager on my hip, antique as a rotary telephone, my breath visible in the car, in the bright sun, and the steely blue surface of Lake Michigan, threaded with whitecaps and birds. I loved the solemnity of the ships, steaming toward the docks, and the train horns of the tugs. It was out of my way, a little, but I'd take Lakeshore Drive nonetheless, and sail along in the off-hour morning, home to breakfast, and finally to the fitful sleep of the exhausted. Throughout those years, those long white nights of sickbeds, young and strong and full of what I thought was promise, I felt that I was struggling for something larger than myself, and greater. I was never sure, exactly, what it was I was moving toward, but I could feel it coursing through me, as if to say, look out, and look ahead, the future is wide open, and someday it will find you. The glory of possibility, the lure of the difficult—it was irresistible to me then, but now it seems like just another thing the world has lit within us.

My younger self would have been shocked to find me as I am. That's all? That's all you've become, and that's what you're going home to? How dismayed he would have been—I could almost see his expression, accusatory, disdainful, and afraid, as if I'd let him down, which perhaps I had. But I've become disdainful of him as well, deluded as he was, full of incoherent work and unexamined ambition, claiming all his wants as his own, incapable of rising above them. So we look at each other, with mutual suspicion, across those years. And if he can't forgive me, so much the worse for him.

In the end I slept well that night. The whiskey was just enough, and not too much, and it led me easily away, far more easily than I would have thought.

CHAPTER FORTY-FIVE

The next day, at the airport, I was determined not to make too much of it. Her flight to Bangkok was an hour before mine, but we went together anyway, and waited through the crowded check-in lines and security lines, through the quick, indifferent glances of the police, their hands stained with blue ink. The wide room, with its battered wooden stations and quivering fluorescent lights overhead, echoed with the muffled chunk of exit stamps, like hundreds of doors being opened, or closed. There were only a few other Westerners among us; for the most part, those waiting with us looked as if they were leaving rather than traveling. Meanwhile Elise stood in front of me, a perfect blond triangle of down at the nape of her neck.

By the gates, with some time left, we sat on rows of battered oval fiberglass chairs bolted together, and looked out at the runways.

She was dressed casually again, in her cargo pants and sandals. Her specimen case hung from one shoulder, and from the other, her solar shower, folded tight, the legs telescoped into themselves and their tips clipped together, like a photographer's tripod. The necklace I'd bought her was nowhere to be seen.

"Are you planning to take a shower on the plane?" I asked her. She smiled.

"I would like to," she said. "But I think they only allow this in first class."

"Why didn't you check it in?"

"Because then it will be broken," she said. "They bent the leg when I came here."

We were quiet for a while, looking out at the lights on the runway. Several times, in the distance, planes landed, but we only saw them in the gaps between hangars. It was getting dark, and all the lights on the field were on.

"Will you write to me from time to time?" I asked her.

"Of course," she said. "And now you must give me your address."

"Remember," I said, thinking again of her black case, "you have to tell me whether my mother should be turning over in her grave because some of her ancestors were African slaves."

"I will not forget," she said.

I took out my wallet, flipped through it, and found another of my cards. I handed it to her, and she studied it for a moment before tucking it away into her bag.

"Thank you, Professor," she said.

"Where are you going in Thailand?" I asked.

"I think I am going to Phuket," she said. "The beach, and also the rain forest. I would like to see them. And I want to ride on an elephant."

I smiled.

She reached into her orange day pack and withdrew her journal and a pen. She opened the notebook carefully to the last full page, and wrote her name, address, telephone number, and e-mail in precise small letters. Then, to my surprise, she handed the book to me.

"This is for you," she said, simply.

"For me?" I asked, puzzled, reflexively taking the book from her.

"Yes," she said, looking at me steadily.

"But it's your journal."

"I have made a copy at the hotel," she said.

I looked down at the book in my hands, confused.

"I wanted to get you something," she said. "And I am not sure what. So I am giving you this."

"But I don't speak German," I said.

"You can translate it if you wish. It is not so difficult now."

I stared at the book for a while. I didn't know what to make of it.

"This is a very personal thing," I said. "I don't know what to say."

"I think," she said, "that this is more important for you than for me. All that happened. And so I would like to give this to you."

I looked down at the book.

"Aren't there things in here that you wouldn't want anyone to read?"

"Yes," she said. "But not so many."

"You can take those pages out, you know. I wouldn't mind."

She shook her head.

"It is okay," she said. "I think it is better to leave them in." She hesitated, then continued.

"Not everything in this book is good," she said. "I wrote some things about you that are not so nice. Maybe it will hurt your feelings a little bit. You should know this."

"Like what?" I said.

She blushed.

"I said that you are always thinking too much, and many

times you are talking too much, and often it is about depressing things, and that sometimes you are boring. I also said that you like giving lectures and telling people what they should do, and that you take everything too seriously."

I laughed.

"Well," I said, "that's all true."

"Some other things, also," she said.

I didn't know how to reply.

"Thank you, Elise," I said finally. "I appreciate it very much."

"I think you gave money to everyone," she said. "Not just Homa. To Sanjit also. More than just paying him. And to Ali's family. I am not sure. But I think so."

"Did Rai say anything to you?"

"No," she said. "And I did not ask him. But I think it is true. He was different when we left his house." She looked at me again.

"I tried to help them," I said finally. "That's all."

"Why were you keeping this a secret?"

"It wasn't a secret. It was private. It's hard to explain."

"How much did you give them?"

I didn't want to tell her. She would measure me with it, just as I measured myself. Their gratitude was cheap, after all. It could be bought with hardly anything.

"A lot for them," I said. "Not so much for me."

"You have done a good thing," she said.

I didn't answer.

"I also want to give something to Ali's family," she continued. "But I only have a little money. And I want to go to Thailand. And one or two hundred dollars is too small, it is nothing. So I gave nothing."

She looked at me steadily.

"Don't be too hard on yourself," I replied.

"I would like to give you some money for Homa and Ali. I would like to send this to you later."

"Don't worry about it, Elise. Let me do it. I can afford it. You're not old enough to give your money away."

"Maybe you are right," she said. "But also you are wrong."

"I won't take it, you know," I said. "And I gave them much more than you ever could."

We were quiet for a while.

"There is something else," she said, finally, reaching into her bag, pulling out the box. It was the necklace, and she handed it to me.

"I got that for you because I wanted you to have it," I said, my voice catching. "Don't make me take it back."

"I know," she said. "But I thought about this very much. I believe this is for someone else. Even if you do not know who it is."

"I don't plan to get married again, Elise."

"Maybe you will not get married," she said. "But you can if you want. You are not too old. You are a good man, intelligent. You are still handsome. It is true. And so I think you should give this to her. It is better."

My cheeks were burning, my eyes stung.

"Tell me," I said, after a moment. "Is Scott Coles meeting you in Thailand?"

She flushed.

"Yes," she said, simply, after a long pause. "For a few days only. Then he is coming here to see what he can do."

"Did you call him?"

"Yes," she said. "I called him from the hotel. After you said you would not come."

"Well," I said. "Please give him my best."

"He is sorry, you know," she said, awkwardly. "He feels very bad for what has happened. He wants to talk to you when you get home."

We fell silent after that. It took me a few moments to compose myself, but I did so, because I am good at doing so. The seats around us had mostly filled up, and then, finally, they called her flight for boarding.

I stood, a bit too quickly. She followed, and offered me a quick, enigmatic look, and I walked with her to the gate. She had the boarding pass in her hand, and just before she handed it to the steward, she turned toward me.

"Good-bye, Elise," I said. I hugged her tightly, then stepped back. I did it as calmly as I could.

"Good-bye, Charles," she replied, with a smile, and then she turned and walked through the door.

CHAPTER FORTY-SIX

A window, near the back. The seats were brown and orange, the cloth worn thin. I smelled the industrial cleaner from the bathroom a few feet behind me. I sat down, buckled the belt, and looked out the window at the ground below. The gray wing in front of me hung out in space. The plane was old, no doubt a worn-out castoff from the West.

Down the length of the cabin, over the seat backs, I could see the other passengers flowing in, peering at the seat numbers in the dim cabin lighting, opening the overhead bins. I saw no Western faces; a few families, with young children, and many men, both young and middle-aged, who seemed to be alone, some in suits, others in warm-up jackets and jeans and tennis shoes. Cabdrivers, I thought, or convenience store clerks, westward toward the dream of a better life.

There was a chorus of thuds as the doors closed. The steward came on the intercom. I could barely hear him. Would we please fasten our seat belts, and place our seat backs and tray tables in the upright position. The flight attendants, young women in blue suits, stood at the head of the sections with seat belts in their hands, and buckled them.

Then we were gliding backward, towed from the gangway, and

the wing out the window was sweeping across the hangars and trucks, and the engines were spooling up, and we began to roll out toward the runways. Somewhere up front, a very young child began to cry—the catlike call of infancy. We taxied in long, slow bounds, the weight of the plane everywhere, laden with all its cold tons of fuel.

Then the sudden turn, and I saw the runway for a moment through the window—a sea of red and blue lights, and the wide black center, stretching out into the dark. For the first time I heard the pilot's voice, in clipped accented English, asking the attendants to be seated.

We came to a quick, shuddering halt, with a low squeal of brakes, and as he pushed the throttles forward, and the thunder of the engines began, I felt my heart thudding and skipping in my chest.

The plane began to move, pressing me against the seat, and the blue lights went by one by one, faster, like a string of illuminated beads. The bins above me creaked and shook, the wing rose at the tip, and then, finally, the slow backward tilt, the thumps and bangs of the gear as it left the ground, and we were off, banking heavily, rightward in a climbing turn. The gear came up, and one of the rumbles left us. For a moment, before the clouds began to shoot by, I had a view of the city, gleaming with the lights of the poor.

Then we were rolling level, and the clouds were flowing heavily past, and the first shudders of turbulence began, the wide gray wing heaving and flexing, the single light at the tip blinking like a metronome. A sudden whine, a reeling in, from the center, and the flaps slid back. The airspeed was rising, we were climbing well, and soon the lights of the city beneath us vanished altogether.

There was a flash as we broke through the high layer of

clouds, but it was a moonless night, and the view I might have imagined—sheets of clouds below us, the stars in their millions—was nowhere to be seen. Instead it was only the dark, and my own reflection in the window, and a few tiny perfect crystals of ice between the layers of plastic and glass.

A few minutes later the lights dimmed, and video screens came on in each section of the cabin. The screens showed the same blue image of the world, with a icon of a plane moving across it like the minute hand of a clock. There were rows of numbers, changing constantly—our heading, our longitude and latitude, our altitude, our airspeed and ground speed, our estimated time to arrival. Forty-one thousand feet. Seventeen hours to go. Half the globe was lit, and half was in shadow, and after a while I realized that our night would be longer than any on earth, because we were moving in the same direction as the passage of darkness across the world.

I thought of Elise, high up in the dark, with her specimen case in the bin above her head. I wondered what she was thinking, and whether I would ever see her again, and I had no idea at all. Meanwhile, in my bag, the necklace gleamed on.

I unzipped my pack then, and took out her journal. I held it for a while in my lap, before turning on the overhead light and opening the book. Each entry was dated in the European fashion. Some lasted many pages, others only a paragraph or two. I saw my name many times, in her tiny, exact hand, and Rai's, and Homa's. Ali as well, toward the end. Other names, also, that I didn't know, scattered here and there. Apart from them, I understood nothing. It resisted me completely, yet never had I wanted to read something so much. It was the same story, of course, told through other eyes, and I was simply another character within it. I was one of many, no better, perhaps, than the rest.

But still she'd given it to me. And if I knew her at all, I must come out all right in the end. It must be true, I thought, because she understood what she'd held in her hands, how raw I'd been, and she'd done it anyway.

I never unwrapped Eric's painting. I left that for him. But I'd hung mine in the guest room where I slept. It was a self-portrait, and I knew which photograph Rachel had used, because I had taken it.

She was in her early fifties, shortly before her illness. She was wearing jeans, and a spattered white T-shirt. She was sitting by her desk, with the studio windows behind her. There were threads of gray in her hair, which was long and tangled and un-done. Her head was cocked, as if someone had just entered the room and asked her a question. A warm, attractive face, intel-ligent, with wrinkles at the corners of her eyes, but not beautiful, not glamorous or elegant—just Rachel as she was, the woman I had loved, looking up at me again.

The hours passed, the icon moved. Dinner was served, and I ate. I dozed, and woke, and dozed again. All through the long, eidetic night—the ridgelines against the sky, the sound of the river, the falling snow, Homa's face, Ali's arms in the water, the rasp of the saw in my hands—for hour after empty hour, the light on the wing blinked on, until Hamburg swam up in the dark like phosphorous. Hamburg, I thought vaguely, had been absolutely flattened. Sixty years earlier it was a pile of bricks and ash.

I sat and waited as they refueled the plane. I had no interest in the terminal, with its duty-free stores and harsh fluorescent lights. I was dulled to all of it by then. I was done with thinking, and sick of remembering, and I just wanted to arrive. It was a familiar feeling, one I'd had over and over as a young man—a few more patients to see, a few more notes to write, another cup of coffee, and then I'd be gone, out to Lakeshore Drive, with all those whitecaps and gulls leading me the last few miles back home.

Two hours from New York, high above the Atlantic, the sun rose. The wings began to glow. At first it was barely perceptible, but soon I could read the letters stenciled on the flaps—DO NOT STAND. Streaks of grease, also, and scratches, the peppering of thirty years of slipstreams. I could feel it wake me up. And I wasn't alone; as the light began pouring in through the windows, the others around me began to shift, and move, and open their eyes.

I rubbed my face, wishing I had a razor. I could smell my breath. I wanted to look decent, on the chance that Eric would be there. I didn't want to shock him; I was thin, I knew, thinner than I'd been in years. I was stronger, also. But my face was haggard, sunburned from the valley, and I was going to look exhausted when I walked off the plane. But it couldn't be helped; I didn't have a razor.

Settle down, I told myself. He won't be there. I'd called him in the middle of the night, and he hadn't answered. Probably he was out of town, or staying with a girlfriend, or any of a hundred other things. It was only a little after six in the morning, and he had work to do. I'd given him no warning, and I was months early. His apartment was small, hardly more than a studio, he had no spare bed, he had only a couch, and what did I expect?

But still my palms were damp, my breathing quick, and I wished I'd brought a razor, and could brush my teeth, and could hold up my side of the bargain a little better.

All through the throttling back, the spinning of dials, the

cryptic voices in the radios, as I imagined them, a whole world of accents in the headings and altitudes and clearances to land, all through the long curve of our descent, I thought about him. I began to see the silver points of other aircraft, a thousand feet above, a thousand feet below. Some of them closed with impossible speed, and were gone, and some of them swelled beside us as our paths converged.

The flaps went down, and the sea grew nearer. Pleasure boats, some under sail, and the wing was starting its slow, pendulous heave, and then the gear was shuddering in the slipstream, and finally there it was, the skyline of New York City, sunlight glistening off the glass facades of the buildings, one by one, as if to say, this is the world we have made.

We were sailing over streets and apartment blocks, our shadow beneath us, a little sideways in the crosswind from the sea, the green grass flowing by, the skip and stutter of the first white stripes, and then the heavy drum-rolling cough of the wheels, on the ground at last, as the cabin shook and creaked once more, and the engines thundered in reverse. Braking, braking again, and they'd done it, they'd taken me all the way back.

Later, after baggage claim, after customs, after the scanned-in passports, after the police with their dogs, after the coffee stands, after all of that, I could not stop myself from shaking. I could not calm down. What's come over me, I wondered, why am I acting this way? And for the first time I realized how afraid I was, and how terrifying it would be to fly on alone, back to my house, and all that I faced there. We were filing out through the last of the barricades to arrivals, one after the other through the gap. I was near the end of the line, pushing my cart, and out in the morning I could see a cluster of drivers standing just beyond the red rope, holding up signs with names on them. The line grew shorter, the gap grew nearer. I was looking everywhere.

And then I saw him. He waited just past the exit, and the rope, near a pillar. He was watching the line; his eyes flicked across their faces. He hadn't seen me. He took a step forward. That was all—a solitary, expectant step.

I felt myself go calm for the first time. He was dressed in a dark suit, with a green tie, which was unlike him. He was searching for me like someone with news to tell, and in that moment he looked like everything I wanted him to be, young and handsome and full of life, with his dark hair, and his bright, alert eyes flowing over us, one by one, there at the end of the journey.

The line moved on through the gap, and then, finally, he saw me. His face lit up, and he came toward me exactly as his mother had done, when she was his age, and had opened her arms for me also.

ACKNOWLEDGMENTS

My deepest thanks to my family, Helena Brandes, Deke and Marina Huyler, Scott Huyler, Holbrook Robinson, and Tracy Hardister, to my friends Tim Steigenga, Johanna Sharp, Chris Bannon, Helen Beekman, Beth Hadas, and Jennifer Brokaw, and to those who generously read various drafts of this book even though we've never met—Stewart O'Nan, Maria Campbell, Michael Williams, Peter Cook, and Toby Tompkins. To my agent, Michael Carlisle, and to my editor, Jennifer Barth, I'm enormously grateful for your support, encouragement, and good advice.

Special thanks, again, to Janet Bailey and to David Sklar.